The Tribute

John Byron

16pt

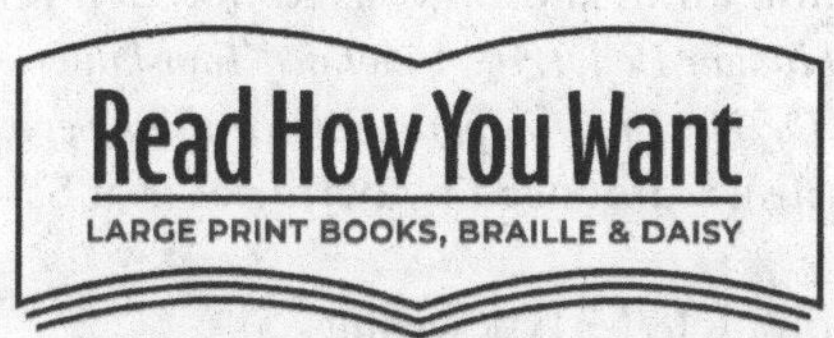

Copyright Page from the Original Book

Published by Affirm Press in 2021
28 Thistlethwaite Street, South Melbourne,
Boon Wurrung Country, VIC 3205
affirmpress.com.au

Text and copyright © John Byron, 2021

The moral rights of the author have been asserted.

Title: The Tribute / John Byron, author

A catalogue record for this
book is available from the
National Library of Australia

Cover design by Sandy Cull, sandycull.com
Cover images: human figure from Andreas Vesalius, *De Humani Corporis Fabrica*, artists Stephen van Calcar and the Workshop of Titian, US National Library of Medicine, nlm.nih.gov; beach image from Anton Gorlin, Westend61 GmbH/Alamy Stock Photo
Author photo by Rebecca Taylor Photography

Illustration on p. 379 from Andreae Vesalii [Andreas Vesalius], *Suorum de humani corporis fabrica librorum epitome*, reproduced by permission of Wellcome Collection, Attribution 4.0 International (CC BY 4.0)

Other internal illustrations and historiated initials from Andreas Vesalius, *The Fabric of the Human Body: An Annotated Translation of the 1543 and 1555 Editions of 'De Humani Corporis Fabrica Libri Septem'*, DH Garrison and MH Hast (trans), reproduced by permission of S. Karger AG, Basel

Typeset in Granjon by J&M Typesetting
Proudly printed in Australia by Griffin Press

TABLE OF CONTENTS

John Byron grew up in Sydney, where he studied medicine for a time before leaving in the interest of the public safety. He has worked as a barman, a factory hand, a help-desk operator and a federal ministerial adviser, and now works in the university sector. His writing has appeared in *The Australian, Meanjin, The Australian Book Review, The Conversation, Time Out* and *Rip It Up. The Tribute* is his first novel and was shortlisted for the prestigious Victorian Premier's Literary Award for an Unpublished Manuscript in 2019. He lives and works on Wurundjeri country, in Melbourne.

For Julienne van Loon:
there you are.

—

He felt his power swell within him, and he loved it as a pregnant woman loves her unborn child.

Elizabeth Harrower
Down in the City

Sunday 8 April – morning

Over the PA came the Midnight Oil surf tune 'Wedding Cake Island', calling the swimmers to order at the northern end of Coogee Beach. The nervous chatter dropped as the guitars swelled on the mild Sydney autumn breeze; then the starting gun fired, and the annual Coogee Island Cool Water Challenge was underway. Jo ran in fast, dived cleanly under a breaker, then surfaced and steamed towards New Zealand.

She swam out past Wedding Cake Island and fought the lurching open ocean swell beyond it for a hundred hard metres, then turned into the channel between the island and the blocky base of the South Coogee headland, the surge behind her now. After passing the Ladies' Baths, the swimmers swam parallel to the beach behind the breakers, and Jo hit the gas. She powered past the tiring field before turning in and catching a rearing wave that propelled her inshore. Exhilarated and breathing hard, she crossed the finish line on burning legs at a shade over forty-six minutes, a personal best.

Jo towelled off, feeling better than she had in ages. She was fit and strong, ready to be in the world again after a long period of emotional retreat. Her small family was thriving, her career nicely on track. Mellowed by a mild, pleasant summer unmarred by fire or flood, Sydney felt vibrant and optimistic. The year had started well, and Jo felt it was shaping to be a good one.

She could not have been more wrong.

Because eleven kilometres away, a strange and intense man was finalising his plan to execute a macabre tribute to the object of his overwhelming intellectual obsession.

His work would begin in three weeks' time, and Sydney Town would be never be the same again.

FRONTISPIECE

Death presides.

The Anatomist has forsaken the professorial chair, and come down onto the floor beside the corruptible flesh. This very stance is a declaration: of war, of science. One hand is inside the ventilated abdomen, the other making a subtle point, but not for the benefit of the noisy crowd around him. He is gazing calmly out of the page, looking straight at the future. He is speaking to us. Speaking to me.

All around him bustle the chattering primates of his time: men of commerce and of politics; men of the book and of the cloth; worthies, voyeurs and hacks. The monkey and the dog of his predecessors' dissections play innocently, displaced by the human corpse; the barbers and butchers stand idly by, banished by this impudent scholar, his own learned hands applied to the physical task. All have been deposed from their ancient roles of brokering ignorance, in favour of the Master's determination to craft a new Anatomy: unmediated, palpable, empirical. They understand no more of this moment than does the cadaver.

A field of calm around the dissection excludes the commotion of the pedestrian and the drone of the self-important. There is only the candidate and the Master.

And the Protégé. Hemmed in by the crowd, above and to the left, near the naked man and his admirer. Peering between two fools debating anatomy without reference to the body. Who might he be?

Above them all, above even Death, a banner unfurled bears the legend:

Andreas Vesalius of Brussels,
Professor in the School of Medicine at Padua,
On the Fabric of the Human Body in Seven Volumes.

This is the frontispiece to the incomparable *De Humani Corporis Fabrica Libri Septem,* the foundation text of modern anatomy, published at Basel in 1543 when Vesalius was only twenty-eight years of age. It not only secured the Master's future – it immortalised him. Along with *De Revolutionibus Orbium Coelestium* of Copernicus, published that same year at Nuremburg, it is one of the most influential books in history.

The *Fabrica*'s break with the past is absolute. Its significance is not in its findings, impressive as they are: its revolutionary contribution is its method. Long before the Enlightenment, Vesalius abjures tradition and received doctrine, looking instead and only to the evidence before him. With this masterpiece, the Master ushers in the empiricism of the scientific age.

His approach is the very model of the new enquiry. He disdains theory and theology. He finds out for himself, learns from the source. He is calm, logical, unsentimental.

He is not afraid to get his hands wet.

His Protégé learns, and emulates.

Monday 30 April – morning

Detective Senior Sergeant David Murphy turned off Parramatta Road and drove up Glebe Point Road, past the fancy cafes and the old Valhalla Cinema, and up onto the butte of hard rock over sandstone that loomed above the surrounding lowlands. He turned into a dignified residential street and parked at the end, overlooking the awful redevelopment below that covered the old Harold Park harness-racing track.

He had to sit for a moment composing himself. He hated this place. The property developers were bastards, but they weren't the problem. What lay directly beneath him through the rock was the problem.

His father had died down there, in the old metropolitan goods railway tunnel, back in the late seventies when Murphy was just a boy. The tunnel was half a mile of sheer determination dug by veterans of Gallipoli and the Somme to take freight off the passenger lines.

It was now a light-rail commuter line for inner-west hipsters.

Murphy had heard a bit over the years about the murder of his old man, and a copy of the file had found its way to him soon after he'd joined the Force. Diarmaid Murphy had been an influential detective at a time when the New South Wales Police had been filthy all the way through, the genuine descendant of the colonial Rum Corps. Murphy didn't know whether his father had been bent or straight, but either way it was crooked cops who'd got him.

Diarmaid Murphy had gone into the goods tunnel late one night – after the freight trains had stopped running for the day – to meet a fellow cop for whatever reason and taken a brace of police-issue bullets for his trouble. A train driver found the body early next morning; an investigation was launched but went nowhere, and media interest soon moved on. The Wood Royal Commission put the broom through the Force in the mid-nineties, but many of the sleeping dogs were allowed to lie. The case was open, technically, but cold as the morgue.

So all his life, Murphy couldn't even drive over the Anzac Bridge without glancing across Blackwattle Bay and thinking of his old man. Of dirty cops on the take, selling out their brothers for coin. Brown paper bags full of cash and nylon sports bags full of heroin. Free roots and free booze; cheap TVs off the back of a truck. Dead hookers and dead addicts; dead civilians and dead police.

Of his mother bereft and grieving, and a five-year-old boy with no father.

So yeah, Murphy tended to avoid this end of Glebe.

Up top today, though, it was your perfect bright, crisp Sydney autumn day. Leaves on the turn and filling the gutters in auburn piles, but a clear blue sky and a warm sun tempered by a faint cool breeze. Murphy pulled himself together, got out of his car and walked past the forensics truck to his crime scene. He ducked under the crime-scene tape and passed a large sign on his way in that said *KEEP OUT – CONSTRUCTION SITE.*

He took his bearings inside the front entrance of the terrace house while slipping on a pair of disposable nitrile gloves. He was standing in a large, open room, inner walls completely stripped back to studwork and brick, floorboards exposed and recently sanded. A clear sheet of heavy plastic hung down from the ceiling in front of the studwork of the room's former back wall. Straight ahead, a steep, narrow flight of stairs hugged the right-hand wall, its balustrade and a couple of steps missing.

Murphy grunted. Fucken home renovation: the latest great Australian obsession, along with cooking like an English wanker. People watched too much crap on television these days. What was wrong with footy?

'Homicide!' he yelled.

'Come through, Spud,' came back from beyond the thick plastic curtain. He knew the voice – it belonged to Dr Michael Kenworth, the most experienced scenes-of-crime officer in the state. He was a medically trained civilian attached to forensic services, working out of police headquarters at Parramatta. Naturally, everybody called him Mack.

A white shape approached the thick plastic veil from behind, which proved to be another SOCO in a paper crime-scene suit. 'Morning, detective,' she said, holding the curtain open for him.

'Morning, Ange. I hear it's a beauty.'

'This one you've got to see for yourself. Unbelievable.'

Murphy raised his eyebrows: SOCOs rarely talked like that, and Angela had seen a fair bit. He crossed the former dining room, empty apart from a bar fridge with a kettle on top, through to a clapped-out kitchen: a mid-century bolt-on that had been last updated thirty years ago. This time, the owner was not mucking around. An internal door at the far end revealed a sparkly bathroom all tricked out in the latest gear. The kitchen itself was still a mess, but it was a mess with intent. The old cupboards had been ripped out, and work was underway on schmick new cabinetry. Murphy shook his head. Fucken madness.

'G'day, Mack. What have you got for me?'

Mack was standing at the sink, his hands out of sight in the basin. He lifted his gaze over his glasses to meet Murphy's eyes.

'Afternoon, Spud.' It being 10.47am, this was Mack's way of giving Murphy shit for being late: since Mack was almost always at a crime scene before him, it was a familiar sledge. 'Male, whitish, forty-odd, in good shape until the weekend.'

'Any ID?'

'Probably the owner, Anthony Williams, but it'll take dental to confirm it. He's not particularly intact.'

'How so?'

'Most of him is upstairs in the back room,' said Mack, indicating the mottled ceiling directly above them, 'but there's bits of him everywhere, poor bastard.' He lifted his hands towards Murphy, presenting the specimen they held like an offering.

Murphy recoiled. It was half a human arm, sawn off just above the elbow and pared right back, all gristle and bone with strips of meat hanging off here and there. 'Christ, Mack.'

'I know. Gets worse.' Mack placed the forearm gently in the sink and nodded towards the draining board, where a tech was taking photos.

Murphy leaned in for a better look at the knuckled segment. 'Jesus fuck, what's that?'

'Cervical spine,' said Mack. 'Neckbones. I don't know what our man was looking for, but he was thorough.'

A voice came through from the front. 'Mack, Tori found the skull-cap, in the upstairs bathroom. Picked clean.' It was Detective Senior Constable Amy Chartier, who'd been on call overnight as Homicide's first responder. 'Wait till you see upstairs, boss,' she said to Murphy as she entered the kitchen. 'I've never seen anything like it.' Her appearance testified in favour – usually bronzed, vibrant and athletic, she looked wan, clammy and deflated by comparison. Chartier was maintaining her professional demeanour but it clearly wasn't easy.

'Who found him?' Murphy asked her.

'Day labourer named Greg Something, just before seven this morning. He's been helping with the renovation; showed up as normal, but the door was locked and there was no answer. He jimmied the front window and went upstairs where he'd left off on Friday afternoon.'

'Alibi?'

'Avoca with the girlfriend's family, all weekend. Unconfirmed at this point, but it'd be a lousy lie.'

'Where is he now?'

'Harris took him for interview, if he can handle it. He's not doing too well.'

'No shit,' said Murphy. He turned to Mack. 'So, all this from the one body, you reckon?'

'Yes. One of everything so far; no remainders.'

'That's something. But still, fucken butchery or what?'

'You don't know the half of it,' said Mack. 'It's a charnel house up there. Soft tissue everywhere, and all the bones chopped up.'

Murphy watched Chartier step to the open window and take a deep breath of fresh air. *Must be bad up there to unsettle her,* he thought: she was one of his best, not easily rattled.

'I tell you this,' continued Mack, 'he's not an orthodox Jew or a devout Muslim.'

'The vic or the perp?'

'The perp.'

'Why do you say that?'

'He underestimated drainage, big time. Five litres of blood goes a long way.'

They all looked up at the old brown patch on the ancient kitchen ceiling and shuffled out from beneath it. No point taking chances. 'What about tissue samples?'

'Nothing obvious so far,' said Mack. 'We've bagged a hell of a lot of material, as you'd expect on a construction site. We'll do another full sweep and then go over it all in the lab. But it looks like he was careful. Nothing's leaped out yet.'

'Just one perp, you reckon? Or a team?'

'Hard to say. The autopsy might tell us, based on the incisions. It's a lot of work for one cutter, though.'

'And what do you make of that?' Murphy asked, gesturing to the forearm in the sink. It was stripped back so far you could see between the bones. The words *ulna* and *radius* floated into Murphy's mind, unbidden.

'I dunno, Spud. He's cut all the muscle away very carefully with a sharp knife, sturdier than a scalpel. He's left some tendon attachments intact and cut others completely away, but it's pretty delicate work. Then he's sawn through the humerus to get the joint out so he can go even finer. Looks like he's used the victim's own circular saw, although it's an extremely fine blade. Not quite surgical, but close. Harris tells me you wouldn't normally see one like it on a building site. Our boy brought it with him.'

Murphy waved towards the chain of vertebrae sitting on the draining board. 'Same for the other bits? Neck and skull?'

'Looks like it. After he's cut the bits out, he's spent a lot of time on them in good light on a stable working surface. He's worked over the lower cranium in incredible detail, after taking the lid off and clearing out the soft tissue.' Mack turned to Chartier. 'And apparently he's taken his time with the top of the cranium, too?'

She nodded. 'Same deal, in the bathroom sink.'

'What about the rest of the body?'

'He's done the torso in situ, after he's removed all the viscera, but you can see the fine cutting,' said Mack.

'Fuck me.' Murphy shook his head.

'Yeah, it doesn't make a lot of sense,' said Mack.

'It's homicide, Mack, it's not meant to make sense,' said Murphy. 'If this shit ever starts making sense to you, let me know.'

'You'd lock me up.'

'Only to protect the community, mate,' said Murphy. 'So how long do you think it would have taken him, all up?'

'A good while. It's a pretty systematic operation.'

'Could it be done in a day, say?'

'I doubt it,' said Mack. 'More like all weekend.'

'Bloody hell, that's quite a risk, taking that much time.'

'For sure, although the neighbours would be used to all the building noise.'

'And there's that big sign out the front,' added Chartier.

Murphy tried to imagine some sick fuck spending the weekend deconstructing his victim while life went on over the other side of the wall. The neighbours probably heard the circular saw rev up while they were cooking breakfast. He pushed the thought aside.

'Let's see what your second pass pulls up. With days on the job there has to be some DNA. Bag everything, okay?'

Mack nodded. 'Always do.'

Murphy turned to his detective. 'Chartier, let's give the SOCOs some room. Start on the doorknock. Call the squad and get some help over here, and a couple of uniforms too. Keep good track of it, come back for anyone who's not home.' She nodded. 'Ask about the entire weekend: any movement or unfamiliar faces from before this Greg character left on Friday until he came back this morning. I want to talk with him once he's ready, too. You should be there, since he's met you. And tell Harris to follow up on that blade thing. I want to know where it came from.'

'Yes, boss,' said Chartier.

'And get Janssen over here, pronto.' Murphy wanted his deputy on deck, right from the start. He had a bad feeling about this one.

'Righto, boss.' The detective turned and fairly bolted for the front door. She couldn't wait to get outside.

Murphy turned back to his forensic specialist. 'So, Mack: what else?'

'What do you mean, what else?'

'Come on, mate, I know you. Something's on your mind.'

'Fair enough.' Mack paused. 'It's just, whatever else you pull up, this is not your normal killing.'

'No shit.'

'No, I mean ... it might be a hit or a jealous husband or something, but the extra stuff, it's not recreational.'

'What are you getting at? Have we seen this bloke before?'

'No. Well, we'll see what CrimTrac throws up on the MO, but I don't think so.'

'So what's your theory?'

'Look at this,' said Mack lifting the length of forearm from the sink and turning it to show Murphy the elbow. 'Can you see where the joint capsule has been opened up, and the cartilage cut away?'

Murphy reluctantly leaned in and tried to concentrate on the anatomy. 'Yeah.'

'It's been done very carefully, with a scalpel.'

'Okay.'

'And he's revealed the joint with extraordinary precision.'

'Mmm...'

'It's expertly done, actually. Meticulous.'

'Yeah, and?'

'Well, it's just a feeling, but it's so ... orthodox. Textbook.'

'Jesus, Mack, use your words, will you? Pretend you're in court.'

Mack sighed. 'Sorry, Spud.' He looked frankly at Murphy over his glasses. 'Look, I couldn't place it at first, but I've seen this before; this exact thing. But not at a crime scene. And not for ages.' He held up the arm, contemplating the painstakingly displayed inner joint of the elbow.

'This looks for all the world like a medical school dissection.'

Monday 30 April – evening

'That was great, Jo!'

Dr Joanna King had just delivered a public lecture at Sydney University on depictions of the body in art and science. She smiled at her sister-in-law. 'Thanks for coming, Sylvia.'

'Wouldn't have missed it. Sorry about Dave, he was held up at work.'

Jo shrugged: her brother was a homicide detective, so he often went missing. It went with the territory. 'Was that all right? Not too academic?'

'Not at all, you pitched it perfectly. Everybody loved it.'

'Yes, we did,' said an elderly woman who'd approached. 'Sorry to interrupt, Professor King, but I wanted to thank you for such an engaging lecture.'

'I'm not a professor, but thank you so much.'

'Well, you should be. You're an interesting thinker and a clear speaker, not like these scrawny old roosters they wheel out. Wouldn't know an original idea if it bit them on the bum.'

Sylvia smirked unhelpfully, but Jo just gave a diplomatic smile. 'You're very kind.'

'Keep at it, dear; your time will come. Those old coots can't live forever!' The elderly woman patted Jo's forearm before making way for a nervy, intense man who'd been hovering at her shoulder, barely suppressing his agitation.

'That was exceedingly interesting, Dr King; thank you.' He was clutching an art book of the Vesalius woodcuts tightly to his chest. 'Most informative, and a daring hypothesis, if you don't mind me saying.'

'Thank you,' replied Jo. 'I see you're something of an admirer yourself.'

'Oh yes, he was the greatest mind of his time.'

Jo's eyebrows shot up. 'That's quite a claim.' Copernicus, Da Vinci, Michelangelo, Erasmus and Galileo all overlapped with Vesalius.

'Oh I'm not belittling his contemporaries; they were Titans. But the Master's legacy is far more profound than the historians generally allow, for mine. Present company excepted, of course.'

'You may have a point,' said Jo, not missing the enthusiast's title for his hero.

The man leaned in, glancing aside at the others waiting. 'I should be grateful if we were to discuss this in further depth. At your convenience, of course.'

This time it was Sylvia who raised her eyebrows, but Jo felt confident this was only the innocent if socially inept advance of a slightly obsessed hobbyist. All the same, this wasn't her first rodeo.

'Why don't you give me your phone number? Perhaps we can arrange a coffee.'

'I'd be very grateful,' he said, pulling out a notepad and inscribing a heavily-underlined *VESALIUS* followed by his name and number. 'It's always refreshing to find a like mind, don't you think?' He tore out the page and handed it to her.

Jo looked at the sheet. 'I look forward to it, Mr Porter.'

He laughed. 'Stephen, please.' A woman at his elbow cleared her throat and gave him a nudge. 'Well, I must be off. I look forward to hearing from you, Dr King. Goodnight.'

Jo smiled faintly at the odd man as he wheeled away, then turned to the next in line. She chatted briefly with a few more loiterers before Sylvia leaned in and said to the others, 'I'm terribly sorry, but we have to go now.' Jo smiled her regret and bundled her papers into a seasoned leather messenger bag. They made their escape, strolling through the mild autumn evening towards Sylvia's car on City Road.

'Good crowd,' said Sylvia. 'You even brought out the trainspotters.'

'He was a bit strange, wasn't he?'

'You're not going to call him, are you?'

'Not likely. I'm sure he's harmless enough, but you never can tell.'

'Well you certainly struck a chord, anyway. The punters loved it.'

'I hope I got the balance right. It wasn't too artsy?'

'Not at all; from a nurse's point of view you hit the mark,' Sylvia assured her as they got in the car. 'Stop angsting about it, Professor.'

Jo stuck her tongue out, then laughed.

They drove to Sylvia's place in Randwick and went through to the big, open living room at the back of the house. Sylvia dumped her keys in a gigantic mortar bowl that Jo had given them as a housewarming present. Its heavy marble pestle lived by the front door, in a drawer of the hall table. Her husband said he liked to have a weapon in every room.

'Tea?'

'Actually, I could use a drink.' Jo slumped into the sofa with a sigh.

'Now we're talking. What'll it be?'

'Do you have any of that Spanish black sherry?'

'Always.' Sylvia found a bottle of Pedro Ximénez and a couple of sherry glasses. 'So did you end up calling that bloke from last week?' she asked Jo while she poured. They'd been to see The Audreys and met a couple of nice fellas who'd shared their table during the set break. One of them had given

Jo his phone number, at Sylvia's covert suggestion.

'No, he wasn't my type.' She was still wary of intimacy with men since her breakup the year before. And with women, for that matter. Humans generally. It didn't leave a lot of options. Maybe she needed a pet.

'What do you mean? He was lovely!' said Sylvia, handing Jo her sherry. 'You had heaps in common.'

'It all just feels so pointless, Sylv.' Jo shrugged and looked into her glass. 'I mean, how do you even reach people?'

'But you have to try, Jo. Otherwise how would anyone connect?'

'Yeah, but it just takes so much energy. Then most of the time it all comes to nothing anyway. Sometimes I wonder how anyone can be bothered, you know what I mean?'

Sylvia was shaking her head at Jo's bleak assessment when the front door opened, way up the hallway.

'Ahoy, me hearties, anyone aboard?' came the cry.

The women looked at each other, parking the conversation for another time. 'You're just in time for a drink,' Sylvia called back.

Murphy bustled into the room, which suddenly seemed to shrink. 'Christ, I could do with one,' he said. 'Landed some new business today.' He took off his jacket then shrugged off his shoulder holster, depositing it into one of the kitchen drawers, revolver and all. He came into the lounge room and leaned down to kiss his wife.

'Jo's lecture was brilliant tonight,' Sylvia told him as he pulled away.

'Oh, great,' he said, kissing his sister on the cheek. 'What was it on again?' He crossed to the sideboard to add his own keys to the mortar and withdraw a beer from the built-in bar-fridge.

'A painting by Hans Holbein the Younger, *The Body of the Dead Christ in the Tomb.* Dostoevsky made a fuss about it.'

'Was he your PhD guy?' asked Murphy as he flopped into the armchair.

'No, that's Vermeer. Holbein was Henry VIII's official painter.'

'So what about this painting?'

'I have a theory about its influence on Andreas Vesalius.'

'Who's that?'

'Oh, nobody, only the founder of modern European anatomy.'

'All right, smart-arse. And what was it in aid of?'

'This new arts-meets-science outreach program the uni's running.'

'It was a big deal to be invited to deliver it,' Sylvia said pointedly.

'Sorry I missed it,' said Murphy, 'but new customers always have priority.' His expression turned serious. 'Shit.' He lunged for the remote and switched the television on. Jo thought he was checking the news regarding his new homicide case. But, no. 'Forgot about the replay.' He flicked the channels until he found the rugby league. 'I missed the Anzac Day game last week. You girls don't mind, do ya?'

The women exchanged a look: *too bad if we do.* Jo finished her sherry and tilted her head towards the front door.

Sylvia nodded. 'Walk you home?' Jo only lived fifteen minutes' walk away, in Coogee. Well, fifteen minutes there, twenty back: there was a decent hill in between. Sylvia could do with the stretch.

'You can stay, sis.' Murphy's eyes were glued to half a dozen shiny white arses, all heaving and flexing, straining against an opposing knot of dark blue.

'Nah, I've got a stack of essays to mark.'

'Righto, then, see ya.' His eyes didn't leave the screen.

Jo came around in front of Murphy, deliberately blocking his view, and leaned down to kiss him on the crown of his head. 'See you, bro.'

'Oh, for...' Murphy ducked his head to the side to keep the screen in view. 'Don't be long, darl,' he told his wife.

***

The Dragons won the scrum but coughed it up immediately in a crunching tackle. A certain amount of chatter went on between the womenfolk in the background, so he turned up the volume. He heard the front door, then silence.

He leaped up and grabbed another beer from the fridge without taking his eyes off the screen, but the Roosters spun it out the backline fast, culminating in a bold cut-out pass to the winger who barged over the try-line right out wide. 'Fuck.' Murphy bolted up the hall and changed into tracky dacks and an old Bintang T-shirt. He made it back for the conversion, an impressive kick from just inside the touch-line. 'Faark.' He flopped onto the sofa, took a swig of beer and let out a fruity belch. This was more like it.

VOLUME I

THE BONES AND CARTILAGES

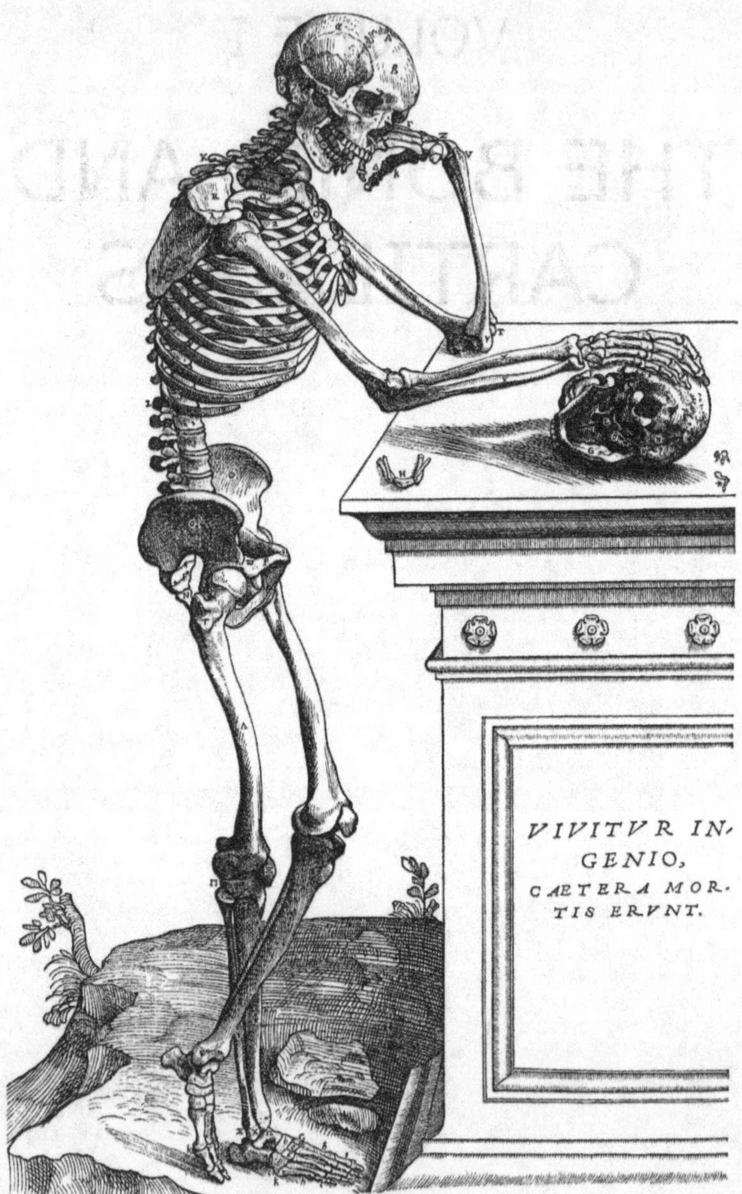
VIVITVR IN-
GENIO,
CAETERA MOR-
TIS ERVNT.

Andreas Vesalius was born in the Holy Roman city of Brussels on 31 December 1514. By his late twenties, he had already attracted widespread acclaim for his teaching and research in human anatomy at the University of Padua. This youthful achievement excited controversy over his disrespect for the established order.

The problem was not that his approach was ineffective or incorrect. Quite the contrary. To try to change the world may be tolerable, even laudable; to be right while doing so, however, is unforgivable.

In 1543, Vesalius travelled to Basel to publish his successful lecture series, in a bid to outflank his critics and secure his reputation. The Swiss city was the centre of European publishing and a significant site of Renaissance debate in scientific, humanistic and religious affairs. Calvin, Holbein, Erasmus, Zwingli and Paracelsus were all associated with the city in the decade or two before Vesalius arrived.

While he was lodged there preparing the *Fabrica* for publication, Vesalius conducted what would become medical history's most celebrated public dissection.

His canvas was the corpse of Jakob Karrer of Gebweiler, who had attempted the murder of his first wife in order to resolve an inconvenient state of bigamy. The criminal's head had been detached from his shoulders on 12 May 1543, *pour encourager les autres,* and the body was donated for the demonstration. The Master continued the dismemberment initiated by the city's executioner, but with far greater finesse and to a loftier pedagogical purpose.

After the dissection, the Master separated the bones from the detached flesh and viscera, assembled the skeleton and presented it to the University of Basel, where it is displayed to this day. Should you ever have the opportunity to inspect it, I highly recommend the experience.

Visually, the first Volume of the *Fabrica* is an exercise in restraint, depicting only bones, singly or in clusters, with arrays of cartilage here and there among swathes of closely descriptive text. The odd resected joint, cross-sectioned long bone or exposed intracranial surface is about as grisly as it gets.

Bones, in any case, are the least confronting of human remains. Every day in museums the world over, hordes of schoolchildren troop past cabinets of bones, and trauma does not ensue. Bones are familiar, inert, harmless curiosities.

At the end of Volume I we find three leaves, each wholly devoted to a complete skeleton posed in demeanours of bleak anguish and existential contemplation. Yet to a modern eye, they appear ridiculous. The right arm slung jauntily across the tomb-spade in the first illustration is almost slapstick; the elegantly crossed ankles in the second plate are more George Clooney than Hamlet, Prince of Denmark; and the cry-baby pose of the third image inspires outright scorn. The Master's sombre *memento mori* is rendered farcical by the modern evocation of cartoon dancing skeletons and lurid Halloween costumes. It is a travesty. The massive, appalling vulgarity of society, as Marguerite Duras has it.

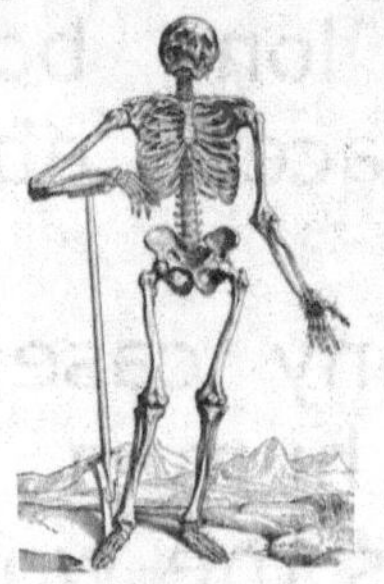

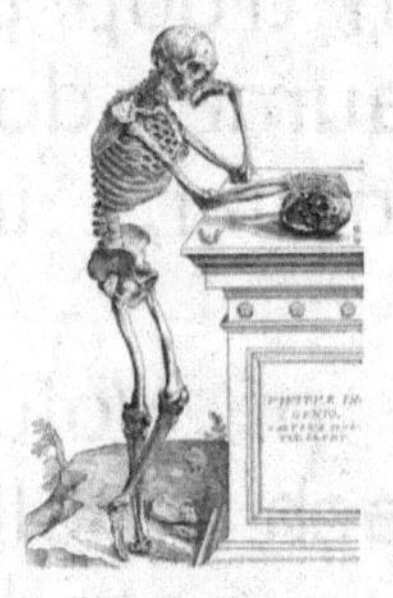

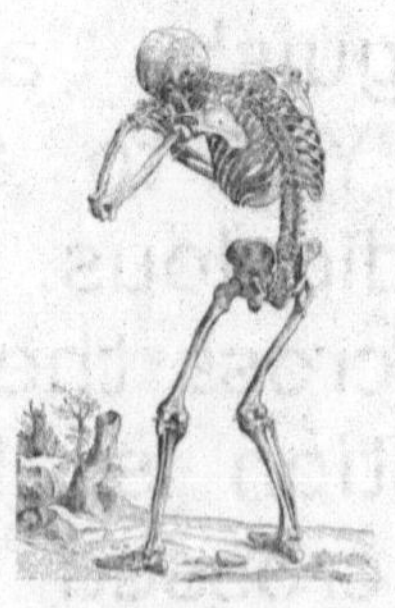

Tuesday 1 May – morning

Amy Chartier wrapped up her crime scene briefing to the Homicide Squad within the Sydney Police Centre at Surry Hills. She glanced over at Murphy and he nodded. Safe pair of hands, Chartier was. He had to admit she'd grown into the job under his supervision, despite the occasional moment of friction when he'd offended her lesbian feminist sensibilities. It didn't hurt that she was easy on the eye, although he kept that to himself.

Chartier switched off the visuals and everyone relaxed palpably: most of her colleagues were hardened veterans, but it was ugly viewing. Even Murphy was relieved to be released from their grisly hold. He swivelled around on the corner of the desk he was sitting on to face the four other detectives, most of them clustered around the briefing table. 'Any questions?'

'Do we have any leads?' asked Nguyễn. The former Drug Squad

detective had transferred to Homicide about a year ago, and was still playing everything by the book. The question was a gimme, but someone had to ask it.

'Nothing from the doorknock so far,' said Chartier. 'Nobody saw anything and nobody even really knew the vic. He lived in Strathfield, worked at home as a day trader. According to his wife he was doing the place up, then they were going to move in.'

'What did she say?' asked Nguyễn.

'She's a bit of a mess, as you'd expect. We'll need to interview her again, but she told me last night she has no idea who would kill him or why. He was a bit of a prickly character, apparently, but he had no real enemies. Not like this.'

'Does he have any form?' asked Nikolaidis, the squad's forensic data specialist. He was sitting in his usual position, atop an ancient battleship-grey filing cabinet, only still in use because it was too heavy to move. 'Maybe he was into something she didn't know about.'

'No, he's clean as far as we can tell,' replied Chartier. 'The labourer didn't notice anything suss, either.'

'What about his mobile phone?' Murphy asked.

'No call activity all Friday afternoon. It seems to have been switched to voicemail that evening.'

'So it was either pre-arranged or a drop-in,' he said. Chartier nodded.

'Who's the chief SOCO?' Nikolaidis asked.

'Mack's running the show for Forensic Services,' said Murphy, to a murmur of approval. 'He'll give us a medical briefing once the autopsy results are in.'

'Any DNA?' asked Harris, the rookie. After three months on the squad he was starting to look the part, Murphy thought, but he still tended to take shelter in technical matters to avoid coming across as clueless. It didn't always work.

'A few biological traces, after excluding the victim and his labourer, but they're minuscule,' said Chartier. 'Could just as easily have come in on building supplies. No DNA matches on CrimTrac, for what it's worth.'

'So, on resources,' added Murphy. 'With the premier's support, Commissioner Carr is making this investigation a priority, so we get two extra uniforms for the hackwork.'

'Yeah, well, there is an election next year.' In addition to crunching the data, Nikloaidis was the house cynic.

'When did you become so jaded, Niko?' Murphy shook his head mournfully. 'Maybe the premier just cares.'

'Takes a serial killer for him to get serious, though,' said Nguyễn, backing up her colleague.

'So that's what we have here, is it, Nguyễn?'

'The newspapers think so,' she replied. 'And the government, apparently.'

'A serial killer. Okay.' Murphy was enjoying himself a bit too much. 'You realise that seriality entails more than one body, right?'

'Sure, boss, but there are other hallmarks.'

'And maybe there's another body out there somewhere,' added Harris.

'All right, let's look at the data before we get carried away,' said Murphy. 'Janssen, what proportion of Australian homicides are serial killings?'

Detective Sergeant Matthijs Janssen stood and faced the room. A tall, pale, rangy man who still carried a faint accent from a childhood in the Netherlands, Janssen was the resident scholar, with a natural seriousness leavened by intelligent bemusement. 'Just under one per cent, in the sense you mean, excluding organised crime and terrorism,' he said.

'And how do serial killings differ from other homicides, statistically?'

'According to the Institute of Criminology, about two-thirds of all homicide victims in Australia are male. The typical scenario is a man in his thirties killing a male acquaintance with a knife, in an argument in a residential setting. Often while intoxicated with alcohol or drugs.

'One-third of homicide victims are female, the vast majority also killed by a male known to them – usually a partner or ex-partner; sometimes a relative – also in a domestic setting, by knife or blunt trauma.

'By contrast,' continued Janssen, '*two*-thirds of serial victims are female, killed by a man not known to them, by knife or strangulation in a *non*-domestic setting. There is commonly a sexual element and often evidence of advance planning.'

'Sound like our guy to you?' asked Murphy.

'Well, he's got a knife.' Nguyễn shrugged, not conceding. 'Sounds well planned, and it's not in the home, exactly. Could be sexual, for all we know. Plus, there's no connection yet.'

'All true, but it's early days,' said Murphy. 'And not only serial killers plan ahead.'

'So, wait: are you saying this is *not* a serial killer?' asked Harris.

'Oh, fuck no,' said Murphy. 'I'd never say that. Not out loud, anyway.'

'Not while the premier's allocating extra resources,' added Nikolaidis dryly.

'I don't get it, boss,' said Harris.

Murphy sat on the edge of the desk and leaned forward. 'I'm sure you've watched your share of television, my boy, and if you'd been paying attention instead of inspecting your undercarriage you would know that, in the public imagination, the key to getting away with murder is misdirection: making Inspector Plod think the crime he's investigating is different from the crime you've committed.'

'People often try to make murder look like an accident,' said Janssen. 'Or suicide.'

'But every now and then, someone goes the full Hannibal,' said Nikolaidis.

'So, yes, this one *looks* a lot like a serial killer starting up,' said Murphy. 'It's very ugly, somewhat ritualistic, methodical and well-planned. *But.*' He lifted a finger and paused for effect. 'Experience suggests that all the melodrama is probably just smoke and mirrors.'

Chartier nodded. 'I haven't worked on anything like this before, but I kind of recognised the scene: not from reality, but from TV. Whether or not it's actually a serial killing, it *looks* like one.'

'As though it's been done for effect,' said Janssen.

'Exactly,' said Chartier. 'Everyone knows the set-up these days.'

'But that's right: everyone knows it,' said Nguyễn. 'Including serial killers.'

'What do you mean?' asked Nikolaidis.

'A serial killer would watch the same TV as the rest of us. It could just as easily be his inspiration for real.'

'That's true, Nguyễn, and we won't be excluding the possibility,' said Murphy. 'But it's probably just somebody's broken heart, or a bad drug deal, or a hook-up gone wrong, and he wants us to think we have a fucken lunatic out there.'

'So what now?' asked Harris.

'Start with the victim's connections,' said Janssen. 'Family, friends, neighbours, colleagues. It's never completely random. Not even with serial killers.'

'It's not that complicated,' added Murphy. 'Homicide always comes down to rage, money or sex. So find out who he knows, who he owes and who he blows.'

Wednesday 9 May – evening

'So you caught this serial killer case, Dave,' said Jo while he refilled her glass with sauvignon blanc. The three of them were eating at a favourite Thai joint in the backstreets of Coogee. The grumpy Sydney autumn had finally shown up, a blustery wind whipping sheets of rain and sodden branches against the restaurant's plate-glass window.

'If that's what it is,' Murphy replied.

'There being only the one body and all?' Jo asked.

He nodded. 'That, and it smells to me like a red herring.'

'Hell of a red herring,' said Sylvia as Murphy refreshed her glass. She shuddered visibly.

'I reckon,' said Jo, grimacing. 'What makes you think that?'

'It was so well planned and executed.' Murphy filled his own glass to the brim. 'No one saw him, he used proper euthanasia drugs and he left no trace at all, from an entire weekend.

He must've been suited up like our crime-scene people: paper suit, booties, gloves, cap. Took everything away with him: piss, shit, garbage, the lot. It looked pretty professional to me.'

'You think it's a hit?' asked Jo.

'Not a spontaneous crime of passion, that's for sure.'

'Who'd go to those lengths to throw you off the scent?'

'I wouldn't put it past the big drug outfits,' said Murphy. 'Shit, I wouldn't put it past the property developers, if the price was right.'

'Can we talk about something else?' asked Sylvia.

But Jo was intrigued. 'Surely this wasn't just business, though. I mean, it's sickening.'

'I'm not saying they didn't enjoy themselves, but it's misdirection. Hoping we'll go all *True Detective,* start chasing shadows.'

'But then isn't a front-page headline counter-productive?'

Murphy shrugged. 'Maybe they're sending a signal to the rivals.'

'Crikey. Overkill, much?'

'People are capable of anything, sis.'

'Yeah, but cutting him up like that.' Jo shivered. 'I mean, that poor man.'

'Mm, maybe.' Murphy shrugged.

'What do you mean, "maybe"?' Jo protested. 'It's horrific.'

'These people aren't always angels themselves, Jo. Sorry to disillusion you.'

'But nobody deserves to be sliced into ribbons.'

'That's enough, you two,' insisted Sylvia. 'Really.'

'Fair enough,' said Jo, holding her hands up.

Murphy smirked at her across the table. 'Don't spread that around, by the way.'

'I won't. You're getting enough attention already.'

'Tell me about it. The journos are all over this, so of course the pollies are all twitchy. The minister's calling the commissioner first thing every morning for an update. Wants something new every day.'

'Must be hard to get on with the job.'

'Fucken oath,' said Murphy. 'Reminds me, I've got a bit of a problem with Sunday.'

Jo's eyes narrowed. 'What sort of problem?' The coming Sunday was Mother's Day, and the siblings made a point of visiting their mother's grave every year. Well, Jo made a point of it, and Dave trailed along: at least he had so far, over the three years since they'd lost her.

'I've got to write the minister's brief for cabinet. There's no other time.'

Jo sat back and folded her arms. 'Really, David?'

'Don't be like that.'

'She's only at Waverley, Dave. Surely you can spare her half an hour.'

Murphy's colour rose. He swirled the wine in his glass, draining it savagely in one draught. 'It's not half an hour, Jo, and you know it.' He poured himself the last of the wine. 'First we go and choose flowers. Then we go to the cemetery and pay our respects, usually in the rain. Then you talk to her, for fuck's sake, then you make me talk to her. Then we go for lunch so we can talk about her some more. At some point we have a fight and my day is a fucken write-off.'

'We fight because you behave like an arsehole.'

'Jesus, Jo...'

'So you're getting in early this year, are you? How efficient.'

Murphy took another slug. 'I'm not going to argue with you, Jo. I have to go to work; that's that.'

Jo regarded him sourly. 'You don't have any common decency, do you?'

'Christ, Joanna, it's not going to make any difference to Mum, is it?'

'Oh, for...' said Jo, pushing her seat back and standing up. She turned to Sylvia. 'I'm sorry, sis. I have to go.'

Sylvia stood and hugged her sister-in-law, then watched as she hurried out into the blustery night without a word to her brother. 'Nice one, Dave.'

'Not another word, Sylvia.'

The waitress chose that moment to ask if they wanted dessert. Murphy shook his head sullenly and handed her his credit card without looking up.

They dashed to the car then drove home in silence.

Thursday 10 May – morning

Stephen Porter poured his second cup of tea for the morning and reflected on the public lecture on Andreas Vesalius early the previous week. It had been audacious to attend, in light of how he'd spent the weekend preceding, but obsession had overwhelmed prudence.

The art historian had discussed Holbein's *The Body of the Dead Christ in the Tomb,* executed at Basel in 1522. 'I'm not going into details, it's too horrible,' she had warned, citing commentary on the paintings by everyone from Fyodor Dostoevsky to Julia Kristeva. These critics all remarked upon the image's devastating existential force, while uniformly struggling to account for it. The lecturer argued that this uncanny power was an effect of Holbein's mercilessly unsentimental physiological accuracy: by painting exactly what he saw – over many days, using a drowned man for his model, the body progressively decomposing before his eyes in the studio – Holbein had achieved a kind of temporal compression within the scene of the painting, with all phases of post-mortem deterioration existing simultaneously inside the frame. This was more than a dead man, which the theology could handle: it was a hyper-dead man, which denied the possibility of resurrection and divinity.

She speculated that Vesalius – who would certainly have seen the *Dead Christ* while in Basel two decades later – would have immediately apprehended the importance of rendering exactly what one saw visually, in addition to describing it textually, ensuring the artistic values of empiricism he set for the *Fabrica* matched his scientific standards.

Porter had been persuaded by the academic's argument, but not her preference for restraint: her thesis turned entirely on those very forensic aspects that caused disquiet, the specific manifestations of death and decay upon the mortal flesh after its abandonment by life and by God. The pursuit of Truth did not brook squeamishness. As the Master himself had demonstrated, anatomical enquiry was not for the faint-hearted.

There was no 'too horrible' about it.

On the other hand, it had been clear from the chatter around him as he had risen from his seat and waited to speak with the academic that her lecture had been perfectly calibrated to its audience, with just a frisson of horror but not too much visceral detail. His own inclinations notwithstanding, Porter conceded that the scholar had the measure of her public.

It had been dangerous to approach this Dr Joanna King, but if she made contact he would relish the chance to pick her brains on the *Fabrica.* He would need to be cautious, however: an intelligent, knowledgeable scholar on a wavelength harmonic with his own, she had the potential to make intuitive leaps that could prove awkward.

He turned his mind to the triumph of his first dissection. It had unfolded almost perfectly, and the results had exceeded his hopes. The working conditions had been ideal, with complete privacy for the duration and excellent light afforded by exquisite weather. The gods had smiled.

The one shortcoming of his otherwise faultless method had been the intensity of the struggle at the outset: he had failed to anticipate the quantum of brute strength required. He had been prepared for resistance, of course – it was no small thing to separate a body from its life – but he had been surprised by the subject's sheer ferocity. Despite Porter's superior physique, it had been an uncomfortably near thing.

His fundamental error had been selecting a young man in prime condition. It had seemed logical to choose the very best specimens available, but in retrospect this was of least importance to the bones, and it had made the operation more difficult.

The study of the musculature, however, would indeed require an outstanding physique, which entailed strength and agility. A female of compact stature was the answer, he realised: one against whom he could exploit his advantages of height, weight and strength, offsetting fitness and survival instinct.

Thenceforth it would become simpler. Physical excellence was less important for subsequent Volumes, beyond a baseline of reasonable health. All the same, he needed to be in vastly better shape than his candidates, to put the result beyond doubt. Tying the laces of his running shoes, he resolved to double the length of his daily circuit, and to extend his schedule with Charlie, his pitiless combat trainer, to six days a week. The current regime was simply inadequate.

Friday 11 May – evening

'Hey, Dave, how was your day?' asked Sylvia as Murphy strode into the living room then flung his bag and jacket onto the sofa.

He only grunted in reply as he crossed to the sideboard, dropped his keys into the mortar and opened a beer. He drank deeply then sighed in satisfaction. 'Fuck, that's better.' He removed his shoulder holster and dropped his enormous revolver into its kitchen drawer.

Sylvia stood up and rested her guitar in its cradle on the wall. She asked mildly, 'Dave, would it be okay if you kept your gun in the safe, please?'

'No, darlin', it lives in there,' he replied, pointing with the bottle at the kitchen drawers. 'Third drawer down. That's where people keep handy utensils. And there's no handier utensil than a .357 Magnum.'

'It makes me nervous, honey, that's all. Isn't it supposed to be secured?' She didn't like to nag about it, but she could never quite relax when that weapon was in the house. It would help if it were in the gun safe.

Murphy drew in a sharp breath, but he blew out his cheeks and rolled out his best Clint Eastwood. 'Little lady, there are two kinds of guns in this world: the ones locked away like the law says, and the ones that'll save your life.'

According to Jo, Murphy had been riffing off *The Good, the Bad and the Ugly* since he was about thirteen, when the other kids were rolling out lines from Ferris Bueller or Monty Python. He'd tried it on with Sylvia the night they first met in a Newtown pub and it had worked a charm, making her laugh after a particularly brutal double shift at RPA. She'd been a sucker for it ever since.

She could see she wasn't going to get anywhere on the revolver business tonight, so she went along with it. 'Could be you know what's best, Blondie.'

'Damn straight I do,' he drawled.

'Supposin' you fix us some drinks, then, and bring 'em to the waterhole?'

'Is it warm enough?' he asked, dropping out of character. It was a pretty fresh night out, clear but cold.

'Should be, I turned the heater on earlier.'

He switched on the outside light and the courtyard appeared beyond the wall of glass doors, the plunge pool shrouded in steam. It looked like a scene from *The Lord of the Rings.*

'All right, then. What'll it be, purty lady?'

'Sauvignon blanc, please, barkeep,' said Sylvia as she shed her slackerwear.

Murphy looked her up and down – although less up than down as she bent to take off her socks. 'Fuck, you're gorgeous,' he said.

'Why thank you, kind sir.' She gave him a mock curtsy then opened the back door. She yelped at the cold night air and dashed for the pool.

***

'Goin' for a slash, Sylv,' Murphy called out as he raced up to the study.

He opened his PC to check that his new wireless spy camera was recording. It was one of a pair: the one on the front door was to record any comings and goings, and this one out the back would keep an eye on what Sylvia got up to when he wasn't here, and capture a bit of the action for posterity when he was. Everything was perfect: the motion sensor had activated and the resolution was incredible. The angle was fine for now, but he'd have to adjust it later to pick up the living room a bit better, especially the sofa. He watched his unsuspecting naked wife for a moment, enjoying her obliviousness as much as the high definition view of her flawless body. He went back to the living room, poured a glass of chardonnay for Sylvia and a bourbon for himself, then headed outside for a piece of the real thing.

By the time he came out she was lying back, nicely relaxed and warmed up, her long coppery hair floating round her head like a halo as she looked up at the Southern Cross through the branches of the tall Sydney red gum in the yard behind. 'Pretty handsome for an old fella,' she said as he stepped down into the pool, giving him a sultry look.

'Cheeky bitch,' he said. He handed Sylvia her glass and angled his own towards it. 'Cheers.'

They each took a drink then put their glasses up on the poolside. Murphy reached for Sylvia's feet, so she started the pool jets, leaned back on the edge and closed her eyes as he started massaging. 'Christ, that feels good.'

Murphy shot a glance towards the video camera, too small to see from the pool, as he worked both of her feet thoroughly, dissolving the knots that had accumulated over days on her feet at the hospital. He kneaded his way up her calves and past the backs of her knees, eliciting further groans, working his way up her thighs towards his true objective, tending inwards and upwards.

But before he could get there, Sylvia glided away and reached for her glass. Murphy took his own and drained the whiskey in one throw. 'Oh no you don't, li'l darlin',' he growled, beckoning to her. 'It's time to repay your debt to society.'

Sylvia put her wine down and floated back to him, her body straight out in front. Murphy's left hand grasped a breast while his right moved down her flank, her hips tilting towards him. If access was on offer, Murphy was inclined to take it – it was just a matter of good policy – so he slipped a finger into her warmth as she stroked him. After a while Sylvia rolled over in the water and floated right up to his face.

'I want you inside me,' she breathed.

There it was: the most exquisite sentence in the entire English language. A lyrical phrase on the lips of any woman, with Sylvia's low, husky delivery it was fucken sublime.

'Glad to oblige,' he said, taking her hand and leading her out of the pool.

Sunday 13 May – late morning

Jo cycled up the lane behind her block of flats, her temper as foul as the weather, which had lashed her all the way home from Waverley Cemetery in gusty curtains full of leaves and grit. She'd hoped a hard physical ride in the steep streets behind the eastern beaches would calm her down, but the rainstorm and the bad behaviour of the car drivers had only made things worse. She locked her road bike then climbed the back stairs and let herself in, water streaming off her onto the carpet inside her back door. She headed straight to the bathroom, where she peeled off every sodden layer and stepped into the shower, washing away the muck from the torrent outside.

That bloody brother of hers. Murphy had been like this her entire life: self-absorbed, instinctively belligerent, and scornful of emotion while oblivious to how driven by emotion he was himself – especially by anger.

Not to mention his complete denial of the huge empty space in their lives where their mother used to be. All in service of his lifelong delusion that their mother had never been present to him in the first place.

As her mum had told it, Murphy senior had never been close to David: an unsympathetic, old-school disciplinarian, he'd been a spectator in all other aspects of child-rearing, regarding it as women's work. He'd called his son 'boy' and had been capable of not even acknowledging him for days on end. Yet the five-year-old had worshipped Diarmaid, and had been utterly devastated by his sudden absence. That pain had never left Murphy, and was only augmented once he joined the Force, gaining access to buried files and the guarded confidences of veteran cops.

By the time Jo came along two years later, her brother was already in open rebellion against both their mother and the kind, generous, patient man she'd married: according to David, his mother was a traitor to a sacred memory, and the usurper was a feeble substitute for his fallen hero father. Jo presented further competition for his mother's attention, so he'd launched a life-long project of antagonism against his baby sister. Older siblings are as demigods to an infant, and it took Jo a long time to realise that the sneaky cruelties and the withering contempt that her brother inflicted upon her were not simply the way of the world. School was a revelation, a place where people liked her and generally treated her well, and where lessons weren't laced with outright falsehoods and booby-traps designed to wrong-foot her and get her in trouble. She thrived on this level playing field, and her self-sufficiency and competence soon neutralised her brother's psychological warfare. By the time he'd hit his moody teens, they were ignoring one another completely.

It was only when Jo's father was diagnosed with cancer that Murphy softened a little, becoming closer to him and their mum in the final year of his life. But after Jo's dad died, Murphy withdrew again from their mother, retreating before her grief at being widowed for a second time. He'd affected indifference ever since, even through their mother's declining health. After her final episode, all he'd had to offer Jo was the observation that a heart attack in your sleep wasn't a bad way to go.

It was vintage Murphy. He refused to be tactful or sensitive. Or to just shut the fuck up.

The water started to cool slightly, and Jo realised she'd been standing under the spray for ages. She stepped out of the shower into the billowing steam and dried herself off, then dashed to her bedroom for a bathrobe and slippers. In the living room, she poured a good dose of Baileys over ice and sat on her sofa, watching the storm thrash the upper branches of the Norfolk pines across the way. She closed her eyes and focused on her breathing. She could use a restorative afternoon of painting, but she needed to get her brother out of her head first.

Thursday 7 June – evening

Arriving home from his twelve-hour day shift, Porter locked the door, drew the curtains and started his stereo, playing Birgit Nilsson's peerless 1966 performance of *Tristan und Isolde* at Bayreuth, opposite Wolfgang Windgassen and conducted by Karl Böhm.

He donned a pair of custom-fitted unpowdered polyisoprene disposable surgical gloves and went to the hall cupboard. He pulled out a vintage Gladstone bag that he'd purchased on the Portobello Road several years ago. Of British manufacture, circa 1925, it was genuine crocodile skin tanned to a deep mahogany, with the initials *ELM* in gold lettering on one flank. He then opened the vacuum cleaner and removed an orange pouch from behind the dust bag. Handmade by Louis Cardini of soft ostrich leather, it held a Browning Hi-Power Mark III automatic pistol, the standard-issue sidearm of the Australian Defence Force. Porter had procured the weapon from an entrepreneur of the enlisted ranks inside the Holsworthy Barracks. He slid the pouch into a sturdy pocket inside the Gladstone bag's front wall and took the whole lot out to the living room.

Next into the bag went a photocopy of Volume II of the *New Fabrica,* a gorgeous new translation recently published by Karger of Basel to celebrate the quincentenary of Vesalius's birth. With freshly rendered illustrations, luminous page presentation and text in English, it was perfect for his project, although both too bulky and far too precious to take on site. He had made separate high-resolution wire-bound photocopies of each of the seven Volumes, in preparation for his Tribute.

He crossed to an antique red-lacquered Chinese cabinet and transferred to the bag an assortment of surgical instruments and supplies: lancets, scissors, forceps, clamps, hooks, chisels, rib spreaders, syringes, probes, retractors, sponges. A basic first-aid kit, an entire box of his custom-fitted disposable gloves, nail-polish remover, tissues, a dozen large plastic bin-liners, two-dozen energy-gel packs, a collapsed plastic expansion bladder, a hooded protective coverall suit, a pair of matching overboots, a hairnet and two N95 masks. He covered it all with a small navy-blue hand-towel.

He took a black syringe case from the Chinese cabinet into the kitchen. He removed an unmarked bottle of freeze-dried sodium thiopental powder from his pantry, stirred a teaspoon into a shot glass half-filled with hot water and drew the solution into a blue-capped syringe. He removed two vials of pancuronium bromide from the dairy section of his refrigerator, transferring the contents of one into another syringe, this one red-capped. He placed both syringes and the spare vial into the case.

The combination of these two drugs was the preferred formula for Dutch euthanasia. The thiopental sedative acted on the brain to induce coma, then the curare-mimetic muscle relaxant stilled the diaphragm and halted the breath. While the pancuronium would be administered intravenously, it had the handy characteristic of being effective via intramuscular delivery. Porter found comfort in the insurance of bringing an extra dose along, just in case.

He took a bottle of liquid midazolam from the fridge, used it to thoroughly soak a pad of soft, absorbent fabric then sealed the fabric in a sandwich bag, ready to deploy. The powerful, short-acting benzodiazepine had a soporific effect nearly as rapid and deep as that inaccurately ascribed by Hollywood to chloroform, allowing him to inject the other drugs. It also had the happy side effect of anterograde amnesia, useful in the unlikely event his meticulous planning somehow failed and he had to abort.

Each of these formulations was regulated in Australia as a Schedule 4 drug: a simple prescription medicine. Considering what Porter was using them for, they had been indecently easy to procure: a few borrowed medical identities, a little homework on sympotomatology, several careless doctors and a dozen suburban pharmacies, and he possessed enough pharmaceuticals to despatch the entire population of Blues Point Tower. It was a scandal, really.

He placed the drugs in the Gladstone bag on top of the navy towel, along with a final pair of disposable gloves ready for immediate access, finishing with a Masonite clipboard on top. He closed the bag and set it by the front door, then took a bottle of clear nail polish from the bathroom cabinet and left it on the kitchen counter, ready for application to his fingertips before the following day's excursion.

Finally, he packed a small overnight bag with clothes and toiletries for his two nights in a bland Manly motel. During his detailed research he had learned that most perpetrators of lethal crimes were identified and taken into custody within forty-eight hours of the act. His rigorous protocol therefore entailed sleeping elsewhere, listening to a police scanner, watching the news broadcasts and surveilling his home and workplace for a couple of days afterwards.

He degloved, satisfied with his evening's work. He ate a light supper then poured a glass of Armagnac, collected the new issue of *Quadrant* that had arrived in the day's mail and took himself off for an early night.

Thursday 7 June – evening

Sylvia came in late from an exhausting twelve-hour day shift to find Murphy on the couch with an empty wine glass, watching some car show on the television while their expensive kitchen steadfastly refused to cook them dinner on its own initiative.

'Hey, Sylv,' he said distractedly.

She bent over to kiss him. 'How was your day?'

'Same old,' he replied. 'Bad guys still doing bad guy shit and the idiots still in charge.' He was always this cheerful when he'd been watching the news. 'What's for tea, anyway? I'm starved.'

She took a deep breath and held it while crossing to the fridge to consider their options. 'How about pan-fried salmon and steamed vegies?' she asked, once she trusted herself to speak.

'Sounds good, darlin'.' An ad came on and Murphy took his empty glass to the sideboard. 'Want a drink?'

'Yes, please,' replied Sylvia, heading for the hall. 'I'll just get changed.'

'Grenache all right?' he called after her. He cocked his ear to listen but there was nothing. He poured her a glass of the red anyway and topped up his own.

She came back into the living room to find Murphy muttering darkly, having embarked on some technical challenge with the home cinema. It looked like he was trying to set the system to record something, but the software had updated and he couldn't work the new menu.

'Oh, before I forget, Dave,' said Sylvia as she gathered ingredients, 'Claire at work asked if she could stay over tomorrow night.'

'Claire?'

'Yeah, she's going to Ireland on Saturday morning. Six o'clock flight.'

'Ireland?'

'Yeah. So I said it was okay for her to stay here,' she ventured cautiously as she started washing vegetables.

'Why? She lives next door.' He was utterly distracted, lost in an obscure sub-menu.

Sylvia struggled not to laugh. 'Not Clare next door, Dave. Claire from work.'

'Oh. But why does she need to stay with us?' He cursed, bailed out to the main menu and started again.

'She lives out west, in Wenty I think. With all the security she has to be there by four. Starting from here will be a lot easier for her.'

'Why can't she stay next door?'

Sylvia silently lost it, but eventually regained her composure. 'They don't know one another, Dave. They just have the same name.'

'Oh, for fuck's sake.' Murphy gave up on the TV and threw down the remote. 'You know I don't like randoms in my house, Sylvia. Definitely not overnight.'

'She's not a random, we work together.'

'Well I don't know her, do I?'

Because we never socialise with my colleagues, Sylvia almost said. Instead, she went with, 'It's only one night.'

'When's this?'

'Tomorrow night.'

'We're going sailing on Saturday. Have to be up at sparrow's.'

'I know. She'll be gone by three-thirty.'

Murphy grunted, having run out of objections. 'Who even is she?'

'You met her at Deb's wedding. Strawberry blonde, amber eyes.' That rang no bells. 'Plum watered silk dress, off the shoulder.'

'Oh yeah, I remember.' Claire had scrubbed up very well that day. 'All right, but I'm not getting up to let her out.'

'You won't know a thing about it,' Sylvia assured him. She laid the fish in the hot pan and the sizzle prevented any further conversation.

VOLUME II

THE LIGAMENTS AND MUSCLES

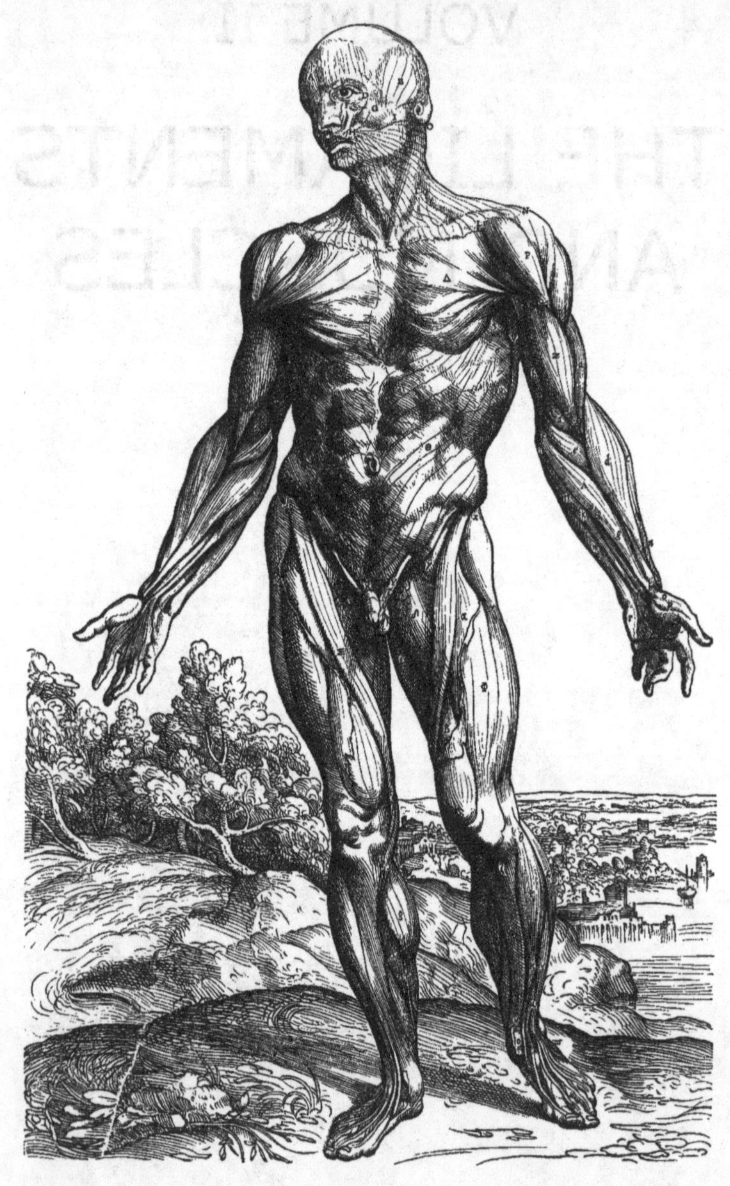

Rendered in exquisite and merciless detail, the depiction of the dissected musculature of the second Volume produces the *Fabrica*'s highest pitch of visual horror. Presaged by a single introductory page of close text, fourteen full-body figures blur into a medieval pageant of violation and misery. The gruesome opening of Foucault's *Discipline and Punish* is a lullaby by comparison.

The first figure, flayed and abject, stands on high ground overlooking Padua, gazing heavenward in an attitude of supplication. Or perhaps we are merely observing the postural effect of the rope that has anchored the model, omitted from the illustration.

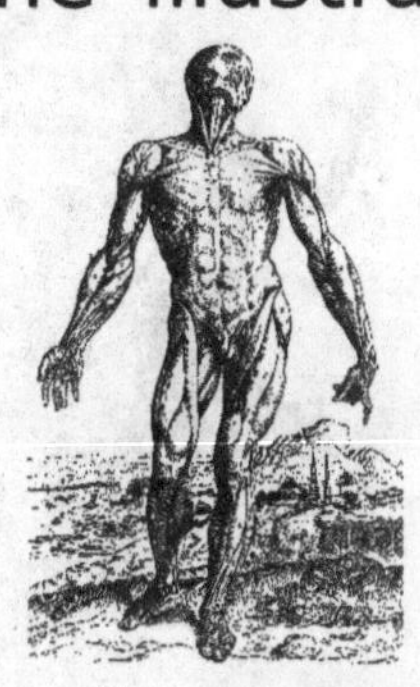

A second figure in an athletic stance and a third in a frank, conversational aspect do not trouble us overmuch, but disquiet is initiated with the awkward posture of the fourth figure (wrongly titled the first – the printer would institute more rigorous quality controls after the production of the *Fabrica*), visibly shamed by the loss of the outer layers of muscle. Many of the long muscles have been severed from their superior attachments and hang, ruined and tawdry, from their still intact lower attachments.

This gruesome procedure of stripping and severing escalates as we advance. The sixth figure's visage is truly terrifying, a kind of anti-mask from an alien horror film, the facial muscles torn asunder. Whole strips of abdominal muscle dangle limp and useless between the legs, almost unnoticed beneath the ghastly head.

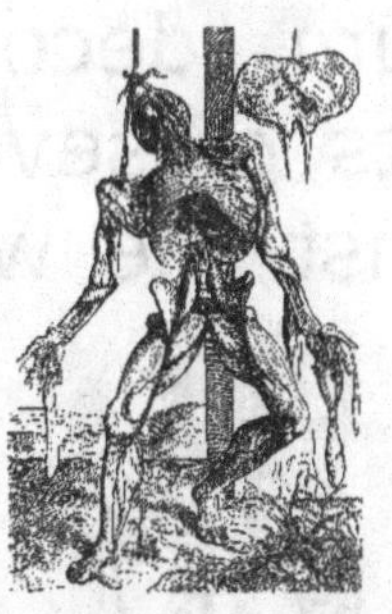

The seventh figure is the most harrowing of all, strung up by rope next to a blank wall. Gutted and stripped of musculature, it is all cavity and barely shrouded bone. Robbed of its jaw, violated by a rope threaded through spaces in the skull, the head screams like a Munch, the resonating chamber inside the ribs echoing and amplifying the existential anguish of the damned. Strips of meat hang from wrists, from fingers, even from toes. Its diaphragm has been completely excised and, horrifyingly, affixed to the wall by its own organic adhesive. No humiliation has been spared this corpse; none spared our common bleak humanity.

The eighth figure is almost too dishabille to truly disturb, slumping in a posture of abjection before its inevitable fate. The arms are nearly detached from the torso, while the resected sternum, decorated with twin gruesome flights of severed ribs, leans carelessly against the wall.

The ninth figure offers us reprieve as we return to an almost complete musculature in posterior view. We begin again, but this time, when the muscles are stripped away and left dangling in the illustrations that follow, it is a nearly cheerful business. The inclusion of an extra leg in the thirteenth plate hardly disturbs the gaiety, although it does portend the sole but powerful discordance in the posterior set: the fourteenth figure, caught awkwardly between standing and kneeling, propped on a low plinth, literally disarmed and contemplating a supernumerary cranium before it. Remember that dust thou art, and to dust thou shalt return.

Friday 8 June – morning

Porter had taken particular care in selecting his second candidate, in search of physiological and aesthetic perfection.

He was utterly committed to a comprehensive anatomical enquiry: every structure and every system of the body was vital to him, without exception. But not without distinction. The human muscular system was what had first united for him science and art, the two halves of his identity.

Although in school he had excelled at art, in which the body played a prominent role, he'd achieved entry to medical school on the strength of his mastery of the beautiful abstractions and intellectual rigours of mathematics and the physical sciences. Biology had little interested him before, so he'd been surprised in anatomy class to find himself overawed by the grace, power and economy of the musculature.

It was the constantly changing shape of muscles beneath skin that had drawn his twofold intellectual attention: the swell and strain of the propulsive flesh engines; the flex and twist of the finer manipulative servos. The perfect union of form and function, mechanical and aesthetic. His interest was consolidated by the superbly efficient tethering of the muscles to the skeleton by the tendons, lending maximum leverage, torsion or finesse of control.

It was then, in the medical school's anatomy museum, that Porter discovered the *Fabrica:* a facsimile of the 1543 first edition, followed by a nineteenth-century English translation in the rare books collection of the university library, complete with Vesalius's glorious illustrations. From the first he had felt that Vesalius was speaking directly to him, and he quickly apprehended the scale of the Master's radical intellectual ambition: to banish from science the illegitimate deference to authority and usher in a new age of empirical fidelity to evidence.

Porter had soon realised that the practice of medicine was not his vocation, but his fascination with human anatomy prevailed, his passion for the musculature finding expression through re-engagement with life drawing. Before long, his intellectual and aesthetic interest was matched by his developing technique: he had found a new calling.

Porter's obsession was tolerated cheerfully by the teachers and students of the Sydney College of the Arts. Despite his bland personality and unfashionable concentration on figurative representation, his technical proficiency and single-mindedness were much admired. Paying work was a different matter. He was far from a natural teacher, and commercial art he spurned on principle, so he'd graduated with consummate technique but poor career prospects. He increased his hours at the part-time job that had seen him through art school, drew from life when he could afford the models, and awaited inspiration.

Porter's tardy muse finally attended him one sunny afternoon in the Mitchell Library rare books reading room. Immersed in Volume II of the library's 1555 second edition *Fabrica,* he had rested his head on the table in an ecstasy of wonder, and fallen into a reverie. His Project came then to him entire, as had *Kubla Khan* to Coleridge: this time there was no visitor from Porlock.

While his Tribute had always been about the *Fabrica*'s anatomy in totality, then, its logic started and ended with the muscles. Each system retained his entire attention, but just as the digestive tract inspired involuntary pangs of disgust, he felt an undeniable aesthetic excitement at the prospect of working on the muscles, tendons and ligaments.

Particularly those of this incomparable specimen.

Even in silhouette at a distance, Laura Newman's musculature had surpassed Porter's aspirations. As she'd approached her locked front screen door from inside the house, moving like an intricate clockwork of inter-coiled springs, she was powerful, agile and poised. Balletic. He had every confidence that her musculature would prove exemplary.

In this anticipation he was entirely vindicated, in due course, but it very nearly didn't come to pass.

Despite explaining himself in detail with an obsequious and servile manner – and despite concealing his capable physique beneath a layer of characterless clothes to match his nondescript face – her demeanour from the outset had been wholly uncooperative, even mildly hostile. While accepting at face value his stated reason for being there, she'd steadfastly refused to open her front door.

Six weeks before, Anthony Williams had admitted him to the Glebe terrace house at this point of the conversation, switching from distracted and slightly puzzled to cordial and grateful: just as planned. Yet Laura Newman had simply refused to comply. It was completely irrational, defying the logic of the encounter entirely. She'd maintained her stance with impressive resolve, almost to the end. It very nearly saved her life.

Standing outside her locked screen door, Porter had found himself abruptly depleted of options. He was rigorous about risk mitigation, which entailed gaining access to the property with the consent and cooperation of the candidates. He decided to abort the operation, perfect musculature notwithstanding: there were other highly toned individuals in the Sydney metropolitan area. Disappointed and angry – with himself more than his candidate – he fired her a sharp parting broadside about the inconvenience she would now endure, having refused his generous offer of assistance.

He was already turning away when the screen door latch unexpectedly clicked open. He froze while the door swung outwards: once its arc passed him, he stepped inside its sweep and wrenched the door open, the handle flying from her grasp.

Instantly realising her error, the candidate turned and sprinted towards the back of her house. More athletic now than balletic, she was a conditioned specimen in flight for her life, as though years of hard training had been directed at this moment. But it was already over.

Porter entered, locking the heavy wooden door behind him while observing the superb body in flight, the bare feet achieving perfect traction on the polished wooden floor, the body's entire kinesis reduced to the vectors generated by its muscles of propulsion and balance. It was mechanical perfection.

Above the lean, sinewy hollow behind the knee, the biceps femoris and the other hamstring muscles reached up to the pelvic girdle, which anchored the whole locomotive apparatus. The shiny blue athletic shorts highlighted each gluteus maximus, catching the sunlight at the top of each stride, at the very moment of zero gravity, as the body exited the hallway into a deep, brightly sunlit room beyond.

Even as Porter made pursuit he felt amply justified in his selection. But later on, well after the unpleasantness, on first direct sight of the musculature freed from its concealment, he exhaled long and deep in sincere appreciation. This: this was beauty.

He went to work.

Friday 8 June – late morning

Sylvia opened the doors and took her coffee out the back into a gloriously mild winter's day – still, clear, sunny and blue, the weather utterly defiant of the season. It had been a revelation when she'd moved here from Western Australia, where winters were short but unsympathetic. Sydney in complete seduction mode.

She decided to exploit it to the full. She skipped breakfast, threw on a bikini and a sarong, grabbed her swimming keys and a towel and headed for the Ladies' Baths, over the road from Jo's flat in Coogee.

Sylvia and Jo both did their serious lap swimming at Wylie's Baths a little to the south, but the exclusively female enclave of McIver's Ladies' Baths was where they went to lounge around. For a gold-coin donation, women could bathe untroubled by the male gaze in the loveliest ocean pool on the Sydney coast.

She dropped her coin in the blue bucket then followed a concrete path down several flights of stairs, making for the wide, flat expanses of rock above the pool itself. She lay face-down on her towel and enjoyed the mild noonday sun on her back. In much of the world this would qualify as a perfect summer's day. So lucky.

After a while, she rolled over and propped herself on her elbows, sighing contentedly as the breeze caught her hair and caressed her skin. Half a dozen sails peppered the stretch of ocean out to the horizon, with Wedding Cake Island nestled in the mouth of the bay in front, the swell slapping languidly across its base as the tide began to turn. This was her very favourite view, anywhere.

It had been love at first sight between Sylvia and the island. Murphy had brought her to Coogee Bay five years ago while he was sweeping her off her feet with his grand tour of Sydney's Greatest Hits. He'd been amused to learn that Perth had its own Coogee Beach – named after this Coogee, he was certain, although Sylvia thought it was a Noongar name – and he'd insisted that Sydney's version was superior, not that he'd ever seen the other one. As much as she loved those wide-open Indian Ocean beaches, she'd had to agree. Wedding Cake Island was a big part of why.

From their vantage on Dolphins Point to the north of Coogee Bay, she'd understood the hydrology at once: the way the island took the sting out of the heavy Pacific Ocean rollers, so that the beach enjoyed all the shelter of an inner reef with the expansive outlook of an open bay. The island seemed perfectly engineered for the amenity of humans, making Coogee the most pleasant swimming beach in Sydney, if not the entire Pacific coast.

Murphy had told her the rock's name was inspired by the rippling foam that perpetually crowned it, and she was smitten. Sensing his advantage, Murphy had chosen that moment to propose. While she hadn't known him long, she'd accepted on the spot. Murphy had his rough edges but he was strong and protective, like the island, and she was grateful for the shelter. They were married within the year.

From then on, the island had been intimately entwined for Sylvia with her ideal of life partnership. Her marriage would be like Wedding Cake Island: a buffer against the unrelenting wildness of the world. A sanctuary from the corrosive environment she'd grown up in, then fled.

So the island had become a talisman of hope and comfort nestled in this Coogee she'd chosen for herself: an anchor to her beautiful new home. Whenever her marriage had been tested, she'd found herself drawn almost viscerally to Wedding Cake Island, back to her faith in its capacity for protection. It had never failed her.

A shriek of laughter from a trio of teenagers pulled Sylvia out of her reverie, and she looked around the grounds of the Ladies' Baths. There were women of all ages and all shapes, mostly in pairs, a few solo, a few with young kids: a family of Muslim women, dressed modestly despite the privacy; a raucous group of young women, all topless, beyond the range of phone cameras or wolf-whistles; an elderly nun from the Brigidine convent being helped into the water by her young carer. The old woman was a local fixture, who'd once confided to Sylvia that the buoyant salt water afforded her aching joints some welcome relief. Sylvia supposed the carer was a nun too, although the slightly racy red one-piece might not be Vatican-issue.

Sylvia stood and crossed the flat rock to the maze of concrete paths and stairs, aiming for the steps down to the pool on the seaward side. A leisurely swim in the salt water, a shower at Jo's then home for a bit of guitar practice. A run in the late afternoon and a glass of wine over a decent novel before her husband came home from work.

All in all, a perfect day off.

Tuesday 12 June – morning

'Jesus Fucking Christ, he did all this right here?' Murphy surveyed the carnage across the spacious, sunlit living room.

'In full view of the entire world,' replied Mack, gesturing to the sweeping panorama beyond the expanse of glass.

They were in North Curl Curl, atop Dee Why Head, with a broad ocean view from Long Reef right around to the Queenscliff bombora, across something like two hundred degrees. It was a very fancy house in a stunning location. The victim had clearly been loaded.

'Yet out of sight,' said Janssen. The architects had avoided any sightlines from land, and the container ships a couple of kilometres out were simply too far away.

They turned back to the scene inside. A long dining table, entirely lacquered in blood, bore a comprehensively flayed body. Here and there the innermost layer of muscle clung to bone, but it was a much-diminished form. Sheets of skin were heaped on the coffee table, while ropes of excised muscle filled the leather sofa.

'*Godskolere.*' Janssen took a deep breath and shook his head. 'Who is it?'

'The speeding fine on the fridge says she's Laura Newman,' said Mack. 'We've taken fingerprints, should have confirmation this arvo.'

Murphy struggled to picture the fingerprinting process. Untidy. He gestured to the sofa. 'Surely that can't be all from one body?' It didn't seem credible that one garden-variety human could pack this much muscle. She wasn't even tall.

'Mm, looks about right to me,' said Mack. 'Subject to tissue matching, of course.'

'Fuck me. And definitely the same guy?'

'Yeah, it's him all right. Same injection scenario, same anatomical fixation, same obsessively clean site.'

'You call this clean? He still hasn't worked out the blood drainage.'

'No, he has,' said Mack, pointing at a maroon slick running up the hall. 'There's a lot of blood in the muscles themselves – gets expressed in dissection.'

'This must have taken him the whole long weekend,' said Janssen.

'I reckon. Maybe more.'

'Fuck. Again.' Murphy sighed in frustration. 'How does he know he has all that time? It's a hell of a risk.'

'Was he interrupted?' asked Janssen. 'Before he got to the bones, I mean.'

'If you're asking whether he's repeating himself, I don't think so. At Glebe he didn't take this trouble before examining the bones,' said Mack.

'So what's your theory?' asked Murphy.

'It's a systems approach,' said Mack. 'He showed no interest in the muscles last time, just cut them away to get to the bones. This time it's the muscles' turn.'

'You're giving him too much credit, Mack,' said Murphy. 'It's a fucken abattoir.'

Mack held the line. 'You can see it in the cutting, Spud. He's really careful with the tissue he's interested in and heedless with everything else. Bones at Glebe; muscles here.'

'But you said he was careful with muscles last time.'

'No, muscle *attachments.* Tendons. Not the muscles themselves.'

Murphy grunted, but moved on. 'Any biological samples?'

Mack shook his head. 'Not yet. We'll see, but I have my doubts.'

'What about sex-type stuff?'

'No, nothing like that. The vagina and anus are intact and undisturbed. It's interesting: he's cut well wide down there, but very closely up here in the head.' Mack approached the face and indicated. 'See, the lips are completely gone, revealing the orbicularis oris muscle, which he's then partially cut away. The eyes, too. See the left socket? Almost down to the bone. He's gone in for a real close look. But he's left the anus and the vulva alone.'

'Why's that, do you think?'

'Well, he's not squeamish,' said Mack, both police snorting in agreement. 'I wonder if he's making a deliberate point about his motivations.'

'To whom?' asked Janssen.

'To himself, maybe. Us. The media.'

'You reckon?' asked Murphy.

'It's a woman this time, Spud,' reasoned Mack. 'He'd know we'd be checking for any sign of molestation.'

'It's the first thing the media will be onto, for sure,' agreed Janssen.

'So maybe he's making it clear from the outset it's not about that,' continued Mack. 'Whatever he's after, it isn't a sexual thing.'

Murphy considered for a moment. 'So, Mack, you're saying he comes in here, kills the girl, skins her completely, spends the Queen's Birthday long weekend cutting her into steaks – but his main concern is that nobody thinks he's a pervert?'

'You could put it like that.'

Murphy grunted again, reserving judgment. 'All right, what else?'

'He's done a very tidy job removing the skin, not just the fine work but in the initial long incisions. *Too* tidy.'

'What do you mean, "too tidy"?'

Mack picked up a sheet of skin from the coffee table, and showed the edge to the detectives. 'See these long, smooth, continuous strokes? Dead-straight, confident, very precise. I'm not sure where you'd get the practice to do that. I know pathologists who can't cut skin this cleanly, and they do it every day.'

'Could he be a forensic pathologist, do you think?' asked Murphy.

'An anatomy professor?' added Janssen. 'Surgeon?'

'Maybe. Definitely maybe,' said Mack. 'He certainly knows his way around a human body. But you'd have to wonder why. If dissection is your thing you get every opportunity in the medical game.'

'What else, then?' asked Murphy. 'Abattoir worker? Roo-shooter?'

'Taxidermist?' suggested Janssen.

'Taxidermist, perhaps,' said Mack. 'The others aren't exactly fine arts. And any of them would have known to bleed Williams out properly at Glebe.'

'Check them out anyway,' Murphy told Janssen. 'Plus the RSPCA and the zoos.'

Janssen nodded. 'What about something industrial, where you learn to cut like that? Lino, or something.'

'Very different texture, but you couldn't rule it out.'

Murphy stared down at the muscular face, devoid of all expression, while the dead eyes stared right back. After a while, her gaze was all he could see. He held it a long while, and made her the customary promise.

Mack went back to cataloguing the pile of discarded musculature. Janssen went outside for a break from the carnage and rang the squad to summon another detective and a couple more uniforms. Murphy stepped onto the balcony and opened a well-used app on his phone to scope the local barista situation. They were going to be here for some time.

Thursday 14 June – evening

Jo stood up and started clearing her dining table. 'Cup of tea?'

'I'd love one, thanks,' said Sylvia, moving to help.

'Stay right there, you,' Jo said. 'No dirty dishes on your birthday.' Sylvia smiled and sat back down.

Jo looked pointedly at her brother but he only handed her his empty plate. She sighed and repeated her question. 'Tea?'

He shook his head. 'Can't handle the caffeine this late.'

'I have peppermint. Home grown, in fact. Organic.'

'Where do you grow it?' asked Sylvia, turning to look out at the small balcony overlooking the park and the ocean beyond. It held only an easy chair, a side table and a bougainvillea, all thoroughly soaked from the steady rain that had been coming down all day.

'Up on the roof terrace,' said Jo as she put the stack of plates down in the kitchen and flicked the kettle on. 'We put in a herb garden last spring.'

'What else do you grow?'

'We have basil, coriander, chives, rosemary, oregano. Garlic. Mark downstairs has a beehive up there, too.'

'I never knew you had the green thumb,' said Sylvia.

'Oh, I don't,' said Jo. 'I'm more your red thumb. Jade next door keeps it going, really. I just help out now and then.'

'Well, I am surprised,' said Murphy. The women looked at him. 'I'd have thought Jade would rather use the terrace to work on her all-over tan.'

Jo rolled her eyes. Her neighbour was a rising film and television actress, and Murphy was a bit fixated. 'No, Jade and I go across to the Ladies' Baths when we want to get our gear off.'

'Oh god, don't torture me,' groaned Murphy. 'I wish I could get inside that place, just once.'

'No men allowed,' said Sylvia, 'and they're militant about it. Cop or no cop.'

'Yeah, what are they going to do?'

'Cut your balls off, if you're lucky,' said Jo. 'And that's just the nuns.'

'Ugh,' said Murphy, screwing his nose up. 'The nuns aren't starkers, surely?'

'You have no idea, brother mine, and you never will.' Jo smiled enigmatically at him. 'Now: to tea or not to tea? That is the question.'

'God, no,' said Murphy. 'How can you drink that crap? Tastes like weeds.'

'You're thinking of chamomile.'

'No, that tastes like cat's piss.'

'Anything instead?' Jo asked Murphy while she crushed leaves of fresh peppermint into the teapot.

'You don't have a decent Scotch, by any chance?'

'Sorry, I don't even have a lousy Scotch. I can offer you gin?'

'Don't worry, I'll just finish off the wine.' He emptied the rest of the shiraz into his glass.

'Hey, Dave,' said Sylvia, straightening in her chair, 'tell Jo what you told me.'

'What? When?'

'This afternoon. About the crime scene. She could help, remember?'

'Nah, you're barking up the wrong tree.'

'It can't hurt to float it.'

Murphy looked sideways at his wife. 'Last time you got the shits with me for talking about it.'

'Last time you were being gratuitous.'

'Yeah, and?'

'And now there's a point to the discussion.'

He looked across at Jo. 'Want to hear about a homicide?'

The news hadn't reported much detail, so she was curious, up to a point. Still, the whole business was beyond ghastly, and she wasn't sure she needed that in her life. 'What do you mean, I could help?'

'Well, I don't reckon you can,' said Murphy. 'That's just her theory.'

'Come on, Dave,' said Sylvia.

'It's homicide, Sylvia. It's a bloody long way from all this.' He waved to indicate Jo's paintings adorning the walls. She'd found modest commercial success painting candid scenes – most real, some imagined – of film actors in costume during downtime on location.

Her living room bore two examples: Harrison Ford and Rutger Hauer in earnest conference inside the Bradbury Building; and Cate Blanchett and Miranda Otto drinking Coopers in Middle Earth garb. She'd given her brother and Sylvia a canvas each from her first solo show: Clint Eastwood, Lee Van Cleef and Eli Wallach playing cards over a bottle of whiskey lived in Murphy's study, while Sylvia had hung Geena Davis and Susan Sarandon pissing themselves laughing with Harvey Keitel in their bedroom.

Sylvia turned to Jo. 'Don't worry. It's a bit graphic, but you'll be fine.'

Murphy looked at his sister. 'I shouldn't even be talking about it, of course.'

'I won't rush off to the newspapers.' Jo started to stack the dishwasher.

'Okay. So you know my killer struck again?'

Jo nodded. 'A woman this time.'

'Yeah. Corporate lawyer from North Curl Curl.'

'Was she...' Jo gestured vaguely at her own body, looking for the words.

'No, nothing like that,' said Murphy.

'Tell her about the muscles,' said Sylvia.

'Forensics tell us that last time he just ripped in and took everything right down to the bone,' said Murphy. 'Discarded pretty much all the soft tissue. Not a lot of finesse to it.'

'I remember,' said Jo weakly. Maybe this discussion wasn't such a good idea.

'This time he took the skin off carefully, then stripped the muscles back, one layer at a time. They reckon it would have taken him all weekend. Made a big pile of muscles on her couch. Not muscle groups: individual muscles, right down to the tiny ones.' He waggled his fingers to illustrate. 'Then, when he reached the bottom layer, he just stopped. That's how we found her.'

Jo let the kitchen counter hold her up. Her blood had drained away somewhere; she wanted to sit down, but didn't trust herself to move. She'd found the story about the man in Glebe distressing – who hadn't? – but she hadn't really visualised it. This was even worse. She looked up to find the others watching her. 'Sorry, it's just a bit vivid.'

Sylvia smiled kindly while Murphy smirked. Jo moved to the kettle, which had boiled while Murphy had described the scene. 'God, that poor woman,' she said. She poured hot water over the peppermint leaves in the pot, then just held the kettle for a moment while the image sunk in. 'Oh,' she said, looking at Sylvia. 'I get it. You mean the *Fabrica.*'

Sylvia sat back and crossed her arms. 'I thought so.'

'What does that mean?' asked Murphy.

'Like I told you,' said Sylvia, 'your description reminds me of Jo's lecture.'

'*De Humani Corporis Fabrica Libri Septem,*' explained Jo. 'It means "Of the Fabric of the Human Body in Seven Volumes". It's a book by Andreas Vesalius of Brussels, published in Switzerland in the mid-sixteenth century. It's considered the foundation document of modern western anatomy.'

'This was the fella who influenced your painter?' Murphy asked.

'No, other way around. Holbein came first.'

'Okay. And?'

'The *Fabrica* was scientifically revolutionary, but it's also a pivotal moment in western art. It transformed depictions of the body.'

'I'm sure that's fascinating, but I don't see how a medieval anatomist is going to help me catch my psycho killer.'

'Renaissance, not medieval.'

'Same diff.'

'Tell him about the muscle men,' Sylvia urged Jo.

'One of the most striking features of the *Fabrica* is the engravings of whole bodies progressively dissected in certain ways. Each one forms the basis for a set of detailed dissections that follows. The scenes you describe sound like those plates.'

'No, he's not making an installation, and he's not doing anatomy,' said Murphy dismissively. 'This is butchery, not sculpture.'

'But doesn't your forensic expert think it's a dissection?' Sylvia pressed.

'Yeah, but he would; that's his frame of reference. He knows about victims' bodies. I know about killers' minds.'

'But even the way you describe it sounds just like the book.'

'I'm telling you, Sylvia, this is murder, plain and simple.'

'But if you saw the images, Dave, you'd—'

'Jesus, Sylvia!' Murphy let the pause hang then continued, cold and pitiless. 'At Glebe he just tore away all the flesh, stripping it off the bones and pushing it into a big wet heap on the floor. All the organs, too. Fucken blood everywhere. Then he cut out a few bones using a circular saw so he could get at them properly and work on them in good light. Almost a whole arm, the top of the skull and half the neck. He did not leave us a neatly arranged display, I can tell you.' Both women were ashen, but he went on. 'This time, okay, he did leave us a body on the table in the middle of the room, but the skin was piled up in a heap on the coffee table and the muscle he'd cut away was just thrown in strips onto the lounge. He drained the body this time but—'

'All right!' interrupted Sylvia. 'You've made your point.' She looked up at Jo, who was staring out through her balcony doors, over the treetops to the sea beyond. 'Jo? You okay?'

Jo snapped out of her reverie. 'Yeah, I'm fine. I just ... this cutting all the muscles away, a bit at a time. It really does sound like a demonstration dissection. That's what the plates of the *Fabrica* are.' She poured the tea and brought the two cups to the table.

Murphy sighed. 'He is not doing this for our benefit, sis.'

'Not yours, maybe. Are you sure he's alone?'

'Forensics say there's only one cutter. If anyone else is there, they're just standing around.'

'Or observing. Learning.'

'I've seen a lot of weird shit in Homicide, Jo, but that's over the top. He's not giving private tutorials.'

'Dave, these drawings are basically the stills from a series of demonstration lectures. Vesalius did dozens of dissections in front of hundreds of students at a time. The process was dynamic.'

'You're coming in at the end of it all,' Sylvia added, picking up the thread. 'Maybe the *Fabrica* is what it would look like if you could see it as he went.'

Murphy shook his head. 'I'm sorry but you're both way out of your depth. You don't know what you're talking about.'

'Maybe so,' conceded Jo. 'I'm just saying, if there is a link to the *Fabrica* you should keep in mind what the book actually is.'

'Well, nobody said there *is* any link. Just you two.'

Sylvia gave it one more try. 'You wouldn't have a copy here, would you, Jo?'

'No. I have a digital version on my computer at work, and our medical school has a facsimile. I think there's a second edition in the state library. Macquarie Uni has a flash new translation called the *New Fabrica,* but you can only view it on-site.'

'How about the slideshow from the lecture?' Sylvia persisted.

'Oh yeah, hang on a sec.' Jo padded down the hall towards her studio.

'So you think an art historian is going to bring down our serial killer, do you?' asked Murphy once his sister was out of earshot.

'Well you don't have any angles yet,' observed Sylvia dryly. 'Maybe you could use a fresh perspective.'

Murphy could hardly argue with that, so they sat in silence until Jo returned with a leather messenger bag. She riffled through and extracted the printouts of her slides, several loose pieces of notepaper falling out with them. Murphy gathered the notes and handed them back to Jo, and she stuffed them back in the bag.

'Here are the woodcuts Sylvia's talking about.' Jo flipped over the pages, showing Murphy a series of ghastly sketches: bodies strung up to gibbets and gallows and scaffolds, held aloft by ropes and pulleys and tackle; others standing unsupported but utterly dismal, stripped of their muscles, which were either completely removed or hanging down in obscene strips. In between were detailed depictions of bones, joints, muscle groups and specific muscles: before, during and after dissection.

'Okay, I can see why you're excited,' allowed Murphy. 'But you've got the wrong end of the stick, trust me. This anatomy stuff is all methodical, colour-by-numbers. Homicide's more random than this: it's law of the jungle, chaotic, deranged.' He turned to Sylvia. 'I'd have thought you'd understand that, working in an emergency department.'

'Working in an emergency department taught me not to prematurely exclude viable explanations,' she replied.

Murphy waved that away and turned back to his sister, who had kept her peace. Her brother's dismissive air had become no more endearing with age, but she wasn't going to get steamed about it. 'This sounds like a nice theory, up here in the warm and dry after a rainy day and half a bottle of wine, but this isn't your art history seminar, Joanna. It's the real world. It doesn't work like this.'

She held his gaze, returning no expression at all. She knew this conversation had hit a wall, and she knew the depth of the resentments that drove Murphy's stubbornness. There was no point arguing.

But Sylvia went around again, ignoring the siblings' stand-off. 'We're not literally saying he's recreating these, Dave. Just that Jo could help get you inside his head a little.'

'Look, enough, okay?' said Murphy, coming to his feet. 'End of discussion. Let's go home.'

Sylvia looked up at Jo, all exasperated, but her sister-in-law just gave her a tiny shake of the head and a wry smile. Sylvia nodded and stood up herself. Their goodbyes were perfunctory, and Jo went straight to bed after they left, leaving the cleaning up for the morning. Her brother just wore her out sometimes.

Saturday 16 June – afternoon

Porter secured a table at the Bathers' Pavilion overlooking Balmoral Beach, with a view down Middle Harbour through the Heads, and Rocky Point Island off to the right. A light shower had passed and the cloud was clearing, everything wet and glittering in the sunlight. He ordered a pot of tea and gathered the Saturday newspapers.

He was gratified to find his Tribute on every front page, in the supplements and even the magazines, the press indulging its sensationalist tendencies to the full. To the salacious city desk editor, this story eclipsed even misbehaving footballers and politicians on trial.

With few facts to report on, though, the outlandish speculations of criminologists and psychiatrists featured prominently. Porter's pleasurable frisson slid gradually into irritation, until he reached a latter-day Freud pontificating on the killer's issues with his mother.

'My mother?' Porter muttered. 'You don't want to hear about my mother.' He threw the newspaper down, poured another cup of tea from the pot and gazed at the slice of ocean horizon between the imposing sandstone cliffs.

No, he had to resist the seductions of publicity. He could not lapse into a flirtation with his coverage, letting it fold back into reality by influencing his behaviour. That way lay disaster. Not only would that see him caught, but it would also completely betray his purpose.

His investigations were private acts, entirely. Contrary to popular opinion, he was not trying to show 'them' anything: there was no 'them'. This was between himself and Vesalius; the exercise was his humble Tribute to the greatest dissections the world had ever seen. That they would have a public dimension was both unavoidable and entirely irrelevant. The Volumes were complete in themselves, with an internal economy of their own. There was no performance. The care he had taken in this last Volume to avoid accusations of sexual molestation was the limit of his consideration for reception. To afford the publicity any thought would be to corrupt his entire Tribute.

He felt somewhat depleted, but that was probably fortuitous: private emotion was as treacherous as public attention. He was no more motivated by gratification than by notoriety. He must be careful to recognise his elation for what it was – a biochemical response to extreme stimulation – and neither condemn nor cherish it. Savour it a little in the acknowledgment, then return to the rational plane on which he chose to operate.

He read a little more in the paper about this Murphy, the homicide detective in charge of the investigation. A highly decorated policeman and a deft media performer, he seemed to have journalists and the politicians alike in awe of him. He'd achieved a formidable arrest rate throughout his career – Bradmanesque, according to one breathless report – culminating in his current streak as the most successful homicide detective in NSW Police history. Porter had every intention of spoiling that record. He would need to conduct some detailed research on this adversary.

He returned the newspapers to the front table and settled his bill, then strolled out onto the beach, the sky above now completely clear, although the light wind was still quite cool. He turned his collar up against the breeze and his mind to the business of candidate selection, which needed to be resolved once and for all.

Laura Newman had nearly rejected him, and it was important to understand why. Presumably she had feared he was a sexual predator, a possibility that had simply not occurred to him, since perversion had no place in his Project. She had been right to be suspicious, of course, if his deductions were correct, but entirely wrong about why.

He'd done everything possible to present as unthreatening. He'd dressed to conceal his strength; he'd worn boring clothes and plain glasses; he'd stood well back; he'd projected an air of diffidence and awkwardness. He was, in fact, diffident and awkward. There really wasn't much more he could have done to put her at ease.

He wandered out onto Rocky Point Island and up the steps. He had the small outcrop to himself. He walked its length and found a seat looking along Middle Harbour, the Pacific Ocean beyond. The ubiquitous sailboats were performing their mysterious ballet out on the harbour, their sails still glittering with the residue of the rain shower. Some of them seemed to be racing one another, but for the most part it looked like an exercise in chaos theory.

Porter sighed deeply as he accepted the unavoidable truth: gender was a problem. The female's suspicion had been founded on a misreading of the precise threat he represented, while his own confidence had been founded on an ignorance of women's expectations of men. It didn't matter that the female response made no sense to him: that response was a material fact, and he had to revise his method accordingly.

So he would concentrate on males henceforth, males in merely moderate physical condition, excepting the specific requirement of a female candidate for Volume V.

He stood and turned his back to the harbour, walking briskly across the little concrete bridge to his car. The parameters had been revised; there was new work to do.

Tuesday 19 June – afternoon

Murphy and Janssen drove out of the basement carpark, heading for the morgue on Parramatta Road. The light rain was in that annoying intermediate range where the only windscreen wiper options are squeaky or blurred. Murphy's phone rang as they turned into Cleveland Street. It was their boss.

'Good afternoon, commissioner. You're on carphone, Detective Sergeant Janssen's with me.'

'Commissioner Carr,' added Janssen.

'Afternoon, detectives. I'll be brief. I've just come from the premier's office.'

Janssen shifted in the passenger seat. This could be anything.

'How was that, sir?' asked Murphy.

'It's an honour and a privilege to serve, as you know, but in other respects it was fairly disagreeable.'

'Sir?'

'Media pressure is ramping up, Murphy. I know you've been managing those bastards. So have I. So's the minister. But the TVs decided among themselves that your ... progress would be the topic *de jour* this morning for the premier's big announcement at the Children's Hospital.'

'Oh, shit,' said Murphy.

'Correct.'

'Please don't tell me he was high and dry.'

'No, he's been reading our briefs, thank God. He held his own. But he signalled emphatically that he wouldn't mind some results. And he has a point, gentlemen.'

The detectives exchanged a bemused glance. Like all frontline cops, they loved it when people who sat on their arses for a living – the brass and politicians, basically – reminded them of the urgency of taking killers off the streets.

'We're doing all we can, sir.'

'So I told him. And requested more resources. He agreed to that, subject to us diversifying our approach.'

'Diversifying how?'

'Apparently he spent the summer holidays working through some sort of corporate leadership self-help reading list. *Hagakure The Art of War,* that kind of thing.'

'*The Prince?*' ventured Janssen.

'I believe he's already across that one, detective. That's why he's premier.'

'Oh, for fuck's sake,' muttered Murphy.

'What's that, detective?'

'Just the windscreen wipers, sir. How does this affect us?'

'He suggests you could make headway by, and I quote, "disrupting your tired old methodologies".'

'Meaning what, sir?'

'Meaning he will devote additional operational funding if we can concoct an initiative that approaches the problem laterally.'

'You've got to be kidding,' Murphy said. 'Sir.'

'Just sort it out, detective. Continue your investigation, but contrive something with genius and originality. Or the appearance thereof. Doesn't matter what it is.'

'But like what, sir?'

'I don't know, Murphy, but that's the nature of innovation, isn't it? Anyway, isn't creative destruction your specialty? I'm sure it will come to you.'

'Yes, sir.'

'First thing tomorrow. Goodbye, detectives.'

Murphy was pensive after that, so Janssen left him alone. He'd learned a long time ago to let his boss think things through in his own time. The rain sputtered out into a background sulk with the odd desultory spit.

They turned off Parramatta Road, but then Murphy turned right again instead of left and parked in front of the Forest Lodge Hotel's forlorn Japanese maple. They climbed the stairs to the pub's front bar.

'New?' asked Murphy. Janssen nodded. Not his preferred beer but that was beside the point.

They sat near the unoccupied pool table. Murphy took a deep draught and emitted a long sigh, then wiped the froth from his lips. They drank in silence until the beer was gone, then Murphy looked at Janssen and tilted his head at the bar. Janssen took the empties up and returned with a couple more schooners. Murphy took the top off his second, picked up a Tooheys coaster and tapped it on the table a few times before grunting and drinking again.

'Okay,' he said finally. 'So, what do you make of Mack's dissection theory?'

Janssen had not expected Murphy's chain of thought to lead here, but he went with it. 'I had my doubts at Glebe, but now I think it has merit. It certainly fits.'

'Yeah, but you know this murder caper, Janssen. It's never that tidy.'

'That's true usually, but these are different.'

'Still. The medicos seem to want it too much.'

'How do you mean?'

'They're nostalgic for their med school years – it appeals to them. From there it's confirmation bias.'

'They're trained to resist that kind of thing.'

'Nobody's immune.'

'Yes, we could all be accused of that,' replied Janssen diplomatically. 'Experience pushing us beyond the evidence.'

'Fair enough.' Murphy tilted his glass in acknowledgment of the tacit criticism of his own stubbornness. 'It's not just the forensics who are on about it,' he confessed.

'Why, who else?'

'Jo and Sylvia were reminded of that medieval anatomy book of hers.'

'Really?'

'You saw her lecture, what do you think?'

Janssen was surprised Murphy knew he'd gone, but he stayed with the topic. 'I think they have a point. Maybe we should look at the images.'

'Yeah, I've seen the slides. I see the resemblance, but I'm not convinced.'

'But if they all think it's related...'

'That's my point. Everybody who sees a link is either a medico, a nurse or a bloody art historian specialising in the body. It's all a bit cosy.'

'And me.'

'And you. Who may or may not be impartial.'

Janssen didn't know what Murphy was insinuating, but he left it alone.

Murphy gazed silently out the window for another five minutes, slowly working his way through his beer. 'Come on, drink up,' he said when he was done, but Janssen abandoned the rest of his schooner instead and they went out to the car. The rain had stopped but it was still gloomy. They drove across Ross Street and parked behind the morgue.

They found Mack in the tearoom with the forensic pathologist who'd performed the Newman post-mortem.

'Anything new for us, Dr Forrest?' asked Murphy.

'You know most of it already, detective,' she replied. 'Caucasian female, mid-thirties, nulliparous, extremely fit. Sexually active but no recent penetration, no pregnancy, no diseases, no suspicious injuries, no abnormalities. She hasn't even had her tonsils out. Killed around midday on the Friday, flayed shortly thereafter, then progressively stripped of her skeletal muscles over the next two or three days.'

'How did she die?'

'Not sure yet, but she has two unhealed punctures in her left median cubital vein with matching wounds in the skin, just like Williams.'

'That's the pattern,' said Janssen.

'I anticipate we'll find pancuronium and thiopental in the blood.'

'When do you expect the toxicology?'

'Supposedly tomorrow, but who knows?'

'Any trauma?' asked Janssen.

'Yes, she put up a good fight,' said Forrest. 'There's a blunt injury over her right ear, with significant subdural bleeding. Dislocated right patella and broken left ankle without associated swelling, so peri-mortem. Bilateral defensive wounds on her forearms. She's also been smothered.'

'But not to death?'

'No. Nil petechial haemorrhaging on the face and lungs, no foaming in the airways. But there's a haematoma around the mid-face and jaw.'

'A pad of fabric?'

Forrest nodded. 'This'll be your midazolam. We're checking remnant fibres under a scanning electron microscope.'

'You have that kind of equipment here?' Janssen was surprised. All they ever heard about were cutbacks.

'New South Wales Coroners?' The pathologist snorted. 'Yeah, nuh. It's at

Lucas Heights.' The nuclear science facility housed a wide range of high-tech scientific equipment, in addition to the nation's research reactor.

'Any tissue samples?'

'Nothing obvious, but we're doing swab analysis.'

'Any other connection with Williams?' asked Murphy.

'Professor McCalman did that post while I was on leave, and he's now in Saint Petersburg at a conference. But from what I hear, the approach and the level of proficiency seem about right.'

'Any possibility it's a copycat?'

'You couldn't rule it out on the pathology, but you tell me: you didn't release his cause of death, did you?'

'No, we kept all that to ourselves,' said Janssen. 'Method and pharmacology.'

'If it's the same drugs, that'll clinch it,' said Mack.

Murphy turned to him. 'I had a strange discussion about this case the other night.'

'Yeah, I've had a few of those.'

'Someone I know has an unusual take on it. I had my doubts, but it fits with your dissection theory.'

'What's the angle?'

'Some famous medieval textbook. Father of modern anatomy kind of thing.'

'You're talking about Vesalius,' said Forrest. '*De Humani Corporis Fabrica.*'

'Do you know it?' asked Murphy.

'Everybody knows it,' she replied, 'it's the urtext.'

'So what's the theory?' asked Mack. 'Our killer's working off the *Fabrica?*'

'Something like that.'

'It's not such a reach. I doubt he's improvising, so he's using *something.* Might as well be Vesalius.'

'Yeah, but I get the sense there's a bit of a cult around this book,' said Murphy.

'People do get excited about the *Fabrica,*' said Forrest thoughtfully. 'There's a new edition in English, actually. It's quite expensive, but apparently it sold well.'

'So there are connoisseurs out there,' mused Janssen.

'Oh, yeah. I'm not sure it's a scene exactly, but there are definitely some obsessives around.'

'Want me to talk with this medical friend of yours?' asked Mack.

'If you don't mind,' replied Murphy. 'Only she's an art historian, not a doctor. Across the road, actually.' He nodded towards the university.

'Oh, right. Might need to avoid the morgue, Spud. Even the average GP would struggle with these remains. An amateur ... yeah, better not.'

'Just a conversation for now, Mack. I'll line it up.'

'Okay. What's her name?'

'Joanna King,' said Murphy. 'She's my sister, actually.'

Wednesday 20 June – morning

'Righto,' said Murphy, calling his unit to order. 'It's official: our man's a serial killer. You were right, Nguyễn, and I was wrong. Fortunately for you, I am a big man in all the ways that count. You may approach.'

The junior detective walked up the front to a cacophony of clapping and whistling. Murphy handed her a remote control, which would get her into the executive carpark. 'That riceburner shitbox of yours better not mess up my nice clean concrete,' he said. 'One month then it's back to the provinces.' Nguyễn held the remote up in victory then returned to her place.

'Okay, enough clowning around,' continued Murphy, gesturing towards a map on the wall featuring two red pins. 'Glebe in April, and now North Curl Curl, with the exact same weird shit. Precedent suggests there's more to come. Eventually he'll make a mistake, or get unlucky, or we'll just accumulate enough data to nail him. But eventually won't cut it, because the taxpayers of New South Wales would prefer to die of old age than being carved into little pieces. So we're officially a task force now. Cox is coming back over from Fraud to help out with our other cases, so we can put most of our energy into hunting down this bastard.'

'So if it's serial, what's the defining theme?' asked Nikolaidis from his usual spot on top of the sturdy filing cabinet.

Murphy nodded at the SOCO, who stood to face the room.

'The puncture wounds are identical, and I'm confident we'll find the toxicology matches when it comes in,' said Mack. 'But the main connection is the strong anatomical dissection theme.'

'I don't really get that angle,' said Harris. 'All I saw was a shit-ton of cutting.'

'I know others who feel that way,' said Mack, tilting his head at Murphy, 'but any doctor would recognise the pattern from anatomy class. A painstaking surgical precision and a textbook orthodoxy.'

'What's the morgue say?' asked Chartier.

'Forrest agrees with me: she did the Newman post. McCalman was the pathologist for Williams, but he's still away.'

'Look, I share your doubts,' Murphy told Harris, 'but there's a classic anatomy book that could be an angle.'

'What book?' Harris asked.

'It's called *De Humani Corporis Fabrica Libri Septem,*' said Mack, gesturing at a copy of an old illustration pinned to the squad's incident board. '*Fabrica* for short. Published in 1543 by Andreas Vesalius, the father of modern anatomy. We think the killer might be working off it.'

'Why that book?' asked Nguyễn.

'The *libri septem* is Latin for "in seven volumes". The first volume's on the bones and cartilages. The second's on the muscles and ligaments.'

'Williams and Newman,' said Chartier. A shiver went through the squad.

'*Gamóto,*' Nikolaidis said. 'That's a whole other level of methodical.' He slid off his filing cabinet and crossed to the incident board to inspect the illustration. It depicted a crowded dissection scene with a commanding figure in the centre looking out at the viewer.

'But what's the significance to the investigation?' asked Nguyễn. 'Is this book super rare or something?'

'No, originals are rare, but many libraries have a facsimile, and it's all over the web,' said Mack. 'And there's a plush new English translation just come out, the *New Fabrica*.'

'You're right, Nguyễn, it might not help, but it's an angle,' said Murphy. 'And we might be able turn it to our advantage in other respects.' He shot Janssen a significant glance. 'So we'll get someone in to take us through the book, help us get our eye in.'

'What about Australian sales of this flash new version?' asked Nikolaidis, turning away from the picture.

'Good idea, Niko,' said Murphy. 'It's published in Switzerland, though; could take a while.'

'I wonder if they're all top-secret like the banks,' said Harris. Everyone laughed. 'What? I'm serious.'

'We know you're serious, Harris,' said Murphy. 'That's what's funny.'

'Forrest said there's a bit of a cult around Vesalius, so there might be enthusiast groups,' said Janssen.

'Oh there will be,' said Nikolaidis. 'If it exists, there's trainspotters of it.'

'How about your abattoir angle, Matthijs?' asked Chartier.

Janssen grimaced. 'It's not a well-documented workforce, and there are thousands of them. Same with kangaroo-shooters. There are not so many taxidermists and they're easier to find, but they all check out so far. The RSPCA has had plenty of sick stuff in the last twelve months, but that's business as usual. Nothing that looks relevant to us. I don't think this approach is going to get us far.'

'What's the hold-up with toxicology?' Nguyễn asked Mack. 'It's been over a week.'

'They're doing the best they can,' Mack replied, defending his laboratory colleagues. 'They're chronically under-staffed.'

'I thought this case was on priority.'

'It is,' said Murphy. 'But we're not the highest priority on priority.'

'Try waiting for a doping assay,' said Harris, evidently trying to recover some dignity. This was something he knew about; he'd been attached to Vice where he'd worked the racecourses. 'Takes them fucken months.'

'Two points define a line,' said Murphy. 'I want everyone to start cross-checking the paper trails for connections – financials, phone lists, email address books, calendars, the works. Triangulation, boys and girls: what do these two have in common? We find that thread, we find our man. There's heaps to do, so get back to work, the lot of you.' The detectives immediately began chattering as they returned to their desks. Murphy turned back to Mack as Janssen joined them.

'How'd you go with my sister?'

'We had a good yarn,' said Mack, 'then Forrest and I had another look at the remains. I think Dr King's right. They really do look like what you'd have left after a system dissection.'

'And there's the order of the dissections,' said Janssen.

'Right. I tell you what, if he goes again, it will clinch it.'

'Why, what's the third volume?' asked Murphy.

'Veins and arteries. It will be very messy, and very obvious.'

'That's all we need,' said Murphy. 'I'm wondering about this angle, Mack. Maybe we need more from Jo than a seminar.'

'Something ongoing, you mean?' asked Mack. Murphy nodded. 'It's a good idea, she knows that book really well. And she's smart. But how would you fund it? Surely you'd have to pay the uni for her time?'

Murphy looked at Janssen. 'I reckon we can sort something out.'

'Well I'd be happy to support that,' said Mack. 'Even if you know what you're looking at, you don't always know what you're looking *for*.'

'Do you reckon she could handle it?' Murphy asked. 'This is pretty hardcore.'

Mack considered the question for a moment. 'I think so. She was squeamish at first, as you'd expect, but once she was looking at it as an expert she seemed better. Not great, but better.'

'Good enough.' Murphy nodded. 'Thanks, Mack, your endorsement will help. I'll let you know how we go.' The SOCO headed for the lift.

'Is this your clever new idea for the premier?' asked Janssen, once they were alone.

Murphy smirked. 'I reckon we pitch this for the premier's bullshit innovation play, cover Jo's charge-out costs and then leverage some extra resources.'

'Hence your change of heart about the *Fabrica.*'

'Never look a gift horse in the mouth, mate. And who knows, it might even turn out to be true.'

'Do you want me to talk to Jo?'

'No, let me handle it. I want to run it past the commissioner first. If he knows the vice-chancellor socially it will all be a lot simpler.'

Wednesday 27 June – afternoon

Jo listened to the voicemail again, considering her options. The dean's assistant had rung while she'd been in the library: his boss wanted to see her urgently. It was well after five, so she could just sneak off home. Or hit Manning Bar for a G&T. On the other hand, whatever he wanted wouldn't simply evaporate. She decided to get it over with.

She regretted it the moment she saw the assistant's sympathetic frown. Conor knew everything that went on, and he had a lousy poker face. He waved her through.

'There you are, Joanna. Good afternoon, how are you today?' enthused the dean. He sounded like a spiv flogging a condemned flat distinguished only by a homeopathic memory of harbour glimpses from the toilet window. His predatory smile was turned up to eleven, his violet eyes were a pair of toxic uranium-mine tailings, and the steely grey of his suit perfectly matched his dorsal fin. Either he'd just had some puppies strangled, or he had an unpleasant surprise for Jo.

But buggered if she was going to be rattled by him. She sat on the chair in front of his desk and looked him straight in the eye. 'What can I do for you, Vincent?'

'I had a visitor a short while ago,' he confided with a look of deep significance. 'A senior figure with the Homicide Squad.'

Her sinking feeling sank further. 'What did my brother want?'

'He has solicited your assistance on this serial killer investigation.'

Was that all? 'Yes, I'm giving his unit a briefing on Andreas Vesalius.'

'Oh, Joanna.' The dean exhaled, using his silverback voice. *Get ready, girlie,* this preamble heralded, *here comes some man-wisdom: you might want to write this down.* 'You must keep me informed of these things. External engagements are gold.'

'I haven't done anything yet. Well, apart from one conversation.'

'You haven't started already?'

'I spoke with some forensic type on the phone. I'll put it on the activity report.'

'No, no, no, no.' He tutted in reproof. 'You have no idea how competitive resourcing is in this place. The scientists are murdering us. The medicos in particular are insatiable. I need evidence to demonstrate our value. This is a front-page story, it gives us significant leverage.'

'Okay, I'll keep that in mind. I'll email you the details.'

'Good, you do that. But there's more to it than a chat and a briefing, you know.'

'What do you mean?'

'The police commissioner has approached the university requesting your ongoing participation. He's been exceptionally persuasive.'

'Persuasive how?'

'Oh you know, community contribution, fellow feeling, Sydney spirit. Research income.' He flourished a document on blue letterhead. 'He has the full support of his political masters.'

An ancient, familiar dread began to stir. What was Murphy up to? 'What are you talking about, Vincent?'

'The police need our help and are willing to make it worth our while. Sooo...' he brandished a university research contract, '...as of Monday, you are seconded to the homicide investigation, working out of the Sydney Police Centre in Surry Hills.'

'But I haven't even been asked!' she protested. 'And I can't, anyway. I'm teaching three courses. I have eight PhD students.'

'The courses will be reallocated.'

'To whom?'

'I don't know, Millie will sort it out,' he said, referring to Jo's head of department. 'The mid-year break is upon us, she has a few weeks to come up with something.'

'But nobody else knows the material well enough!'

'There are plenty of indispensible people in graveyards, my dear, and yet the world still turns.'

'One's an honours course. I can't abandon them mid-year.'

'You're not abandoning them, you're being called to higher duties.'

'What about my research students? Everyone's already over capacity, nobody can take any more load.'

'There's latitude in the contract for ongoing commitments. A day a week. But you hold their hands too much, anyway; some independence will do them good.'

She sat back, astonished.

'Don't knock it, Jo, it's a juicy piece of external research funding. Well done.'

'It's not research, Vincent. It would only be a consultancy.'

'No, I have assurances that this will be assessed as high-impact applied research.'

'Assurances from whom?'

'Never mind from whom.'

'But there's nothing to assess, Vincent. There is. No. Research.'

'You'll have to write something up, of course. But that's not difficult, is it?'

Jo sat back, stymied. 'May I see the letter?'

The dean slid it across his desk. 'As you'll see, it will all count as external research funding, for the purposes of the block grant formula.'

It was all there in print, everything pre-approved right up the political line – state and federal. Somebody had pulled some serious strings. It was dodgy as all get-out.

'It's a handsome bit of income for the faculty, once we apply our premium,' said the dean, leaning back in his chair and addressing the ceiling. 'I think we'll use the corporate tariff, rather than the public sector rate. They won't even notice.'

Fuck this. 'What if I won't do it?'

His attention snapped back to her. 'This is exceptionally lucrative for the faculty, Joanna, not to mention the reputational value. You're in no ethical position to decline.'

'Ethical?' She leaned forward on the edge of her seat. 'Ethical would have been discussing it with me before I was assigned, Vincent.'

He looked stunned for a moment, then his face softened into a smile. 'Oh, I see. Very good, Joanna. My apologies, it hadn't occurred to me that you had it in you.'

Jo returned his gaze blankly, mystified.

'All right, then,' he continued, 'do you think five per cent would be fair?'

Jo finally caught on. 'What? No! I'm not looking for a cut.'

'Oh,' he replied, perplexed. 'For your department, do you mean?'

'No! I just mean, what if I decline? You can't make me do it.'

'Actually,' he said, selecting Jo's employment contract from the documents on his desk, 'I think you'll find I can.'

'I can't believe you'd do this!'

'I can't believe you'd argue with me. I thought you'd enjoy a break from this place. The students, the colleagues. The committee meetings.'

The prospect of not dealing with the dean himself was appealing, admittedly, but she resented not being given even the illusion of choice. Bloody Murphy.

'Oh, come on, Jo. Don't you want to help stop the killer? Isn't that enough?'

He had her. 'Yes.' She sighed. 'Fair enough.'

'How about that?' muttered the dean.

'What?'

'Your brother told me to lead with that angle. I should have listened.'

Jo shook her head and got to her feet. 'Can I go now?'

'Yes, you may. You'll have to get your skates on to hand over. Talk to Millie, she's always on top of things. Then report to Detective Murphy at Surry Hills on Monday morning. He'll give you the full details.'

'Oh, I'll be seeing him before Monday, don't worry,' said Jo. In fact, she was going to head around to his house right away.

As soon as she'd had that gin and tonic at the Manning Bar.

Wednesday 27 June – evening

Murphy held the door a little unsteadily, and Sylvia stepped out of the Greek taverna onto the footpath. '*Efharistó,* Dave, that was lovely.'

'A pleasure, *erastís.*' They headed towards King Street, Murphy smacking his lips. 'That mastika is fantastic. Must get a bottle.'

'I do miss Newtown,' she said. 'We should come here more often.'

'It just reminds you of your youth.'

'Yeah, it was fun living here, but it's still pretty great.'

'You're romanticising it. You forget how hot it gets in summer.'

'Maybe. It's a little cool now, though.' The night was mild for the season, but it was still winter. And she wasn't wearing much.

'Here y'are.' Murphy draped his jumper across her shoulders, pulling her in close. 'So who was that bloke you were talking to?'

'I don't know, it was just small talk.'

'Why do you need to talk to someone to go to the toilet?'

'He spoke to me as I went past, that's all.'

'What'd he say?'

Sylvia sighed. 'He said he liked my dress.'

'Liked what's under it, more likely.' Murphy smoothed his hand over the curve of her arse and hitched up the fabric.

Sylvia's hand went straight to her hem, and she tilted away from him slightly. 'Stop it, Dave,' she said, laughing. 'This dress is short enough by itself.'

'That's why it's my favourite.'

'Why, so you can get annoyed when other men notice me?'

'Nah, I like the tease. And you've got great legs, Sylv. All the way to the top.'

'That's kind of you, but you don't want all King Street knowing what colour undies I'm wearing.'

'Personally, I'd prefer you went commando,' he said, trying again to lift her dress.

She pulled right away from him this time. 'Not in this dress, mister. I can't afford the bail.'

'Don't worry about that, I have connections.'

'There's one,' she said, stepping towards the kerb to hail a vacant taxi.

'Not yet,' said Murphy, pulling her back. 'Let's go get a daiquiri.'

'I think I've had enough, Dave.' She knew he had.

'We haven't had an anniversary cocktail yet.' He waved the cab driver on. 'You don't even have to work tomorrow.'

'Let's just go home, honey.'

'We hardly go anywhere these days.' He took her by the wrist. 'Come on, just the one.'

'A Murphy "just the one" or a mathematical "just the one"?'

'What do you mean?'

'Your idea of one doesn't always stop at three or four.'

'Really, just one. Promise.' She said nothing but allowed him to pull her along the footpath to Corridor. They entered the bar and climbed the steep wooden stairs, Sylvia leading. They found a small table on the back terrace.

'So: blue, eh?' said Murphy, examining the drinks menu.

'Blue what?'

'Your undies.'

Sylvia slapped him with her menu. 'Pervert.'

'It's only natural.'

'What are you having?' she asked.

'Manhattan. What about you?'

'A cosmopolitan.'

'Not a daiquiri?'

'Dave, I haven't had a daiquiri since Pardon won the Cup.'

'Is that right?' He stood up. 'Back in a sec.' He went downstairs to order.

Sylvia shook her head at her husband's persistent misremembrance. It wasn't just because he was half-cut: he was always trying to feed her daiquiris. Admittedly, the one time she'd overdone them – at Kuleto's on the corner, not here – was the night she'd finally rewarded his persistence by going home with him, so it was no wonder it had lodged in his brain. But she'd not had a daiquiri since: her body had neither forgotten nor forgiven her the hangover.

She pulled out her phone to check her feed. Lucia from work had finally had her baby, six days overdue. No pictures yet, just an excited update from the boyfriend – a healthy boy, 3.6 kilos and 52 centimetres (slightly overcooked), a seven-hour labour (not bad for her first), mother and baby both doing fine.

Sylvia was typing her congratulations when she heard angry shouts downstairs, followed by crashing furniture and the unmistakable wet crunch of flesh striking something solid.

Murphy.

Sylvia was halfway down the stairs when she saw three men lift Murphy off someone writhing on the scuffed saloon-style floor. She recognised the man who'd spoken to her in the taverna.

Someone yelled, 'Call the cops!' but the tattooed hipster barman was already on the phone. Sylvia could see a baseball bat across the chopping board. He'd armed himself but stopped short of intervention.

'I *am* the fucken cops,' snarled Murphy. He looked across at the barman and barked, 'Put the phone down.' He shook one arm free, pulled out his badge and shoved it at the man still holding the other. 'Back the fuck off, arsehole.' The man let go and stumbled backwards. Murphy turned back to the barman. 'I said, put the fucken phone down. Bro.' Cool and menacing this time, sarcastic on the *Bro*. The barman complied.

Murphy was still for a moment, surveying the wreckage while the man on the floor whimpered and held his crotch. Murphy visibly pondered giving him a final kick for the road, but another bystander took a half-step forward, in an access of courage or decency or recklessness. It was enough.

'Come on,' said Murphy, stalking towards the door without looking back. He hadn't looked up at Sylvia once. The crowd shrank from his path as Sylvia clutched his jumper around herself and followed him into the street, keeping her eyes away from the man still squirming on the floor.

Thursday 28 June – evening

Porter had been out of sorts all afternoon, dreading his evening shift. The elation of his early successes had collapsed into melancholic frustration as his search for a candidate for Volume III had gone nowhere.

He dragged himself to the garage and out into the thick Sydney traffic. It took thirty-nine minutes to get to work – he could literally walk there faster – and now he was ten minutes late for his 7pm shift. This town was becoming unliveable.

'Evening, Tom,' he greeted the security guard while scanning in.

'All right, young Stephen?'

The retired soldier was English but had transferred to the Australian Army in the early 1980s. Rumour was he'd needed to get far away from Ireland in a hurry.

'Not bad,' Porter replied. 'How's it been?'

'All quiet on the Western Front.' The old soldier said this every single time: it was one of his many mantras.

Porter respected Tom, so he humoured him: 'Good show, let's keep it that way.'

'Peace in our time.'

'Hope it works out better this time around.'

'I'll do my bit if you do yours,' said Tom.

'Yes, sir.'

'Don't call me sir, I work for a living.'

'Yes, Sergeant. Sorry, Sergeant.'

Tom chuckled delightedly. 'See you up there later, mate.' Porter pushed through the inner glass door, entered the lift and scanned his fingerprint again.

On the second floor, he crossed through a dozen rows of cubicles to the area occupied by his section, Systems First Response. They were fortunate to be located by the intersection of two walls of floor-to-ceiling windows, although the view was not exactly bucolic: on one side was the railway line with a row of warehouses beyond;

on the other a floodlit shopping-centre carpark decorated with skip bins, a shopping-trolley corral and a loading dock. If you crossed your eyes and squinted, you could evoke a kind of Jeffrey Smart aesthetic.

But any distaste was amply offset by the sense of space bestowed by all that external glass: the cube farmer's equivalent of harbourside water frontage. This was Sydney, after all – it was all about the real estate.

Porter passed through a wide-open work area containing eight broad desks for the day-shift staff and proceeded to the corner of the floor, where the windows converged. Facing out through the apex sat an Aeron chair at a wide, angled command desk with five large computer monitors. Mounted on the partitions that sectioned off the immediate area were smaller terminals displaying command screens or process logs of the systems in action. Beneath them were benches housing half a dozen line printers for error reporting and numerous volumes of dusty documentation manuals, a few key folders clean from constant use. Several office chairs were tucked beneath for use in emergencies and for training, but the area was fundamentally a one-person workspace.

This was the systems monitor's domain, from which the entire IT first response operation was run. There was someone in this chair around the clock, every day of the year, without fail. In reality, the networks ran themselves most of the time: the systems monitor was there to intervene quickly and accurately when something went wrong. The five staff who worked these twelve-hour shifts were the organisation's top operators, qualified personnel experienced enough to act solo in the middle of the night when specialist help was an hour away. Systems First Response had other operators on regular eight-hour dayshifts, doing routine IT support, but occupancy of this chair was the real job.

'Heeeey, Stevie, my man, there you are!' said the incumbent as soon as he caught Porter's reflection.

'Sorry I'm late, Nathan. How's it been?'

'Good, good, not much to hand over.' Nathan jotted a few final notes in the shift journal, evidently bursting to flee in his ridiculous boy-racer motor car. He would most likely have a quick shower then head to the pub to celebrate four and a half days off, hoping to beat the poker machines, win at pool, drink a lot of beer and take home some attractive young woman. Porter never socialised with his workmates, but his understanding of the situation was that his affable, handsome and rampantly single colleague was typically successful in three of these four ambitions.

Nathan rattled off a few telegrammatic remarks to Porter, mostly acronyms and obscene euphemisms the systems monitors had devised over the years to describe the infinite varieties of weird phenomena the systems were prone to. Things had been quiet today, Nathan said, with no sign of drama. Porter was relieved: you could never completely discount the possibility of a sudden systems crash, but it was seldom unheralded by the subtle portents that raised the hackles of a seasoned systems monitor. This sixth sense was what set them apart from their lesser colleagues, and Nathan was one of the best.

Good enough for me, thought Porter, as his colleague bounded for the lift – and a fine thing, too. He had a lot of research to do on Detective Senior Sergeant David Murphy.

Five hours and two pots of Grand Yunnan tea later, Porter sat back and regarded the impressive dossier he'd assembled on the homicide detective. He knew now where Murphy lived, where his wife worked, what they each earned, how much their house was worth, what they drove, what they did on weekends, where they bought their groceries, how much alcohol they drank and what day their cleaners came.

And he had discovered the piquant fact that the Vesalius expert from the university, Joanna King, was David Murphy's sister. She even lived near the detective, in Coogee. The sibling connection had brought him up short, but he'd stumbled on the next-of-kin entry just as a flurry of calls had come in, and he'd had to wait until the rush subsided around 10.30 before he could give it some serious thought. He sensed danger – his meticulous plan was all designed around police procedure and forensic practice, but this academic was cut from an entirely different cloth. If Murphy had the wit to consult her, she could offer a perspective on him and his Tribute that the linear process of the cops could never achieve, and that Porter himself would find difficult to anticipate. The scholar was a wildcard, one to watch. In light of this revelation he now found himself relieved that she had lacked the courtesy to arrange their coffee meeting.

He was satisfied with a good night's work. He went into the kitchen and made another pot of tea to help him through until dawn. His evening of scholarship had made the first half of the shift pass quickly, but twelve hours were twelve hours.

Sunday 1 July – morning

'Then he shows me this official letter saying the feds will treat it like proper research, impact assessment and all.' Jo was debriefing with her regular Sunday morning brunch crew: Sylvia and two old friends from Jo's university days.

'The fix is in,' said Sylvia. 'That's creepy.'

'Exactly!' said Jo.

'Surely they can't force you?' asked Katie.

'They probably can, actually,' said Freya gloomily.

'They can't just make her do *anything,* though, surely. Muck out the dunnies or something,' said Katie.

'But if this is applied research within her field of expertise,' said Freya.

'It isn't bloody research!' exclaimed Jo.

'All right, but even you said it was a consultancy.' Freya paused to slurp the last of her orange juice through the straw. 'That relies on your specialist knowledge.'

'They really want you,' said Katie. 'It's a compliment, really.'

'Yeah, right.' Jo snorted. 'Like having a stalker is a compliment.'

'And Murphy lined this up without asking you?' asked Sylvia.

'Without so much as telling me.'

'No wonder you were spewing,' said Freya.

'Too bloody right. I went to the bar to calm down, then I came around to have it out with him but there was nobody home.'

'What day was this?' asked Sylvia.

'Wednesday.'

'Our anniversary dinner.'

'Yeah, I remembered after trying his mobile about eight times. Didn't even ring.'

'I made him turn it off.'

'I bet he timed it that way on purpose, the bastard.'

'I forgot about your night out,' Freya said to Sylvia. 'How was it?'

Sylvia pulled a face. 'It was okay.'

'Wasn't the famous Greek taverna up to standard?'

'No, Steki was fabulous – you really should go.' Freya never went west of Kent Street if she could help it: she thought the black stump was located somewhere around Ultimo. 'Murphy just made a scene afterwards.'

'What happened?'

'He got upset with some bloke for talking to me.'

'Why? What'd he say?'

'Just trying his luck. Nothing untoward.'

'What did you do?'

'Gently deflected, of course. And he was totally cool.'

'So what was Murphy's problem?'

'The standard alpha-male bullshit?' asked Jo, somewhat rhetorically.

Sylvia nodded. 'And he's such a hypocrite. He can rave about some woman's arse, but when a bloke admires my dress...'

'The blue one?' asked Freya.

'Oh, *that* dress,' said Katie. 'Hmm, well.'

'Not you, too!' Sylvia scowled. 'Murphy gave me enough shit, after practically ordering me to wear it.'

Katie put her hands in the air. 'No, you're right, I'm sorry. I didn't mean anything.'

'Anyway, it didn't end well. By the time we got home it was all my fault.'

'Happy anniversary, baby.'

'I know, right? Then he makes nice on Thursday with next door's camellias. Thinks I don't notice what Clare grows in her front yard.'

'No way,' said Freya.

'I came around yesterday to try again, but your place was quiet,' said Jo. 'I thought you two must've been out sailing.'

'No, Dave's away for the weekend so I did a relief shift.'

'Where is he, anyway?'

'St George are playing Brisbane, up there. It was a last-minute thing.'

'Go Broncos,' said Freya. They all laughed.

'I'm sorry you've been shanghaied,' Sylvia told Jo.

'Ah, it's not your fault.'

'It is, kind of. It was my idea to bring you into it.'

'That's not the problem, Sylv,' said Jo. 'The problem is that Murphy still thinks he's the boss of me.'

'I feel you, sista.'

'And you're probably over-sensitive,' said Katie.

Jo flashed her a look – Katie could be a bit liberal with the armchair psychiatry – but then her face softened. 'You're probably right. Anyone else I'd shake it off. With him, it pisses me off automatically. He doesn't even have to try.'

'Siblings,' said Freya, who had two of her own. 'You can't live with 'em, and you can't shoot 'em.'

'When's he back?' Jo asked Sylvia.

'I'm picking him up at eight. Do you want to come with me and say your piece?'

'No, it'd only ruin my night. Might as well leave it to the morning.'

'All right then, let's get on with the quiz.'

'Wait, I'm going to need more caffeine,' said Katie.

'Me too,' said Freya.

'Not for me – I'm cutting back,' said Jo.

Sylvia waved to Lexie at the counter, held up three fingers and indicated herself, Katie and Freya. That'd be a macchiato, a latte and a black filter.

'Oh fuck it, all right,' said Jo. Sylvia waved again and added the fourth finger. Lexie smiled and nodded. And a strong flat white.

'Okay, on we go,' said Freya, retrieving the magazine. 'Where were we?'

'Twelve.'

'Right. "In what year was an apparition of Mary seen at Coogee Beach?" Ha!'

'Our Lady of Coogee,' said Katie. 'Early two thousands, wasn't it?'

'So what's the story?' asked Sylvia. 'I was still in the West.'

'You know the reserve at the other end of the beach?' asked Jo. Sylvia nodded. 'There's a white two-rail wooden fence along the edge.'

'Yeah, I've see the shrine.'

'Okay. So from a certain position near the Pavilion, if you looked along the fence when the light was just right, it made the shape of a statue of Mary.'

'Flowing robes, headscarf, arms held out from her sides, the whole bit,' said Freya. 'It was a pretty good optical illusion.'

'But then someone claimed it was an actual visitation,' said Katie.

'Seriously?' said Sylvia.

'Hence "Our Lady of Coogee",' said Jo. 'Rather tongue-in-cheek.'

'It's not still there, I gather.'

'No, some dickhead knocked it over,' said Freya. 'The council rebuilt the fence but it doesn't work anymore.'

'It's a shame, I liked it,' said Katie.

'But what year was it?' asked Jo, referring back to the quiz.

'It was an Ashes year,' said Freya. 'I was seeing that Barmy Army bloke. He thought it was hilarious.'

'Before or after New Year?' asked Katie.

'Hmm. After, I reckon. Just before he went home.'

'So that's, what, early 2003,' said Katie.

'Sounds good. Next?'

Jo nodded. 'Okay, thirteen: "Who's the only prime minister to have done prison time?"'

VOLUME III

THE VEINS AND ARTERIES

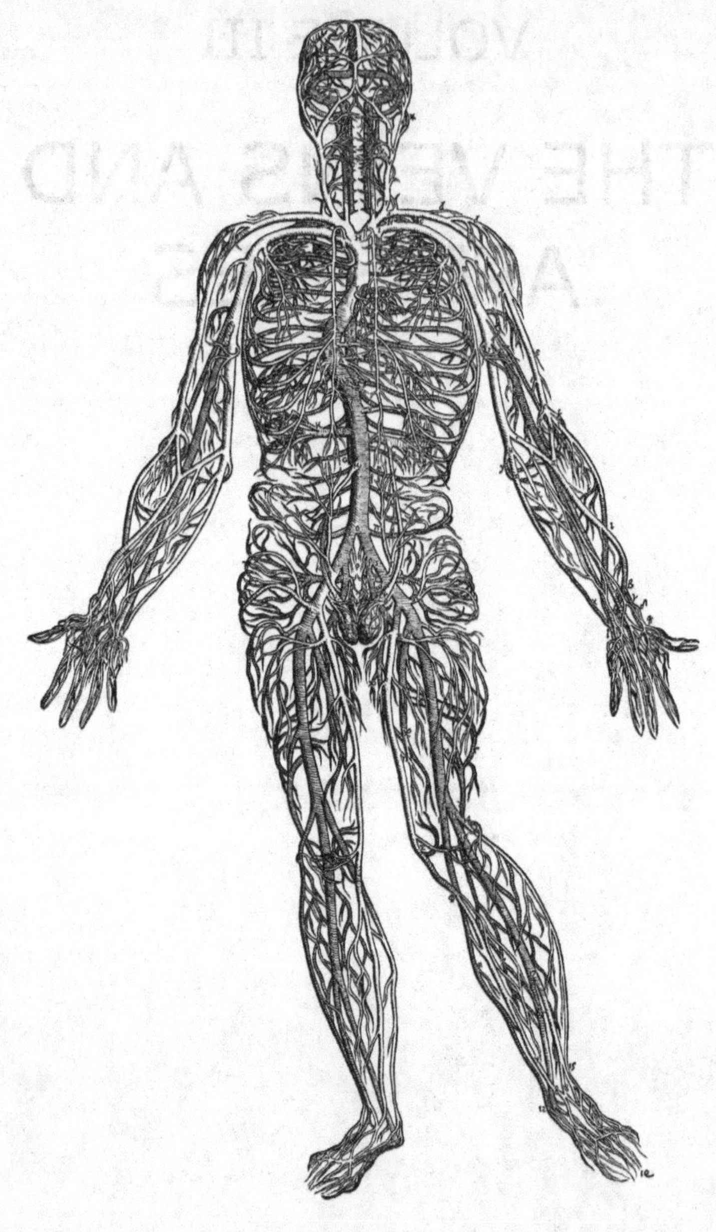

Contemporary artistic tastes may favour the horrors of Volumes I and II, but medical history holds that it was the *Fabrica*'s study of the vascular system that did most to propel medical knowledge into the modern era, by disproving numerous misapprehensions that had prevailed since the second century on the strength of a mighty name: Galen of Pergamon.

The premier medical authority since Hippocrates of Kos, Galen navigated a middle path between the feuding sects of the Dogmatic and the Empiric schools of medicine, founding a tradition that dominated for well over a millennium. Yet for all his reputation for mastery of human anatomy, Galen never once dissected a human cadaver: his knowledge came solely from work on animals.

Serious errors were thus introduced or consolidated in Galen's corpus, enduring until Vesalius's close study of his predecessor – and of human bodies – exposed the twin follies of theoretical orthodoxy and proxy empiricism.

Vesalius approached the colossus of western medical knowledge with respect and humility. He translated Galen into Latin from the original Greek, and defended him against Dogmatic hostility. Yet the Master did not harbour any reverence for Galen's standing: to Vesalius, the only human authority was that of the body itself. He corrected without triumphalism a series of misconceptions, introduced by Galen's flawed method and perpetuated by thirteen hundred years of intellectual cowardice.

The Master demonstrated that the great blood vessels did not originate in the liver, as Galen had declared, but instead constituted a distributive system with its nexus in the heart. (The Arab polymath Ibn al-Nafis had already rectified this error in 1221, in his encyclopaedic *Al-Shamil fi al-Tibb*, ignored by Europe for centuries.) Vesalius also mapped the blood circulation to the foetus, and discovered the venous valves within the liver.

Vesalius made the definitive description of the azygos vein – from the Greek, meaning 'unpaired' – an asymmetrical formation that runs alongside the thoracic spinal column, offering an alternative route for deoxygenated blood from the posterior thorax and abdomen to the superior vena cava. Because of its atypicality in both structure and function – being at once unilateral and redundant – it had presumably been dismissed as anomalous, if it had even been noticed by earlier anatomists. Through his revolutionary method of conducting numerous dissections and recording scrupulously all that he saw, Vesalius realised that, far from being abnormal, the azygos was in fact ubiquitous.

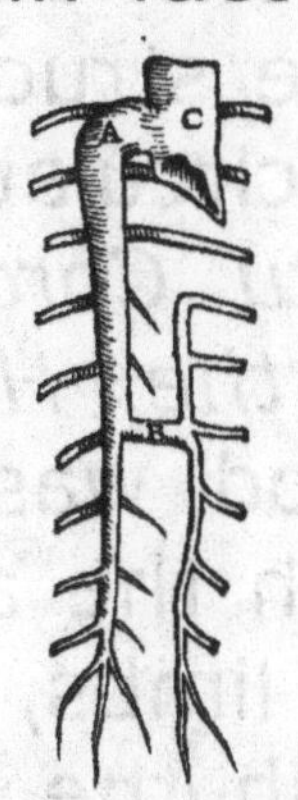

Yet even history's greatest empirical mind made the occasional error. So it goes. (Indeed, Vesalius embraced fallibility as inevitable, encouraging his students to take nothing on authority – including his own.) Vesalius propagated Galen's error that the veins and the arteries carried different fluids, although he contributed to the ultimate correction of the error, after a fashion, through his incapacity to resume his professorship at Padua in 1564. Denied their preferred candidate, the Venetians installed the eminently capable Fabricius, who held the chair for four decades. One of his students was a bright young Englishman by the name of William Harvey.

Harvey established for European anatomy the true structure and precise function of the circulatory system, set forth in *De Motu Cordis* in 1628. *On the Motion of the Heart and Blood* proved that blood was propelled from the heart through the arterial supply to the organs and limbs, cycling back to the heart through the venous return – resolving the misapprehension under which Galen, Vesalius, and thousands of European physicians, surgeons and anatomists had laboured since antiquity.

Monday 2 July – morning

Jo entered the Sydney Police Centre in Surry Hills and approached a long counter. A portly uniformed policeman with his back to her pivoted with a touch of gravitas and greeted her with a courteous smile.

'Is it about a bicycle?' he asked.

'I beg your pardon?'

'Your enquiry. Is it about a bicycle?'

'Ah. No.'

'Are you sure?'

'Yes. Why?'

He indicated the helmet in her hand. 'Been a spate of thefts lately.'

'Oh. No, my bike's fine. I'm after David Murphy.'

He picked up the phone and pressed a button. 'What's your name, miss?'

'Joanna King. I'm his sister.'

He replaced the phone. 'You'd best leave a message. They're flat chat just now.'

'Yes, I know, it's not a family matter. I'm here on business.'

He dialled again. 'Whyever would anyone tell the desk sergeant what's going on?' He shook his head ruefully. 'Gately here, Niko. I have a Joanna King for Spud. Righto.' He hung up and slid the visitors' log across to Jo. 'Fill this out, please.'

'My bike's locked up out the front,' she said while she wrote. 'Is it okay there?'

'Sorry, miss, worst place for it. Local thieves have it in for us; can't imagine why. I'd move it if I were you.'

'Where to?'

'The racks at the milk bar are pretty safe.'

'Bugger that, Gately, this one's a VIP,' said a plainclothes policewoman who'd materialised beside Jo. 'Amy Chartier, Dr King: detective senior constable.'

'It's Jo,' she said as they shook hands.

'You were quick,' said Gately.

'Walking past.' Chartier turned to Jo. 'Recognised you from your photo.'

'What photo?'

'In Spud's office. The two of you with Sylvia, all dressed up.'

'Huh.' Jo was surprised her brother had her photo on his desk. Maybe she didn't give him enough credit. But then she remembered how she came to be here this morning. Prick.

Chartier signed Jo in, and Gately handed across a plastic ID badge. 'Wheel your bicycle down the driveway. Chartier will buzz you in. There's a bike rack near the lift.'

'Thanks, mate,' said Chartier. 'Do me a favour and let them know I've got her?'

The policeman nodded and they went outside.

'We'll set you up with carpark access,' said Chartier. 'Visitor tags can't get in.'

'No space left for the brass?'

'How'd you guess?'

'I imagine that stuff is the same everywhere.'

'I thought universities were bastions of civility. Dreaming spires and all that.'

Jo just snorted as she keyed the bike lock.

'Nice wheels,' said Chartier, admiring Jo's Dutch commuter.

'You should see my road bike.' Jo was an enthusiastic road cyclist with an unhealthy appetite for speed, but she'd woken up still pissed off with her brother, so it had seemed prudent to ride the sensible bike in. 'Sounds like you reckon I'm going to be with you for a while.'

'If we catch him tomorrow, it'll only be his own fault. Your angle's our most promising, so far.'

'I'm not sure how much I can help,' said Jo, wheeling the bike down the driveway. 'I'm happy to brief you, but I don't know anything about what you do.'

'At this point you have the best shot at getting inside his head,' replied Chartier as she swiped them into the carpark. 'You could recognise things the rest of us don't see.'

'Hmm. Your forensic fellow said the same thing.'

'Look, Jo,' said Chartier, stopping her with a hand on her forearm. 'I heard how this secondment was set up. I'm sorry about that.'

'Yeah, well, my brother's only part human. More your monster truck.'

Chartier smiled. 'But we do need your insights. I'm sure they'll review things if it goes nowhere, but we have to try.'

'And meanwhile he's out there killing people, I get it,' Jo said. 'Thanks, Amy, I appreciate it.'

They locked her bike then took the lift upstairs to Murphy's office, a glass-and-plasterboard box in a corner of the open-plan floor. Chartier rapped on the open door and walked in. Murphy was on the phone, facing the other way, but he twirled in his seat and waved Jo to a chair before turning his back and continuing his conversation. Chartier left Jo to it.

She looked around her brother's domain. Messy, but not as chaotic as she'd expected. There was indeed a photograph, and not in a modest desk frame but as a large print on the wall. It was from the night of Jo's PhD graduation, when Murphy and Sylvia had taken her and Lachlan to Tetsuya's to celebrate. The two were not obvious siblings – Murphy had his father's dark brooding Irish looks and stocky build, while Jo had taken after her own father, all fair hair, blue eyes and athletic frame – but on that particular night they must have both been channelling their mother, and they looked for once like they belonged together. It was her own favourite picture of the two of them.

But more surprising was a painting of hers on the other wall, from her second solo exhibition. He'd missed the opening and she never knew he'd gone to see the show, let alone bought a picture. It showed Guy Pearce, Nick Cave, Ray Winstone and John Hurt drinking beer in front of a boxy old television in the iron-red desert. It was called '*The Proposition:* The Ashes'. She was touched.

But then Murphy swivelled back around, hung up the phone and said, 'Thank you for coming in, Jo,' all formal and officious.

Her little bubble of sibling affection burst. 'You didn't leave me much choice.'

'Nothing to do with me; that's between you and your boss. The commissioner just pitched her an idea.'

So the order really had come down from the top. 'And you knew exactly what would happen.'

'Not everything is a conspiracy, Joanna.'

'No, only when you're involved. Anyway, you could have at least asked me.'

'No time for that. We're on the clock here, you know.'

She knew the real reason was that Murphy couldn't bring himself to ask her for help: that would involve crediting her expertise, after years of writing off her work as frivolous bullshit. But there was no point going down that road. She drew a deep breath and tried to leave it behind her.

'Well, anyway. Here I am. What now?'

'Do you have your briefing ready?'

'Yeah. It's a modified version of the lecture, with Holbein dialled back and Vesalius beefed up.'

'Good. We'll do it after lunch when the whole unit's assembled.'

'What about in the meantime?'

'I'll introduce you, we'll sort out the paperwork, get you a desk.'

'Okay.'

'And you'll have to give us a bio sample.'

'What for?'

'To exclude any DNA you might leave behind at a crime scene.'

'Oh.' She hadn't considered that. 'You're not going to need me there, are you?'

'We don't catch crooks with archival research, Jo. This is the business end.'

'Fair enough.' She hoped it would only be a formality. The discussion with the forensic fellow had been vivid enough. 'Is it a blood sample?'

'No, they swab inside your cheek. Piece of piss.'

'Okay.'

'Let's go.' Murphy led her across the floor to the opposite wall, which was filled with notes, floorplans, maps and pictures of buildings, and an array of brutal crime-scene photos that she avoided looking at. Murphy pointed to a spot on the floor: to her own great surprise, Jo stopped at the position he'd indicated. People gathered.

'Homicide,' said Murphy, 'meet our anatomy art consultant, Dr Joanna

King.' Jo felt the curious gaze of the detectives. 'Jo, you've met Chartier, and you may remember Janssen from the police awards last year.'

She certainly did. 'Hey, Thijs.' He smiled tightly in reply.

'That's Nguyễn, and Nikolaidis, our data cruncher, and Harris, our apprentice,' he said, pointing to a young man with an unruly head of ginger hair and an apologetic smile.

'Hi, everyone,' Jo said, barely resisting the impulse to wave. She felt like a complete idiot.

'This is the core unit,' said Murphy. 'We're getting some uniforms for the hackwork: they'll be here for your briefing this arvo. So will Mack.' He clocked Jo's blank look and added, 'The SOCO.' When that still didn't help he spelled it out. 'The scenes-of-crime officer you spoke with the other day. Kenworth.'

'Oh, right.'

'Why don't you tell everyone about your work?' suggested Murphy.

'No, I'll save that for this afternoon.' A couple of the cops smirked and Murphy looked peeved. Evidently people didn't say no to him much around here. Well, she'd had years of practice and had become quite good at it. If he didn't like his team seeing it, he should have thought of that before dragooning her.

This reminded her that she was still standing on the spot he'd designated. She moved away, joining the crowd and turning to face him. It was his show now. He looked stranded. She sensed the grins around her widening a little.

'Fine,' said Murphy in his gruff, suit-yourself voice. 'Janssen, what's the update on the new English edition? Did you get the list of buyers from the publishers?'

'Yes, they've sold eleven copies in Australia directly, all to libraries,' replied his deputy. 'But they say that most non-institutional sales are going through third-party websites. Untraceable.'

Nikolaidis snorted. 'Nothing's untraceable.'

'Any news on extra resources, boss?' Nguyễn asked.

'As you know, we got another run on the evening news last night. The commissioner rang me as the story went to air.' The assembled detectives shuffled grimly. 'It went well, actually. Our, ah, innovation play came through.' Murphy shot a glance at Jo. 'On top of the uniforms and the consultancy, we have a standing call on additional manpower including after-hours, up to a certain point but at my discretion, plus a small expense line for unconventional leads. Premier's funding it out of contingency reserves.'

'Nine months out from an election and getting smashed in the polls,' said Niklaodis. 'Gotta love democracy.'

'Let's meet again after lunch,' said Murphy, ignoring the taunt. 'Chartier, show Jo around and run her through what we have so far. See if you can find something she might care to work on. Janssen, sort out a desk for her.' He stalked off to his office, obviously still annoyed about Jo's little act of rebellion.

Janssen and Chartier stayed as the squad dispersed.

'Don't worry about him,' said Amy.

'Oh, I don't,' replied Jo. She didn't need them to explain her brother to her. It would be like this on and off the whole time: it always was. Besides, his prickliness was partly due to the weirdness of having her in his workplace. She felt exactly the same. They'd both get used to it. Mostly. Maybe.

'So I'm an innovation play, huh?' she asked Thijs.

He saw that she'd worked it out, and he had the grace to be embarrassed about it. 'He's just talking about funding. This is a genuine line of enquiry, Jo. Forensics are convinced, and they're the experts.'

Jo let him off the hook. 'It's okay, Thijs. I know what he's like.'

'So what do you want to see first?' asked Amy.

'Your espresso machine,' she replied. 'I'm dying for a coffee.'

Wednesday 11 July – evening

Murphy handed Rocky another schooner of Reschs. He'd come down the Diggers to watch the State of Origin decider on the big screen, and had run into the half-back from his weekend rugby league side. Lang Park had worked its usual magic on New South Wales, though, and by half-time it was over. There was nothing to do but drink.

'Cheers.' They watched the first-half recap.

'Christ, what a shocker,' said Rocky. 'We hardly had the bloody ball.'

'Yeah, we're fucked now,' said Murphy. 'You can't come back from this.'

'We can't, anyway.'

'Missing Bastian badly.'

'Missing Ireland, is who.'

'Gotta hand it to Queensland, they're on fire.'

'How good's McLaughlin?'

'Sheil.'

'Shrives.'

'Bastards.'

They groaned at each Blues blunder and sarcastically cheered the odd Maroons fumble. The ad break was sheer relief.

'Up to much on the weekend, Rock?'

'Just the usual. Soccer, Little Athletics, some kid's birthday party. You?'

'Sailing on the harbour,' said Murphy. 'Tip run. Watch the footy. Saturday night at the movies.' *Sunday afternoon fuck in the pool, produce some new footage for the private video collection.* This last to himself.

'Haven't been to the flicks in ages,' said Rocky. 'What're you going to see?'

'Dunno. I'd like the *Sicario* sequel, but it's Sylvia's choice.'

'She doesn't like crime?'

'It's not that. She has this rule about women in film. The Bechdel Test.'

'How's it go?'

Murphy counted off with his fingers. 'A movie has to: one, have two or more women in it; who, two, speak to one another; about, three, something other than a man.'

Rocky shook his head. 'Chick flicks, basically.'

'It's not that bad. You only need the one scene. *No Country for Old Men* passes. *Pulp Fiction*.'

'Still. That must rule out half of all movies, surely?'

'That's about right, actually.'

'Oh, well, half the movies for them, half for us. Sounds fair.'

'That's not really how they see it, mate.'

Rocky grunted. 'Bit of a feminist, is she?'

'Don't fucken start me. But it's my sister's rule, actually. She's an academic.'

'Oh, fuck.'

'Yeah, "Oh, fuck" is right. She won't see a movie at all if it fails. At least Sylvia watches when it's my choice.'

'And this weekend it's her pick, eh?'

'Her pick, her rules.'

'Becktell Test.' Rocky snorted. 'Typical.' He stared sourly into his beer, shaking his head, then his face lit up. 'Actually, we need one for parents.'

'One what?'

'One of them tests. Call it the Rocky Test.'

'How d'you mean?'

'Take my place, for instance. Me and the missus can go days without talking about anything other than the kids. I mean, at all.'

'Bloody hell.'

'Living in a houseful of kids is bullshit, Spud. It's a fucken zoo.'

'I thought you only had the two?'

'Two's a houseful, mate, believe me.'

'What about Cath?'

'Nah she's right into it, mate. It's like it's her bloody life's work or something.'

'How about when they're asleep? Don't you talk then?'

'Nah, that's my issue. It goes quiet all right, but then we talk about the kids, or we clean up after them, or we're knackered and crash out.'

'Hence the Rocky Test.'

'Exactly. A pass is a day when the parents talk about something other than the fucken children.'

'A benchmark for adult living.'

'Actually, I'm starting to see your sister's point, Spud.'

Murphy raised his eyebrows sceptically over the rim of his schooner.

'No, really,' said Rocky. 'It's like what the femos say about blokes.'

'How so?'

'The kids rule the fucken roost,' said Rocky, animated now. 'They're so in control they don't even realise it. They're like, I dunno...'

'Tyrants?' suggested Murphy. He could see where this was going.

'Yeah, tyrants, exactly! Everything's all about them when they're around, and it's fucken still all about them even when they're not.' Murphy tilted away, magnetically repelled by Rocky's vehemence. 'I mean, they're great and all, don't get me wrong – they're the best thing on earth some days, but other times they're like miniature fucken emperors with the power of life and death.' Rocky took a long draught of beer then sighed deeply.

'But, mate, you can't be surprised,' said Murphy. 'It's not a state secret.'

'What do you mean? What isn't?'

'That children will take over your life. It's been widely publicised.'

'Yeah, but Christ, not like this.'

'Yeah, like this,' Murphy insisted. 'Fucken, exactly like this.'

'I knew it wasn't gunna be easy, but fuck me...'

'Come on, mate, it's been going on since we came down from the trees,' said Murphy. 'That's why I had the snip.'

'Half your bloody luck, Spud.'

'Wasn't luck, I saw it coming. Not for me, I can tell you.'

'Well I got blindsided mate, fucken T-boned,' said Rocky. 'They have their moments, like I say, but Jesus you pay for them.'

'You weren't shotgunned, though?' asked Murphy. Rocky shook his head. 'So you knew the deal going in.'

The half-back mumbled into his beer. 'Yeah, s'pose.'

Murphy weighed the insensitivity of his next question. Bugger it: he started it. 'So why the fuck'd ya have 'em, Rock?'

There was another sigh as Rocky straightened up. 'I dunno, mate. Cath ... yeah. I really don't fucken know.' He stared morbidly at the bottom of his glass. 'Oh, well.' He drained his schooner, and when he came up for air his face had brightened. 'Such is life, eh? Said the actress to the bishop.' He smiled and wiggled his empty glass at Murphy. 'Anothery?'

Thursday 12 July – afternoon

Jo was sitting at the big briefing table with the detectives, trying to get a sense of how she was supposed to fit into their operation. Murphy was in his office, and Thijs was out somewhere, but after a flurry of conversations in the wake of her briefing, the others were still unsure of how to engage with her. They had been interested in her expertise and for the most part seemed genuinely alive to its potential contribution to the investigation, but after the initial questions they had mostly returned to their familiar rhythms.

Amy Chartier looked up from across the table and smiled at Jo before returning to the recent case files she was working her way through, looking for links. Amy had been the most welcoming to Jo, showing her around and lunching with her most days. She'd opened up about her struggle to be taken seriously coming into what had previously been an all-male Homicide Squad. She'd faced the usual package that came with being not only female, but also gay – open doubt about her capability combined with unwanted sexual attention. But Amy was an old hand by the time she'd made detective, having dealt with that attitude since she'd entered her teens, so she'd just focused on the job and deflected the odd advance until the men of the squad accepted her as she was.

Angelo Nikolaidis rose from his place to Jo's left and walked across to the incident board to inspect a forensic report. She watched him stretch out his tall, narrow frame with a deliberate, fastidious movement that had the air of ritual about it. He had greeted Jo as he greeted the world, with a reflexive, knowing cynicism, but the squad's resident philosopher had soon impressed her with his alert intelligence and openness of mind.

At the end of the table Liệu Nguyễn had drawn her feet up onto the chair in front of her slight frame while she leafed through the second victim's financials. Liệu had been the most sceptical about Jo's role in the case, which Jo had put down to her preference for dogged adherence to textbook investigative procedure. Jo could well imagine that an orthodox bent would be prudent for a petite Asian-Australian woman working in a rough, white, blokey police culture. For all that, Liệu had been friendly and helpful to Jo, not allowing her professional reservations to become personal.

That left young Cooper Harris, sitting to Jo's right, his leg bouncing up and down in some exotic staccato time signature known only to him. From what Jo could see, Cooper was still finding his way in the squad, in equal parts eager to make the hero's breakthrough and desperate to be accepted as one of the gang. A fit young blond surfer type, he was all restless energy and enthusiasm. He had to be at least half golden retriever.

Not that there was anything much for them to devote their energies to yet. There were no forensic leads; the doorknocking had been fruitless; the families and colleagues knew nothing;

the hotline attracted only cranks and conspiracy theorists; and the victims had nothing in common. The squad's copy of the *New Fabrica* had not yet arrived from Basel – the police commissioner had approved the $2000 purchase on the proviso it went to the state library after the case – so Jo couldn't even dive into that. It was hard to concentrate when there was nothing to concentrate on.

Maybe it was time for an espresso. She texted Thijs:

—*Coffee?*

His reply came almost immediately.

—*Yes pls! Can't go far tho at court can you come down?*

That's right, he'd been called to give evidence on an old case. He was at the Downing Centre in the old Mark Foy's building, a few blocks away.

—*Sure! Courthouse or cafe?*

—*Cafe next door. Barista-at-law (haha) do you know it?*

Jo replied one-handed while packing up:

—*Ill find it on my weayh*

The detectives ignored her completely as she took off out the door.

She wondered what Thijs felt about her being around. She hadn't thought much about him since their brief dalliance the previous year – a surprising one-night stand that had rolled on agreeably for a few weeks. It had been a restorative encounter after many months of post-breakup blues. This last week or so had reminded her how much she enjoyed his company. Maybe she'd test the waters.

He was standing out the front of Barista-at-Law, next to a defiant winter-flowering wattle, its gnarled trunk surrounded by asphalt. Inside, the cafe was filled with cops and lawyers, a mash-up of guns and technical webbing with wigs and robes.

'When do you have to be back in court?' Jo asked.

'They just adjourned, actually, so there's no rush.' They ordered and found a table in a corner. They made small talk until their coffees arrived.

'So, Thijs, did you enjoy my public lecture in April?' asked Jo.

His spoon halted above his long black. 'I didn't think you'd seen me. The room was full.'

'An hour's a long time to look at the faces.'

'I suppose so.' He stirred in his sugar. 'It was very good. Your argument is convincing, about Holbein. I've been thinking back on it lately.'

'It's a shame Dave wasn't there.'

'Yes. He asked me about the dissection theory, in light of your lecture.'

'Really? I thought he just pulled me in here to please the brass.'

'I wouldn't go that far,' said Thijs. 'He's coming around to your angle. He just doesn't trust theory.'

'Especially anything complex.'

'Well, he's seen a lot of homicides that come down to pretty basic factors.'

'Human nature, red in tooth and claw.'

Thijs nodded. 'It's very often like that.'

'But you're not an anatomy sceptic.'

'No, I'm not. I think Forensics are right about the dissections, and I think there's a good chance the *Fabrica* is involved.'

Jo nodded. 'Anyway, at the lecture. You didn't come and say hello.'

Thijs looked down. 'I wasn't sure what you'd think.'

'I was glad you came. And a bit surprised.'

'Why?'

'I didn't know of your interest in sixteenth-century anatomical representation.'

'Vesalius was one of my most accomplished countrymen.' He sat back and sipped his coffee, looking her straight in the eye.

'So your interest in Habsburg Dutch humanism brought you to a lecture theatre on a balmy autumn evening?' She leaned in and raised an eyebrow.

'Why do you find that so hard to believe? I wasn't the only one.'

True, the lecture had been popular, but that wasn't the angle she was working. 'I'm just wondering about ... alternative theories.' Surely he could see the sparkle in her eye.

Thijs sat forward. She hadn't realised how far across the table she'd been leaning until his motion brought him near, much nearer than people normally come to one another's eyes, faces, mouths. His breath on her lips was very pleasant. She watched his eyes as he looked into one of hers, then the other, then at her mouth, then her eyes again. His eyes were so many blues: ocean, sapphire, sky at dusk. Shards of Yves Klein. He opened his mouth to speak, smiled instead. She felt a hammer pulse in her neck – he must see it – felt her mouth go dry while everything else became humid. The tip of her tongue ran lightly across her lower lip before she realised what it was doing. She smiled in return.

'All right,' he confessed. 'I wanted to see you again.'

'Hmm?'

'I came to see *you.*' *There you are,* his blue eyes said: *are you satisfied?*

'But you didn't say hello to me,' she repeated.

'I thought you might not be pleased to see me.'

Jo slid her hand over his, and the sensory memory flooded back: how lovely his hands were; how well he used them. She cupped his fingers in her palm.

'I'm pleased to see you, Thijs.'

He smiled back at her. 'Me too.'

She opened her mouth again slightly, breathing in. He closed the final inch. She kissed him lightly with that lower lip, the very tip of her tongue meeting his.

Friday 27 July – evening

'Sharon, can we have the bill, please?' Sylvia asked as the restaurant owner cleared their dishes.

'No dessert tonight?' the Thai woman asked with a cheeky smile.

'You still trying to ruin me, Shaz?' Murphy said.

'But you love the black sticky rice, Mr David.'

'Exactly. That's the problem.'

'How about a glass of port?'

He shot a glance at Sylvia, who looked pointedly at the full glass of wine in front of him. 'Nah, not tonight. Up early tomorrow.'

Sharon shook her head and went to work out the bill. Sylvia opened her purse and rummaged for a moment. 'Bugger.'

'What's the matter?' asked Murphy.

'Can't find my credit card.'

'When'd you use it last?' Ever the policeman.

'This afternoon. Renewed my union membership online. I'm sure I put it back.'

'But it's not there?'

'Doesn't seem to be. Can you get this, Dave? Sorry.'

He sat back and crossed his arms. 'No, I can't, actually.'

She looked up at him. 'Why not?'

'Didn't bring my wallet. You said you were taking me out for tea. Didn't think I'd need it.'

'Neither did I.'

'Typical, though.'

'Come on, Dave, it was just a mistake.'

'Yeah, but you always count on me to pick up the slack.'

'Here, I have a twenty. I can give her that now and we'll pay the rest later.'

'You want all the freedoms and privileges, but not the responsibilities.'

'So now you want to discuss the patriarchy?' Sylvia snapped.

'Happy to get bought drinks all night. Free entry for the ladies, complimentary glass of prosecco. Leave your wallet at home, some man will pay your way.'

'I *have* my wallet, David, I just accidentally left my card at home.'

'Same thing, darlin': you still can't pay. Then you expect a man to cover it.' He drained his glass. 'Lucky for you, Sharon knows us.'

'Lucky for both of us.'

'How's it my problem? It was your shout.'

'Your belly's just as full as mine, mate.'

'That's not the point.'

'Can we just go now, please?'

'Fine.' Murphy scraped his chair back, stood up and walked outside without a backward glance.

Sylvia went up to the counter and explained. Sharon waved away the twenty-dollar note, scrawled an IOU on her duplicate order pad and gave one leaf to Sylvia, taping the other onto the wall next to the till. There was already another one there, alongside dozens of bits of sticky tape of varying vintage. Clearly this happened all the time. She thanked Sharon and left.

By the time she caught up with Murphy he was halfway up the hill. They walked the rest of the way in silence, and nothing more was said until she came to bed.

'Find your credit card?' he asked from behind his paperback.

'Not yet. It's definitely here, though. Has to be.'

'You need to pay more attention, Sylvia.'

She huffed and rolled over.

Murphy continued reading until she fell asleep, then gave it another fifteen minutes of rhythmic breathing before retrieving Sylvia's credit card from beneath the mattress. He went out to the living room, poured himself a Lagavulin, then slid the credit card between the sofa cushions. He took his whisky back to bed, finished the chapter then turned out his light.

Tuesday 7 August – early hours

Stephen Porter was at his desk, entirely absorbed in researching Joanna King, which had become more urgent since the premier's announcement that the Vesalius expert had been co-opted to the homicide investigation. He'd had a busy night, and the usual sources of information were not very forthcoming, so he'd not made much headway. He threw his pen down in frustration, only to notice that he'd been neglecting an incoming call for almost three minutes. He put himself on queue and the call dropped in.

'Good evening, Denison Bank. This is Stephen.'

'Finally. Thank Christ.'

'I'm sorry for the delay, sir. How may I help?'

'I've been on hold for ten minutes, you know that?'

Well, not quite, thought Porter, *but it was not ideal.* 'I'm sorry, sir. I'm the only one here, at this time of night.'

'More bloody cutbacks. Jesus. Record profits every quarter but nobody around when you need them.'

'What seems to be the problem, sir?'

'My credit card's been stolen. You need to shut it down right now. I don't want you bastards blaming me when some prick's out there using it.'

Oh, perfect, thought Porter, *another entitled, belligerent fool. How tiresome.*

No problem, sir, the bank indemnifies you against liability when you report a loss promptly,' he said. 'Can I start with your full name and home address, please?'

'Patrick Hall, 17 Crown Street, Castle Hill.'

Porter typed and the dozens of Patrick Halls appeared. There was only one in Castle Hill. 'I'm speaking with Mr Patrick Arthur Hall, is that right?'

'That's what I said.'

Porter asked several identity questions, Hall answering impatiently but correctly.

'Thank you, Mr Hall. You say the card was stolen?'

'My whole bloody wallet was nicked, with my Fort card inside,' said Hall, using the bank's marketing nickname.

'And where did this occur?'

'The Fiddler.' That would be the old Mean Fiddler Hotel, up the Windsor Road.

'Very well. We can lodge a missing card report, if you're sure it's gone.'

Porter always checked one final time: sometimes the imminence of cancellation quickened a memory. Most customers appreciated the prudence of a final confirmation. Not Mr Patrick Arthur Hall.

'For fuck's sake, of course I'm sure. I just spent a quarter of an hour on hold listening to fucking Kenny G, and I'd rather be asleep at three o'clock in the morning than talking to morons. So yeah, I'm pretty bloody sure it's gone.'

Porter bristled at the insult: not to him – he was accustomed to abuse – but the hold music was John Coltrane. He nearly terminated the call on aesthetic grounds.

Instead he took a breath and smoothed his voice. 'Of course, Mr Hall. I'm only checking because we can't reverse a cancellation if the card turns up.'

'Well it's not turning up because some bastard at the pub stole it, and right now he's probably spending your money on hookers and booze. So why don't you do your fucking job and cancel the fucking card?'

'Very well, sir. Would you mind holding, please?'

'Fine.'

'I won't be long.' Porter placed the call on hold, stood up and walked to the kitchen and back, breathing deeply. Over the years he had learned how to let hostility flow past him, but of late he'd implemented an even more effective method for dealing with belligerence.

And this Patrick Hall was making an excellent case for participation in the Tribute. Although being a nasty piece of work was only the first criterion: there were many hurdles to clear yet, chiefly relating to operational security. But Porter was encouraged: the subject appeared to confirm a correlation between a defective personality and a net worth that provided the working conditions required for the Tribute.

Porter sat back down and opened a missing card report, so he could look into Hall over this shift and the next. The system wouldn't let you browse a customer's file in detail just because you felt like it – you had to have an open query on them. If research indicated that conditions were unfavourable, Porter would simply cancel the card in the system, and Hall would never know how close he'd come to donating his body to science. If the prospects looked good, however, Porter would delete the open missing-card report and proceed with Volume III.

He returned to the call. 'Thank you for holding, sir, your card is now cancelled,' he lied.

'Thank Christ, what a bloody rigmarole. I'd ditch you lot if the other banks weren't just as bad, you know that? You're all a bunch of crooks.'

'Denison Bank appreciates your business, Mr Hall.'

'Whatever. When do I get my new card?'

'The card will be imprinted within the next twenty-four hours and mailed out on Wednesday morning. It should arrive on Thursday.' This timeline would work whichever decision Porter made.

'Bullshit, it won't arrive until next week, at that rate. I need it down the snow this weekend. Just mail it tomorrow.'

'We've missed the plastic card generation cut-off for tonight, I'm sorry. It's all automated. Yours will be in tomorrow night's batch.'

'For fuck's sake.' Another big sigh. 'Can I pick it up instead?'

Porter cursed silently. If Hall opted for pick-up, the Tribute was off: it had to be by mail. But he had to play it straight; let the chips fall where they may.

'Certainly, Mr Hall. Which branch would suit you?'

'I don't know, I run all over town. Dunno where I'll be.'

'We'd have to specify a branch for collection, Mr Hall.'

'Can't I just drop in when I go past one, get them to sort it out?'

'No, sir, the card is embossed centrally and couriered out. They can't print them on site.'

'Okay then, where do they get made? Maybe I can drop by there.'

'I'm sorry, sir, there is no public access to the card facility.'

'Where is it, anyway? Is that where you are now?'

'I'm afraid security protocols prevent me from discussing that, Mr Hall.'

'So you're Jason Bourne now, are you? Unbelievable.'

'Would our Castle Towers branch do, Mr Hall?'

'Nah, by the time you bludgers roll out of bed I've been on the road for two hours. Could be anywhere.'

'Is there a branch of the Fort you pass frequently?'

'Shit, I don't know. You've closed half your branches, anyway. In case you didn't notice.'

They were at an impasse. 'Shall we send it straight to your home, then, Mr Hall?'

'All right, then, just bloody mail it. Shit. I'm going to be stuffed if it doesn't show up by Friday.'

'Once you receive the card, please sign it right away, then follow the instructions to activate it.'

'Oh, for fuck's sake, what a bloody bureaucracy. Why do I have to activate it?'

'If your wallet was stolen...' Porter began.

'It *was* fucken stolen. Are you deaf?'

Porter considered repeating himself but forewent the cheap antagonism. There was a far more satisfying rite of redress in prospect. 'Your driver's licence was in your wallet, I take it?'

'Yeah, so?'

'It has your address on it. An experienced thief will know we are having this conversation. They've been known to skim mailboxes and steal replacement cards. So they go out unactivated.'

'Then why do you halfwits mail them out at all?'

'I am very happy to send your replacement card to a Denison Bank branch, Mr Hall, if you care to nominate one.'

'Mate, we've just been through all that, I don't know where I'll be. Christ, you people shit me to tears. Are you even fucking listening to me?'

Porter was very calm now. He had passed through repugnance and irritation, and reached a kind of serenity. There was a lot of vetting to do yet, but he had a feeling that this was all going to end well. For himself and Vesalius, if not for Mr Hall. Although realistically, featuring in the Tribute was the only worthwhile contribution this man would ever make, so in a sense Porter would be doing him a favour.

'So are we mailing it, then, sir?'

'Yes, I said. Put it in the bloody mail.'

'Okay, then, that's all set. It should arrive on Thursday.'

'It fucken better,' said Hall. 'If I don't get my card on time there'll be hell to pay.'

'I understand, sir.'

'Are we done?'

Not in the usual course of events, they weren't: normally the operator would provide the new card number so the customer could start updating their regular billers. But Porter couldn't do that, because he hadn't cancelled the card in the system, so it hadn't generated a new number. Not that it mattered: subject to vetting, any future use of a credit card by Mr Patrick Arthur Hall of Crown Street, Castle Hill was vanishingly unlikely.

'Yes that's all we need, Mr Hall.'

There was one final muttered curse, then the disconnect tone.

Porter breathed in deeply and removed his headset. He held that breath for a long time, then slowly let it out. He really hoped this one would work out.

He hated people when they were not polite.

Monday 13 August – morning

Janssen spotted the house with the crime-scene van through a veil of pelting rain and parked in front of the identical McMansion next door. An umbrella was pointless, with the rain rebounding waist-high off the bitumen, so he ran flat-out for the house, straight through the crime-scene tape strung across the driveway.

Murphy came through the white wrought-iron screen door just as Janssen made the verandah. 'Where the fuck have you been, Janssen?' he barked. 'Even the TV cameras have been and gone.'

'Sorry, boss, I came as soon as I heard.' He and Jo had flown to Noosa for the weekend, planning to sneak home early Monday morning, but the violent electrical storm had other ideas. Their plane had circled Mascot for an hour, and by the time they'd landed, the airport was in complete chaos. Then the long drive out to the Hills District had taken forever. It was almost noon.

'It's a Homicide Squad we're running here, detective sergeant,' Murphy continued. 'In our industry, the suppliers tend to work outside traditional business hours. Know what that means?'

'Yes, boss. Do not leave my telephone unattended.' Janssen's English, never particularly vernacular, tended to the formal when he was stressed.

'That's right, mate, answer your fucken phone.'

'Give him a break, Spud,' came Mack's voice from inside the screen door. 'It's not like Mr Hall's getting any deader.'

Janssen appreciated Mack's intentions, but it would only make matters worse. He kept to business. 'Morning, Mack. What have we got?'

'Another dissection. Your boy again.'

But Murphy was having none of this. 'Chartier and I have been here since fucken sparrow's fart, Janssen. We went over it all while you were admiring your morning wood. You'll have to wait for the unit briefing.'

Janssen nodded meekly. *Mea maxima culpa.*

'I'm going back to Goulburn Street. You start knocking on doors.' Murphy pointed at Janssen, right up in his face. 'Every single house on this street and a block each way. It's a bloody long drive out here to fucken Woop Woop, Janssen, so you stay until you're done. Got that?'

'Yes, boss,' said Janssen, relieved at the moderate punishment. Murphy had a quick and unpleasant temper, but he tended to get over things. He was tough but more or less fair over the medium-to long-term; short-term, it could go either way.

'And no uniformed minions today, sport: it's just you.' Murphy stalked off to his car.

'See you, Spud,' said Mack to Murphy's back, before turning to Janssen and raising his eyebrows.

The detective shrugged then nodded at the door. 'Is Chartier here still?'

'Out the back,' said Mack. 'Come and have a look.' They went inside as Murphy spun his tyres in the wet. An angry roar of the V8, and Murphy was gone. 'You picked a hell of a morning to go AWOL, young fella.'

'Arteries and veins, is it?' asked Janssen.

'Yep. Volume Three.'

'Is Spud convinced?'

'He is, finally. Probably contributing to his mood.' Murphy didn't much like being wrong. 'That and a kick in the balls playing footy on the weekend, apparently.'

They entered a formal lounge and dining area featuring a half-metre-wide smear of rust curving into the room from the hallway beyond. The body was on the table, more intact than the other two but still deeply excavated, the scene recognisably consistent to Janssen's increasingly schooled eye. The skin had been incised this time, folded back along the limbs and up the sides of the neck to the skull. The abdomen and thorax had been completely excavated from neck to pelvis, the ribcage chopped away and the viscera removed. The large blood vessels running up the back wall rang a faint bell for Janssen, with their complexes of tributaries. Then it came to him, and he wished it hadn't: the Pompidou Centre.

'*Verdomme,*' said Janssen, quelling a wave of revulsion. 'This must have taken longer than a weekend.'

'Definitely. Three or four days, I reckon.'

'Damn.'

'He's just moving things out of the way now, see?' continued Mack. 'He's only after displaying the vessels. He's chopped away the viscera specifically to get to the blood supply. And there's something else. Come here.' Mack led Janssen to a cupboard in front of a wide window overlooking a tall hedge. An assortment of carefully dissected tissues was spread across the top.

'So that's where it all went,' said Janssen, wincing. They were looking at the remains of the victim's genitals, alongside his liver.

'You noticed.'

'It was hard to miss that he'd been castrated, Mack. What's the story?'

'Unfinished business from Volume Two. Chapters Thirty-Three, Thirty-Four and Forty-Nine: muscles of the testes and the penis.'

'I see. Surely this clinches it, then, that he's following the *Fabrica?*'

'Certainly does, although it's interesting he didn't give Laura Newman the corresponding treatment. Chapters Thirty-Three and Thirty-Four canvass the uterus and muscles of the ovaries as well.'

'Maybe he's planning to come back to it. Is there a section specific to the reproductive organs?'

'Yes, it's shared with the gut, Volume Five.'

Chartier came through from the kitchen, smiling wryly. 'Hey, Matthijs, I heard your welcome ceremony from out the back.' Janssen nodded bashfully.

'How well do you know Joanna King?' Mack asked the detectives.

'Yeah, a little,' said Chartier. 'We have lunch most days.'

Janssen's pulse quickened, but he remained outwardly calm. 'Why, Mack?'

'I think she should see this for herself, to best utilise her expertise. But.'

He didn't need to expand on the last word. The two detectives looked down on the very untidy corpse. It looked good only in comparison to the two previous victims. They looked at one another and held a brief exchange without saying a word. It wasn't pretty, but Jo would know what to expect. Anatomical drawing wasn't reality, and a crime scene was more confronting than a medical scenario – still, a body was a body. It would be tough on her, but this was the job. The silent dialogue ended in agreement, and they turned back to Mack.

'Fair enough,' said Chartier. 'Have you spoken to her about it?'

'Can't reach her. Spud tells me she's at the uni today, but her mobile's off.'

'Might be lecturing,' said Janssen, although he knew exactly why she'd been out of range all morning. 'Try her office phone.' He gave Mack the number.

'Come on,' said Chartier, looking through the window. The wind had dropped and the rain had settled into a steady shower. 'Let's get started on the doorknock.'

Janssen raised one eyebrow. 'I'm supposed to do that by myself.'

'Yeah, but since the boss departed in a huff, you're my lift back to civilisation.' She selected a pair of golf umbrellas from their gear stash by the door and handed him one.

'Any chance we could get an espresso first?'

Chartier shook her head sorrowfully.

'Nothing outside the shopping mall,' said Mack, dialling Jo's office number. 'It's all just houses.'

'*Verdorie,*' said Janssen. It was going to be a long afternoon.

Friday 17 August – afternoon

The detectives stood in the briefing area, caffeine in hand and raiding the big packet of Tim Tams that Jo and Chartier had brought back from lunch, hoping to inspire a breakthrough. The idea was to hold the killer's method up to the light and see if they could find the right angle. There had to be a diamond in there somewhere, but so far it had all the sparkle of a lump of coal.

'We just don't know enough to connect them,' complained Harris.

'We don't know *anything*,' said Nguyễn.

'We know he's targeting wealthy people,' said Chartier. 'That must mean something.'

'Perhaps it just correlates with the time and space he needs,' said Janssen.

'They all seem to be arseholes,' observed Nikolaidis from his perch on the filing cabinet. 'According to the neighbours and relatives, anyway.'

'They didn't actually say that, Niko,' said Chartier.

'A couple practically did, and most of the others implied it,' said Nikolaidis. 'Don't you reckon, Nguyễn?'

'Yes, the families seem less bereaved than usual, apart from the gruesome aspects.' Nguyễn had done a good deal of the family and workplace liaison. 'The friends and colleagues don't seem to be too cut up, either.'

'So to speak.' Nikolaidis pointed at the Tim-Tams. 'Give us one of them, will you?'

'A bit of respect for the dead?' Chartier objected, while holding out the packet for him.

Nikolaidis shrugged. 'Even arseholes die. Not soon enough, I grant you, but still.'

'It's all so smooth, too,' added Harris. 'He must be doing heaps of work beforehand.'

'Yeah, it's like naturalism,' said Jo.

'What do nudists have to do with it?' Murphy said, smirking.

'Naturalism, dimwit, not naturism.'

'Same thing.'

'Like fashion icon and fascist icon are the same thing?'

'What are you getting at, Jo?' asked Chartier, slicing through the sibling banter.

'It takes a lot of artifice to make a movie look realistic. The more real it looks, the less real it is.'

'Okay, I get it,' conceded Murphy. 'He's expending all his energy before he goes in so he leaves no trace for us after.'

'But you can't expend energy without emitting heat and light,' said Nikolaidis.

'So what does his heat and light look like?' Chartier waved a chocolate biscuit around for emphasis. 'Why haven't we seen it?'

'He's someone who has the time and the solitude,' said Janssen. 'Lives by himself, works flexible hours, comes and goes without being noticed.'

'Yeah, but he also knows a hell of lot about his targets before he rocks up,' said Murphy.

'Like the layout of the houses, you mean?' asked Harris. 'Security cameras?'

'Yeah, but more than that,' said Murphy. 'How does he know they're alone? And that he'll have that much time.'

'Maybe he doesn't,' suggested Harris.

'But mate we've had no near misses and no dead bystanders,' reasoned Nguyễn. 'He must already know it's safe, before he starts.'

'So how does he reduce the odds to practically zero before he even knocks on the door?' asked Chartier.

'He has to have access to their data,' said Nikolaidis. 'Maybe where he works?'

There was a flurry of suggestions from the detectives: a telco, an internet provider, an energy retailer, a security firm, the motor registry, the tax office.

'An intelligence agency?' proposed Harris. His colleagues all laughed, except Nikolaidis, who just raised his eyebrows and puckered his lips.

'Let's save the deep-state conspiracies for later,' said Murphy.

'What else is bothering you?' Jo asked the cops.

'The entry method,' said Janssen. 'How does he get into the houses without being known to his victims?'

'What makes you so sure they don't know him?' asked Jo.

'If he did we'd expect to find some common thread between the three victims,' explained Chartier. 'But there's nothing there at all. No childhood link, no uni days together, no workplace in common. He's just come at them out of the blue, as far as we can see.'

'We know he's not making appointments with the vics, either,' said Nikolaidis. 'There's nothing unaccounted for in their diary entries, or the phone and email records.'

'So what does he have to offer that gets him inside?' Harris took a Tim Tam, bit off the opposite corners and sucked his coffee through it as though it were a straw, then popped the result into his mouth. He moaned with pleasure.

'We've been around and around on this; it's a dead end.' Murphy huffed with impatience, but the rest of the squad ignored him.

'Ah.' Jo's eyes lit up. 'It's a MacGuffin.'

'That Hitchcock thing?' asked Janssen.

'That's right, Thijs. It's an object that drives the narrative, something valuable or powerful. People behave in ways they normally don't, because they want it so much. They lose judgment and perspective, do desperate things.'

'Like the Maltese Falcon,' he said.

Jo nodded. 'The briefcase in *Pulp Fiction*. The Ark of the Covenant in *Indiana Jones*.'

'You're saying he has something they want,' said Chartier. 'Something they'll put aside their usual caution for.'

'What if it's not an object?' Nguyễn asked. 'Could it be information?'

'But information can be passed through a closed door,' Jo said. 'A physical object at least gets the door open.'

Murphy waved his hand dismissively. 'Opening the door is not the issue, Jo,' he said. 'People do it all the time.'

Jo turned away to look out the window. This was typical Murphy. Reject anything that doesn't fit his thinking.

Look for the short cut, the flash of inspiration.

And he was punishing her for not making it to the crime scene: by the time Mack had reached her at work, the body had been on its way to the morgue, so she'd only been able to observe the autopsy. That had been absorbing – and clinical enough to take the edge off her initial revulsion – but it had not inspired any insights. Her brother was annoyed with her for missing the chance to examine the corpse at the scene, so he was ridiculing her contribution. He'd been doing this kind of thing all her life.

She took a deep breath and turned back around. Janssen offered her a sympathetic smile, but nobody else had noticed.

'Say you're right,' she told her brother. 'It still doesn't solve your problem. Williams and Newman fought well inside the house, not inside the front door. And Hall didn't struggle at all. So how does he get such an advantage on them? I'm telling you, Laura Newman's not inviting a stranger in for just anything. Something made her take the risk.'

'Maybe she didn't think it was a risk,' said Harris. 'She was in great shape.'

'But look how it ended for her,' said Nguyễn.

'So she was wrong, doesn't disprove the point,' said Murphy. 'She opened the door—'

'But why?' asked Chartier.

'Doesn't matter why, she just did,' said Murphy. 'Point is, she didn't think he was a threat. It's that simple.'

'I still don't see her just opening the door to him,' insisted Jo.

'But why not?' asked Harris. 'Sure, in hindsight, but at the time it was no big deal. I mean, are you saying she was worried he was a rapist?'

'Not necessarily, Cooper. It's broader than that, more like a default setting. She'd have been more wary than you think.'

'Anyway, not all men are rapists,' her brother added, the opening line to many an argument between the siblings over the years.

'That's true, Murphy,' Jo said, rising to the bait despite herself, 'but the ones who are don't wear big, red rapist badges, so you never can tell.'

'Yeah all right, Jo, cool your jets,' Murphy replied. 'Bloody hell.'

He looked at the others for a supporting reaction, but their smirks were at his expense, not hers. They were obviously enjoying Jo giving the boss a touch-up.

'It's Schrödinger's rapist, okay?' continued Jo. 'The cat is dead; the cat is not dead – you have to look inside the box to find out.'

'By which time it's too late,' added Chartier.

'Actually, it's not quite a perfect analogy,' said Harris. Everyone went a little still, but he failed to notice. 'The cat is both dead *and* not dead until you open the box, causing the wave function to collapse into one state or the other.'

'What's your point, Cooper?' asked Jo tautly.

Nikolaidis nudged the rookie in the leg with the toe of his shoe, but Harris ploughed on regardless.

'If you apply that to your scenario, right, every man is both a rapist and a non-rapist until the woman opens the door, causing him to become one or the other.'

Everyone just looked at him for a long, silent moment.

'Unbelievable,' Jo said eventually. 'Hashtag Not-All-Men, mansplaining and victim-blaming, all inside a minute. That must be a record.'

'Welcome to the New South Wales Police Force,' said Chartier dryly.

'Moving on from quantum mechanics,' said Murphy, shooting Harris a what-the-fuck-was-that look. 'Even if Newman had her knickers in a twist about a man at her door, that wouldn't have been an issue for Williams and Hall. Not unless our guy is a bikie or an enforcer of some kind.'

'It's still about the MacGuffin,' Jo maintained. 'It doesn't just get him in the door: it gets him inside and distracts them somehow.'

'But a MacGuffin can be anything, can't it?' asked Janssen. 'It has no meaning.'

'Not exactly; it's only arbitrary to the audience,' said Jo. 'To the participants its meaning is self-evident. And significant. It's always valuable, at least to them.'

'So it's something valued by the victims, but completely innocuous to us,' said Nikolaidis. 'Perfect.'

They all stared at the floor in silence as they imagined the MacGuffin in their killer's hand – after he's been invited through the door, when his victim's back is turned, their attention drawn away from the unthreatening visitor. It glowed softly golden in Jo's mind, like that briefcase in front of John Travolta. *What the fuck could it be?*

Wednesday 22 August – evening

Sylvia opened her front door, keen to get in from the cold, dark night. As soon as she entered, she was enveloped in a rich, warm, comforting aroma wafting down the hall from the kitchen. 'Hey, gorgeous,' she heard Murphy call.

'Hello, Dave,' she replied as she walked through. 'No footy training?'

'Nah, I decided to leave them to it and cook tea for my best girl instead.'

She dropped her keys into the mortar and slung her bag onto the table, next to a tall vase of spectacular oriental lilies.

'For you, darlin'.' Murphy wore a linen shirt, cotton shorts and a wide smile.

'Thanks, Dave, they're beautiful.' She could smell their perfume even over the cooking. 'What's in the oven? It smells great.'

'I'm trying Cath's lasagne recipe.'

'From scratch? Bechamel and all?'

'Yep, made it from the ground up.'

'Oh, lovely. Any vegies?'

'Steamed broccolini with toasted almond slivers.' He wiped his hands on the tea towel and came around the counter. 'And baby carrots.'

'Sounds great.'

He smiled again and opened his arms for her. She moved inside the arc and he pulled her close, wrapping his arms around her.

'Sorry we got out of sorts on the weekend, Sylv.'

That was one way to put it. 'That's okay, Dave.'

'You just riled me up again with all that radical crap.' He left a pregnant pause.

'I didn't mean to provoke you, honey.'

'But you know how that stuff gets to me, Sylvia. It's not the first time.'

'I'm sorry, Dave. I was just in a mood.'

'All right, love,' he said. 'Let's not let it happen again, eh?'

'Okay.'

'All better, now?' He stroked her hair.

'All better, now.' She reached up and kissed him on the cheek.

'That's my girl,' he said, turning to kiss her on the mouth, one hand running scales up and down her spine.

Keen to move on, she moved her body into the shape of him. 'So what's for dessert?'

'I thought every man for himself.' A hand slid inside her scrubs to caress her arse, the other wandering up beneath her top. 'I'm thinking pussy, myself. Hot pussy in pussy sauce.'

But Sylvia wheeled away when his fingers began working her bra catch. 'Not so fast, cowboy, you'll burn the lasagne.'

'It's in there for another hour yet!' he protested, but she was already moving.

'I really need a shower,' she called back from the hall.

Sylvia closed the bedroom door behind her then went into the en suite and started the water running. She shed her work clothes and leaned against the wall, just clearing her mind, until the space steamed up, then she stepped into the shower. She knew how it was going to go, and that was fine. She just needed a moment to settle first.

VOLUME IIII

THE NERVES

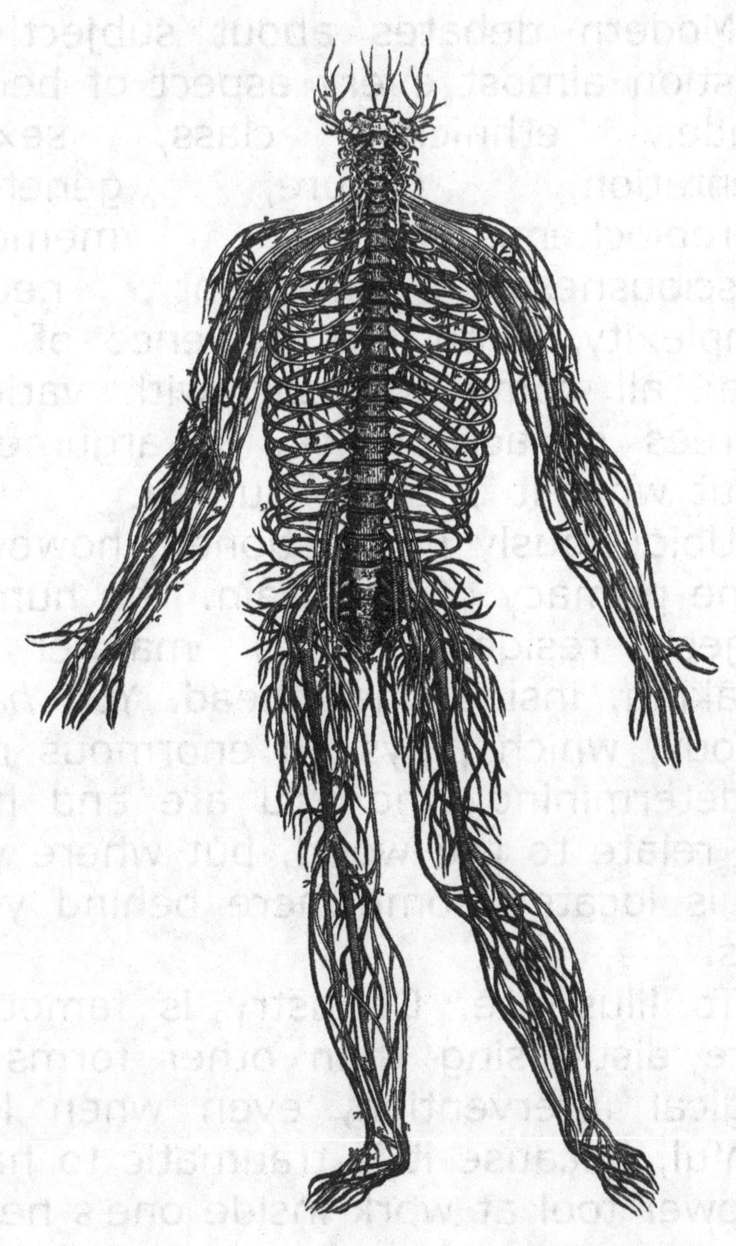

Modern debates about subjectivity question almost every aspect of being. Gender, ethnicity, class, sexual orientation, culture, genetics, neurobiochemistry, memory, consciousness, emergent neural complexity, even the influence of gut flora: all come to bear, with various degrees of acceptance, in arguments about what it is to be human.

Ubiquitously *un*questioned, however, is the primacy of the brain. The human subject resides, in a manner of speaking, inside one's head. You *have* a body, which plays an enormous role in determining who you are and how you relate to the world, but where you *are* is located somewhere behind your eyes.

To illustrate. Dentistry is famously more distressing than other forms of surgical intervention, even when less painful, because it is traumatic to have a power tool at work inside one's head.

This fear is not only a function of objective pain: it is simply too close to home.

Philosophers invent ontological thought experiments to test our loyalty to our flesh. The consensus holds that were our brains to be removed from our bodies and kept in vats, we ourselves (whatever that means to each of us) would still be essentially present, in a way we would not were the surviving artefact instead a well-tended left leg. That assumption is today held to be so obviously and axiomatically true as to be invisible to most interlocutors.

It has not ever been thus.

The orthodox Aristotelian theory, prevailing in Europe for two millennia until Vesalius overturned it, held that the heart was responsible for intellect and affect. The heart did not serve the vascular system: it was served by it. The heart was where you were, while the nervous system – including the brain and the spinal cord – were merely conduits driving motion and sensation. The nerves were classified together with the ligaments, with interdependent and parallel functions, in the manner of the arteries and veins.

Then the Master demonstrated that the nerves originate in the brain, not in the heart, including those nerves serving distal structures of emotional expression: tear ducts, facial muscles, sweat glands, the hairs on the back of the neck. The heart, by contrast, consisted entirely of muscle, lacking the foundry to originate emotion and intellection. Vesalius hypothesised that the brain and the nervous system were responsible for thought and affect, as well as motion and sensation.

This was a minority view at the time, opposed by experts and the masses alike, to whom the proposition was ridiculous. Yet Vesalius did not flinch. He challenged orthodoxy in the very structure of the *Fabrica,* considering the nerves in isolation in Volume IIII, while examining the ligaments in Volume II alongside the muscles, tendons and aponeuroses, relegating them to the realm of locomotive leverage and anchorage, rather than impulse transmission.

Wednesday 12 September – afternoon

'I've found the connection, boss!' said Harris, bursting in from the stairs.

'Apart from being rich arseholes?' said Murphy, standing up from the worktable in the Homicide Squad's open area. 'What've you got?'

'All three victims are with Denison Bank!'

Murphy rolled his eyes and sat back down heavily.

'Why not?' protested Harris.

'Do you have a Denison Bank account, Harris?' asked Murphy.

'Yeah.'

'Does Niko? I know you've asked him.'

'Yeah, he does.'

'What did he say about your theory?'

Harris drooped visibly. 'He doesn't like it. Told me to try it on you.'

Murphy rummaged in his back pocket and pulled out his wallet. He slid a credit card emblazoned with the image of Fort Denison across the table.

'Yeah, but all three,' said the rookie. 'What are the odds?'

'Short, Harris.'

'Come on, boss. It's a hit for sure.'

Murphy tilted his head like George Kennedy regarding Paul Newman in *Cool Hand Luke* as he hauled himself out of the dirt: *I like your pluck, son, and I don't really want to hit you again, but if you keep getting up ...* 'Janssen?' he called out.

'Yes, I have one.'

'Chartier?'

'Me too.'

'Jo?'

'Nope.' She left the commissioner's *New Fabrica* and wandered over.

'Anyone else?' Murphy knew the uniforms were listening. There was a chorus of yeses, a couple of noes.

'Oh,' said Harris, deflated. He turned and started trudging towards the stairs.

'Thirty-four point three per cent,' said Jo.

'What's thirty-four point three per cent?' asked Murphy.

'The odds of all three victims having a Denison Bank account. Give or take.'

Harris stopped and turned, and everything went quiet. Murphy tilted his chair back and examined her sceptically. Despite decades of experience, he still couldn't reliably tell whether his little sister was taking the piss out of him. Janssen and Chartier each put down what they were doing and tuned in.

'Really?' Murphy said dubiously.

'Uh-huh.'

'How would you know?'

'Worked it out.'

'What, just then? In your head?'

'Yep.'

'You're an art historian.'

'We're allowed to use the mathematics, you know. As long as we put them back the way we found them.'

Chartier coughed to conceal a laugh.

Murphy gave Jo his well-rehearsed 'you little smart-arse' look. She held a neutral gaze in return. 'All right, I'll bite. Talk me through it.'

'Population of Sydney is five million, right?'

'Less the children.'

'They've all got Fort Denison moneyboxes, Dave.'

'Yeah but they're not his demographic.'

'Okay, minus the children but plus Newcastle and the Illawarra. Five million.'

'How about people in hospitals? Prisons? Barracks?'

'Come on, Dave, you're nitpicking. This is ballpark.'

'Okay, okay.' Murphy held up his hands. 'It's just, you say "point three" like it's precision engineering.'

'Fair enough, I'll round off. So Denison Bank has three and a half million individual customers in the Sydney area. It's their best market by a country mile.'

'How do you know that?'

'I'm a shareholder. It's in the annual report.'

'You little capitalist,' said Murphy. 'Who knew?'

Jo stuck her tongue out at him. 'The university credit union demutualised when the Fort swallowed them whole. They issued us shares.'

'But you don't bank with them?' asked Janssen.

'I was pissed off and took my banking elsewhere.'

'So any given citizen is more likely to have a Denison account than not,' said Chartier, returning to the point.

'That's for each one separately,' urged Harris. 'I mean for all three together.'

'That's the right thinking, Cooper, but the numbers don't stretch that far,' said Jo. 'Not with the Fort's market share, and not with only three victims.'

'I don't get it.'

'The odds in Sydney of being a Fort customer is three and a half out of five, right?'

Harris nodded.

'So that's seven out of ten. For any three particular Sydneysiders to all bank with them, it's seven-tenths cubed. That's 343 on a thousand.'

'Thirty-four per cent,' said Janssen.

'Point three,' added Chartier.

'Wait, why cubed?' asked Harris.

'Because we multiply each of the odds together. With three the same, it's a cube.'

'Okay.'

'And the odds of none of them being with the Fort are three-tenths cubed,' added Chartier. 'Under three per cent.'

Murphy looked at her in surprise. 'How the fuck'd you work that out?'

'Jo just explained it, Spud,' said Janssen.

'Oh, right,' said Murphy, clearly not following.

'So there's a one-third chance we'd find all three victims had Denison Bank accounts,' concluded Jo. 'I'm no statistician, but that could be random coincidence.'

'Yeah, fair enough,' said Harris, defeated.

'Sorry, mate.' Jo offered him a sympathetic smile.

'They're all in the NRMA, too,' Harris revealed. 'And Qantas.'

'Not to mention the electoral roll, drivers' licences, Medicare cards, tax-file numbers...' added Murphy dryly. He'd never been particularly impressed with this kind of dragnet fishing: it was as meaningful as saying they all ate Vegemite on toast and drank Toohey's New. It might be true, but it didn't help you catch anyone. 'Tell you what, though, I wouldn't mind having access to Denison Bank's database,' he added.

'Why's that?' asked Jo.

'Head of security over there is Tom Adams, my old partner from Armed Rob. You wouldn't believe the kind of information they have on their customers. There's no such thing as privacy when it comes to commercial data, and no one gives a shit. Actually, the regulators encourage it, to help the banks estimate risk. But as soon as it's a government database, everyone freaks out about invasion of privacy. I tell you, if we had access to half that much intel we'd double our arrest rate overnight.'

'Yeah, government surveillance of innocent citizens, what could possibly go wrong?' quipped Jo.

'Righto, comrade, but meanwhile you and your civil liberty mates are keeping this bloke on the street while we flail about in the dark.'

So how many would it take, Jo?' asked Chartier, steering them back on track again. 'Just out of interest.'

'What do you mean?'

'How many Fort customers as victims before it's implausible that it's by chance alone?'

'Depends on what you mean by implausible. Scientists go for five per cent, sometimes even one per cent.'

'We're looking for leads, not the laws of physics,' said Murphy. 'Let's say ten.'

'So seven-tenths to the power of whatever. Hang on.' She scribbled on a notepad for a minute. 'Yeah, seven. Once you have seven victims all with Denison Bank accounts, it's only an eight per cent chance of being random.'

'*Klote,* let's not get to seven,' said Janssen.

'Amen to that,' said Chartier.

Jo turned to the young detective. 'This is good work, Cooper. Keep track of it.'

'Thanks, Dr King,' replied Harris. 'But I'm still hoping to stop him at three.'

Jo smiled and nodded. Weren't they all.

'I'm seriously impressed, Jo,' said Janssen.

'Me, too,' said Chartier.

'Nice work, sis,' said Murphy, although he was clearly only saying it for the benefit of his colleagues. He turned his chair back to the worktable and opened a file, pretending to read until everyone went away.

Monday 17 September – afternoon

Sylvia left the hospital, crossed Avoca Street and wended her way through the residential streets towards home. She stopped for milk on the way, then again on the steps at the end of their street to admire a magnolia in full profusion of ivory and pink. She was passing the riot of azaleas in their elderly neighbour's garden when she heard a cry of distress from inside. She went through Clare's gate and knocked on the door.

'Just a minute,' she heard from the depths, then the door opened. 'Hello, Sylvia, how are you?' Her neighbour seemed fine.

'I'm well thanks, Clare. Sorry to disturb you, but I thought I heard something. Just seeing you're okay.'

'Oh! Yes, it's nothing. It's kind of you to check.'

'What happened?'

'I found a crack in my favourite teacup. I was being melodramatic.'

'Oh, no, I understand.'

'It was the last survivor from a set I bought in Lisbon decades ago. Vista Alegre.'

'It's lovely to use precious things in your everyday life,' ventured Sylvia. 'But sooner or later they come to grief.'

'Yes, I'm reconciled to that principle,' said Clare. 'But you also reach an age when you're never going back to places. It lends some objects a heightened significance.'

'I hadn't thought about it like that.'

'No reason you would, at your age. Everything's still possible.'

Sylvia smiled. 'I suppose so.'

Clare pulled the door open. 'Would you like to come in for a cup of tea?'

'Oh, no, that's okay.' Sylvia didn't want to be a bother.

'Don't worry, the backup crockery is quite up to scratch.'

Sylvia laughed, and reconsidered. It was only a cup of tea, not a four-course meal. Anyway, Clare was impressively independent for ninety, but also alone a good deal. She might like the company. 'Why not? Let me put the milk away. I'll be right back.'

'I'll put the kettle on,' Clare said. 'Come straight through.'

Sylvia went out one gate and in the other, and entered her front door just as Murphy was leaving his study. He looked a little furtive.

'Oh!' she exclaimed. 'I wasn't expecting you.'

'Why not?'

'Your car's not out the front. Hasn't been stolen, has it, detective?'

'Nah, it's back in the shop. Still has that rattle in the drivetrain.' He went ahead of her into the living room, straight for the sideboard. He waved a bottle of red at her with a raised eyebrow.

'No thanks, I'm going next door to have a cuppa with Clare,' said Sylvia as she put the milk in the fridge. 'I'll make dinner when I come back.'

'What does she want?' grumbled Murphy. He harboured an unspecified – and as far as Sylvia knew, unprovoked – aversion to their neighbour.

'Nothing, just catching up. So did you get the bus again, working man?'

'Fuck, no.' He shuddered as he poured. 'Janssen dropped me on his way to Jo's.'

'Isn't she working at Surry Hills?'

'Yeah, but she had to see a PhD student this arvo.'

'What couldn't keep until tomorrow?'

'I dunno. Something about search results.'

'Hmm.' Sylvia was sceptical. 'You don't need me to drive you in tomorrow morning, I hope?' She was finally on her weekend, and was looking forward to a sleep-in before a quiet day to herself. She'd been learning a tough new flamenco guitar piece and wanted a good few hours to work on it, well rested and alone.

'No, he's picking me up on his way in,' said Murphy.

'Who, Matthijs?'

'Yeah. Why?'

'Doesn't he live in Bondi?'

'So?'

'How is Randwick on his way to Surry Hills?'

'I dunno.' Murphy shrugged. 'He offered.'

There's definitely something fishy about this, Sylvia thought. Enquiries would have to be made. 'Just don't bring him inside tomorrow morning,' she said. 'He scared the daylights out of me last time.'

Murphy smirked. 'He got a nice eyeful, but. You in all your glory.'

'You set us up, you bastard.'

'Didn't hurt anybody. Anyway, the Danish are chronic nudists.'

'He's Dutch, and that's not the point.'

'I don't know who was more embarrassed, you or him.' He laughed.

'Not you, that's for sure.'

'I was fully dressed.'

'Well, tomorrow just go out front and get in his car, will you? No funny business.'

'Just trying to put a little sunshine in a young fella's life.'

I reckon he's probably doing all right for sunshine, thought Sylvia, although she kept it to herself. *Right now, and not that far from here.*

Thursday 20 September – afternoon

The police filed into their minister's office, the top brass all spit-polish and dark navy serge, Murphy in a rumpled grey suit with a pie stain on the left lapel. He'd been a last-minute inclusion and had not had time to change. He hoped the effect was of streetwise authenticity. At least Sylvia had ironed his shirt.

The police minister was at the head of the rectangular coffee table, his chief of staff next to him, and on the other side the attorney-general, a silk of the Sydney bar who thought he was Cicero and everyone else a fucking idiot. This would be interesting: the attorney-general was a committed factional enemy of both the police minister and the premier, who in turn hated one another passionately, despite – or perhaps because of – their factional alliance.

Murphy let his commissioner, deputy commissioner and superintendent make their greetings and select their seats. While they were still milling, he noticed that one of the several staffers present was being treated with a particular deference by everyone else. In his early thirties, fit, sharply dressed, modish hair – could pass for anything from a tech entrepreneur to a special forces sniper – he turned out to be the premier's principal adviser.

This was not good. Somewhere in the no-man's-land between these various political agendas sat Murphy and his homicide case. He was resigned to the political class doing its plotting and scheming, but he did not want to be nearby when it happened. Coppers who kept this kind of company tended to come to grief.

He took the last remaining chair and looked up to find all eyes on him.

'Detective Senior Sergeant Murphy,' said his minister. 'They call you Spud.'

'Yes, sir, they do.'

'Why's that?'

'The boys called me that in school. It stuck.'

'They must've had a reason.'

Murphy offered his altar-boy face. 'Best known to themselves, sir.'

'Well, "Spud" is a common enough soubriquet for a male of Irish extraction,' contributed the attorney-general. 'Although the association with Erin is as specious as it is banal, given the tuber's origins in the Peruvian Andes.'

That pearl of erudition struck the room silent, so the police minister grunted ambiguously and turned to Murphy. 'Why don't you lead off, detective?'

This was a surprise – Murphy had not actually been told what the meeting was for – but he was used to being put on the spot, so he unrolled a crisp operational update on the case. Superintendent Manning added an aura of calm competence with some textbook platitudes. The police minister asked the others if they had anything to add. Deputy Commissioner Hughes passed, letting the men play their cards before making her contribution, while Commissioner Carr spread his hands munificently and said, 'We are eager to hear how we can help, minister.'

'Thank you, detective,' said the police minister, 'I've learned more in five minutes from you than from five months of morning digests.' He glanced significantly at the commissioner. 'The lack of progress is frustrating, though.'

The attorney-general leaned in to add his two bobs' worth. 'We have three grief-stricken families, five million frightened citizens, and six months until the election, detective.'

'It *is* frustrating, minister,' agreed Murphy, ignoring the attorney. 'These are the cleanest crime scenes our forensic people have ever seen – he's meticulous and extremely well-prepared. We've doorknocked like the Salvos, but we've found no eyewitnesses. There is no apparent link between victims, other than that they're reasonably well-off.' He decided not to mention the resource constraints that added autopsy and toxicology delays to their woes. Not in front of the Klingons.

But the chief Klingon smelled his hesitation anyway. The attorney-general leaned forward. 'You have also comprehensively failed, have you not, detective, to account for his confident access to the premises, and his capacity to occupy them with apparent impunity over such extensive durations?'

'Yes, attorney, they are both unknown factors at this stage.' This was interesting – only the briefings for the police minister and the premier had gone into those concerns in detail. Murphy wondered how the attorney-general was accessing them, and what else he knew. 'But we're confident those aspects will provide the key leads once we pinpoint them. That's why we are downplaying them in the media.'

'The media, yes,' said the police minister. 'We'll come to that. But first can you tell us how you are deploying the additional resources the premier and I have placed at your disposal?'

'We've benefited significantly from additional uniformed officers to help with the substantial volume of analytical work,' said Murphy. 'If we crack those elements we were just discussing, it will be due to that assistance.'

The police minister beamed.

'What about the premier's funding?' asked the principal adviser.

'That's enabled us to acquire certain materials essential to the research. Again, absolutely pivotal to success.'

'And we certainly appreciate your advocacy to the premier for those additional resources, minister,' said the commissioner, throwing their boss an extra bone.

The police minister nodded benevolently. 'I'm particularly impressed with how early you latched onto this anatomy angle, detective. I understand you've brought in an expert consultant?'

'That's correct, sir,' said Murphy. 'A specialist from the University of Sydney.' Both politicians puffed out their chests at the mention of their alma mater.

'The premier asked me to convey how pleased he is to see you using such creative initiative,' said the adviser. 'It's the future of policing.'

'And of universities,' added the attorney-general. 'It's time those leftists rendered their contribution. You mention that your killer is targeting the affluent, Murphy. It seems probable he's a communist, wouldn't you say? Have you consulted ASIO yet?'

Oh good, a witch-hunt will help no end, thought Murphy, but he kept his reply civil. 'That is the victim profile so far, attorney, but there could be either positive or negative selection principles at play, sir. Or both.'

'Meaning what?'

'It could indicate that he is pursuing rich people deliberately, for whatever reason—'

'Envy, Murphy, it's the politics of envy.'

'—but it's more likely that poorer people drop out of his selection process, because they don't enjoy the conditions he needs to undertake his dissections,' said Murphy. 'Privacy, distance from the neighbours, big empty houses, and lots of time at their command.'

The attorney-general was clearly not happy with this but the police minister cleared his throat to signify an end to the preliminaries. 'So a lot is being done but there's not much to show for it, and the entire city waits in dread. He will continue, I suppose, if not apprehended?'

Murphy nodded. There was no denying the facts. 'He's embarked on a series and he won't stop until it's complete, we catch him or he walks in front of a bus.'

'There's been a rich discussion around the cabinet table,' said the police minister, with a sideways frown at the attorney-general, 'with some, ah, imaginative options canvassed. The cabinet has proposed an alternative course of action that might help bring this case to a conclusion. The premier would like you to consider it.'

So that's what this was all about. Cabinet was up in arms, egged on by the attorney-general; someone'd had a brainwave about how to do a copper's job, and the premier had decided to let some air out of the tyres by advancing the proposal. The police minister would've objected to the meddling, so the attorney-general was here to make sure the minister stuck to the script; the premier's spook was here to ensure the attorney didn't verbal the rest of them. What a clusterfuck.

Not for the first time, Murphy reflected that the political preselection ecology in New South Wales had to be the last frontier of human understanding. Infuckenscrutable.

Once the police personnel had digested the political play, the commissioner said, 'We are open to all practical suggestions, minister.'

The police minister turned to the premier's adviser. 'Angus?'

'Thank you, minister, and with your permission, attorney?' The attorney-general signalled his consent with a long blink, and the adviser turned to the police. 'The ministerial offices have been enlisted for ideas on this one,' he said, nodding in the direction of the police minister's chief of staff.

God help us, thought Murphy. That prick was about as useful as an ashtray on a motorbike.

'The policy advisers have sketched out the main challenges,' the adviser went on, 'but it was the press secretaries who came up with the solution.'

'Not exactly, Angus,' admonished the attorney-general. 'Credit where it's due, please.'

The adviser nodded. 'True, the attorney's press secretary thought it up then workshopped it with the others. The problem is we're being slaughtered in the media for lack of progress. You don't want to share details like this anatomy angle, fair enough, but that leaves a void and the broadcasters just make shit up to fill it. The premier is starting to take some lead, and the backbench is getting antsy. It was regrettable when the police force was under fire, of course, but now it's become a political issue it's time to act.'

Murphy felt his poker face beginning to slip.

'So the press secs have developed a whole integrated strategy,' this Angus character continued. 'The short version is we drop a major media splash across several outlets. Give one of the TVs an exclusive up-front, then back it in with the other networks – plus radio, print, socials.'

'To what end, Angus?' asked the commissioner.

The adviser sat back and spread his hands. 'We go your lad big-time: trash his brand, piss him off, flush him out.'

‘That's just too random,’ objected the superintendent. ‘He could do anything.’

‘Yeah, nah, we're onto that,’ the adviser replied. ‘See, this is essentially a political comms op, and that's something we do extremely well.’ Murphy nearly laughed aloud at that claim, but he managed to suppress it. ‘You want to provoke a reaction, yes, but you *direct* his aggression. You inflame him so he acts without his usual preparation, but so he comes at you in a particular direction. Where you'll be waiting for him.’

Murphy had been watching the two cabinet ministers’ contrasting reactions: the attorney-general leaning in and nodding along open-mouthed, his stumpy pink tongue on his bottom lip; the police minister sitting back, arms folded with a scowl on his face.

‘This harnesses all the media aggro and turns it to our advantage,’ continued the premier's adviser. ‘It directs the spotlight away from criticism to action, making us look decisive and proactive. Who knows, it might even bring him down. I think it addresses all our needs.'

Murphy considered his options. It was colossally risky, of course, but not the worst idea he'd ever heard – in fact he'd done something like it himself once or twice. But it was the sort of the thing a cop would cook up on the quiet with the help of a trusted journo mate, not a roomful of dodgy political hacks. He knew for a fact his brass would never go for it. It had major operational flaws: anticipating the behaviour of an unknown perpetrator would be a lot harder to achieve in the field than on a whiteboard, for one. They still didn't have any idea how their perp was selecting his victims, so steering his reaction would be all speculation. It wasn't going to fly, not without a lot more intel on their target. In any case, with so many cooks around the broth something was bound to go wrong. And he knew who would carry the can when it did. Nup.

The room had been quiet while the police absorbed the plan. All eyes turned to Murphy for a reaction. *Oh well,* he thought, *in for a penny.* He leaned forward.

'Listen, Machiavelli, I really don't give a fuck what you think.'

The commissioner groaned and the superintendent slumped visibly in his seat. The premier's man was completely unperturbed, returning Murphy's gaze with polite curiosity about what he would say next. Murphy was curious about that himself.

'You're batting well out of your crease, detective,' observed the deputy commissioner. 'You might want to rephrase that.'

It was the first thing she'd said since entering this shark tank, and it was excellent advice. *And remember who butters your bread,* Murphy told himself. 'With respect,' he lied, 'the premier's support is invaluable, and our minister's role is obviously fundamental, but amateur opinions are not pertinent to this operation.' The attorney-general bristled at this, but the police minister smiled widely and the commissioner revived a little. 'And the fantasies of your press secretaries are dangerously misguided.' He was well ahead and under the laws of sustainable gambling, ahead was where you quit. 'This investigation is strictly a police matter,' he wrapped up, gesturing to his bosses and the police minister. 'It will be executed by police personnel, within police procedures, under police authority.'

Murphy having divided, the commissioner proceeded to conquer. 'And with the unpredictability of the subject's behaviour, combined with the operational fluidity that characterises any open criminal investigation, the introduction of such a dynamic, uncontrolled variable would only imperil the outcome, rather than securing it.' Nicely put, if you went in for that kind of language.

The politicians and staffers had clearly not considered that angle: this could backfire in ways impossible to imagine, let alone prevent. In any case, the police minister clearly regarded his detective's fine fuck-you to be the end of the matter. He had discharged his obligation to propose the idea, and the result was clear. There would be no provocative press kit released into the wild.

But the attorney-general could not quite let it go. '"But it is not the place of the Police to convict guilty men, as it is by them they get their living",' he intoned. 'Ned Kelly, *The Jerilderie Letter.* The Taig was not impercipient.'

'Attorney, our sole objective is to stop this man before he kills again,' said the commissioner, barely controlling his fury. 'Any other suggestion is outrageous.'

'Yes that's unworthy, Leonard, even of you,' admonished the police minister.

The attorney-general turned to Murphy. 'Proceed as you must, detective, and apprehend your quarry with despatch. You can be sure we will be observing closely.'

Murphy considered making a proportionate response but merely nodded in reply. He bade the police minister farewell, directed a loose, ironic salute to his brass, and fled the room.

Saturday 22 September – night

Porter quickly completed his routine shift duties and triaged some extra hackwork. He made a pot of tea then turned to his latest prospective candidate.

Damien Henley had nominated himself for Volume IIII late in Porter's previous shift, delivering a protracted tirade of vile aggression. As soon as the dreadful man had slammed the receiver down, Porter had set to work. His early impression had been favourable, but the shift had ended before he could be sure. He had to either finish his assessment tonight, or release Henley: he could not hold up the credit card cancellation any longer.

Henley had refinanced with Denison Bank two years ago to renovate a house overlooking the Georges River, although 'renovation' completely failed to capture the scale of the exercise. The plans showed a perfectly sound and sensibly proportioned house making way for a grandiloquent mansion: of the original Californian bungalow, only the vintage façade remained. There were now five bedrooms, four bathrooms, a library, a conservatory and a home gym – all fully wired, climate controlled and tastefully lit, with European fittings throughout – with a three-car garage and cellar beneath and a broad deck, an enormous hot tub and an extensive Japanese garden out the back.

This had cost an absolute fortune, but as a highly remunerated executive for Recondite Technologies, a boutique local front for a global defence technology firm, Henley could well afford it. The final product was certainly impressive, but all that destruction and reconstruction was a colossal gamble on the market's willingness to disregard common sense. On the other hand, Porter reflected, when had a bet on a luxury home with expansive water views ever gone wrong? In the Ponzi scheme that was the Sydney real-estate market, the reckoning was always indefinitely deferred.

Porter returned to the layout, considering sightlines to the windows and doors, then brought the house up on both satellite and street views. The building's disposition looked promising, subject to reconnaissance, but he was concerned about security systems. In a house this plush, especially one belonging to a wealthy defence contractor, they would be a logical inclusion, yet there was no reference to them in the plans or the insurance documents. It didn't make sense.

Porter dived into the murkier recesses of this vast reservoir of information, which was held by private enterprise and tacitly – if illicitly – available to the bank. As consumer data had become increasingly digitised, and as the pricing of products and services had increasingly become a function of accuracy in risk assessment, most commercial entities had realised that it was in their interests to allow mutual access to all manner of harmless customer data. Notionally illegal, of course, all it required was a studied carelessness regarding data security on certain commercial interchange channels. A technically savvy operative inside one of these companies could discover a great deal about any private individual, as long as they knew where to look. And Stephen Porter knew.

He quickly discovered a technician's run sheet showing the installation of a back-to-base alarm by a sister company within Henley's corporate group, just after lock-up stage. Henley had not recorded its existence on his house-and-contents insurance policy, foregoing a modest discount on the premium, which was all but proof that the unit was stolen. Sure enough, Porter verified by serial number that the base unit had been reported to the manufacturer 'damaged on delivery': it would have been written off without return. The crooked job had doubtless been contra for an equally dubious favour.

People were dreadful.

Happily, there were no surveillance cameras, only motion sensors and reed switches, which would not trouble Porter.

Still at large in the Borgesian data ocean, Porter searched for other pitfalls, as well as routine behaviour that might suggest times to avoid, or approaches that could influence risk. He checked for deliveries to Henley's address (clothes, wine, protein supplements); searched for the existence and range of fixed cameras on nearby buildings (one at the local newsagent, easily avoided); assessed the diligence of the neighbourhood watch group (comatose); checked ride-sharing logs for unusual pickup times (none recently); looked at Henley's current airline bookings (nothing for weeks); and found the cleaning contract (no problem, this would all be over well before Friday).

No red flags.

Porter turned back to the Fort's own system to make a final check on the executive's domestic spending habits. Henley didn't go out much, although he didn't really cook either – it was all delivery and takeaway – and he drank too much vodka and ate too much ice-cream. He spent most evenings watching movies, including a moderate diet of tediously predictable porn. Every Saturday he rented the company of a young woman furnished by a discreet establishment in Sutherland. It added up to a single man who spent a lot of time at home, mostly alone.

Henley was well insured for disasters that would leave him alive, but there was no life insurance, nor any declared beneficiary for his superannuation. There was no sign that anyone in this wide, brown land depended on Damien Henley – not whom he cared about, anyway. Just as well, because Mr Henley was needed for a higher calling.

The final matter was timing. Porter went back to the commercial realm and navigated through a porous firewall into Henley's ineffectually encrypted telecommunications data. He skimmed the candidate's recent emails and text messages, establishing that he would in all likelihood be home alone from Sunday evening. He checked Henley's diary for the coming week and found no commitments that would create any problems. He determined that Henley tended to organise his work life using the scheduling tool in his company's desktop calendar program, mostly through the mobile phone app. Perfect.

So it was on. Porter would go in late on Sunday night, after the burghers of Taren Point had turned in for the night, and he'd have almost a week of splendid isolation with only Mr Henley for company. They had a significant quantum of detailed study to work through together. Porter sat back contentedly and nursed his tea, surveying the results of a good night's work.

'All right then, young Stephen?' came a voice from right behind his chair.

'Christ, Tom!' Porter shot to his feet and wheeled around to place himself between the security guard and the main screen. The manoeuvre just about sent him tumbling, but it was entirely pointless anyway, with printouts on every surface and scrolls of data on the other terminals. Damien Henley was everywhere.

He needn't have worried. Tom evidenced his usual indifference to what actually went on in the business he was paid to protect. Instead, he watched with amusement as Porter recovered.

For his own part, Porter sat down again, tilted his chair back and took a long, measured breath. 'Whew!' He grinned up at the guard, holding his hand over his heart for dramatic emphasis. 'I didn't realise you were there.'

'Yeah, I can see that,' said Tom. 'Sorry, mate.'

'It's okay, I've been chasing down some transaction errors and became engrossed.'

'Inattention's a bit risky in this job, though, innit?' Tom chastised. 'Blimey, if I'd caught you like that in the army, I'd've put you on report. Nothing personal – I wouldn't've had any choice.'

'Eternal vigilance,' suggested Porter, happy to proceed along this tangent. This was Tom's special subject: the Improvement of Civilian Life through the Application of Military Principles.

'Absolutely. The sentry has one job and one job only: keep watch for the enemy. All your mates are relying on you. Your country's relying on you. You have to be completely alert, every moment.'

'I agree, Tom, but you tell that to management. They deploy us to keep a close watch on the whole empire, and to immediately rectify any problem on any of these systems.' He waved his hand, taking in a score of terminals and a dozen printers. 'But at the same time, they think we're doing nothing all night, so they allocate all the fiddly work to us. Transaction errors, processing anomalies, file cleansing, card activations.'

Tom nodded sagely, having heard all this before. It was not his problem. The bank managers were not even his bosses anymore: he worked for a contract security firm nowadays. *We each have our cross to bear,* his expression said.

'Well, sorry to have startled you. Not a guilty conscience, then?'

'Not at all,' said Porter. 'I sleep like a baby.'

'That's the way to a ripe old age, my boy. A solid eight in the rack.' Tom stretched and yawned. 'Anyway, pumpkin time for me. I came to tuck you in.'

Porter had to hand it to the guard: he was as reliable as clockwork. He'd probably been an excellent soldier. 'All right, then,' he said. 'Have a good night.'

'You too, hope your shift is quiet as the grave and smooth as a baby's bum. And don't concentrate so hard. They don't pay us enough.'

Tom shuffled off to complete his rounds, while Porter collated his printouts and packed them in his bag.

Sunday 23 September – evening

'That was great, darlin',' said Murphy, sighing contentedly.

Sylvia returned his smile. Her smoked salmon pasta was dead-easy, actually, but it made him purr like a cat. It didn't hurt that they'd enjoyed the gorgeous spring morning sailing on Pittwater, then the afternoon in the pool at home, where nature had run its course most agreeably. She reached for his plate and he for the bottle, taking it over to the sofa and switching on the television.

She quickly cleaned up in the kitchen while he finished the shiraz in front of a doco about the Great Barrier Reef. When that finished they scrolled through the movies. They landed briefly on *Bridget Jones's Baby*. Murphy just snorted and moved on, but Sylvia decided it was pretext enough. She'd drained his balls and filled his belly, and he was lightly toasted now: his mood was as good as it would ever be. She grabbed the remote and scrolled back to Renée Zellweger.

'You must be joking,' said Murphy. 'I'm not watching that.'

'All right, but doesn't it make you think?'

'Think about what?' He retrieved the remote and scrolled on again.

'About having a baby.'

'Don't be daft.'

Sylvia burrowed into his side. 'I just think maybe we could discuss it.'

'There's nothing to discuss.' He stopped on the *Blade Runner* sequel. 'What about this?'

'But come on, honey, wouldn't you like to teach your son how to kick a footy?'

'For fuck's...' Murphy recoiled as though she were electrically charged. 'You're actually serious, aren't you? For real?'

'Yes,' she replied, calmly but firmly. 'I'd like us to consider it.'

Murphy gaped then shook his head in a performance of incredulity. It was like a switch had flicked. 'Jesus, Sylvia, you're a piece of work.'

'What's that supposed to mean?'

'Last year you wanted to take five years off to go to fucken medical school—'

'Four.'

'Whatever. First you want to take four years off work because some doctor's trying to flatter his way into your pants—'

'Iain's gay, Dave. And Christel said the same thing about my potential.'

'And she's probably a dyke. She certainly loves looking at your twat.'

'She's my gynaecologist, David.'

'Yeah, well, trust me, this has nothing to do with your "potential" darlin', they just want to fuck you. Anyway, it's beside the point.'

'Really. And what is the point?'

'The point is that this is why I can't take you seriously. You were going to be a professional musician, remember? How'd that work out for you? Then it's your life's ambition to be a doctor. Now it's a baby. Next you'll be wanting to trek across Antarctica or some fucken thing.'

'People do have medical careers *and* children, you know. Even the lady doctors.'

'Oh, right, you're going to do both, are you? You think you can take a kid to lectures? Onto the wards? "Mrs Murphy, please demonstrate how to palpitate the patient's liver." "Certainly, professor, as soon as I get this infant off my tit." You've got no fucken sense, Sylvia.'

Murphy stood abruptly and lurched to the sideboard to pour a long whisky. 'You know what your problem is? You listen to all that fucken "women can do anything" hippy shit. Life's not like that. You need to separate fantasy from reality.' He drained the glass, refilled it and reeled back to the sofa. 'Truly, if it weren't for me you'd be completely rooted.'

'Reality,' she repeated.

'Yeah, fucken reality.'

'And what is "reality" according to you?'

'Reality is what we are *living,* not all your unicorns-and-rainbows horseshit. It's our fucken *life,* right here, right now. You're a nurse, I'm a cop. I deal with dead people and you deal with sick people. We live in a bloody nice house that costs me a fortune. You swim at

Coogee, I play footy for Maroubra. You play your guitar and read your books and watch your pretentious foreign movies with your film wankers' group. I follow rugby league and motorsport and the cricket. On weekends you have brunch at Industry Beans with my sister and those other two chicks, and I go to the Diggers or the pub. We fuck, we get pissed, we have the odd misunderstanding. Then we make up, and on Mondays we do it all again.'

'So that's all life is to you? Just that, week in, week out.'

'Nah, course not. We go sailing when we can, we go to the flicks, we see the odd band, eat at flash restaurants, take nice holidays, drive up the mountains or down the coast ... fuck, I dunno. What more do you want, Sylvia?'

'I want a child.'

'You don't want a child, you want a fucken baby.'

'What's the difference?'

'See, that's my point exactly.'

'What are you talking about?'

'You want a pet, like a kid who wants a puppy without thinking about what happens when it isn't cute anymore. It might feel all nice and glowy while you're knocked up, with your baby showers and your maternity leave and your girlfriends egging you on, but once the fucken thing's out and screaming night and day, shitting everywhere and chewing your tits raw and keeping you awake all night, then all bets are off. Where are the bitches then, eh? You're on your own. It'd be penal fucken servitude, and not just for eighteen years – it's for the term of your natural life. You've got no idea what's involved, darlin', no idea at all.'

'I take it you wouldn't be getting up in the night, then?'

'Fucken oath I wouldn't – fuck that. A baby is the last thing this household needs. Anyway, it's all academic. This is the one thing left a bloke can still control—'

'What do you mean, "the one thing left"?'

He waved that away: a debate for another day. 'I'm not reversing the vasectomy, Sylvia. It doesn't matter how much you bitch and moan, it's my right of veto. Thank Christ. And it's not fucken happening.'

Friday 28 September – morning

Murphy and Janssen walked up the driveway of the palatial house in Taren Point. Mack met them at the front door.

'You sure you're not our serial killer?' asked Murphy, by way of greeting.

'Now why would you want to say a thing like that?'

'You're always here first. It's like you know in advance.'

'Ah, well, I'm not carrying your old football injuries, Spud,' replied Mack. 'There are some benefits to the contemplative life.' He nodded at the coffee cup in Janssen's hand. 'That wouldn't be for me, would it, Matthijs?'

'Certainly is,' said Janssen. 'Strong flat white.'

'You are a gentleman and a scholar, my boy, and a prince among men. Keep away from the likes of this one and you'll go far.'

'What have we got, Mack?' asked Murphy. 'Volume Four?'

'Yep. The nervous system. No question.'

Murphy turned to his deputy. 'Get hold of Jo, will you? I don't care what she's doing – pull her out of class if you have to – I want her at the scene this time. Now.'

Janssen peeled off to make the call while Murphy followed Mack to the body.

'Detective Senior Sergeant David Patrick Murphy, meet Damien Rufus Henley, Esquire.' Mack waved with a melodramatic flourish at the sliced-up cadaver lying on the long plateau of polished concrete that served as a dining table.

'Rufus?' asked Murphy, ignoring the brutalised corpse to take in the room's sleek Scandinavian feel. The aesthetic might have been minimalist, but there was a lot of it. The wide smear of blood where Henley had been dragged from the central bathroom only added to the arty tone.

'That's what it says on the phone bill.'

'Sure it's him?'

'His cleaners found him this morning, reckon he's the right build.' Mack shrugged. 'The photo on his staff card isn't much help, obviously, but the company's going to decrypt the biometrics on the chip so we can cross-check the irises and fingerprints. We'll know today.'

'Any struggle?'

'No sign of one. We'll check in the post-mortem but the house is in order.'

'Fuck, again.'

Murphy crossed to the window and parted the curtains. It was a magnificent Sydney spring day, the best time of year in a city that did not want for agreeable conditions. They were in that perfect fortnight that Sydney laid on every September, going all-out to impress: sunny and warm beneath clear blue skies, the air fragrant with everything in bloom. Right now it was probably the finest place to be on the planet.

The outlook was even better than he'd expected: looking straight across the Georges River, over Tom Uglys Bridge to Blakehurst behind. The panorama took in a long inlet and the western side of San Souci, a riot of green and gold with all the wattle in full glory. 'Nice view.' He let the curtains fall back into place. Their skirts were flecked with blood and particles of flesh.

Janssen came back in. 'Jo's on her way. Twenty minutes.'

Murphy nodded. 'All right, Mack, show us what you've got.'

They approached the ravaged corpse from its right. 'See here, detectives,' said Mack, pointing with a pen at the near arm. 'On the right side he's gone all the way in, just cutting everything away to find the nerves *in situ*.'

'Okay.'

'But come around this side.' Mack walked around the head of the table and bent the flexible neck of a battered forensic services floor lamp to throw more light onto the other shoulder. 'Here on the left he's gone in much more carefully, gently lifting the nerves up and right out, can you see?'

'Oh, yeah.'

'Christ.'

'He's started right up in the neck, dissecting down to find the brachial plexus and track it under the clavicle into the axilla, here. He's cut away ahead so he can work it all the way down the arm. He's lost track of the posterior cord, back in here, but he's found it again in the radial nerve down here, see?' Mack pointed at the forearm.

'Uh-huh,' said Murphy, not really following. Janssen grunted ambiguously.

'Then here – this part is astonishing. You see how delicately he's displayed the lateral cord? Cutting ahead and threading the pectoral nerves back out, excising everything else to reveal the union of the medial and lateral cords. Then he's worked the median nerve right down—' Mack tracked down the arm, tracing a thin brown filament with his pen, '—through the cubital fossa and into the carpal tunnel.'

'Okay, I see,' said Murphy, beginning to appreciate Mack's point. Once the homicide victim turned into an anatomy specimen, you began to inhabit the medicos' perspective. And the killer's, presumably.

'It's very detailed work,' added Janssen.

'It's extraordinary,' said Mack. 'This is the most accomplished nerve dissection I've ever seen outside an anatomy atlas, in my entire career. If I'd seen a brachial plexus demonstrated like this in second year, I'd have saved myself a week of exam prep.'

'It must have taken a good while,' said Janssen.

'No, it must have taken *ages*,' said the SOCO. 'And the lumbar plexus is just as good. That's why all the guts are in the living room. After he's finished with the intestinal nerves, he's pulled it all out and mapped the lumbar plexus off the back wall and right down the left leg.' Mack pointed from the hollowed-out cavity down towards the left foot.

'How long do you think, Mack?' asked Janssen.

'Four, five days. Until he started to ripen.'

'How the fuck does he buy himself that much time?' asked Murphy in frustration.

'He must know their every movement for days to come,' said Janssen.

Murphy shook his head then leaned in to peer inside the abdominal cavity. He was surprised to see daylight through the other side. 'Have you turned him over yet?'

'No, we're waiting for photography. But I can already see he's opened up a stretch of spinal cord. Upper lumbar and lower thoracic, by the look. And you can see the same detail on the face, here.' Mack moved up to the head and outlined the familiar pattern of patient excavation and extraction on the right side of the face.

'What's up with the other side?' asked Murphy.

Mack circled around to the left and pointed with his pen. 'He's pulled back the skin and fascia very carefully to get underneath. He's cut away the mandible entirely, and carved away the maxilla and the zygomatic bone to get to the base of the skull.'

'What's he after?' asked Janssen.

'The cranial nerves.'

'What are they?' asked Murphy.

'Twelve pairs of nerves that feed straight out from the brain through a series of apertures in the skull.' Mack leaned in underneath and pointed to a thin, bloodied cord hanging out of the bone. 'This is the mandibular nerve, the third branch of the trigeminal; cranial nerve five.'

'Is this one?' asked Janssen, pointing to a thicker cord emerging into the vacant eye socket.

'Yes, the optic nerve, cranial two. That's the easy one. He's had to resect all the soft tissue almost to the median line to get to the others. See: oculomotor, facial, abducens, glossopharyngeal, vagus, accessory,' said Mack, pointing as he went. To the policemen they were just strings of bloody sinew of different thicknesses hanging out here and there from the base of the skull. Mack chuckled to himself.

Murphy regarded him with distaste. 'What could possibly be funny, Mack?'

'I'm just remembering a bad med school joke.'

'Okay, spill.'

'You won't get it.'

'Come on.'

'What do the vagina and the chorda tympani have in common?' He indicated a thread exiting through the earhole.

Murphy sniggered. Janssen showed no expression.

'They both supply taste to the anterior two-thirds of the tongue,' said Mack, unable to suppress a smirk.

Murphy laughed. After a slight pause, Janssen asked, 'Were there not too many women in your class, Mack?'

The medico shrugged. 'The dean said our generation would have the distinction of practising twenty-first-century medicine with nineteenth-century minds.'

'Perhaps that was generous,' suggested Janssen.

'You haven't heard the cranial nerve mnemonic yet.'

There was a loud, sharp intake of breath behind them, and they all turned at once. Jo was standing in the doorway, utterly alabaster, staring at the remains on the table. She was holding the door jamb, anchoring herself at the room's entry. Thijs offered her a kind smile, but she never saw it.

'You all right?' her brother asked.

She nodded, unable to tear her eyes from her first *in situ* murder victim. She turned at last to the forensic scientist, finding a gentle compassion within his professional demeanour.

'Morning, Mack,' she said in a wavering voice. She let go of the woodwork and pushed off, walking stoically towards the table and its obscene burden. 'So tell me: how does the trochlear nerve dissection look?'

Friday 28 September – afternoon

Jo was still deeply shaken when they arrived back at Surry Hills. She walked in behind Murphy on autopilot, but Amy came across to intercept her before she could follow her brother into his office.

Jo sat for a while in Amy's chair, staring vacantly at a photograph of a pensive American detective with the caption *What would Lester Freamon do?* Eventually she looked up.

'Fucking hell, Amy.'

The cop gave Jo's shoulder a light squeeze. 'I know. I still remember my first. Everybody does.' They sat like that for a minute, then Amy looked at her watch, scooped up her keys and her bag and said, 'Come with me.'

They swung by Jo's desk to collect her bag and headed for the lift. Amy hit the lowest button, marked *SB.* Jo had thought they were heading for the carpark, but that was the button above. She asked where they were going.

'We're going to shoot some villains,' said Amy.

Jo pondered what this could mean while they descended to the sub-basement. They stepped into a concrete corridor and walked towards an irregular banging noise. Eventually she realised Amy had been speaking to her.

'...have it all to yourself some days,' she was saying. 'I don't know why, because it's the best damn stress relief known to humanity. Well, second-best, anyway.'

Jo surprised herself with an abrupt laugh and looked up at Amy, who briefly met her eyes before turning ahead. Jo noticed a slight flush to Amy's neck.

They reached a heavy metal door. 'It's going to be a bit loud,' said Amy with a wide smile. She swiped her pass and the door swung open, and the distant jazz percussion became the Battle of Stalingrad. This was the Sydney Indoor Light Arms Training Range. 'Come on.' Jo hesitated, until Amy said, 'Trust me, this'll help.'

They approached the armourer's desk. Jo wasn't cleared for this floor, so the duty constable admitted her as a visitor after she read through the safety rules in front of him.

'Are you sure we should be doing this?' asked Jo as she signed in.

'Yeah, don't worry about it. Best keep it to ourselves, though.'

'You won't get in any trouble?'

'No, it's allowed, but Spud wouldn't like it. He disapproves of civilians coming in, but they do it all the time. Study tours. Politicians.'

'Politicians?'

'We had a prime minister down here once. Couldn't decide whether he was Arnold Schwarzenegger or John Wayne. A pretty good shot, though, I must admit.'

The armourer leered at Amy. 'So, Detective Chartier, you ready to try something with a bit of heft?'

Amy scoffed. 'It isn't the calibre, Constable Vanderlaan, it's how you use it. Just a couple of 22s, please.' He went to collect their weapons.

'You use 22s?' asked Jo, surprised. 'Aren't they kind of lightweight?' All she knew about guns she'd learned from the movies – Hollywood University, as her brother put it – but it wasn't exactly an authoritative source.

'No, that's point-two-two calibre. This is the Glock twenty-two pistol. It's actually a .40 calibre.'

'I'm confused.'

'So the .22 you're talking about refers to the calibre. It means the barrel bore is twenty-two hundredths of an inch. And you're right, not a lot of stopping power. The 22 in the Glock is just a model number, like a Boeing 747. It takes the .40 calibre Smith & Wesson round.'

'Okay, so calibre is just a fraction of an inch?'

'It can be metric.'

'Oh, like James Bond's 9-millimetre Beretta?'

'Right.'

'What's that in inches?'

'Well, that's where it gets confusing. It's equivalent to both the .357 and .38 rounds in the American money.'

'As in three-fifty-seven Magnum and thirty-eight Special?'

Amy laughed. 'Spud's right, you do watch too many movies.'

'Is that what he says?'

Amy let that go through to the 'keeper. 'Anyway, the Glock 22 is the standard issue sidearm for uniformed police and most plain-clothes. They're easy to use, safe, accurate...'

'...weak as piss and made of plastic,' said Vanderlaan as he returned with their gear. He pushed the weapons across the counter, along with a handful of red magazines full of bullets and two pairs of bright-orange earmuffs.

'Why so threatened by plastic?' asked Amy. 'Scared you'll be made redundant?'

'Not me,' he said with a cocky smile. 'Ain't nothing like the real thing.'

Amy grimaced and shook her head. 'Not for me, Constable.'

'Don't know what you're missing.' He sighed regretfully. 'Stall four.'

'Come on, Jo, I'll show you what I mean.'

They each picked up a pistol, and Amy collected the training magazines while Jo grabbed the ear protection. Jo couldn't believe how light the gun was.

'Yeah, it's amazing,' said Amy as they entered the gallery. 'I mean it's unloaded, but still. It's a real godsend in uniform – you have to carry so much crap, and the pistol is the heaviest item by far. Makes it easier to use too, especially for women, which is forty per cent of the force now. And no doubt for unfit fat old blokes, which is probably another forty per cent.'

They reached their stall and Amy gave Jo the safety run-through over the racket around them. Then she showed her how to check the chamber was empty, load it with one of the red training magazines and rack the slide. 'Now there's a round in the chamber, ready to fire.' Amy quickly performed the safety check on the other Glock, then handed it to Jo. 'Now you have a go.'

Jo took up the pistol and repeated Amy's actions. She hefted the gun, noticing the extra weight. 'It's a lot heavier with the magazine.'

'Yeah, it's an even kilo, loaded,' said Amy. 'About a third of that's bullets.' She noticed Jo gripping the gun with her left hand. 'Ah, you're a lefty. I hadn't noticed.'

'Is there a difference?'

'Nothing that matters. It's good, actually: you can mirror me. Stay there.' Amy put her gun on the shelf and moved around behind Jo before picking up her pistol again. 'You want to stand comfortably. Some people like a side-on stance, others prefer straight on. I'm kind of in-between. You want your feet shoulder-width apart and your knees slightly bent. Keep your back straight...'

'...abs in, shoulders back and down,' continued Jo. Amy gave her a quizzical look. 'You sound exactly like my trainer, Amanda.'

Amy laughed. 'It's the same principle: you want to be braced and strong, but relaxed and flexible.' She moved one foot diagonally behind her then lifted her pistol. 'Always use a two-handed grip. Leave the gunfighter bullshit to the glory boys. It just isn't stable enough. Cup your palm and cradle the firing hand, like so.'

In mirror-image, Jo took her stance and copied the shape of Amy's hands around the pistol. It was completely different to the one-handed cops-and-robbers stance, but it felt highly stable. And kind of deadly.

'Okay,' said Amy. 'Any questions?'

'Yeah, where's the safety, and what's with the split trigger?'

Amy smiled. *Good girl: you're paying attention.* 'That *is* the safety,' she said, pointing to the component Jo had noticed, sitting in a groove in the front part of the trigger itself. 'You have to pull it in first before the trigger will move.' Amy put her earmuffs on. 'You ready?'

Jo nodded and followed suit. The detective picked up her pistol and took her stance again, sighted along the top of the barrel and fired. Even though Jo was expecting it, she still jumped at the noise. Amy fired three more times in quick succession, without resighting between shots. She repositioned once more and fired another salvo, this time four or five bullets: Jo lost count. Amy placed her pistol on the shelf and flicked a toggle switch on the wall, bringing the paper target forward on a runner. There was a cluster of shots on the chest, while several shots surrounded the head.

They pushed back their earmuffs. 'Always, always, go for the chest,' said Amy. 'You're much more likely to hit something.' She pointed at the halo of holes around the head. 'Head shots are for heroes, usually dead heroes. A bullet to the chest will give him plenty to think about.'

This was all academic to Jo, who had no intention of shooting anybody, but she could see the logic of it. 'So the idea is to put them down rather than kill them.'

'No, not at all,' said Amy, suddenly serious. 'You never shoot at someone unless you're willing to kill them. The point of the chest shot isn't to minimise harm, it's to maximise your chances of putting a round in them.'

'Oh. Okay.' Suitably sobered, Jo looked at the pistol on the shelf in front of her while Amy removed the riddled target from its clip.

'Your turn,' said Amy. Jo hesitated, and Amy laughed at her expression. 'Don't worry, it's only paper.' They slid their earmuffs back over their ears.

Jo picked up the pistol, took her stance, wrapped both hands around the pistol butt and took her aim at the fresh target. But before she could shoot, Amy touched her wrist and pushed gently down.

'Your right thumb's around the butt: it's going to get hit by the slide when you fire. Just support your left hand; it's not a tennis grip.'

Amy stepped behind Jo, circling her with both arms to raise the weapon again, and guided her hands into the correct position. Amy was all around her for a moment. On a sudden impulse, Jo pressed back against her ever so slightly. Then Amy stepped away, and Jo sighted onto the target's chest area. She pulled the trigger and the pistol came alive in her hand, kicking up and back with a great *boom*. She'd fired wide of the chest, and a bit below.

'That's okay, you blew his mate's nuts off,' shouted Amy. 'Try again.'

Jo reset herself and fired, putting the round into the target zone. Not in the middle, but still on the body.

'Got 'im!' Amy whooped. 'Try a few in a row.'

Jo aimed again and fired four times in quick succession, getting used to the recoil. She put all four inside the outline, one right in the middle.

'He's totally fucked!' Amy cheered.

Jo laughed. For a lifetime pacifist, she was enjoying this far too much.

'Want to keep going?' asked Amy with a grin.

'Shit, yeah!'

They spent another half-hour taking turns. Amy fired consistently into the target zone, a good proportion in the centre, except when she went for the head, where she managed a hit less than half the time. The point was not lost on Jo, who stayed mostly on the torso, missing her few head shots completely. Jo reloaded each time for both of them, until she was working the mechanism like a pro.

By the time they'd burned through the training magazines, Jo's arms ached, her ears rang, her heart thumped and her brain buzzed. Her traumatic afternoon was forgotten. They checked the chambers of both weapons, gathered the empty magazines and earmuffs, and took the whole lot back to the armourer.

'How was that, Dr King?'

'Oh, brilliant!' replied Jo. 'Thanks heaps!'

'Next time you should try the Smith & Wesson 686.' Vanderlaan lifted up a gigantic revolver with a six-inch barrel.

'Still with the metaphors, Constable?' Amy said.

'Hey, sometimes a cigar is just a cigar.'

Amy just shook her head and signed them out. 'There's your .357 Magnum,' she told Jo as they entered the corridor. 'That's Spud's weapon of choice.'

'His barrel's even longer, I reckon.'

'Yeah, it's eight and a half inches or something. The full Callahan.'

'What does he even need a cannon like that for, rhinos?'

'Don't ask me. A Glock has enough firepower for anyone.' They stepped into the lift and Amy pushed the button for the carpark above them. 'So, feeling better?'

'Oh, yeah. Thanks, you were so right.'

The lift door slid closed, and it suddenly went very quiet. Jo caught Amy's eye. 'Second-best stress relief known to humanity, eh?'

Amy blushed and looked down. 'Yeah, well.'

Jo moved towards her. 'What's number one?' she asked, low and husky. Waiting.

Amy lifted her face and caught Jo's gaze, a tiny smile playing at the corner of her mouth. 'You know,' she whispered. Amy's eyes glanced down to Jo's mouth, then back up. Her smile widened.

Jo closed in and kissed Amy lightly on the mouth, and moved to stroke her short dark hair. But just then the lift stopped, and they parted self-consciously as the door opened. The two of them looked out at the carpark, like cat burglars caught in a sudden pool of light.

Empty.

They exchanged a glance and laughed, then walked towards Amy's car.

'So now you know our dirty little secret,' said Amy.

'What's that?'

'Shooting makes you horny.'

Jo laughed. 'It's not just me, then.'

'Not at all.'

They were at the car now, standing in shadow by the driver's door. Nothing was said for a while. Even when she came up for air, all Amy could manage was, 'Mmm.'

'Oh, no,' said Jo, lightly biting Amy's lower lip. 'My bike has a flat tyre.'

'You can't even see it from here,' said Amy, nipping back.

'It's one of my superpowers.'

'I suppose you'll be needing a lift home?'

'Yes, please.'

'Do you have any other superpowers?'

'Oh, yeah,' said Jo, soft and sultry. 'Yes, I do.'

Wednesday 3 October – afternoon

Jo was giving a presentation to the squad on Damien Henley's post-mortem, which she and Mack had observed that morning. She paused about halfway through to take a sip of water and to collect herself. Beyond the brutal images that she could not put out of her mind, it was the cold, relentless progression of the dissections that really disturbed her. Immersing herself in the technicalities helped, but the horror never went away. She couldn't understand how the detectives could sit through it with such apparent sangfroid. Experience, perhaps. Or maybe they just lived with it. Buried it. She rolled her shoulders to loosen her neck muscles and took a sip from her glass. 'Any questions so far?'

'Why did you ask Mack about the cochlear nerve at the scene?' Murphy asked.

'Trochlear nerve. I was just coming to that. It's the fourth cranial nerve.'

'What's a cranial nerve?' asked Nguyễn.

'Most of the nerves in the body come off the spinal cord, but cranial nerves come straight out of the brain itself.'

'What are they for?'

'Mainly motor and sensory supply for the head and neck – sight, smell, taste, muscles of the face and tongue, speech and so on. Although the vagus also operates lots of stuff in the chest and abdomen – heart, lungs, most of the gut.'

'And how many cranial nerves are there?' asked Harris.

'Depends who you ask. Galen described seven pairs, and Vesalius had a slightly different seven. Sömmerring established the modern twelve-pair list in 1778, and that's still the pub trivia answer today.' Jo turned to her brother. 'Mack's mnemonic is a twelve-pair list.'

'Do you know it?' asked Murphy.

'Yes, but I'm not repeating it,' she said. 'It's sexist and puerile.'

Murphy rolled his eyes. 'So what's the point of all this, Jo?'

'The point of looking at the trochlear is that it was Vesalius's big contribution to the cranial nerves. It was isolated for the first time in the *Fabrica,* although he called it the "slender posterior root" of the third cranial nerve.'

'And what does it do?' asked Nguyễn.

'It operates the superior oblique muscle. Makes the eyeball look down and in.'

'Is that all?'

'Yep. It's exceptionally specialised.'

'And what did you find?' Chartier asked.

'The trochlear was extraordinarily well-dissected, even relative to the very high standard overall.' Jo turned to Murphy and Janssen. 'You saw the brachial plexus dissection in the arm, right?'

'Mack told us it's the best he's ever seen,' said Janssen.

'He said this was even more impressive. Our killer treated it like a holy relic.'

'So maybe he's more into the book itself than anatomy as such,' suggested Nikolaidis.

'That's right, but it gets better,' continued Jo. 'The pathologists reckon he first dissected the cranials the way Vesalius described them, very carefully. Then he went back over them and separated them out in the modern arrangement, as twelve separate nerves.'

'And what do you make of that, Jo?' asked Chartier.

'I think it shows he's primarily interested in the *Fabrica,* as Angelo says, but he's also a committed empiricist, which is Vesalius's overarching project. So after following the *Fabrica* roadmap, he then completes the dissection with more modern knowledge.'

'I guess that's what Vesalius would do if he were here now,' mused Janssen.

'Exactly,' said Jo. 'And then our boy went after the thirteenth.'

'I thought you said there were twelve?' asked Harris.

'That's the standard model, but there's also the terminal nerve, which has been known in humans for over a century. It's in position zero, anterior to the other twelve.'

'What's it do?' asked Nguyễn.

'Nobody really knows, Liệu, which is one reason for its obscurity. It might be involved with pheromones. But it's also extraordinarily fine and easily missed, and may not even always be present, so it's often disregarded. But when Dr Forrest went back to check, she discovered that our killer had not only found it, but very skilfully demonstrated it. I mean, it's literally just a thread; it was incredibly meticulous.'

'Doesn't that conflict with your theory about his treatment of the new material?' asked Nikolaidis.

'Maybe it's the discovery thing,' Chartier suggested. 'The twelve cranial system has been known since whenever, so that's boring. But this terminal nerve is obscure and interesting, and worthy of his time.'

'Yeah, I like that,' said Jo. 'It's unmarked territory, possibly done without a visual dissection guide. To boldly go, and all that.'

'Like his hero,' Janssen said.

'Is that all of them? Thirteen?' Harris was like a dog with a bone.

'Sort of,' said Jo. 'There's an ongoing argument about classification – a lot of anatomy is like that. The intermediate nerve is an offshoot of the facial nerve, for example, which is cranial number seven, but some argue it's a cranial nerve in its own right. But our killer either doesn't know about that debate, or he doesn't care. We checked.'

'Who checked?' asked Murphy, patently doubtful of Jo's unsupervised judgment.

She sighed and addressed a point above her brother's head. 'In light of the history of the description of cranial nerves in the anatomical literature and the careful treatment of the terminal nerve in the dissection of the victim, I asked Dr Forrest to investigate whether there was any sign of exploratory dissection that might indicate a particular interest in the intermediate nerve. She conducted a further secondary post-mortem investigation and advised there was no physical evidence of any inordinate attention to the facial nerve, including that branch, beyond the degree of care exercised generally.'

The cops were clearly impressed with the evenness of Jo's response – she could have been giving evidence in court against hostile cross-examination – but Murphy just grunted. 'What about McCalman? What does he say?'

There he goes again, Jo thought. *Why would you trust a fully qualified woman's expertise when you could ask someone equipped with actual testicles?* But Jo had a simple answer. 'Professor McCalman was there the whole time and agrees.'

'Okay, fine. So what's the significance?' asked Murphy. 'What does it all mean?'

'He's not just doing anatomy with the *Fabrica* as his chosen guide: he's performing some sort of re-enactment.'

'Like a tribute?' asked Chartier.

'That's it, Amy, exactly. This is a tribute.' Jo endured a wave of revulsion at the notion of people dying for what amounted to a hobby on steroids. 'It's all about Andreas Vesalius himself. Our killer's allegiance is to Vesalius and his values, including empirical enquiry. Anatomy per se is not really his priority: he's not all that interested in the standard developments since the *Fabrica*. Anything still obscure, though, and he's in there – just like Vesalius would be.'

'Why haven't we seen this obsessive detail before, do you think?' asked Janssen.

'Good question. The bones and muscles were well described by the time of Vesalius, so there wasn't much to trace over there. We did see his careful work on the azygos vein, which Vesalius first described. But my guess is we probably missed something like this last time. The veins in the liver, say.'

'Too late now,' said Nguyễn. Patrick Hall's remains had been released and cremated.

'Yes, fascinating, sis,' said Murphy, openly impatient now, 'but how does this help me catch my bad guy?'

'Apart from getting inside his head?' Jo thought that had some value in itself, but she continued. 'I think his scholastic approach and sheer proficiency are the products of formal anatomical instruction, probably to a fairly sophisticated level. You'll want to look at medical practitioners, as well as science graduates with an anatomy specialisation.'

'Is that difficult, Niko?' Murphy asked his data specialist.

Nikolaidis leaned forward, resting a foot on the open bottom drawer of his filing cabinet. 'The medical registries are easy enough, but for anyone else we'll need to go uni by uni. There's no national database. It'll take a while, but it can be done.'

'Get some uniforms on it. We can cash in some overtime from the premier's account.' Murphy turned back to Jo. 'Anything else?'

'Yes, I reckon he's working off the *New Fabrica,* rather than a facsimile. I've been using it a lot myself, and the production values are brilliant. You just wouldn't attempt this fine cranial work with a facsimile of the old versions when the *New Fabrica* is available.'

'So we should have another go at tracking down any copies in Australia?' asked Nikolaidis.

'I know it's laborious, Angelo,' said Jo, 'but I'm virtually certain he has one of his own. There can't be many out there.'

'Can't hurt, I suppose,' said Murphy, clearly unconvinced. 'Anything else?'

'Yeah, he's going to need more time than ever from now on. The remaining chapters have a lot more along these lines. He bought himself a week for these last two, instead of the weekends on the first two. That'll continue.'

'It'll put pressure on his operation,' said Janssen. 'He'll make mistakes.'

'He fucken better,' said Murphy. 'He hasn't so far.'

'He must've known from the start he would need this much time,' said Nguyễn.

'He's so confident,' said Chartier. 'It has to mean something about who he is.'

'Yeah, but what, exactly?' complained Murphy. 'Without a link between the vics we're still stuck with our two big fucken mysteries: how does he buy so much time and how does he get their guard down?' He came to his feet and turned to his sister. 'I'm sure this is fascinating to you, Jo, but I need something more concrete we can use to track this bastard down. Until then it's all just academic.' He left the briefing area and stalked away to his office.

The detectives were apologetic about Murphy's attitude, but Jo wasn't bothered by it: if anything she shared her brother's frustration. Amy went off to return a phone call, and the others drifted away to their desks.

'How did you find the post-mortem?' asked Thijs, once they were the only ones left in the briefing area. Jo was glad to have him alone for a minute. She had no idea what she was doing in her personal life but staying connected felt important right now.

'Not too bad,' she replied. 'Heaps better than the crime scene, that's for sure. I don't know how you do it.'

'It never gets easy, I can tell you that. But it works the other way around for me. I've watched a lot of autopsies, but I still find them upsetting: they're so sterile and alienating. It's ugly at the scene, but at least I'm there with the victim. On their side, trying to help them.'

'I felt more like I was there with the killer; it freaked me out,' replied Jo, her hackles raising again at the recollection. She had felt the traces of the killer's movement through the rooms, his hands on the furniture, his breath in the air. 'I much preferred the clinical setting. I could tell myself it's all just tissue to be studied.'

'Anyway, you seem much better than the other day,' said Thijs.

'Definitely, thank you.'

'No need to hit the shooting range this time.'

Jo looked away, wondering what he knew, but there was no special weight to his tone. False alarm, she decided. Although it was only a matter of time. 'No, I'm good.'

'So would you care for some company over dinner?' he asked.

A wave of relief went through her. She looked up at his kind, open face and felt a sudden surge of affection for him.

   'Yes, thank you, Matthijs, I would love that.'

Saturday 6 October – evening

'What's that supposed to mean?' Jo asked her brother. He'd had a skinful down the Diggers watching the Bathurst motor race before arriving home late for his own birthday dinner with her and Sylvia. He'd been dispensing provocations all night, and she'd finally had enough.

'You academics think about everything too much—'

'Dave,' Sylvia warned.

'You prefer thinking too little?' countered Jo.

'—and you have no fucken idea what goes on in the real world.'

'Oh, really.' Jo had heard this a million times over the years: the theme of her general pointlessness. He was probably still annoyed about the statistics episode.

'Yeah, really. You get stuck on the detail and miss the big picture.'

'You wouldn't have an example, would you?'

'Yeah I do, actually.' Murphy froze, deep in drunken concentration. 'That yarn about Shakespeare.'

'Do tell.'

'Oh what is it?' he grizzled, trying to retrieve the memory while half-cut. 'Fuck fuck fuck. You know it, sis. Remind me.'

So she was to be witness for her own prosecution. Again. She decided to let him flounder. 'There are quite a few yarns about Shakespeare, mate.'

'You know, the one Willsy told that weekend in Blackheath. What was it, Sylvia?'

'I have no idea, Dave, I wasn't there.'

He screwed his eyes shut, snapping his fingers as though the cadence would dislodge the memory. And then it did – his eyes shot open and he leaned forward. 'The one where he scores first with the tart, cuts the other bloke's lunch.'

That pissed Jo off. 'Tart, was she? Okay, I'll play.' She drained her own glass and turned to her sister-in-law.

'This is almost certainly apocryphal, by the way. But the story goes that during a performance of *Richard III,* a woman in the audience becomes so enamoured of the lead actor, Richard Burbage, that she comes on to him backstage and invites him back to her place later. To preserve their honour, he is to announce himself as Richard the Third. Shakespeare overhears this, turns up first and talks his way into her bed. He is "at his game", I believe is the wording, when they're told Richard the Third has arrived. Shakespeare sends back the response, "William the Conqueror preceded Richard the Third."'

Murphy roared with laughter. 'What a champion! Best line he ever wrote.'

'It is kind of funny,' Sylvia said, smiling apologetically. Jo shook her head and sighed.

'What's your problem with it again?' asked Murphy, wiping away tears. 'That's fucken brilliant.'

'Where do I start?' exclaimed Jo. 'One, why is she a tart? Two, the woman is reduced entirely to something for the boys to rub their cocks up against. She might as well be a hole in the fence. Three, did she even consent to Shakespeare's overtures—'

'Of course, and that's why she's a tart!' roared her brother.

'—or did he trick her into thinking he was Burbage? That's clearly the implication of the overheard password. But if he tricked her that's *rape,* detective, as you well know. Four, even if Shakespeare was greeted with open arms—'

'Open legs, you mean.'

'—she's just a trophy in some juvenile, macho pissing contest. Five, she's so thoroughly erased that we don't even know her name.'

'It's called chivalry! They were protecting her reputation.'

'Even if that's why, which I seriously doubt, and this is point six, why does her reputation need protecting, but not theirs? Why is he a champion and she a slut for the same behaviour?'

'I didn't say slut, I said tart.'

'Oh for fuck's sake, Murphy. Point is, it's a double standard.'

'See? This is what I'm saying. You always want to make a fucken murder trial out of some harmless funny yarn.'

'But it's not just a funny yarn. And it's not harmless. That's seven: what's the purpose of inventing and then retelling this story? Its function is to erase the agency of women and define them as objects for men to exchange for sexual gratification and one-upmanship.'

'For fuck's sake, get a sense of humour, Joanna,' said Murphy, eliciting a snort of derision from his sister. 'Anyway, like you say, it's probably not even true.'

'What if it is true?'

'Then it's even funnier, and Shakespeare's a fucken legend. Besides, it doesn't sound like she was complaining, does it?'

'We'd never know, Dave, we don't find out if she enjoyed herself. You can call that point eight. These stories are never concerned with women's pleasure.'

'You just want to take all the fun out of things.'

'Do you think Anne Hathaway would find it so amusing?'

'What's she got to do with it?'

'Not her, the other one. Shakespeare's wife.'

'Oh, don't be so bloody naive!'

'What do you mean?'

'It was just a bit on the side. Trivial. Happened all the time.'

'Trivial?' asked Sylvia. 'Really?'

Murphy suddenly realised how far out on the ledge he was. 'Just that he was an actor and all, you know? And men in those days were less...'

'Faithful?' prompted Jo. She was enjoying her brother's discomfort.

'Well, yeah. With women not having as much freedom and that.'

'Oh so you do agree the story illustrates gender inequality?'

'Nah, I just...' Murphy stopped. 'Huh.' He looked at Jo. 'Maybe it does, yeah.'

Jo and Sylvia exchanged a glance of surprise. Sylvia was clearly impressed, but Jo wasn't going to let him off the hook that easily.

'But you think all that's past now?' she prompted. It was a bit mean of her, but if a copper didn't spot an exercise in entrapment then that was his own bad luck.

'Too right I do,' said Murphy with a passion that burned straight through any credit he'd just won. 'If anything, things have gone too far.'

'What, you want to be able to sneak around fucking anonymous women to score points off other blokes, do you?'

'Of course not,' said Murphy. 'You're putting words into my mouth.'

'Then what? In your own words.'

'It's just that there are differences between men and women, right, and society works best when those differences are respected.'

'By offering women up as tribute to their mighty male overlords, eh?' Jo shook her head and laughed ruefully. 'I'd better go home before I tell you what I really think.' She came around behind her brother, wrapped her arms around his shoulders and kissed the crown of his head. 'Happy birthday, you troglodyte.'

'Go on, get out of here,' grizzled Murphy, only half-joking.

***

Sylvia walked her sister-in-law to the front door. They said more through body language than words, but it was all at Murphy's expense. They embraced and Jo mounted her bike, riding off into the warm, dark night.

Despite her best intentions, Sylvia couldn't help catching Murphy's eye as she came back into the room.

'What?' he asked. 'It's not my fault.'

'Really.' She started clearing the table.

'That's my whole original point. They take an innocent story and prosecute it like a fucken crime against humanity.'

'But that's what she's saying, it's not such an innocent story.'

'But it's just funny, Sylvia. You said so yourself.'

'I thought so at first, but maybe she has a point.'

'Christ, whose side are you on?'

'It's not about sides. I'm just ... what are stories like that for?'

'It's just a yarn! You'll be banning bloody fairy tales next.'

'Well maybe they're not so innocent, either. Like Jo says, they must be performing some function, or we wouldn't still be telling them.'

'Oh for fuck's sake, they're just kids' entertainment,' he said with a sudden vehemence. 'They're not bloody mind control. The only brainwashing going on around here is all this feminist bullshit everyone gets in the universities these days.' He waved savagely in the direction of his departed sister.

'Okay, Dave, it's okay.' She returned to the table and took his clenched hand.

'That's why I don't want you going back to uni,' he continued. 'You'll come home spouting all this fucken lesbian propaganda.'

'It's all right, honey,' she said soothingly, stroking his wrist.

'I won't fucken have it, not in my house.'

'I know, it's okay,' she said, leaning her head on his shoulder. She murmured softly and stroked gently, until his muscles relaxed and his breathing slowed. By the time he got up to pour himself a whisky, he was calm again.

Saturday 20 October – afternoon

'So why is he really called Spud?' asked Amy, passing Jo the sunscreen and reaching for her water. They were standing on Pulpit Rock in the Blue Mountains, the Grose Valley wilderness sprawling before them. They'd hiked along the clifftop from Evans Lookout via Govetts Leap Falls, so while it was a mild, lightly overcast day, they were looking forward to a cold beer at the Hydro Majestic on the way back.

'What does he say?' asked Jo.

'He just gets evasive. That's how we know there's a story.'

'Okay, but you can't tell anyone. And don't even hint that you know – he would fucking kill me.' Jo could see Amy struggling to suppress a laugh. 'Promise me.'

'Okay, I promise. Now spill.'

'So they're on school camp, Year Eight or Nine. He went to the Marist Brothers, so it's boys only. Thirteen or fourteen – as horny as they are stupid.'

'So, pretty bloody horny.'

'Exactly. So after lights-out they get into the booze and porno magazines.'

'Oh God, getting themselves even more worked up.'

'I know, right?' Jo laughed. 'And then it's strip poker.'

'No!' Amy hooted.

'Gets better. The rule is, once your clothes are gone, if you lose another hand you have to perform a forfeit. First kid gets off easy – he's the lookout for the head brother doing his night patrol.'

'At least someone was thinking.'

'Then the losers have to run around outside naked, wank themselves, chuck brown-eyes, that kind of stuff.' They were both constantly sniggering by now, Jo only just holding it together. 'Dave runs out of clothes then loses a round, so the others get in a huddle and decide his forfeit is to...' but she broke up and couldn't speak.

Amy prodded her. 'Is to what?'

Jo wiped tears from her eyes. 'Fuck, it's too funny. I have to back up a bit first. Murphy had been suspended that year for shoving a potato in the tailpipe of some teacher's car. You know how it fires out like a cannonball when you start the engine?'

'I didn't know that, but go on.'

'So at camp his forfeit is to...' but Jo cracked up again, unable to continue.

'Is to what?' Then Amy's eyes opened wide, and she gasped. 'Wait, it isn't to shove...' before she lost it too.

Jo nodded, painfully gulping in air between heaves of laughter, and finished Amy's sentence, eking out each word with a high, tight voice, '...a potato ... up ... his arse!' The pair doubled over laughing, setting off a kookaburra in a nearby Sydney peppermint tree.

'The story took off like a grassfire. Everyone called him Spud from then on.' Jo wiped away tears with her T-shirt. 'He's very sensitive about it.'

'No shit! He'd never live that down.'

'He tried to shut it down but that only made it worse. You know, boys' school. So he embraced it instead. I mean, he's a Murphy, so it makes sense.'

'Did you give him any shit about it?'

'Are you kidding? I once asked him how big the potato was and he belted the crap out of me. After that I couldn't even look sideways at him while peeling potatoes for tea.'

'I won't say anything, but damn. What ammunition.'

'You better not or we're both dead,' said Jo. 'I'm not even kidding.'

They recovered briefly, then Amy said, 'Spud,' and set them off again.

VOLUME V

THE ORGANS OF NUTRITION AND GENERATION

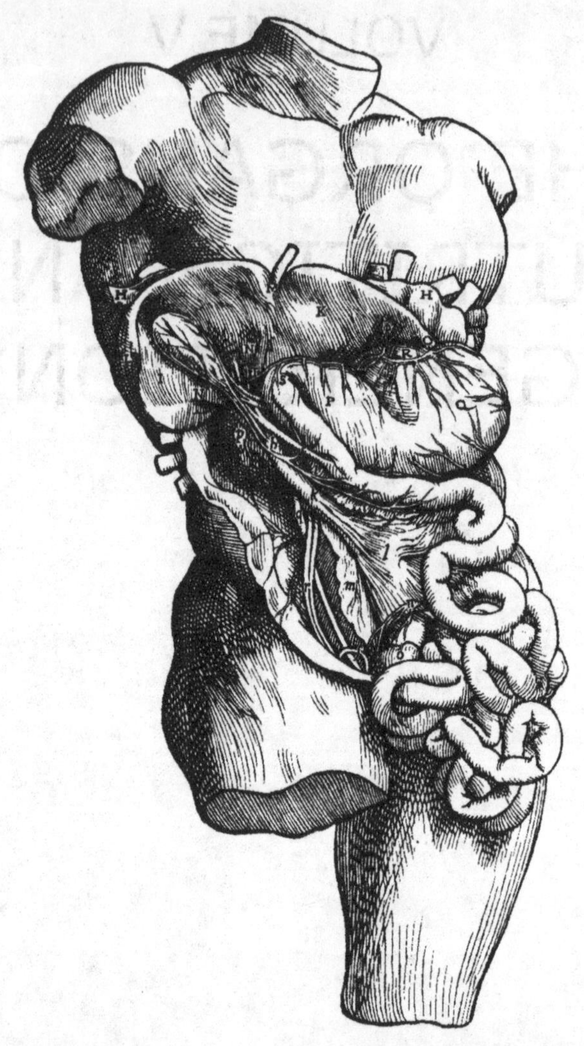

Education and discovery – the Master's twin goals – find harmony in the final chapter of Volume V, the longest chapter of the entire *Fabrica*. A workshop manual for the greasier elements of the human machine, it not only describes the organs of nutrition and elimination, and both styles of reproductive apparatus, but painstakingly expounds the mechanics of their dissection. Through his meticulous tuition, Vesalius plays Virgil to the novice's Dante, guiding him through this diabolically confusing realm.

When the time comes, he will do this for me.

Vesalius pithily demonstrated the utility of direct observation when he soundly debunked the prevailing myth that the normal human uterus was formed of two branches, instead of a single chamber. By reference to human cadavers, rather than drawing inferences at one remove from animal specimens, as had been the practice of his forebears, the Master established the truth of the matter.

Vesalius made a reproductive impression upon the world in the usual way as well, albeit to lesser renown thus far. His issue was well documented at first, before passing into obscurity – but not oblivion.

The Master married at the late age of thirty in 1544, the year after the *Fabrica*'s publication. At the peak of his celebrity, Vesalius had just secured his lucrative appointment to the Imperial court of Emperor Charles V, a position involving constant travel and political intriguing. A marriage tie cannot have been convenient.

The chronicle of his marriage speaks three other facts of note: the Master's young wife, Anna van Hamme, bore him a child with impressive post-nuptial rapidity; their daughter, also Anna, was the sole issue of their twenty-year union; and Vesalius was still warm in the ground when his widow remarried.

One surmises from all this that the wedding was solemnised beneath the supervision of an arquebus.

Sixteen years after his daughter's birth, from the distance of the court of Philip II in Madrid, Vesalius secured her marriage to Jan de Mol, who numbered among the Serroelofs, one of the seven noble houses of Brussels. Anna *fille* lived until the age of forty-three and bore de Mol two sons and three daughters. Adriana, their fourth child, made an equally advantageous match with Hugo de Croeser, the eldest son of a prominent family of Bruges, with ancestral holdings in Zeeland. Adriana produced her own daughter, Ernestine, who secretly married her cousin Cornelis van Hulsberg (Adriana's sister Elisabeth was married to Charles de Bausele, the brother of Cornelis's mother, yet another Anna). The scandal was not ruinous, as the pair were not blood-related, but it was notorious enough to see the couple banished from the dynastic home in Gouden-Handstraat, and their line fall from the family records.

Two centuries later, a descendent of that love match named Hendrick Peeters migrated to the Victorian goldfields, where he found only mud and oppression and grinding toil, and the pyretic society of resentful men. At Ballarat he stood among the miners in early skirmishing with the police and infantry, and participated in the torching of the Bentley Hotel in October 1854. When the rebels began fortifying their position at the Eureka Lead, however, Hendrick opted for strategic withdrawal. By the time he arrived in brash, chaotic Sydney Town, he was calling himself Henry Porter. Twelve years later, he sired his fifth child and second son, William.

My grandfather's grandfather.

Thursday 1 November – evening

Stephen Porter parked at the Lane Cove River end of Roseville, in a position carefully chosen during his earlier reconnaissance: a moderate distance from the house, not in line of sight; adjacent to public land, on a lightly trafficked street; and near to Grosvenor Road, which furnished several flight routes.

He walked quickly through the leafy, fragrant suburban streets, the jacarandas in riotous bloom. There was a modest degree of neighbourhood activity, typical for the after-dinner hour on a pleasant spring weeknight. Nobody would look twice.

Porter confirmed the registration number of the Audi Quattro parked down the side: the candidate was in. There was no one in sight as he went through the gate and onto the verandah. He put down his Gladstone bag, removed a clipboard and opened the flyscreen door, then knocked crisply.

Footsteps approached, then the door opened.

The candidate looked older than his online presence, unkempt and more fatigued. A worn white T-shirt bearing a monochrome image of a near-naked woman hung above loose cotton shorts. The body itself appeared in reasonable shape: more wiry than muscly, but still moderately fit. Porter would have to choose his moment well.

The candidate slouched against the door frame, radiating boredom. 'Yeah?'

'Good evening, Mr Evans,' enthused Porter. 'I'm Stephen, from Denison Bank. We spoke last night.'

'And?'

'I thought I'd bring you your card, since you mentioned you were going to Melbourne for the spring carnival.'

'Hmm.'

'So rather than relying on the post, which might not deliver your card in time...' He tapered off, encouraging Evans to pick up the thread.

'That's ... uh, yeah, good.' Evans nudged the front door wider, opened the screen door and extended his hand towards the envelope.

'Oh, sorry, Mr Evans. I'm afraid I have to see some photo ID first, and a recent bank statement. Then you'll have to sign for it.' Porter smiled inanely. 'Procedure.'

'Fuck,' Evans said with a grunt. 'All right, come in.' He turned abruptly and walked away down the hallway. Porter picked up his Gladstone bag and followed, closing the door behind him. He eased the latch home then flicked the snib to secure the lock. He moved quickly but lightly along the hall, passing four open doors: two bedrooms, a study and a bathroom. All empty, all quiet, all dark. He caught up with the candidate where the extension opened out at the back of the house. An enormous television dominated one wall, displaying the asinine proceedings of a football panel show. There was nobody else there.

'I hope I didn't disturb you,' said Porter.

'No, it's fine.' Evans sighed. 'Can we get this over with?'

'Of course. Just some photo ID, please.' Porter opened his blue plastic clipboard to a sheet bearing a list of names and numbers, with a few signatures down the right column.

Evans turned around and opened a drawer in a heavy antique sideboard. Porter reached into his pocket and removed the soaked cotton pad from its sandwich bag. He fitted it into his palm and quickly crossed the space.

The candidate heard his approach and started to turn, but Porter was there first. He landed the thick pad onto the middle of the face in one fluid movement. Surprise provided both an intake of breath – consisting chiefly of midazolam – and a delayed reaction. Porter applied a headlock with his other arm and pushed the legs out from beneath. He turned and heaved, pushing down hard on the torso, keeping his own feet spread wide and his weight above their combined centre of gravity.

The body lurched violently, fighting with a rugby player's instinct: the legs were buckling but the feet remained grounded. The head twisted desperately, hands clawing at Porter's grip as they stumbled together into a floor lamp, sending it flying. Porter braced and pressed harder on the face, the benzodiazepine finally taking effect, the struggle dissipating into random lunges. The feet lost traction and the body fell to the floor, pulling Porter down on top of it. The flailing lost coherence and strength until the body finally slumped into submission with a muffled sigh.

Porter held the pose for a moment, then eased the head onto the floor. He quickly retrieved his Gladstone bag from inside the front door and donned his surgical gloves. He opened the syringe case and selected the sodium thiopental, then crossed to the unconscious body. He found the median cubital vein inside the left elbow, inserted the needle, pulled a thread of blood into the barrel to confirm the strike, then pressed the plunger. The drug would induce coma within a minute, taking over from the short-term aerosol.

Porter could finally relax: the candidate was not coming back. He put on his isolation garments then inspected every room, confirming there was no one else home. He chocked the front door with a sturdy wedge and armed it with a portable intruder alarm.

He found the mobile phone charging on the kitchen bench. He applied the candidate's right thumb to the home button, the phone unlocking on the second attempt. Porter scrolled through recent text messages and found an exchange with the Melbourne friend who was expecting Evans the following afternoon, for a long weekend of debauchery culminating at Flemington Racecourse on Tuesday. The discourse was even more impoverished than Porter had anticipated.

He formulated a text, typing and deleting until he achieved the required degree of depravity and illiteracy.

—Change plans bro – scored w fkn hottest babe!! Im goin off grid all wknd wont be @ melb til late mon nite hope its ok?

The reply came swiftly. Evidently Porter had chosen his words well.

—Champion!!!! U fkn playa evo thurs nite drinx rulz eh bro? No worries legend fuck her ass 4 me. C U when im lookin at ya

Where did men learn to be like this? Did they go to a special school? Had they been lobotomised as children? He sent a fitting response.

—*Ok sweet @ hers now even hotr chick just cum out showr nkd total slut 2!! Game on m8 over n out!!!!*

The predictable reply was immediate.

—*Fuck mate 241 go evo!! Send pix or didnt happen want 69 lez action \i/EVIDENCE!!!! Dont ware out ur dick hahaha*

Porter diverted all calls to voicemail then returned the mobile to its charging stand.

Now they really were alone, and would be for days and days.

He returned to the becalmed body and injected the pancuronium bromide. Soon the tidal movement of the chest ceased altogether; a moment later, a small flow of urine signalled the body's final release.

Porter looked longingly at the long dining table, but it was just too exposed for this kind of work: the dining room's wide glass doors opened onto a tall back fence that screened the yard, but there were no blinds or curtains.

He considered the other rooms and settled on the master bedroom, well back from the street frontage and looking out at a blank brick wall. A mattress was a poor surface for dissection – too low, too absorptive and too tensile – but it couldn't be helped. He could risk the kitchen for the close work, perhaps. It would be a fair proportion of this Volume's labour.

He dragged the body up the hall to the bathroom, pleased to find it equipped with a bath. He made the necessary incisions and left the body to bleed out. He moved his Gladstone bag to the bedroom and carefully unpacked everything onto the top of a wide chest of drawers, then went back to the bathroom and rolled the body over. He took off the bloodied gloves, removed the nail polish from his fingertips, then regloved. While he waited for the last of the fluid to drain away, he opened his wire-bound photocopy of Volume V and reviewed Chapter XIX: 'How it is best to perform an anatomy, and how to dissect each of the parts that are mentioned in this book.'

Saturday 3 November – afternoon

'Do you get back to the Netherlands much?' Jo asked Thijs. They were walking in the warm sunshine alongside Circular Quay towards the Sydney Opera House.

'I do. Mum moved back after Dad died, and my sister followed.'

'Where do they live?'

'Mum went back to Delft. Anneke and her kids live in Amsterdam.'

'Oh, I love Delft, it's a gorgeous town. What a lovely place to grow up.'

'It was. It's on such a human scale, you know?'

'Those beautiful canals. It's the home of my first true love, actually.'

'Johannes Vermeer?'

'Yep. He's why I became an art historian. Those exquisite moments from household life. His control of light is incredible.'

'I'll show you the house I grew up in some time. It's in the *View of Delft*.'

'No way! Since 1660!' Jo was blown away. 'To my ear that's like saying you were wandering through the Senate one day when up popped these fellas and stabbed Julius Caesar.'

Thijs laughed. 'Yes, it's a different time-scale. Here history is either very recent or vastly ancient. I prefer it, actually.'

'But we can be afraid of our deep time here. And our recent history, for that matter. There's this terrific gallery of Australian Aboriginal art in Utrecht, do you know it?'

'No. I know Utrecht, but not your gallery.' Thijs took her hand in his.

'It feels like a compliment when you first see it – I mean, I was literally walking past, not knowing it was there, and suddenly there were these Vernon Ah Kees in a window – but at the same time it's ... I don't know, an admonition? Like, "You Aussies come here to fuss over a few hundred years of rubble while we Europeans are exploring this continuous art tradition that's tens of thousands of years old and still powering strong."'

'So you've been in Delft and Utrecht. Amsterdam, I imagine?'

'Such a great town, especially for art. But my favourite gallery is in Den Haag.'

'The Mauritshuis,' Thijs said. 'Isn't it incredible?'

'I went there to see the *Pearl Earring,* like the predictable undergraduate I was, but I fell for Judith Leijster.'

'Your second love?'

'Yep, head over heels. I ended up writing my honours thesis on *The Proposition.* Feminist mise-en-scène of the Dutch Golden Age.'

'So you abandoned your first love!'

'Heresy! I have never forsaken Vermeer and never will. That has nothing to do with Colin Firth, I might add.'

Thijs laughed. 'I can't say I'm entirely indifferent to Scarlett Johansson.'

'Oh, I'm not indifferent, but my devotion to Vermeer predates him.'

He drew her closer. 'We should go to Holland together some day.'

'I'd love that.'

'We might even see something besides paintings.'

She poked him in the side and laughed. 'Philistine.'

'But we should go when it's warm. It's too gloomy in winter.'

'Hah! So you *are* an Aussie then.'

'Sure. When we arrived I couldn't believe the warmth and the light. It felt like I'd been shivering in the dark for fourteen years without even realising it. I love the Netherlands, but I don't know if I could give up all this.'

He gestured at the Harbour Bridge over the shimmering water, framing the inner harbour and Blues Point. Jo told him about Wendy Whiteley's secret garden in Lavender Bay, just out of sight behind Luna Park. Thijs told her how the bridge's muscular pylons actually bore no load, and were not part of the original design. They were added to make people feel secure. Jo considered them necessary for visual balance, irrespective of the engineering. They took in the panorama, watching the Manly ferry cut its way to Circular Quay, amid the swarm of sailboats dashing across the wide stretch of water.

Jo wondered if Sylvia and Murphy were out there in front of them right now, under one of the colourful sails. She'd never gone out on the water with them, wary of her brother in ship's-captain mode; Sylvia said it relaxed him, but Jo just couldn't imagine it. The prospect was even less appealing these days, with his increasing surliness.

She nudged Thijs's hip with hers, and they walked on in the shadow of the Opera House towards the botanic gardens.

'So, Thijs. I need to tell you something.'

'What is it?'

'I'm seeing someone. Else.'

'I know, *schatje,*' he said, brushing hair from her eyes.

'How?' God, had they been that obvious?

'You've been a little distracted lately.'

'Oh.' She was relieved he didn't seem to know it was Amy. This didn't feel like the time for that detail. 'It's only new. I wasn't sure what would happen, but we ... it's nice.'

'I'm glad for you, Jo.' He hugged her reassuringly. 'You don't owe me any explanations.'

'I know, I just want to be up front with you. I still like being with you, Thijs.'

'Me too, *mijn liefste*. It's okay.'

She stopped and kissed him, then they stood at the Man O'War Steps watching the colourful throng of yachts and ferries crossing the blue harbour. Jacarandas and Illawarra flame trees and late-blooming wattle refracted the full spectrum of colour among the infinite shades of green. The Palm Beach seaplane banked into its final approach on Rose Bay, wings wavering and correcting as it disappeared behind Shark Island. Anchoring the entire vista was the golden, solid, vigilant sandstone of Fort Denison, its solitary date palm leaning away from the Martello tower, as though trying to escape.

Wednesday 7 November – afternoon

'Where are you, Mack?' boomed Murphy from the front door of the Roseville house. 'What aesthetic delights do you have for us today?'

A muffled greeting came from halfway down the hall as Janssen, Chartier and Jo followed him in, stepping over a wide swathe of rusty red that ran across the hall, reminding Jo of the signature painting style of Kazuo Shiraga. She wasn't sure if that made her feel better or worse, but it was something to anchor her.

She followed the trail and paused at the master bedroom door, closing her eyes and picturing for a moment Vesalius's frontispiece, to get into character. Inside, she found the police gathered around a bed, like relatives in a hospital room. She blanched at the carnage before her, but focused hard on the technicalities.

The arms and legs were entirely intact, albeit bloodied, the head and thorax untouched apart from an excavation of the throat from jaw to sternum. But the abdomen had been plundered, the muscle and skin pulled up and out like the jagged remnants of a contained blast. The deep concavity was anchored up the middle by the vertebral column, framed by the corrugations of the lower ribs and a pelvis stripped nearly to the bone.

Jo grasped the reference immediately. In its utter unsentimentality, in its compelling, relentless brutality, the tableau was straight out of the *Fabrica.* They were looking at a sculptural interpretation of the Vesalius woodcuts, as though rendered in flesh by HR Giger. This was not the remains of a dissection; it was an anatomical demonstration in itself.

This was new.

With a vast effort of will, Jo pulled away from the gothic scene to find everyone watching, waiting for her to either speak or faint. 'Volume Five,' she croaked.

'Yes,' said Mack gently. 'The organs of nutrition and generation.'

'Made a right fucken mess of him, anyhow,' said Murphy, giving his sister's sensibilities no quarter. 'Who was he?'

'Brendan James Evans, mining index analyst. A quant.'

'That's a bit harsh,' Murphy chided. 'You didn't even know him.'

Mack ignored him. 'Early thirties, good shape, lived alone. Took a few days off to go to the Melbourne Cup, then failed to show up at the office this morning. Someone came around and hopped the fence, saw the results of a scuffle out the back and rang Chatswood station.'

'Definitely our killer?' asked Janssen.

'Yep. Fresh punctures in the left median cubital, blood in the bath and the dragline across the hall. And the anatomy lesson, of course.' Mack leaned in to point. 'He's opened the neck to access the oesophagus. He's left off through the thorax to save time – it's all the same anyway, and spreading ribs is hard work. So the main action is below the diaphragm. He's resected the organs one by one and examined them on the kitchen bench.'

'Let's have a look,' said Murphy.

They filed out the back and clustered around the kitchen island like students at a cooking school. Its timber surface was covered in a miscellany of organs, blood seeping into the grain. One sink was full of intestines, all blood and shit and seeping fluids. The other was empty of organs but smeared with streaks of blood and flecks of gore. The whole mess smelled terrible. Jo retched once, sharply, turning her head and breathing in deeply through her mouth. She looked outside at a large jacaranda tree in full profusion by the back fence. In a few weeks, the lawn would be a carpet of indigo. Janssen passed around a small jar of menthol salve for everyone to smear on their upper lips. It helped.

'There's your struggle.' Mack gestured towards a felled lamp and several pieces of disarrayed furniture, which a SOCO was dusting for prints.

'Any security cameras, Ella?' Murphy asked the SOCO, peering through the broad expanse of glass doors. Anything mounted out there would have a clear view of the kitchen.

'Doesn't look like it, detective.'

Mack resumed his lesson. 'We found most of the viscera here in the sinks. After photography I pulled it all out for inspection, except the guts. They take up too much room and slide all over the place. Almost ended up on the floor.'

'Mack,' said Chartier, glancing at Jo.

'Oh, right. Sorry. But the intestines are all intact: Evans even had an appendix before our boy opened it up. He's also sectioned the gut in places, but it's all accounted for.'

Mack turned to the organs on the bench. When Jo finally looked she found a collection of sleek, wet bruises, all slippery and alien, in livid hues of yellow and purple and green and brown. Lars von Trier meets David Cronenberg. She very nearly lost her breakfast.

'Everything here is gastro-intestinal and reproductive. Removed, cleaned up and dissected on that glass chopping board,' said Mack, pointing at a large, bloody rectangle set across the gas burners in a bright pool of light from the rangehood.

He turned back to the viscera, indicating each organ. 'Liver, pancreas, stomach, bladder, right kidney, right adrenal, gall bladder, prostate, left – no, *right* epididymis, right testis, oesophagus, penis, left kidney with adrenal, left testis with epididymis.'

'What about these?' asked Murphy, indicating a collection of slender tubes and small bulbs.

'Vasa deferentia, ureters, seminal vesicles, Cowper's glands, urethra, bile duct.'

'And how long would this all take, Mack?' asked Janssen. 'Days, surely?'

'Definitely. Hence the extra-long weekend.'

'Anything out of the ordinary?' asked Murphy, bracing against the benchtop and leaning in carefully to inspect the viscera.

'Well, there's early cirrhosis of the liver, and his bile duct's inflamed.'

'I mean "anything out of the ordinary" in the being-killed-and-butchered sense.'

'Oh, right,' said Mack. He hesitated.

'No sex-type stuff?' prompted Chartier.

'Not at all. I mean, everything's been cut out and apart, which makes my eyes water, but there's no funny business.'

'What, then?'

'There is one weird little quirk, Spud. He's taken the spleen out.'

'Hasn't he taken everything out?'

'Yeah he has, but the spleen isn't here,' said Mack, waving at the organs before them.

'Maybe he didn't have one,' said Chartier. 'Don't people have them removed?'

'They do. Mostly due to impact rupture.'

'Does that cause problems?' asked Janssen.

'Not really. It has a blood-conditioning function, but you can get by without it.'

'So maybe he played footy,' said Murphy. 'I've had my share of hits to the guts. Not a spleen, but I know blokes who've had them out.'

'He might have been a footballer, but Brendan Evans had a spleen all right, up until the weekend.'

'How do you know?' asked Murphy.

'I employed the arcane mystic ritual of organ divination, handed down through the ancient occult guild of the forensic arts.'

'You what?' asked Chartier.

'I looked around.'

'Smart arse,' replied Murphy, pushing up from the bench. 'Show me.'

Mack led them back into the hall, across the bloodsmear and into a front room, the police photographer leaving as they filed in. They fanned out around a queen-size bed, where a piece of offal sat delicately on the pillow. It was the red-brown of iron ore, trimmed of intra-abdominal fat, and with the blood vessels severed flush to the surface.

'So that's a spleen,' said Janssen.

'What's he done to it?' asked Chartier.

'He's opened it up along the rear of the renal surface, then sliced straight through beneath the hilum, almost to the front edge,' said Mack, pointing with his pen. 'Then he's spread the wings and laid them flat on the pillow.'

'Like he's butterflied it,' said Janssen.

'Huh. Has this Evans guy been on a cooking show or something?'

'Don't watch them.'

'It'll turn up if he has.'

'Interesting angle.'

'Bizarre.'

'Why would he butterfly the spleen?' mused Chartier. The cops all shook their heads in bafflement.

'He didn't butterfly it,' said Jo quietly, speaking for the first time since she'd seen the remains across the hall. Everyone looked at her. 'He vented it.'

'He vented his spleen,' said Murphy. 'Bugger me.'

'Well, it's a clue,' said Chartier. 'In a way.'

'Clue.' Murphy snorted. Jo knew it was a word he never used. He always said it reminded him of little old lady sleuths doddering around quaint but lethal English villages.

'It means something, though, surely,' said Chartier.

'Maybe it's a critique,' said Janssen. 'Perhaps he had a run-in with Evans.'

'Like a car accident.'

'Hell of a case of road rage.'

'Social media?' Everyone grunted. Certainly a possibility.

Murphy looked up at Janssen. 'Put Niko on recent interactions. Work, internet, social life. Neighbours. Any misdemeanours or complaints.'

'There is another angle,' said Jo. 'I was thinking about this in the bedroom, too. Maybe the spleen isn't important in itself, so much as the gesture.'

'What do you mean?' asked Janssen.

'The medium is the message. It's not about *what* he's saying, it's about the fact he's saying something at all.'

'Say it again in English, Professor,' said Murphy.

Mack got it, though. 'Yeah I agree, Jo, this was done for an audience. Like the nerve demonstration. He's talking to us, Spud.'

'The presentation of the corpse was the same,' continued Jo, tilting her head towards the main bedroom. 'He didn't just dissect it and leave. It's a montage in the style of a plate from the *Fabrica*.'

'Yeah, nah,' said Murphy dismissively. 'It's just a leftover body.'

'No, the first three were leftover bodies,' said Jo. 'Then last time he gave us perfect dissections of the brachial and lumbar plexi. This time he's left us an entire installation. Like he knows we're onto his *Fabrica* obsession, and he's taunting us.'

'I disagree,' Murphy insisted. 'It's not a fucken diorama.'

'I understand you disagree, Dave,' Jo replied gently. 'But you're wrong.'

'You're reading too much into it, Joanna.' He waved impatiently at the violated spleen. 'He was settling a score and amusing himself, that's all.'

They all looked at one another and then down at the organ sitting atop its crimson tailing, gradually soaking the pillow. It meant something, but what?

Tuesday 13 November – evening

Sylvia was knocking off a few chores before heading out with her European film group. It was more a way to get outside their mundane working lives than an exercise in high culture, and the effort required to get to the cinema only proved its necessity.

She heard the front door just as she hit the start button on the washing machine. She took a deep breath to compose herself. Dave didn't like her going out with this crew, and lately he'd been finding reasons to stop her. But she played it straight, leaning out of the laundry alcove and calling out a greeting.

The washing machine started to fill, obscuring any reply. She emptied the dryer into the laundry basket and turned around. Murphy was standing not half a metre behind her.

'Oh shit!' she gasped, falling back against the machine. 'You scared the daylights out of me!' She put her hand over her heart and tried to calm herself. He was standing stock-still, arms by his side, hands clenched, his face a grim mask. She could smell booze on the breath he expelled through flared nostrils.

She needed to get out, but he had her blocked in. She feinted left, and when he moved with her she darted right and around him. She filled a glass of water at the kitchen sink, drinking it slowly with a shaky hand.

He followed her over, both fists out face down.

'Pick a hand, Sylvia.'

'What?'

'Just pick a hand.'

'Why?'

He exhaled impatiently. 'Pick. A *hand.*'

She swallowed. 'Right.'

He turned his right hand over and opened it. Empty. 'Wrong.' He breathed into his curled left fist. 'What do you think I have here?'

She suddenly couldn't be bothered with the whole charade. 'I don't know, Dave, what do you have there?' she asked wearily.

It was a mistake.

He smashed his hand down on the counter, along with its contents: her Wylie's Baths tag and three keys – to Jo's place and their own – on a Sydney Uni keyring.

'My swimming keys,' she said meekly, her heart pounding again.

'Yeah, your fucken keys. You know where I found them?'

It wasn't hard to guess. 'In the front door.'

'Yes, in the front door. A-gain.'

'I'm sorry, Dave.' She needed to calm this down.

'I'm sorry, too, Sylvia. I'm sorry some random intruder could've snuck in here and violated my wife. I'm sorry they could've followed up with my sister, a few streets away.' She opened her mouth to respond. 'No, I'm not finished. I'm sorry I could have been ambushed in my own home. You know how many crooks I've sent away? These are not pleasant people, darlin'. They'd pay good money to watch me die in excruciating pain. Fuck knows what they'd do to you while they waited. You'd just be a juicy piece of fuckmeat to those boys, sweetheart. Then they'd slit your pretty throat.'

'I didn't mean it.'

'Well you're hardly going to do it on purpose, are you? But why does it happen at all?'

'I don't know.'

'It's because you don't pay *attention*, Sylvia.' But his voice was losing some of its edge; she sensed he was losing interest. It was probably 'fuckmeat' – even by his standards that was over the top. If she remained meek enough this could still peter out.

'I'm sorry.' She looked at him with glistening eyes. 'I'll try harder.'

He softened, then. 'Did you go overboard with the laps again?' She nodded, and he tucked a strand of hair behind her ear. 'So what should you do?'

'Remember to check.'

'That's right. Just make it routine, like when you take off your cossie.'

She nodded. There was no point reminding him she changed and showered at Jo's place.

'Say it for me.'

'Have I got my keys?' she intoned.

'When do you ask yourself?'

'When I hang my swimsuit up to dry.'

'See? It's easy, Sylv.' Soothing voice, hand stroking her hair. 'Now, go make us our tea, eh darlin'?' He poured himself a whisky and left her to it. There'd be no European films for her tonight.

She stared at the Wylie's Baths tag. It was true she often went into a trance during a long swim, but it wasn't the laps that had done it today. It was the gins she'd downed at Jo's place after showering, fortifying herself before coming home to Murphy and his increasingly dark moods. The secret drinking had to stop, from today. Alcohol was not going to help.

One drunk in the house was enough.

Monday 19 November – morning

Jo and Janssen were laughing as they walked onto the unit's floor on Monday morning. Chartier stood up at her desk with a finger to her lips.

'What's going on?' asked Jo.

She pointed beneath a nearby desk. 'Nguyễn's asleep.'

'Big weekend?' asked Janssen.

'She phoned me yesterday afternoon. Said she was onto something with this time-on-premises question.'

'That's great,' Janssen said. 'What's it about?'

'She wouldn't say until she was sure, but she was here all weekend on it.'

It was a quarter to eight: Nguyễn wasn't going to get much more sleep. 'I'm going to make coffee,' said Jo. 'Anyone know how she takes it?'

'Same as me,' said Chartier. 'Maybe bring the biscuits.'

By the time Jo returned, Nguyễn was awake and rubbing her eyes.

'You're a lifesaver, Jo,' she said. Strong flat white with one.

'So what's the story, Liệu?' Jo handed Chartier and Janssen their coffees then opened the biscuit tin.

'I sat up late Friday night watching *Rage,*' Nguyễn said, helping herself to an Iced VoVo, 'but I couldn't get my mind off how he has all that time, you know?' They all nodded. 'I thought he must be seeing into their diaries, but buggered if I could work out how. And I must've gone to sleep because next thing I'm waking up to the film clip of "Streets of Your Town", you know the one with all those rapid little scenes around the city? And I'm still half-asleep, right, so in the dream logic it's all connected, how he gets around town and can see everything and control everything, and it just comes to me: he's not just accessing their diaries, he's *changing* them somehow. And I realise he must be doing it there, in the house – it's too dicey to set it up beforehand. So then I thought of their phones—'

'Oh!' said Jo, snapping her fingers. 'Fingerprint activation!'

'Bingo.' Nguyễn smiled. 'He's getting into their phones using their fingerprints.'

'I thought that didn't work once you're dead,' said Chartier.

'Yes, something to do with skin conductivity,' said Janssen.

'Doesn't matter,' said Nguyễn. 'He has them unconscious first.'

'So he gets into their phones before he kills them,' said Chartier.

'Nice thinking, Nguyễn,' said Janssen.

She shrugged. 'I just had to get out of my own way. So I came in on Saturday and went back through all the victims' text messages and emails and calendar entries around time of death, and I found a bunch that looked pretty suss.'

'Like what?'

'So, Laura Newman, for instance. Curl Curl. Friday morning she sends a couple of texts to cancel her plans for the Queen's Birthday long weekend, which was mountain-biking and wine-tasting up the Hunter. She's got the flu. Just like that, her weekend's freed up. Those friends leave her alone because they think she's sick and everyone else thinks she's away. So she's alone with him until her ex drops in on Monday night to see if she needs anything.'

'That's brilliant.'

'You can't be completely sure it's him, because the texts have to sound like the vics for it to work. But the final messages are about clearing the time ahead, without fail, all sent within the window for estimated time of death. Then radio silence.'

'How did we not pick this up? Didn't the uniforms go over these already?'

'Yeah, they did, and Niko had a look too, but all our victims are forever rearranging things. It didn't look out of the ordinary. This last one for Brendan Evans looks obvious now, once you think of it, but in context it just looked typical.'

'So you've tracked them down for all the vics?'

'Yeah, I came back in yesterday and went through the rest. Most are texts and emails, so we have those, but there weren't any at all for Henley. Then I remembered that Hall emailed his assistant asking her to clear his diary:

he's crook as Rookwood; doctor says he needs the rest of the week off. I realised the work diary could be cleared manually in the phone app, which would explain Henley.'

'So he's deleting diary commitments just before he kills them. Genius.'

'Yeah, or adding red herrings to account for their absence from work. We can't be sure until we get the time stamps for those electronic updates from their employers.'

'This is bloody good work, Nguyễn,' said Chartier. Jo agreed.

'It's excellent,' said Janssen. 'Although it won't lead us to him, unfortunately.'

'I don't know about that,' said Jo. 'I mean, he already knows at least some of their plans before he arrives. That's a privileged position.'

'That's right,' said Nguyễn. 'Newman for instance. She worked from home every Friday, and that's when he went in. He knew she'd be there.'

'And presumably he knew about the Hunter Valley plans, so he could exploit them,' said Chartier. 'That's got to help narrow down who he could be.'

'Well done, Nguyễn,' said Janssen. 'Why don't you go home for some proper sleep? You've done your bit.'

'No, I'll stick around to brief the boss. Where is he, anyway?'

'He had to drop Sylvia at the doctor's,' said Jo.

'No worries, I have to write it up anyway,' said Nguyễn. 'And I want to follow up the calendar amendments with the companies.'

'Okay, if you're sure,' said Janssen. 'This is your baby now.'

'Bloody oath it is!' She accepted a fist bump from Chartier, then took another Iced VoVo as a reward.

Saturday 24 November – afternoon

When Jo couldn't take any more, Amy drew back and blew gently, watching her pulsate with pleasure, then wriggled up the bed and draped her arm across her lover's heaving torso. 'Happy birthday, love,' Amy said.

'Bloody hell, Amy,' Jo said, when she'd recovered the power of speech, 'you certainly know your way around a cunt.'

Amy laughed. 'Years and years of dedicated practice.'

'Ten thousand hours, do you reckon?'

'At least. I've been in constant training since the year nine tennis camp.'

'I'm impressed. Maybe you could help me get my hours up?'

'Looking for volunteers, are you?'

'Always.' Jo blushed suddenly. 'That sounds pretty slutty, doesn't it?'

'Not to me.' Amy laughed. 'I'm in no position to judge.'

'Do tell?'

'I have my moments. But surely you haven't been on a desert island yourself?'

'Almost, actually, until recently.'

'Really?'

'Yeah, I spent the last eighteen months in my cave, with the odd foray into the wild. I wasn't fit for consumption; the whole marriage catastrophe did my head in.'

'What happened?'

'The romantic-industrial complex. Lachlan's a decent man, but all that coupledom shit made me miserable. Made us both miserable.'

'Yeah, I've been there. Not for me. *The romantic-industrial complex* – I like that.'

'Red roses, diamond rings, Valentine's Day, candlelit dinners, silk lingerie. Weaponising love for profit.'

'Woah, too far. Back up, sister.'

'How?'

'You cannot seriously be against silk underwear.'

'Fair call, I take that back. But I stand by the rest of it. And the whole construct is just toxic for women, even though we're the ones expected to police it.'

'I wouldn't know about that.'

'You've never been with a bloke?' Jo asked.

'Nup. I had a male flatmate once, closest I'll ever get. He was a complete pig.'

'Bet you did all the washing up.'

'Yeah I did,' Amy said, laughing. She propped herself up on her elbow and looked down at Jo. 'So you got divorced and you've left the convent and now you want to explore.'

'Something like that.'

'Good on you, Jo.'

'What about you? Are you seeing anyone else?'

'I have a few friends. And I don't mind a little novelty now and then.'

'Sounds all right to me.'

'Yeah, it's nice. But you have to work at keeping it low drama. Doesn't stay that way by itself.'

'That's what I mean about the culture.'

'So what about men?' Amy asked.

'There is one, at the moment.'

'And what about men's expectations?'

'I'm just being really clear. I define myself socially, but not inside a unit of two.'

'Yeah, that's it. It's like, I have lots of friends I have sex with...'

'Just how many of us do you have on the go?' Jo laughed, pushing Amy onto her back. 'A round number will do.'

'It's not like that,' Amy said, smiling. 'My point is that nobody has a claim on me.'

'I want to be able go with whatever feels right. It's not like it's always about sex, but I don't want to arbitrarily rule it out either, you know?'

'Yeah. I love that spark, and it doesn't care who else I'm fucking, that's for sure.'

'So why are we expected to only explore it with one person at a time?'

'The romantic-industrial complex,' said Amy.

'Right.'

'So, this man; does he know about us?'

'No. He knows I'm seeing someone else, but that's all.' Jo didn't like keeping secrets from Amy and Thijs, but in each case they'd instinctively known to keep the relationship quiet, at least while Jo was seconded to the squad. Amy wasn't going to press her for the man's identity while expecting Jo to keep her own name out of despatches. It was the same for Thijs. Keeping faith with those tacit undertakings avoided the whole awkwardness issue, too. But it wasn't ideal.

'What is it, hun?'

Jo realised she'd been staring out the window. 'Does that bother you?' she asked Amy. 'That I'm seeing a man?'

'You don't need my permission.'

'I know, I'm not asking for that. But how do you feel about it?'

'It's your choice, Jo. I don't get a say. I don't want a say.'

'Fair enough.' Jo shook her head. 'I'm not quite used to it yet, sorry.'

'It's not going to scare me off, if that's what's worrying you,' said Amy, rolling onto Jo's chest. 'Even if I don't need cock like you do.'

Jo laughed. She kissed Amy and slid her hands down the length of her back to cradle her arse. 'I don't need cock, honey. Not when I'm with you.'

'For an anti-romantic you say the sweetest things.'

Jo rolled them over so she was on top. 'It's not just talk, you know.'

'Whatever could you mean?'

'Allow me to demonstrate,' said Jo, heading south.

Friday 30 November – afternoon

Murphy stalked towards the briefing area. He made no sound, but his intensity produced its own gravitational field. Jo had sensed it from the moment he'd put his office phone down: she had a finely calibrated radar for her brother's moods, and it seemed his detectives were almost as sensitised. He stood looking at the incident board while everyone assembled to hear the bad news.

'I just had a call from Commissioner Carr,' said Murphy when he turned around. 'The media unit says the *Sydney Envoy* is going to give us a touch-up on the front page tomorrow morning.' That wasn't good, but it wasn't surprising either. The case had been running for seven months without a significant breakthrough. Media criticism had been building, and a major serve in the newspaper was only a matter of time. In some respects it was overdue.

But Murphy's next remark explained his displeasure. 'The yarn's going to be framed around a big scoop on the killer's use of fingerprints to access the victims' mobile phones.' He looked pointedly at Nguyễn.

'I never spoke to anyone at the *Envoy,* boss,' she said in a quavering voice.

'So I understand, Nguyễn, and it's just as fucken well. Because anyone who talks to a journalist about a case without my explicit approval gets transferred to the Back of Bourke West fucken dog-catching unit. No exceptions, no second chances. Does everyone understand me?'

There was a murmur of concurrence. Jo felt it best to mumble along.

'My old mate Hollier says some fucken graduate punk trying to steal his crime patch got the story from Recondite Technologies.'

Nguyễn flushed all over again. Recondite Technologies was Damien Henley's employer – she'd obtained from them the update history for his electronic diary scheduler.

'I don't...' Nguyễn began. 'How could...?' Then she stopped cold.

'They might have worked out the fingerprint angle themselves,' suggested Chartier. 'It's not such a leap from the data request.'

'Yeah, they might've,' said Murphy, gazing levelly at Nguyễn. 'Did they?'

'No, boss,' she admitted miserably. She'd shared her theory with Henley's boss while sweet-talking him into giving her the data.

Murphy softened his tone – an honest confession went a long way with him. 'Look, I realise we need to give people something to get their cooperation. That's the reality. But we're on a fucken hair-trigger here, and the media will use any pretext to murder us.'

'It's dishonest of them to use an inspired piece of police work to frame an attack about lack of progress,' observed Janssen.

'It's fucken horribly ironic is what it is, and it's grossly unfair, but that's how it works,' said Murphy. 'They're going for all-out panic – the story will suggest that anyone in Sydney who cancels an appointment electronically could be the next victim. The despatch team is bracing for a surge of 000 false alarms.'

Nguyễn groaned.

'The ambos and the fireys are going to love us,' said Nikolaidis.

'At least they're not editorialising against us yet,' said Murphy. 'The commissioner reckons one more victim and they'll let rip. You think I'm pissed off, you should hear him. He was off to tell the minister about it next, soon as he finished giving me six of the best. Fuck knows what mood he's in by now.'

'Where to from here, boss?' asked Harris, who had broken out in a cold sweat of sympathy. *Thank fuck it wasn't me this time* was written all over his face.

'From now on we go full cone of silence. Commissioner's orders. No pillow talk, no front-bar chat, no locker-room banter – no matter how trivial. No exceptions, at all. Not your missus, not your mistress, not your priest. Even the morgue: keep it to absolute essentials only. Jo, you're inside the tent, and Mack's cleared, but otherwise it's sworn police only. That clear?'

Everyone muttered in assent.

'Nguyễn, I'm not holding you personally responsible – it could have been any of you – but this is the last time it happens.'

'Yes, boss. Thank you.'

'After this story breaks tomorrow you'll be quizzed by everyone from the lowest-life fucken gutter-press hack camped in your backyard shithouse to your Uncle Fuck-Knuckle at your next family piss-up. It doesn't matter what they ask you, there is only one right answer and it only has two words. What are they, Janssen?'

'No comment.'

'Correct: no fucken comment. Now back to work, the lot of you. And if you run into the commissioner having brunch this weekend I suggest you try another cafe.' Murphy turned and stalked off to his office.

The detectives all returned to their desks except Nguyễn, who just stood there, mortified.

'I'm going out for a coffee, Liệu,' said Jo. 'You want to come?'

Nguyễn smiled gratefully 'Thanks, mate.' They headed for the stairs.

Friday, 30 November – evening

Sylvia was slicing onions when she heard the front door open and close. 'Hi, Dave!' she sang out. There was no answer. She stopped cutting and stood still, but there was only silence. She had definitely heard the front door, though. She was suddenly aware of how vulnerable she was, and how alone.

She approached the hall cautiously, long knife in hand, and turned into the doorway just as Murphy came through it. They very nearly collided.

'Jesus, Sylvia, what the fuck?' exclaimed Murphy. 'Be careful with that thing!'

'Sorry,' she said, lowering the knife. 'You didn't answer.'

'Who'd you expect it to be?' He stalked into the kitchen and deposited his revolver in its drawer, slamming it shut. He leaned back against the bench, rubbing his temples with his eyes screwed shut.

'I'm sorry, Dave,' she repeated. She set the knife down on the chopping board.

'Sorry's not much help if you disembowel me, is it?'

She decided against asking about his day, going with the old reliable fallback. 'Would you like a drink?'

'I'd fucken love one.' He sighed, taking off his tie.

Sylvia moved to the sideboard and uncorked the Lagavulin. 'Whisky?'

'How about a G&T?'

She swapped the malt for a bottle of Four Pillars and pulled out a glass.

'Have one with me.' His voice had a little gravel in it now.

'I'm good,' she replied. 'I'll have wine with dinner.'

'Not very sociable to let someone drink alone.' It was not a suggestion.

She withdrew another glass, filled both with ice, then free-poured a shot into each, one long and one short. She added the tonic water then went back to the kitchen, where Murphy was still leaning against the bench. 'Why don't you sit down,' she said. 'I'll bring it to you.' She selected a lime from the fruit bowl on the kitchen bench.

'I'm fine here.'

'Excuse me, then.' He moved aside slightly, and she opened the top drawer and reached in for the old paring knife she always used for slicing limes. A long-dead great aunt had introduced Sylvia to gin when she'd visited her in Tasmania the summer she'd finished university. She'd given Sylvia the knife to remember her by.

Her hand found the knife, but before she could pull it out Murphy leaned against the drawer, hard, crushing her fingers above the second knuckle and trapping them there. She cried out in pain, tears springing immediately to her eyes.

'What's up, love?' he asked, eyes front.

'Dave, please,' she whimpered.

Murphy made a show of looking down at her hand in the drawer. 'Oh, how'd you manage that, darlin'?' He pushed off the drawer with a bounce. She opened it with her left hand and extracted the wounded right. There were unhealthy white stripes across the indented flesh, and swollen purple flesh beyond the compression points. 'I bet that smarts,' said Murphy as he cut a wedge of lime for his drink.

Her fingers throbbed visibly, and it hurt to move them even slightly. At least they seemed intact this time, although she could already tell she'd need an X-ray. She concentrated on her breathing, not trusting herself to speak.

'You need to take more care around the kitchen, Sylvia.' Murphy took his glass to the living room. 'They're dangerous places, you know.' He sprawled on the sofa and reached for the remote. 'And you are a bit prone to accidents.' He turned on the television and flicked until he found a grand prix replay.

Sylvia stood still for a few minutes with her back to her husband, her head resting on a cupboard. She ran the tap and found a gentle tepid stream that seemed to help. She held her hand under it until the throbbing subsided and some tactile sensation returned. She remembered her gin and downed it in one go, the warmth spreading across her chest and numbing the pain a little.

Eventually she went back to preparing dinner, holding the knife awkwardly in her left hand, two of its fingers slightly crooked on the handle. The memento of an earlier lesson on the price of resistance.

There'd be no guitar practice for a while. She'd probably have to find another accompanist for the kid's ward Christmas concert. She wondered what she could tell them.

Murphy barely spoke to her for the rest of the evening, other than to order another gin. Then over dinner he drank a bottle of shiraz, less the glass he poured for her, while grizzling about the homicide case, politicians, the Dragons' shithouse season, Sylvia's lack of interest in the concerns that burdened him. Over fruit salad he finished the leavings of a chardonnay in the fridge door, then moved back to the sofa with the first whisky of the night and switched on the news channel. He didn't even notice when Sylvia said goodnight and went to bed.

Tuesday 4 December – afternoon

Murphy was giving Jo a lift home on a classic Sydney scorcher when the traffic lights went amber on Anzac Parade, just past the SCG. He floored it.

'Dave,' said Jo, in their mother's voice. He grumbled but came to a halt.

A wiry character with prison tatts and a squeegee lurched out from beneath a Moreton Bay fig and smeared the windscreen with muddy water.

'He must be fucken ripped to do a cop car,' said Murphy. It was unmarked, but still.

'He's pretty strung-out,' observed Jo. The man's eyes were glassy, and his jerky limbs were on full auto. The damp rollie in the side of his mouth had long gone out.

'Dunno whether to run him in, take him to hospital or give him a couple of bucks,' said Murphy.

'You're not serious...'

'What, about running him in? It's illegal, this routine.'

'At least he's trying. Anyway it's baking out there. Give him a break.'

'I'm not saying I'm gunna, just that I oughta.'

Jo opened Murphy's glovebox. 'Any coin in here?'

'Reginald Scott Southee,' Murphy said, instead of answering.

'Who's that?' Jo lifted out the Holden owner's manual, a Police Force logbook and an abused paperback: Don Winslow, *The Power of the Dog.*

'Your friendly fucked-up window washer.'

'How do you know?' Next came a slab of black polymer that Jo recognised as a spare Glock magazine, full of bullets.

'He's got a record as long as your arm, and my name's on half the arrests. Known him for years. He asks for me whenever he gets collared. Last year I booked him for robbing that servo over there.' Murphy pointed across the intersection. 'Srinivas Aravamudan, nicest man in Sydney. Reg here tried to hold up the one punter soft enough to let him shit in a clean dunny.'

'So he's trying to go straight; you should encourage him.' Jo found a hoard of coins at the back of the glovebox.

Murphy eyed the murky streaks across his windscreen as Southee came around his side. 'You don't call this robbery?' He lowered his window to the fierce heat.

'How ya goin', Sergeant Murphy?'

'All right, Reg?'

'Didn't notice ya till you was already wet.'

'Our secret then, eh, Reg?' Murphy turned to Jo. 'You got that coin, sis?'

Jo picked out five twos and handed them to her brother, who shot her a look over his sunnies. 'Go on, tightarse,' she said. He dropped two into his lap and handed the rest to Southee.

'Thanks, Sarge! I always said you're a top bloke. Don't care what everyone else says.'

Jo laughed out loud, but Murphy just shook his head. 'Do me a favour and leave Srinivas alone, will you?'

'Nah, we're tight as, Sarge. Jes' a misunderstandin'.'

The lights went green. 'Better get off the road, mate.'

'See ya, Sarge!' called Southee as he scampered in front of the car for the shade. Murphy raised his window as they took off.

Jo piled everything back into the glovebox except the novel. 'Don Winslow, eh?'

'Yeah, for surveillance. Those shifts get fucken long.'

'Any good?'

'Oh, shit yeah, you should read it. Only I have to keep back-tracking to pick up the thread. Too long between stakeouts.'

'Have you tried short stories?'

'No, I haven't. Good idea, sis.'

'Try Lydia Davis. Some of hers are really short.'

'How short?'

'A few pages. Some just a page.'

'What's the point? You wouldn't even get going.'

'No, she can pack entire movies in. They're brilliant.'

'Yeah?' Murphy sounded sceptical.

'Or Lucia Berlin, if you want them gritty.'

'She a crime writer?'

'Not exactly. Sort of. You might be surprised.'

Murphy was quiet a couple of beats. 'Not sure we share the same tastes, sis.'

Jo laughed. 'You could be right.' She crammed the novel back into the glovebox as Murphy pulled over in front of a row of shops.

'What's up?'

'Just getting Sylvia some flowers.'

'Oh, aren't you nice?'

'I do me best,' said Murphy. 'Need anything?'

Saturday 15 December – evening

Averse to crowds at the best of times, Porter disliked the city, detested extended-hours shopping and loathed Christmas. Yet here he was, in Anthony Hordern & Sons department store in Pitt Street, doing his late-night, last-minute Christmas shopping.

He had to be insane.

Everyone was abrasive and intemperate, angry to be spending money they didn't have on pointless trinkets for people they didn't even like very much. Adults were abusing their spouses and children; children were annoying their parents and siblings; customers were haranguing the staff; and staff were snapping at their colleagues.

When *Joy to the World* started playing, he found the irony intolerable. He needed a cool shower, a glass of sauternes and a decent sleep before the twelve-hour dayshift to come.

Porter settled on a soft-toy globe for his niece's four-year-old and found a queue feeding two cash registers. He was fourth in line when another shopper stopped to the left of the head of the queue instead of joining its tail. She clearly had designs on the cashier in front of her: her back was ostentatiously turned to the queue, right shoulder angled between them and the cashier. The interloper knew exactly what she was doing, although she was feigning ignorance.

The man in second place leaned over to the newcomer and said, 'Excuse me, there's a queue.' Porter heard him distinctly from two positions back, but there was no visible response from the woman.

'Excuse me?' the man tried again. Still nothing. He turned to the others in the queue, and was encouraged by supporting sighs and eye-rolls. He reached to his left and tapped the interloper lightly on the elbow.

'DO. YOU. MIND?' boomed the woman.

'Yeah, um, there's just the one queue here for both registers,' he said civilly.

'Rubbish.'

'Uh, sorry, but there is. We've all been waiting for some time.' He gestured down the line. The customer in front of him was called forward, promoting him to head of the queue.

'There was no queue for *this* register,' she said.

By now the cashier in front of her was aware of the argument. She looked like she needed a cigarette, a foot-rub and a glass of red wine, instead of an encounter with some wretched sociopath looking to start a brawl. Porter shuddered in sympathy. Hell was other people, all right. Manifestly, Sartre had once worked in customer service.

'You may not have seen the queue, but it was here,' said the man, his voice hardening. 'I'm next in line.'

'You may well be next over *there*,' she insisted, waving to her right. 'I am next *here*.'

'Look, it's just a mistake, no big deal. Just take your—'

'Do *not* tell me what to do; do *not* touch me; do *not* speak to me,' she bellowed.

The outburst was loud enough to stop passing foot-traffic. Anyone could tell at a glance what was going on and who was at fault, yet the newcomer maintained her pretence. Porter felt hackles rising right along the queue. This person was, as they say, a piece of work. The young woman in front of Porter decided to give it a try.

'Look, you can't just push in,' she said to the interloper.

'I am not pushing in,' came the breezy reply. 'I don't know what you people are doing, but I am waiting for That. Girl. There.' She pointed at the exhausted cashier in front, who had just bagged the previous purchase and was waiting for the receipt to print. She looked out at them with a kind of resigned dread.

The new combatant turned to Porter and said, 'Mind my spot,' then stepped out of the line towards the invader. 'Listen, you entitled arsehole,' she hissed with impressive venom. 'You can pretend all you like, but you know fucking well we were here first. We're just as fed up as you, and we all just want to go home. You're not helping. Now get in the line and wait your fucking turn like everyone else.'

The interloper quaked and fumed in her confected fury. In her wrath she became very Brünnhilde, summoning the Teutonic pantheon. The vampire slayer stepped back into line in front of Porter and resumed nonchalantly scrolling on her phone. Porter felt like shaking her by the hand.

Then the cash register on the left became free, and the moment for physical action had arrived. But the fellow in front looked at the quivering intruder, muttered, 'Oh, who cares,' then walked off in search of a demilitarised cashier elsewhere. Porter looked to the heroine in front of him, but the cashier on the right called her forward, and she went over shaking her head.

The monster smiled triumphantly and advanced on her chosen cashier.

Porter stood at the front of the queue, enduring the awkward silence that had descended. At least nobody had appended themselves to the interloper's one-woman queue, innocently or otherwise, to extend the misunderstanding.

The woman who had been in front of Porter only had the one item, so his turn came quickly. While the cashier scanned his gift, he looked across and noticed the interloper berating her poor cashier. He was not surprised – character was always revealed in the treatment of service staff – although the cashier endured, and before long the fiend was on her way.

Porter concluded his own transaction and headed for the elevator, but spied the villain waiting there, so he rode the escalators instead to the third floor and had his present gift-wrapped. He took the elevator back to the ground floor, heading for the exit.

And then fate intervened, as it will when the old gods have been woken from their slumber.

He was weaving between the cosmetic counters, enshrouded in their miasma of sickly musk, when he saw the Valkyrie in deep conference with a sales consultant. Curious and still vexed, he sidled closer. Being both the main thoroughfare of the ground floor and a densely populated retail zone in its own right, the area was a seething crush of ill-tempered, impatient, overburdened shoppers, so neither woman noticed Porter standing a metre away. As the sales consultant turned to retrieve a vessel of the agreed concoction, the malefactor opened her Birkin bag, extracted her purse and withdrew a Hordern's store card.

From beside a Denison Bank credit card.

Well, now, thought Porter. *How about that.*

Not since he'd conceived his entire Tribute had he experienced such a moment of celestial inspiration. The idea didn't develop: it simply manifested, fully formed. It had been there all along, like a tiny orchid in the middle of the desert, waiting to be found.

His Project was presently in need of a female to complete the study of the generative organs for Volume V. And now here she was, volunteering at precisely the crucial moment.

It was her destiny.

Porter observed the transaction, resisting the Brownian motion of the jostling crowd. Just as the target was moving to slide her store card into her purse, he deflected a passing father of two small children into her back with a well-timed bump, causing her to lose her grip on both the purse and any remaining composure. She berated the man mercilessly, while one child wriggled from his grasp and the other started wailing. Apologetically, the man bent to retrieve the purse, but Porter was already there. He palmed the store card and handed the purse to the father, who unwittingly muttered his gratitude to the author of his evening's latest woe. Porter stood up in a spiral motion and navigated to the exit without a backward glance.

Only when he was safely at home did he take the card of Mrs Amber F Darcy from his pocket, then thoroughly washed and dried it before sliding it into a plain white window-envelope.

***

The following day was agony, staying out of Darcy's file until 2pm when his help-desk colleague would depart. He found himself incapable of conversation, despite Nicole's best attempts, and he could not bring himself to read the Sunday papers – not even the breathless updates on his own activities. Compounding matters, the networks were all working properly, so it was unusually quiet for the season. By 1pm he was beside himself, so he gave Nicole an early mark, citing the lull. She offered only token resistance. As soon as he saw her car turn into the traffic, Porter opened Amber Darcy's customer profile to examine the prospects.

Patience, care and scepticism, he kept telling himself.

She had a husband, living at the same address, while their son attended university in Brisbane. The Darcys did most of their banking with the Fort. They'd both spent liberally in the current statement cycle on their joint credit card, although Porter conceded it was the season for it. The husband had a separate credit card in his own name, as well as a savings account in rude health, with both statements being mailed to the office. Reliably a sign of bad behaviour.

Porter found that the husband was presently travelling, having used his solo card the previous afternoon at a lavish new hotel in Fremantle, then at an upscale restaurant nearby. He was booked to return from Perth on the following night's red-eye, landing in Sydney early Tuesday morning. While Porter was in the airline database, he checked the son's travel plans: arriving home next Saturday, just before Christmas.

Son studying in Brisbane; husband philandering in Perth; Mrs Darcy home alone. He could undertake this auxiliary dissection for Volume V the very next day. There would be little time, but the abbreviated work programme rendered it feasible. He found his way into Darcy's email and calendar – to view only, not to amend: with his method of clearing diaries now in the public domain, it would be foolhardy to rearrange her commitments. Fortunately, her next scheduled engagement was a tennis lesson on Tuesday afternoon. His excitement began to build.

Now just settle down, he admonished himself: *this is how people make mistakes.* Using the full array of data sources available to him, he spent the rest of his shift conducting his painstaking due diligence on the candidate and the site.

He established that she would by all indications be alone the following day in a large, well-screened house that sat behind a high wall, well back from the road and far from neighbours and cameras. So it could be done.

But should it be done? He'd be killing her and leaving her husband to find her, a week before Christmas.

Was that bad? he wondered.

Compared to what? he replied.

So that settled it.

He would take her Hordern's card to her house early the next morning, simply a fellow patron of her favourite department store who'd seen some brute barge into her at the cosmetics counter. He had found the card on the ground and deduced it was hers; not trusting the feckless department store staff to see it safely returned, he had taken this task upon himself. He'd found her in the telephone directory, and of course now he recognised her. *You are indeed Amber Darcy? Yes,* she would say; she would be cautiously grateful. Or if not actually grateful then at least gratified. He would pour on the misanthropic scorn, casting himself as the last bastion of a dying chivalric code. When he offered her the charge card, visible through the envelope window, she would open the door: she had to.

The plan wasn't perfect, but it was adequate. He only needed to turn on the charm well enough and long enough for her to flick the latch. Once she'd made that fatal mistake, the rest would ensue.

On his way home from work, Porter reviewed it all from first principles, but in his heart he knew he was going to do it.

And he did, the following day. He dissected Amber Felicity Darcy on her family dining table, the Monday of the week before Christmas.

And he had to admit, as he drove away through the tastefully lowlit streets

of Neutral Bay, he had rather enjoyed
it.

Monday 17 December – afternoon

Fresh from swimming laps at Wylie's Baths, Sylvia crossed quickly to Jo's apartment block to escape the blazing heat. On weekends she always knocked, but on weekdays she just let herself in, since Jo was never home. So Sylvia was as surprised as Jo when she walked in to find her sister-in-law making tea in the kitchen. What was more surprising was that Amy Chartier from the Homicide Squad was sitting on the sofa strumming a guitar. There was a palpable air of relaxed intimacy that stopped Sylvia in her tracks.

'Oh, Sylvia,' said Jo. 'Hi.'

Amy turned and smiled. 'Hey, Sylvia,' she said.

'Amy, hello.' Sylvia looked across at Jo, who hadn't moved a muscle. 'Hi, Jo.'

Then Jo laughed and the mood relaxed. 'Come in, sis.'

Sylvia entered the room and closed the door behind her, setting her beach bag down on the kitchen bench. Amy came over and slid her arm around Jo's waist, erasing any residual doubt.

'Want a cuppa?' Jo asked Sylvia, her eyes sparkling with mischief, her skin glowing with something electric and fresh. She turned her head and kissed Amy's temple.

'I'd love one,' Sylvia said, 'but I'll just grab a shower first.'

Jo nodded. 'No worries.'

Sylvia raised an amused eyebrow at the pair, then headed for the bathroom. She rinsed her swimsuit then soaped up. This was an intriguing development. She must have been wrong about Matthijs, or else it had blown over. But this was obviously doing Jo good. Either way, it was all best kept on the down-low.

Sylvia finished her shower and put on her dry clothes. Back in the living room, she found Jo and Amy on the sofa sipping their teas.

Sylvia grabbed her cup of tea from the bench on the way past and sat on the floor. 'How have you been, Amy?' she asked.

Amy glanced at Jo and stroked her ankle. 'Pretty bloody good, lately. How about you?'

'Yeah, all right,' replied Sylvia. 'Aren't you two supposed to be at Surry Hills?'

'I'm on my academic day,' said Jo. 'But my office at uni has no air conditioning so I'm better off at home. There'd be nobody there to miss me, anyway.'

'Getting lots of research done then, Dr King?'

Jo stuck her tongue out but didn't attempt to defend herself.

'And I'm taking a day in lieu for working on Labour Day,' said Amy. 'It's all legit.'

'Although we'd rather you didn't mention it,' added Jo.

'Yeah, no, I'd assumed that,' said Sylvia. 'Don't worry; not a soul.' She hesitated. 'But I will say how well this suits you both.'

Jo returned her smile lovingly. 'Thanks, Sylv. That means a lot to me.'

She stroked Amy's arm. 'This one is taking very good care of me.'

'That's the way it should be.' Sylvia cleared her throat and sat upright. She couldn't afford to think too much about that sort of thing right now. 'Have you been playing guitar long?' she asked Amy.

'No, I'm still learning, really.'

'Me too,' said Sylvia.

'That's such bullshit,' said Jo. 'Sylvia is performance-standard,' she told Amy, while Sylvia shook her head. 'She's had paid gigs and all.'

'That's awesome! Whereabouts?'

'Oh god, I was pretty ordinary,' said Sylvia. 'I had a residency at the Tilbury, year before last.'

'You were not ordinary!' said Jo. 'You were a bit nervous at the start, but once you relaxed you were terrific. Your last two shows were packed out.'

'Anyway they shut it down after me,' said Sylvia wryly.

'That was the noise complaints!' Jo shook her head and laughed.

'Have you considered doing it again?' Amy asked Sylvia.

'I have, but it's pretty nerve-wracking. I'd need to practise a lot more first.'

'You should, though, you're a natural,' said Jo.

'Maybe,' said Sylvia. Radiography had been positive but the persistent throbbing in the bruised fingers of her right hand told her it would be another week or two before she'd pick up a guitar. She looked at Jo's kitchen clock. 'I'd better get going, I have some errands to run.' She got to her feet and scooped up her bag.

The other two stood as well. 'Thanks for being so lovely, Sylv,' said Jo as she hugged her. 'You're the best.'

'It's nice to see you so happy, sis.' She gave Jo an extra squeeze, then turned to give Amy a light hug. 'Welcome to the family, Amy. Or half of it, anyway.'

'Might be best left at that for now,' said Jo.

'I reckon you're right,' Sylvia replied, opening the door. 'But I'm glad to be in the picture. I hope we can hang out.'

'Yeah, I'd like that,' said Amy.

'Hey, let's all go to the Ladies' Baths,' said Jo, her arm around Amy. 'One day over the holidays when we're all not working.'

'That'd be great,' said Sylvia. 'Have fun!'

Jo smiled. 'Oh, we will,' she said as Sylvia closed the door.

Tuesday 18 December – morning

The twelve-seat dining table in Neutral Bay was an elaborate mahogany antique with the aura of an heirloom piece, although this was probably the end of the line, with all the fluids from the owner's corpse ruining the finish.

'Who is she, Mack?' asked Murphy. He'd brought the whole squad with him today, plus Jo. It was well past time for all hands on deck.

'Amber Felicity Darcy. Passport in the bedside table checks out. Fifty-four, married with one, husband found her when he returned from a business trip.'

'Looks like you got your sex-type thing, boss,' said Harris, bent over the table inspecting the crater where her pelvis used to be. He pulled back and shook his head. 'That's seriously fucked up.'

'No, I don't think it is like that, actually,' said Mack. 'This is strictly the lady version of the bollocking at Roseville. Wouldn't you say, Jo?'

Jo summoned to mind Hazlitt's observation that technical interest overcomes repugnance even at the sight of a maimed corpse, and looked again at the remains with an analytical eye. With the exception of a thoroughly dissected left breast, the rest of the body had been disturbed only to the extent necessary to gain access to the reproductive organs. The killer had removed these and dissected them in detail at the other end of the long table.

'Yes, this is a straight dissection of the female reproductive organs,' she confirmed. 'Volume Five, Chapters Fifteen and Eighteen: the uterus and other female organs, and the breasts.'

'Not Sixteen and Seventeen?' asked Janssen.

'I'll defer to Mack, but I'm guessing the pregnancy chapters don't apply.'

'No, you're right, Jo. She was most likely beyond that, anyway.'

'So no violation, then?' asked Harris.

Mack shook his head. 'There's no foreign material, he's proceeded in his customary orderly fashion and he's shown the genitals a strictly professional anatomical interest.'

'You call this orderly?' asked Murphy sceptically, looking at the pile of organs and the jagged cuts on the body. 'Professional?'

'I'll grant you it's untidier than the last few. But I've seen plenty of dissections and plenty of sex murders, Spud. Believe me, I know the difference.'

'Fair enough, just asking.'

'Bloody methodical with that book,' said Nikolaidis. 'He's a machine.'

'Two volumes to go, isn't it?' asked Nguyễn.

Mack nodded. 'Heart and brain.'

Chartier groaned softly.

'There will not be two more,' said Murphy in a low, hard, even voice. 'We're going to fucking catch him.'

'It's strange he's left everything else alone and stuck strictly to the gynaecology,' said Jo.

'Makes sense, if he's just scoping out the new stuff,' said Nguyễn.

'Yeah, it's methodical and all, but I wonder if it's to do with time,' Mack said. 'He's just left it as is, instead of arranging things for us like he'd been doing recently.'

'As though the full-time siren went,' said Nikolaidis.

'How long do you think this would've taken?' Chartier asked Mack.

'Nothing like the others,' said Mack. 'A day, maybe? Less?'

'Why choose a post-menopausal woman for female reproductive organs?' asked Harris. 'Seems odd to me.'

'Good point,' added Murphy.

'No, the organs don't change much, anatomically,' said Mack.

'But did Vesalius know that?' asked Nikolaidis.

'Fair question.' Mack looked at Jo.

'Vesalius's specimens seemed to be of child-bearing age, like his dissection of the lactating breast,' she said. 'But he makes no comparative remarks to distinguish pre- and post-menopausal characteristics.'

'Which he would have, if he'd had the chance,' added Mack.

'Definitely,' said Jo. 'He commented on everything he saw with his own eyes.'

'Nah, but Harris is right,' insisted Murphy. 'If you want to inspect the reproductive system, surely you'd use a viable one.'

'By that logic, our killer should go for a pregnant woman,' said Chartier.

'Ah, well, Vesalius never managed to dissect the pregnant uterus,' said Jo. 'That would be a big departure from the program.'

'Perhaps he was avoiding another physical struggle with a fit young woman,' suggested Janssen.

'So no presents for us this time, Mack?' asked Chartier.

'There is, Amy, as it happens,' said Mack, leading them across the lounge room to the fireplace. 'When I said he just packed up and left, that wasn't entirely true. He did leave us one little gift.' He indicated a glass of greenish liquid on the mantelpiece.

'Looks like chartreuse,' said Janssen.

'Too viscous,' said Mack. 'And by the whiff, a little too organic.'

'What do you think it is?' asked Murphy.

'Obviously we'll test it, but my guess is it's another bit of character assessment.'

'Oh, god,' said Chartier. 'It's not bile?'

Mack nodded. 'He's milked the gall bladder.'

'Good fuck,' said Murphy.

They were each quietly processing this choice detail when a telephone shrilled, and everybody jumped. They all turned to the cordless handset on a side-table.

'You answer,' Murphy told Chartier. 'Be her.' He nodded at the corpse.

Chartier held the handset out so the others could hear. 'Hello?'

'Good morning, may I speak with Mrs Amber Darcy, please?'

'What is it regarding?'

'It's Jen from Anthony Hordern & Sons department store, Mrs Darcy, in Pitt Street. You spoke with Annabelle on Sunday about your lost Hordern's card?'

'Oh, yes?'

'I'm afraid we've been unable to track it down, Mrs Darcy.'

'Right...'

'So it's Hordern's policy to cancel a lost card immediately. I can organise—'

Murphy took the phone from Chartier's hand. 'Jen, is it?'

'Oh. Yes. Who is this, please?'

'Jen, this is Detective Senior Sergeant David Murphy of the New South Wales Police State Crime Command Homicide Squad. I'd like a word with your supervisor, please.'

Tuesday 18 December – afternoon

Two hours later, Murphy and Chartier were with the head of security at Anthony Hordern & Sons. Graeme Archer was an ex-cop who'd moved into the private sector for twice the salary, half the stress and one-tenth the risk.

'Bloody hell, Archie, is that the best you can do?' asked Murphy.

They were looking at grainy black-and-white security footage of a woman standing at the cosmetics counter. The picture was shithouse. Murphy couldn't believe the contrast with the video from his high definition spy cameras at home.

'How do you even know that's Amber Darcy?'

'Time stamp,' said Archer. 'And that's Taasha, serving her.'

'Come off it, there's no way you can recognise that cashier.'

'You would if you'd seen her in the flesh, mate. She's a little hottie.' He looked at Chartier. 'Sorry.'

'Just play the collision again, please,' said Chartier.

Archer started the video. A man with two children approached Darcy just as she was putting her store card away. He bumped into her, knocking her purse to the ground. He bent over, surfaced with the purse and handed it to her. He paused to apologise, but his children escaped and he took off after them.

'That's the moment, but it's the weirdest snatch I've ever seen,' said Murphy. 'Two kids under five to slow him down, then he hangs around to cop a mouthful. Not exactly a criminal mastermind, is he?'

'Is there a better image of him later?' asked Chartier.

Archer called up some footage from adjacent cameras, but the quality was so poor the man might've been anyone from Pope Francis to Humphrey B Bear.

'I dunno,' said Murphy. 'It doesn't add up, does it?'

'What about her other transactions?' asked Chartier. 'Can we look at them?'

'What's the point?' asked Archer. 'She still had her card at cosmetics.'

This is vintage Archie, thought Murphy. *Why go nine yards when four will do?* 'Just roll them, will you, mate?'

Archer brought up the kitchen appliances department, but it added nothing. Next he cued the toy department, with Darcy standing alongside a line of customers, obviously intending to cut in. She managed it, too, after a dispute with those in the queue.

'That would have pissed them off,' said Murphy.

'That's Erin who's served her,' said Archer as Darcy completed her transaction and left. He stopped the video.

'No, keep going,' said Chartier. Archer hit play again. 'Go back to when she shows up, then play it through.' Archer complied. 'Stop,' she said after Darcy left the frame. Chartier pointed to a figure at the adjacent cashier, who'd been in the queue during the argument. 'This man was down at the cosmetics counter,' she said.

Archer didn't need any further instructions. He ran the cosmetics footage from the beginning in another window. A figure they hadn't noticed earlier was hovering near Darcy and Taasha during their discussion.

'Fuck me, you're right,' said Murphy. They couldn't make out any features, but it was definitely toy-counter guy. He made brief contact with the father just before he knocked into Amber Darcy.

'He's given the dad a nudge,' whispered Murphy. They watched both men go down to retrieve the spilled items; the father came up with the purse, while toy-counter guy stood, turned and headed for the doors.

'He's stolen her card right there,' said Chartier.

'For sure,' said Archer.

'Faaaark!' groaned Murphy in anguish. 'We fucken had him! Where do you buy your security kit, Arch? Fucken Vinnies?'

'Mate.'

'This is the halfest-arsed setup I've ever seen. And I work for the government.'

'Believe me, I know,' said Archer. 'I take this into court and the magistrates want to put *me* away instead.'

'Are all the stores like this?' asked Chartier.

'Nah, course not. Pitt Street's last on the upgrade rollout. Fucken Launceston's high def is so good they can probably tell people's eye colour. But the profit forecast threatened the executive bonuses, so there's a freeze on expenditure. Probably wiping their own arses up on the top floor, poor dears. We're all doing our bit.'

Murphy pushed his seat back. 'I sympathise with you, Archie, I do. But that's no fucken help, is it? We have the killer of six citizens right there on camera!'

'Come on, Spud. It's not that bad.'

'Arch, this prick has been invisible so far, then we get him on fucken video and it's about as useful as a cave painting!'

'At least you know he's white and male. Probably middle-aged.'

'Practically every serial killer in the entire fucken history of serial killing has been white, male and fucken middle-aged.'

Archer shrugged. 'Now you know for sure.'

Murphy sighed lengthily. He was not to be mollified.

'Here's your MacGuffin, anyway,' Chartier told him.

'What, he takes the card round her place, talks his way in?'

'Yeah, I reckon. Explains how he's getting inside.'

'Can't see this working six times, though, can you? Picking their pockets?'

'Yeah, I don't like that bit,' she admitted. 'Way too risky.'

'You would have seen this before, if he'd been pulling this caper all along,' chimed in Archer.

At the interjection, the two sworn officers realised they'd been thinking aloud in front of an outsider. Ex-cop, but still.

'Keep all this quiet will you, Arch?' asked Murphy. 'I can't afford another leak.'

'Yeah, I saw the fingerprint thing on the news.' Archer chortled. 'You must have copped some shit over that.'

Murphy smiled grimly. 'I could do without a repeat.'

'I won't breathe a word, Spud.'

'Could you make us a copy?'

'No worries. I'll bring it over myself.'

'We're going to need to interview those two cashiers,' said Chartier.

'And the one who served our man,' added Murphy.

'Young Andrea. I'll line it up.'

'Thanks for this, Archie. It's a big help,' said Murphy. 'Sorry for being shitty.'

'It's all right, Spud. I understand.'

'How's the festy season going, anyway?' Murphy asked.

'Same as always. I fucken hate Christmas.'

'It's not that bad.'

'Spud, you got no idea. Being a cop was bad enough, but retail crushes your faith in human nature. This industry would turn the Dalai Lama into Vlad the Impaler.'

Wednesday 19 December – morning

Chartier and Murphy had just finished filling in the squad on the Hordern's tapes. They passed around someone's homemade shortbread.

'This is great, but it doesn't get us anywhere,' said Nikolaidis.

'Are you kidding, Angelo?' said Jo. 'He got himself caught on camera!'

'My old Commodore 64 had better resolution than that crap,' he said, waving at the blurry stills on the incident board from atop his grey steel throne. 'It's completely useless.'

'But we have a method,' added Harris. 'That's a huge lead.'

'No, it's an aberration,' said Murphy. 'London to a brick it's not his usual MO.'

'Why do you say that?' Harris asked.

'There's no way he's doing this every time; we'd know about it for sure.'

'But we only know about it by coincidence, because Hordern's rang,' said Jo. 'He was just unlucky this time.'

'That wasn't a coincidence,' said Chartier. 'They rang because he took her card.'

'Everything gets to us sooner or later,' said Murphy, dunking his biscuit in his tea.

'And there's been nothing like this for the others,' said Nikolaidis.

'So far,' persisted Harris. 'It could still come in.'

'Glebe was eight months and six bodies ago, Harris,' said Murphy through a mouthful of sodden shortbread. He paused to swallow. 'If he was routinely knocking off credit cards in department stores we'd have been onto it ages ago.'

'Yes, he's much more methodical than this,' added Nguyễn.

'That's the real lesson here,' said Janssen. 'This is quite unsophisticated.'

'You're right, Thijs,' said Jo. 'If he's changed, why has he changed?'

'Letting emotions come into it,' suggested Chartier. 'That argument in the queue.'

'The cold, rational planner getting hot-headed,' Nikolaidis said.

'That's when people make mistakes,' said Murphy. 'They lose their finesse.'

'The emotions are not skilled workers,' Jo said.

'I agree the snatch is an anomaly, but I like the entry method for the other victims,' said Janssen. 'Showing up with something they want, getting them to open the door, maybe let him in.'

'It fits,' said Nikolaidis. 'The lift may be clunky but the entry is slick.'

'What else might he have that they want?' asked Janssen.

'A telegram?' suggested Murphy.

'There are no telegrams anymore, van Winkle,' said Jo.

'Really? When did that happen?'

'Only about a decade ago.' She shook her head.

'Well, bugger me. End of an era.' He reached for another biscuit.

'Online shopping?' asked Nguyễn. 'Food, books, technology, something like that.'

'No, we've gone through every single transaction,' said Nikolaidis, his boot heel clunking against the steel in emphasis. 'There's nothing unaccounted for.'

'What about flowers?' suggested Jo. 'You don't order them yourself.'

'They've been mostly men, so I'm not sure about flowers,' said Murphy. 'But I like the idea of transactions the vics don't initiate.'

'It doesn't even have to be real, just plausible,' said Chartier. 'Enough to open the door. To check an order docket, say.'

'Maybe, like a fake delivery error?' Harris suggested.

'What if he's mixing it up,' said Janssen, 'tailoring his approaches?'

'If he's following them around like he did with Amber Darcy, working out his best angle, then there's bound to be more footage,' Nikolaidis said.

'Yeah, that's good,' said Murphy. 'Let's see what CCTV we can get in the days leading up. We haven't really looked into a stalker angle yet.'

Nikolaidis grunted in approval. It would be labour intensive, but it was action. 'We're already getting the city council footage near Hordern's on Saturday night.'

'Let's do the same on all the others, too, going back,' said Janssen. He drained his coffee and stood up from his chair.

'We'll need more uniforms,' said Nikolaidis. 'That's a lot of hack work.'

'I'll talk to the commissioner; it won't be a problem,' said Murphy.

'Did the others have Hordern's cards?' asked Nguyễn, trying another angle.

'Only Newman, from memory,' said Harris. 'But Darcy had a Denison Bank card. And Qantas, and NRMA.'

'Six from six is starting to feel relevant,' said Chartier.

The cops all looked at Jo. She blinked at them. 'What?'

'What are the odds up to, sis?' Murphy asked.

'Oh. I don't know. Hang on.' Jo moved to Chartier's desk nearby and sat down to work it out on paper. She looked up after a couple of minutes, calculations in hand. 'Based on rough market share there's still a twenty-six per cent chance of all six being NRMA members, so forget that. The Fort's at twelve, but Qantas frequent flyers is down to six.'

'Maybe they were all on a flight together once,' suggested Harris.

'Jesus, spare me the Agatha Christie!' said Murphy. 'Fucken – no, Harris.'

Harris hung his head and shrunk a little. Jo passed him the biscuit tin with a smile. He rummaged beneath the shortbread and extracted two Anzac biscuits.

'Anyway there's nothing there with the airline,' said Nikolaidis. 'We've checked and checked again.'

'What if it's the combination?' asked Chartier.

'How do you mean?' asked Nguyễn.

'If the numbers are tightening on each one, what's that mean for the whole set?'

Jo nodded. 'You're right, Amy, but it just narrows it to the affluent, mobile, well-established – people like that.'

'We already know they're all loaded,' said Janssen.

'That's why things like Qantas are not random,' said Jo. 'They're all well-off, they'll all be frequent flyers.'

Murphy had been standing beside Chartier's desk, off with the pixies and gazing sightlessly at the promo shot from *The Wire.* He eventually came back to himself and focused on the caption. '*What would Lester Freamon do?*' he read aloud. 'Damn.'

'What's that, Dave?' asked Jo.

Murphy seemed to come to a decision. 'Fuck it.' He patted his pockets and pulled out his keys. 'Never mind,' he answered Jo. 'I'm going out.'

'Where to?'

'Follow up this commercial angle,' he said, heading for his office.

'Want some company?' asked Janssen.

'No, I'm good.' He grabbed his jacket and was out the door. The others shrugged and moved off to their desks.

Jo stood to give Amy back her chair. 'So what *would* Lester Freamon do?' She'd never watched *The Wire.*

'He'd install an illegal wiretap and nearly get himself killed.'

'Not encouraging,' said Jo. 'Did he bust his gangster, at least?'

'He did, but then his gangster walked. And everyone got fired.'

Sunday 23 December – morning

Jo woke from a deep sleep in a disorienting rush. She opened her eyes and listened intently: a truck was reversing down near the beach, but inside the flat the only sound was her own pounding heart.

She pulled on a long T-shirt and opened her door carefully. Nothing. She crept across the squeaky hallway floorboards to the living room. Empty. But something was definitely off, some weird ripple in the background radiation. She shivered, despite the clammy heat.

Maybe it was the accumulated weight of all the horror getting to her. The truncated lives, the sundered bodies. Or maybe it was the memory of the unadorned, depthless grief of Amber Darcy's son, with whom Jo had spent a wrenching hour after his formal police interview on Friday, until he felt able to go outside again. That poor, inconsolable boy. It would surely be dysfunctional of her *not* to freak out.

Or maybe it was just early and she needed a coffee. 'Oh, fuck it,' she said aloud, consciously shaking it off. Then she turned to her espresso machine and found a note:

Hey Jo
crashing here tonight
hope you don't mind?
See you at brekkie

S xx

It had been a delayed reaction, then. Great survival instincts, Buffy. Had Sylvia been an intruder, Jo might've been dead for hours before realising it.

She padded along the hall to her studio and opened the door. Sylvia was sleeping soundly on the guest bed, a couple of stalled paintings on easels behind her: Lizzie Schebesta and Joel Edgerton making shadow-puppets on the set of *Felony;* Rose Byrne and Heath Ledger drinking steaming mugs of tea on the *Two Hands* shoot. Jo really needed to finish those paintings.

She left her sister-in-law to sleep. While closing the door, she spotted a large pink rubber wedge beneath the apartment's back door. She bent down and retrieved it. Jo owned the same item in yellow but had never seen this one before. She took it to the kitchen and placed it on the counter, then glanced at her front door – but there was nothing chocking it. Jo couldn't work out why Sylvia would want to fortify her flat in the first place, but it made even less sense to barricade only the one door.

Jo turned to make her coffee and became absorbed in the routine. Once she was done, she stood at the counter nursing her flat white, looking through the balcony doors, over the treetops to the glittering sea beyond. Then it came to her:

Murphy.

Sylvia and Murphy had a full set of keys to Jo's flat. Sylvia kept the front-door keys with her Wylie's tag, so she could shower at the apartment after a swim. But Jo's spare back-door key lived on Murphy's keyring.

Sylvia was barricading Jo's apartment against her own husband.

Just then, Jo heard her sister coming up the hall and tried to figure out how to play it. But first, espresso.

'Morning, hun,' said Jo, turning to make Sylvia's coffee. 'How are you?'

'Morning, Jo. Sorry if I disturbed you last night.'

'Didn't hear a thing.'

'Thanks for letting me crash.'

'Any time.' Jo glanced over as she filled the basket with ground coffee. 'Is everything okay, Sylv?'

'We just had an argument. I couldn't stand the sight of him.'

Jo waited for more, but Sylvia looked away and kept her silence. Jo finished making the coffee and handed it to her sister-in-law.

'Ah, that's good,' said Sylvia, inhaling the coffee aroma and forcing a smile.

Jo gestured with her mug towards the pink door wedge on the end of the counter. Sylvia blushed.

'Are you all right, love?' asked Jo, her voice softening.

Sylvia nodded and tried to smile, but couldn't quite make it work. She looked down and shook her head slightly.

Jo put her mug down and took Sylvia in her arms. She held her friend as Sylvia breathed deeply and wiped her eyes. Sylvia pulled back and shook her head again. 'It's nothing, I'm fine.'

'Come on, Sylv.'

'I'm just being melodramatic.'

'I doubt that. You're the most collected person I know.' She let the silence hang for a moment, weighing her next words carefully. 'Sylvia. Did Murphy hit you?'

'No, nothing like that.'

'Did he threaten you?'

'No.'

Another pause. 'Has he ever hit you, sis?'

'Of course not,' said Sylvia quickly, shaking her head. She was silent a moment, then looked up. 'Why? Has he ever hit you?'

Jo paused a moment, not expecting the question. 'Only once, when we were kids. Mum was totally strict on that. There was pinching and hair-pulling, but nothing serious – apart from that one time.' Jo hesitated, then added, 'But I always thought he could. And he got more intense as he got older. Kind of ... ominous.'

'I know what you mean.'

'He'd look at me with this cold eye, like he didn't even know who I was. Scared the shit out of me.'

'Like he's the hunter and you're the kangaroo.'

'Exactly! How do you live with it? I was so relieved when he left for the Academy.'

'It's not often. I've learned how to avoid it, mostly.'

Mostly. 'Still...' Jo said.

'Anyway, it's good to know it's not just me.'

'What do you mean?'

'He says it's my fault. Says I bring it out in him.'

'Oh, it's not you, honey, he's always been a deadshit. Honestly, I don't know what you see in him.'

'Come on, Jo, he's your brother.'

'Yeah, well, there wasn't much sweetness and light growing up, I can tell you,' said Jo. 'He didn't have to hit me to make me pay.'

Sylvia nodded grimly. 'I know it.'

'You can't live that way, Sylv. It isn't healthy.'

Sylvia looked up. 'But he's not always like that. He looks after me; he makes me laugh. We have a good time.'

'Do you, though? Still?'

Sylvia shrugged. 'He's under a lot of pressure right now. With the case.'

'It doesn't matter, he's meant to be on your side.'

'It's not so bad. We just need some clear air. Maybe we can get away once the case is finished.'

'Why didn't you tell me, Sylvia? I know you two fight, but I had no idea it was like this.'

Sylvia frowned. 'It's complicated. You're his sister.'

'Fuck that. Don't even get me started. I'm always here for you.'

Sylvia smiled. 'Thanks, Jo.'

'Stay tonight, at least?'

'No, I need to work it out with him.'

Jo was unconvinced, but didn't want to press. 'Okay. But this door is always open to you, no questions asked.'

'Really?'

'Of course.'

'No questions asked?'

Jo blushed at that. 'Fair enough. I'm sorry for the inquisition. You can tell me anything you want, but you never have to explain yourself to me. I promise.'

Sylvia reached for Jo and hugged her. 'Thanks, sis.'

'And I'll get my back-door key back.'

'No, please don't. Who knows how he'd react. You know how he is.'

'Yeah, I do,' said Jo. 'The prick.'

Sylvia's grim frown turned into a cheeky grin. 'Anyway, what's going on with *you?* I need to know.'

Jo laughed and waved her hand. 'It's just an easy thing with Amy, that's all.'

Sylvia gave her a dramatically raised eyebrow. 'That is not all, Joanna, and you know it. What about Matthijs?'

'What about him?'

'Oh, come on. Bringing you "documents" in the evening then driving Dave to work next morning?'

Jo groaned. 'Oh god, don't tell me he knows.'

'No, he's oblivious. But I can still add two and two.'

'Okay, so Thijs and I *rekindled,* you could call it, once I started with the squad. I was just keeping it low key.'

'But then Amy swept you away? Poor Matthijs!'

'Weeeell...' Jo smiled on one side of her mouth. 'Not exactly.'

The penny teetered, then dropped. 'What, both of them?' asked Sylvia, then gasped at a further thought. 'Not together?'

'Ah, no. Definitely not.' Jo laughed. 'Strictly in parallel.'

'Oh.' Sylvia looked relieved and disappointed in equal measure. 'Do they know?'

'They each know there's someone else, but not who. It's all fine.'

'Bloody hell, that must be fraught.'

'It's not, actually. It's pretty informal. They're both cool about it.'

'Keeps you busy, though, I bet.'

'Yeah, finding time for myself turns out to be the main challenge. Besides feeling a little guilty.'

'Why? You're not hurting anybody.'

'I know, but it's like I'm getting away with something.'

'Nah, bugger that, good on you. It's about time someone had it all her own way.'

Jo laughed ruefully. 'I guess thirteen years with the nuns have left their mark.'

'Well, enjoy it while you can,' Sylvia said. 'One's more than enough for me, but I can see why you like them both. I hope it works out.'

'Thanks, hun.' Jo shelved discussion about what 'working out' might mean. Another time.

Sylvia glanced at the clock. 'I should get going. I have an early.'

'You first in the shower,' said Jo.

'That's all right, I'll go home.'

'You sure that's a good idea?'

'He'll be sleeping in. Anyway, my uniform's there.' Sylvia put her cup in the dishwasher. 'Thanks for everything, Jo. I don't know what I'd do without you.'

'Well, you don't have to do without me.'

'I know.'

'Don't imagine for a second I'd back him over you. You're the best thing about that bloke by a country mile.'

'Thanks, Jo.' Sylvia stepped in and gave her a long hug. 'When do you leave?'

'First thing tomorrow.' Jo was going to Hobart for Christmas with Amy's family, then they would be motoring around Tasmania for a while.

'I won't see you then – I've got a double today. Have a great time, won't you?'

'We will,' said Jo. 'I hope Christmas is all right.'

'It'll be fine.' Sylvia kissed Jo on the cheek. 'I'm really happy for you, Jo.'

'Thanks, Sylv. Call me, okay? And remember, *mi casa, su casa.*'

Sylvia grabbed the pink wedge and went through the front door, waving before pulling it closed.

Jo leaned against the counter and listened to Sylvia descend the stairwell until the lobby door clicked shut below, then let out a breath she hadn't realised she'd been holding. She shook her head.

That fucking bastard.

Monday 31 December

Sylvia and Murphy had a long Christmas lunch at Rocky and Cath's, eating like Romans and knocking over half a dozen bottles of wine between the four of them, so they left the car there and walked home. On Boxing Day, Murphy retrieved the car and met a bunch of old cop mates at the Watsons Bay pub to drink their body weights in New while waiting for the Sydney to Hobart yacht race to start. Sylvia was watching the fleet from the Ladies' Baths when Murphy rang from the Watto, sunstruck and way too pissed to drive. She took a taxi over and drove him home, where he fell asleep on the sofa watching Australia pile on the runs at the MCG. He was still there when the Test concluded four days later, with Australia mowing down a demoralised English tail.

New Year's Eve began heavy and sultry, the low leaden clouds roiling impatiently, the air damply electric. The morning light was the unpleasant yellowy-violet of a tender bruise; the greenish sea choppy and restless; the wind squally and menacing. The tension built through the afternoon, the intense weather holding, waiting, summoning its forces.

Murphy drove to the Domain at noon, where he stood for a while in front of his father's name on the Police Wall of Remembrance. He grabbed a bagel at Paradise Lox across from the station then tidied up some paperwork in the office. Around six, he headed to the Glenmore for beers and a counter meal ahead of the night shift. The New Year's Eve gig in The Rocks was the state's largest single police patrol operation after the Bathurst touring car race in October. In these politically correct times it presented a rare legal opportunity to let off steam, old-school, upon the city's most deserving. Murphy hadn't missed it in years.

Sylvia went to Jo's place late in the morning to water the plants and ran into Jade from next door, the apartment block's resident green thumb. The women ate lunch at Industry Beans then considered swimming some laps at Wylie's, but the conditions were ominous, so instead they took the low road and retreated to Jade's balcony with a bottle of sav blanc and a wedge of French cheese. Sylvia just had the one glass of wine, since she would be heading in later for Emergency's biggest night of the year.

Mid-morning, Jo and Amy hiked over the saddle in the Hazards, the granite spine of the Freycinet Peninsula, and spent a few hours at Wineglass Bay, swimming and dozing under a clear blue sky. After lunch they crossed the low isthmus to a long, deserted beach on Promise Bay. They skinny-dipped for a while until a yacht came over for a look, then quickly dressed and hiked back to Amy's brother's car, which they drove to their hotel in Swansea. They ate in the front bar and kicked on with the locals, until a pair of Bicheno boys commenced their spade-work in earnest. Jo and Amy excused themselves to the bathroom and ran laughing up the back stairs to the sanctuary of their room.

In the late afternoon Matthijs returned from Adelaide, where he'd spent Christmas with old family friends. He changed into a uniform and strolled down to Bondi Beach for his crowd-control shift.

Porter drove to the art gallery at midday to admire François Sallé's *Anatomy Class at the École des Beaux-Arts.* He paused before *The Sons of Clovis* on his way out, then went home for a short run and a light supper. He listened to *Die Walküre* over a glass of Roederer, to mark the birthday he shared with his ancestor, Andreas Vesalius. Then he drove beneath churning clouds to the Denison Bank computer centre. He always volunteered to cover the New Year's Eve shift so his colleagues could go out and celebrate. The festivities held no attraction for him.

He wasn't really a people person.

VOLUME VI

THE HEART AND ASSOCIATED ORGANS

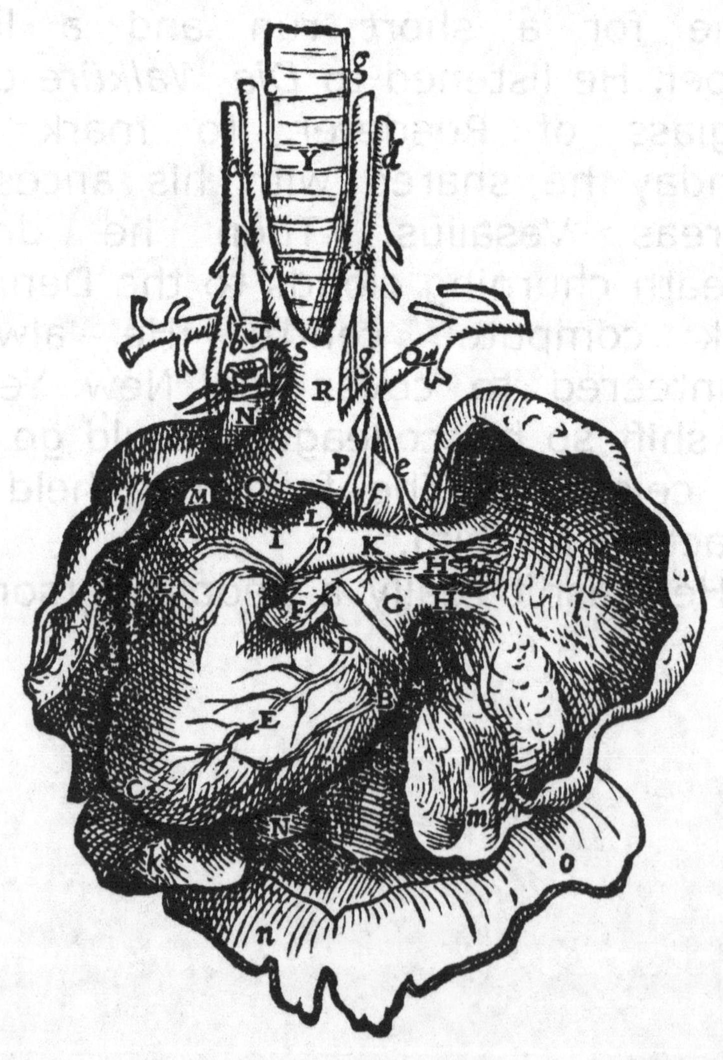

Vesalius was the victim of a vicious slander at the Imperial Court, circulated after his embarkation on a pilgrimage to the Holy Land. The gossip held that Vesalius had been compelled by Philip II of Spain to undertake the pilgrimage in lieu of a death sentence, imposed by the Inquisition for dissecting the body of a Spanish nobleman before the heart had ceased beating. Historians have long since discredited this slur as a fiction. The story is now considered an invention of the diplomat Hubert Languet, created for tactical advantage in court politics.

In his magisterial Volume VI, the Master penetrates the chest in an orderly progression, proceeding methodically through the diaphragm, the membranes of the thorax and the lungs. Not until Chapter X does the Master address 'the substance of the heart', spending four chapters enumerating its constituent parts. The penultimate chapter, on the function of the vascular-pulmonary complex and its relation to structure, is a mighty corrective to centuries of intellectual error.

After extensive investigation, Vesalius broke with Galen over the question of the interventricular septum. Galen had asserted the existence of apertures in the ventricles' common wall to account for the blood flow, but in his second edition of the *Fabrica* in 1555, Vesalius demonstrated conclusively that the wall was impermeable. Searching for an alternative explanation for the flow, he described and named the mitral valve that regulates the current between the left atrium and ventricle.

But it is the final chapter, on the 'method of dissecting the heart, lungs, and other organs serving respiration', that is most revealing of Vesalius's temperament. For thoracic dissection is a messy business, and a brutal one. It is impossible to divide the thoracic cage without assuming the bearing of a common butcher.

Vesalius understands that while his readers are scientists, we are also human beings, all too aware of the hearts beating within our own timid bosoms. He guides his dissection in disinterested but never indifferent scientific objectivity. His detachment is neither sentimental nor callous: he is true to his method and his intellectual commitments, without alienating his new audience for anatomical knowledge.

Vesalius famously proposed the brain as the seat of intelligence and sentiment, rather than the heart. Asked to nominate the seat of the human soul, Vesalius contemplated the merits, but found the matter beyond empirical observation. Under the theocratic conditions then prevailing, he found it politic to leave the question open.

Sunday 6 January – afternoon

Sylvia looked up to find the concrete wall rushing at her, too fast and too close. She pulled out of the stroke and feathered her hands, bleeding off speed then rolling into a flying tumble. She kicked off the rough concrete and powered through the salt water on another lap. She'd lost count after twenty-four. That was a while ago.

She caught a glimpse of the lap clock. She was still averaging just under her old record after smashing it in the first lap. She was in good shape, but not that good – it was all agitation driving her today. She glided to the wall and pulled up, panting hard. This wasn't working.

She left the pool and rubbed down briskly, catching a few men eyeing her off without any attempt at subtlety. Was a little discretion so much to ask? She decided to leave before someone really ticked her off.

Wrapping the Turkish towel around her waist, she climbed the stairs and left the baths, heading down the hill for Jo's place. She'd take a shower, water the plants – Jo and Amy were still in Tassie – and have a glass of wine on the balcony. Oh – no, not wine. Tea, then. And she'd figure out what the fuck to do.

But when she came to the Ladies' Baths, she turned in there on impulse instead. Still pissed off with the pervs at Wylie's, she wanted to reclaim her right to enjoy sun and salt water without male evaluation. She settled on a slope of lawn she and Jo called the grassy knoll, which sat above the wooden steps leading down to the western side of the pool. A deep sorrow welled within her as she surveyed Wedding Cake Island, a view that had sustained her for years. She blinked away tears and put aside her grief for what was lost. It was time now to focus on what was to come.

Sylvia had been slow to identify the gusts of nausea, the weird corporeality, the tenderness in her breasts. Her period was a bit late, but that was not unusual under stress, and feeling ordinary around Christmas-time was no rarity. The plain facts were that her husband had been sterilised years ago, and she had been faithful: the possibility had simply not occurred to her.

But early on New Year's Day a distraught teenager had fronted Emergency with the familiar syndrome, and Sylvia had reeled under the vertigo of recognition. Two red lines in the staff toilets confirmed it.

Her husband's vas deferens must have recanalised. It only happened rarely – she'd looked it up after doing the test – about once in every two thousand vasectomies. It tended to be triggered by an injury, like the kick to the groin he'd suffered in a football game last winter. The possibility hadn't occurred to her at the time, but it was the only explanation.

Fuck, this was complicated. She'd put it all off during the week, but her condition could no longer be ignored, and not much longer hidden.

The immediate problem was telling Murphy without starting a blazing row.

Any discussion was a minefield these days, let alone this one. In the first place, Murphy would not believe he was the father. Proper testing would be conclusive, obviously, but her concern was not with how things might resolve in the long run: she was worried about the first hour, the first day. He would instantly assume she'd been with another man. He'd always been utterly clear about his expectations on that score, and who knew what form his initial response might take, in his present state. A shiver ran through her, her skin all goosebumps and cold sweat.

Then, even if he accepted the fact of his paternity, Murphy would never allow her to keep the baby. He'd insisted their last discussion was final, and she had every reason to take him at his word. She knew without testing him that he would be utterly unyielding.

The third problem was the most serious. She'd been in denial for months about Murphy's descent into a cruel, seething anger. He was like a peat fire now, smouldering underground all the time, waiting to flare on contact with dry fuel and oxygen. His spiralling alcoholism only fed the beast. Driven by the pressure of the *Fabrica* case, his withdrawal from her had accelerated, his aggression becoming more frequent and more frightening, his exercise of control and dominance more unhinged. She'd tried to ask him whether it was something she was doing wrong, something they could work through together, but he'd put up a barrier and fended off her attempts to reach him. Whatever the cause, it all pointed in the same direction.

She wiped away her tears, realising she'd been sitting with one hand on her belly as though she was eight months along. She laughed at herself, surprised by a swell of optimism about this life within her body, despite her situation. Their situation.

She looked beyond Wedding Cake Island to the open water. At that moment, the rhythmical undulation of the Pacific Ocean felt powerfully maternal: the rolling swell, the fluid motion, the briny amnion, the teeming life beneath, the birth and death and rebirth, all connected. She turned towards the beach, full of people enjoying the sun and the sea: young women and men; couples; families. She watched a tall, thin, tattooed man dunking a toddler in the shallow waves. Even from a distance she could see the child's joy – fancied she could hear the squeals. She looked at the sand and knew for certain which of the women there was the mother. The bond between the woman and her child was like a steel cable: there was no mistaking it.

Sylvia straightened, breathing deeply and cyclically, closing her eyes to focus on the gentle sea breeze across her skin. A clear, level calm enveloped her as she realised her situation was actually very simple. She finally admitted the truth that she'd denied every day for months: the only change in her marriage would be for worse, not for better. Murphy was liable to do anything. While the shift had been gradual she'd ignored it, even hoped for a reversal, but now she no longer could.

She felt more powerful than she had since entering Murphy's orbit. More powerful than when she'd been a teenager, full of piss and vinegar, escaping her toxic family then putting herself through uni and crossing the continent to start her own life. She felt restored to herself, centred and calm.

She was going to safeguard this pregnancy and raise this child. She was not going to be denied the chance to be a mother. She was not going to be punished, for sins actual or imagined. Murphy's pathology put it all in perspective, and the baby raised the stakes beyond negotiation or self-deception.

She was going to leave. There was no point telling him about the baby, no point managing his wrath while they did the DNA test, no point reasoning, pleading, begging, cajoling. He would not believe she'd become pregnant by him; even if he believed her, he would not permit the birth of their child; and even if he permitted it, she realised, she would not bring a child into a home such as theirs had become.

She would no longer sacrifice her own wellbeing; she would not submit that of her unborn child to the furies and frailties of this degraded man. She had left before, when she was just a teenager: she could do it again now.

She was going to escape once more, into life.

Monday 7 January – afternoon

A double-rap on the hollow door was followed by Tom Adams, Murphy's former partner on the Armed Robbery Squad, now chief of security for Denison Bank. 'Ah, Spud. Thought you might be here.'

'What are you doing all the way out here?' Murphy was in a crappy abandoned, unairconditioned office on a remote corridor in the Fort's anonymous western-suburbs logistics warehouse. It was not a glamorous place, a far cry from the dazzling corporate tower in the city where Adams worked, or even the shiny new computer centre in the inner suburbs.

'Routine visit,' Adams said. 'Thought I'd drop in, see how it's going.'

Murphy was slouched in a decrepit office chair, surrounded by computer terminals and reams of paper, with a half-empty bottle of whisky by his coffee mug. He knew he looked shithouse: unshaven, hair awry, his shirt soaked through with sweat, streaks of highlighter and pen ink on his hands and face. He'd been back and forth out here over the last few weeks scouring data and cross-referencing everything he could about his six victims, looking for any correlation. Nothing so far.

Murphy had been astonished at the volume of private commercial data the bank could access. Adams had told him all about it but he hadn't been prepared for the sheer scale of the transgression. It made the paranoid fantasies of civil liberty types look benign. Best of all, technically and legally the vast database didn't even exist: it was purely an effect of a universal unspoken agreement between organisations to leave a back door open and look the other way. There were oceans of information out there about absolutely everybody.

All strictly off-limits for law enforcement, of course – which was why he was doing this alone, and in secret. People would tolerate invasions of privacy by these corporations that they would never permit their governments. Even confirming known facts by these means would not be allowed, let alone a fishing expedition like this. Murphy was definitely not meant to be here.

'He's fucken in here somewhere, Tom. He's gotta be.'

'Yeah, mate. I hope you get him soon.'

Murphy looked up. 'Why, am I making you nervous?'

Adams laughed his shaky little pissant laugh. 'Mate, the bosses would shit bricks if they knew you were here.'

'I'm not going to fuck you up, Tom.'

'Yeah I know, mate, just ... don't get caught, all right?'

'Don't worry, nobody will ever know I was here.'

'It's just, I can't explain all this searching.' Adams waved at an old orange-on-amber mainframe terminal. 'You're logged in as someone who doesn't exist.'

'Why, do they keep track of your searches?'

'Mate, they keep track of fucken *everything*.'

Murphy pushed his chair back and indicated the orange screen. 'Show me.'

Adams came around and pulled out the keyboard tray. He found the security operations login screen and entered a username and password. 'I've got spook access to the whole system,' said Adams as he navigated through the menus. 'I can read any customer file I like without opening a contact report. I can see building entry and exits, the trades of the securities cowboys, the cash load of any ATM, how much your house is worth today. I can see what lingerie the CEO bought for his secretary this morning.' He selected an item from an obscure menu. 'And in here is the staff search activity monitoring system. I can see exactly what any user has been looking at, inside the bank's network, on the internet, out in the swamp.'

'What's the swamp?'

'What you've been trawling through. It's what we call all the back-door stuff that companies share about the punters. Look.'

Adams keyed in the fake user ID he'd assigned to Murphy, and all his activity inside the Fort's systems appeared: every bank file for each of the six victims and their families, his day's work scrolling past line by line. 'You've been busy,' said Adams. 'I can search on date ranges or data type, set up an automated report, even.' Murphy was impressed: this was a lot more access than his fake ID had granted.

'It works for the internet, too,' continued Adams, typing. Murphy hadn't spent much time online while searching through the system, but he saw the cricket commentary he'd looked up earlier scroll by. A chill ran through him as he realised how exposed he was.

'See?' Adams saw Murphy's reaction. 'It's not just the metadata: I can see your exact query, the results, what links you followed – everything you've looked at while you were logged in. And if I can see it, so can the bosses.'

'Fuck. Will this report to anyone?'

'Not unless there's a red flag.' Adams logged out. 'But you getting caught on our system would be one hell of a red flag, Spud.'

Murphy leaned back. 'Okay, I can see why you're edgy. But you've got nothing to worry about, mate. I'm like a ghost.'

'Famous last words. And if you do find him, you're going to need a whole another story for the court about how you worked it out. You can't breathe a word of this.'

'I know, Tom. Leave it to me: you'll be amazed.'

Adams hesitated. 'Look, Spud. Could you wrap it up in a day or two, eh?'

Murphy sighed. It hadn't been easy to convince Adams to give him access in the first place. Murphy had been forced to remind his old partner of a certain debt he owed from their time together in Armed Rob: one of those owe-you-for-life obligations. Adams had given in, but now he was nervous.

Murphy sat still and held Adams's eyes, saying nothing. At first Adams returned his impassive gaze, then his eyes started to waver, then his will collapsed and he looked down at the floor. Murphy waited until the ex-cop glanced back up at him, defeated.

Murphy spoke quietly. 'I will be discreet. I will be careful. I will be here as long as it takes.'

'I didn't mean—'

'Yeah, you did mean,' Murphy cut him off. He leaned forward and spoke, low and vicious. 'Listen, cunt. You owe me. And I fucken *own* you. You are never off the hook, you hear me? Not until I say. One word from me and they will put you away for life. And you won't last long inside.'

'Oh jeeze, Spud, there's no need...'

'You're right, *mate;* there is no need. Because we understand each other, don't we?'

Adams nodded weakly.

'Look, Tom,' continued Murphy, his tone placatory now. 'Nothing else is working, all right? He's leaving nothing behind. He's buying his snuff drugs at the chemist, we think – untraceable. Nobody who knows him has a clue. He goes in and out without anyone seeing him. He talks his way in and buys heaps of time. He's selecting his victims for minimum risk. He's a fucken wraith, mate. If we don't try something different, he's gunna keep killing people. If I can just find the link between the vics, we'll nail him. To do that, I need data. I need *all* the data. And I need your help.'

Adams nodded again. 'All right.'

'Look, I won't take the piss, but stop giving me shit, okay?'

'Okay, Spud. I'm sorry.'

'I know this makes you nervous. I know your bosses get toey about the rules. Mine too. But you have to hold your nerve. I'll find what I'm after then I'll disappear, and it will be like I was never here.'

'Thanks, mate.'

'All right.' Murphy turned back to his desk. 'Now fuck off, I've got work to do.'

Monday 7 January – afternoon

Sylvia walked slowly home from work, daunted by the scale of her task. Getting out would be difficult and dangerous. The news was full of what happened to women when they left, or tried to leave. Every week a woman murdered; every day an abuser charged, tried, sentenced. All those dead and beaten and broken women.

Every single day.

And she saw at the hospital what the stats didn't capture: the abuse beneath the radar. Domestic violence accounted for as many emergency department attendances as alcohol and drugs combined. God help the women living with all three. It was like there was a war on.

Not that Murphy was going to kill her ... but then, who knew what he'd do in his rage? He'd never fully lost it with her, although he'd come close, one terrible night three years ago. Since then he'd worked out subtler ways to keep her in her place, methods of control and coercion, adding physical intimidation and the odd not-quite accident as required. But in his current mood, with the right trigger, she couldn't rule anything out.

And nothing was beyond him financially and legally – he wouldn't hesitate to send her to the wall. She knew he would never let her go on civil terms. She remembered what he'd said when she'd threatened to leave that one time he'd struck her: 'Where are you going to go, Sylvia? I'm a cop, you can't fucken hide from me. There is nowhere I won't find you, I promise you. Nowhere.'

She had learned the lesson of that episode: there would be no talking this time. She had to prepare for escape, make detailed plans then move decisively when the time came, before he had the chance to undermine her. And it had to be soon, before she began to show. She needed patience, stealth and cunning; she needed expert advice.

And she needed Jo, once she had her plan worked out. She knew her sister-in-law would back her, but it was a huge step to come between siblings in such a definitive way, and she wasn't going to go there until everything was ready.

'Hello, Sylvia, how are you?' Sylvia snapped out of her reverie to find her elderly neighbour watering the banksias along their shared nature strip.

'I'm all right, thanks, Clare. How about you?' She put on a smile she hoped was casual but that probably looked brave.

'I'm well, thank you,' said Clare, turning her full attention on Sylvia. 'Care for a cup of tea?' Sylvia's neighbour was as tactful as she was astute.

'I'd love to but I need to make a few calls right now. Maybe later?'

'Any time that suits you. Today, tomorrow, whenever you like.'

'I'm sorry I haven't been over much lately.' The woman only lived next door, and she had been so good to Sylvia since they moved in.

But Clare wasn't having any of it. 'Nonsense,' she said, waving her hand. 'I like my own company, you don't have to worry about me. Just come when you can; you're always welcome.'

'Thanks, Clare,' said Sylvia, unlocking her screen door.

'And, Sylvia: my door is always open to you, any time you need it. Day or night.' Clare engaged Sylvia's eyes. 'Do you know what I mean?'

Sylvia flushed. She looked down as tears welled, nodded and turned her key in the front door. 'Thank you,' she croaked as she pushed inside.

She leaned her back on the closed front door, almost undone by the kindness and the shame, in equal measure. But she couldn't afford to give into any of it right now. She calmed down and tuned in to the quiet, cool house, infused with that particular silence of emptiness. She dropped her keys in the mortar and put the kettle on. She found a notepad, pulled out a stool at the kitchen bench and started her laptop.

The web search was eerily easy: she typed in *leaving husband* and the Domestic Violence Resource Centre came up first. It depressed her that the algorithm was so on-point. She started writing down the details before realising it was a Victorian service. She found a link to organisations in other states, clicked on NSW and found the Women's Legal Service. She explored the website while the tea steeped. Once she had a mug in her hand, she picked up her mobile phone, trying to ignore the butterflies in her stomach.

She called her gynaecologist first. They'd had a cancellation for the following day, so she made an appointment and jotted down the time to put in her calendar later. She drew a breath and dialled the other phone number.

It was a long wait. A recorded voice urged her to hang up and dial 000 if she or anyone else was in immediate danger; otherwise, the voice apologised for the delay. For once, the apology sounded sincere. Sylvia was on the sofa finishing her second cup of tea by the time she got through. A woman named Hilary apologised and thanked her for holding. Not enough funding to staff the hotline properly, she said. *Quelle surprise.*

Hilary asked concise, practical questions and quickly steered the conversation to concrete action. She had clearly heard it all before. Hilary was unfazed by things that Sylvia had never before said aloud, things that felt impossibly momentous. Sylvia confirmed she was ready to leave. Hilary congratulated Sylvia on her resolve and talked about developing a departure plan. 'A safe path to safety,' she called it.

'This is the most dangerous moment, Sylvia: right now and what comes next.' Sylvia's anxiety escalated – shit was getting real. 'You need your wits about you and you need bloody good advice,' Hilary continued. The next step was a face-to-face discussion with a lawyer. When Sylvia said she was pregnant, there was an intake of breath. 'Righto, you're going on the priority list.'

'Why?'

'Pregnancy's a major risk factor. Does he know?'

'God, no. He'd be livid.'

'Okay, good. Research shows it can escalate the situation. Our advice is that the pregnancy is best kept to yourself for now, while you sort everything else out.'

'Don't worry, there's no bloody way I'm going to tell him.'

'How far along are you?'

'Not long. I'm not showing.'

'Okay. Since you're a nurse, I don't suppose you need advice on terminations?'

'No, I'm going to keep her. Him.' She was pierced by a spike of joy at the simple act of speaking aloud about her child. It made it all so real. She gave in to a visceral surge of love for the being growing inside her body. A rich bronze warmth suffused her, settling in as though it was going to be around for a while. A good, long while.

'All right then, let's get you sorted,' Hilary was saying. 'Now, I know you're in Randwick but we only do face-to-face in Western Sydney.'

'Why is that?'

'Funding, again. This is the least-bad arrangement, given our resources.'

Where did women from Dubbo go for help? Sylvia wondered. Or Brewarrina? 'Okay. Where, exactly?'

'Blacktown, Liverpool and Penrith.'

'Liverpool's probably best, on the M5.'

'How's Thursday the seventeenth? Georgie is free at 12.30.'

'There's nothing sooner?' It was over a week away. And this was the priority list.

'Not right now. Are we able to contact you if there's a cancellation?'

'Umm, how would you do that?'

Hilary knew exactly what she meant. 'We send a text or an email that looks like it's from a friend. But only if you think it's safe.'

'No it's okay, let's just make the time and stick with it.' It was too risky, the way Murphy treated everything like a lead. Occupational hazard.

'Okay then, 12.30 on the seventeenth.' Hilary gave her the address and some directions, and told her what documents to bring. 'We recommend you bring copies if you can, rather than remove the originals.'

Sylvia was just hanging up when she heard the front door. *Fuck, that was close.* She ripped off the page of notes she'd made and slipped it into her pocket. She was too agitated to face Murphy now: he'd definitely guess something was up. She closed the laptop, leaped up from the sofa and dashed past him as he came down the hallway, telling him she was going next door for a cup of tea with Clare.

Tuesday 8 January – morning

A six-pack, half a bottle of shiraz and a three-finger whisky nightcap ensured Murphy slept through the wild southerly storm that battered Sydney in the early hours, but the peace woke him up around dawn. Everything was quiet out the back, the air scrubbed clean, only sodden leaf litter from next door's Sydney red gum left behind. He'd have to clean the pool this evening, rake up the leaves out the front, check the spy cameras were still working.

While the espresso machine warmed up, his eyes fell on a glossy notepad on the coffee table. The early-morning sunlight threw into relief a set of scratchings left over from a page since torn away. Murphy went across and picked it up. The impressions were deep and urgent, messier than Sylvia's usual neat hand.

What was she up to now?

Murphy found a 2B pencil in the bottom drawer and lightly shaded across the sheet. He returned to the machine, drew the espresso shot and sipped it while examining the revealed script. It was two separate notes. The one at the top was an appointment with Sylvia's gynaecologist:

Christel/2.45 – 8 Jan

But further down the page was a larger block of text:

DVRC 03 WLS 5550-7010 Hilary Livpl Thurs 17 Jan – **Georgie** *12.30 18 McArth St ~ Westfld bank stmts/tax 5 yrs/* **SUPER**

Comprehension and caffeine kicked in at once. *Divorce,* then an appointment and a list of financial documents. He fired up the tablet and typed the phone number into the browser.

The Women's Fucking Legal Service of New South Fucking Wales.

His anger rising, Murphy clicked on *about.* Sure enough, it was a specialist service helping women seek justice relating to domestic violence, discrimination, reproductive rights, fucken blah blah blah typical anti-male feminist victim bullshit. Women helping women fuck over men, at taxpayer expense. And who paid most of the fucken tax in this country? Fucken men did, that's who. It was outrageous.

So his wife was going to divorce him and take him to the fucken cleaners. With the help of some fucken dyke lawyer named Georgie. Well, fuck that.

Murphy felt a surge of rage pass through him like a bolt of electricity, but he very deliberately calmed himself and channelled the anger to his dark place, where it could ferment and grow, gathering force, ready to be directed at its proper target at the right time. He tore off the page of rubbings, along with the next few sheets, and returned the notepad to the coffee table.

He didn't know what was next – he would take his time working out the exact shape of an appropriate response – but he was going to beat her to the punch. She was about to get the shock of her fucken life.

Sylvia had never really liked surprises, but that was bad fucken luck.

Tuesday 8 January – morning

Jo put the phone down and let out an almighty *whoop.* She crossed the office to Chartier, who rose from her chair just in time to receive a crushing bear hug.

'What is it?'

'We found a *New Fabrica!*'

'What, how?'

'From the customs list Angelo put together.' To find the Australian purchasers of the *New Fabrica,* Nikolaidis had asked the customs service for a report on high-value imports of books between the date of publication and the first murder, where the packages were of low weight or volume. Most had turned out to be high-end art books, but the process had been validated when it identified copies of the *New Fabrica* that went to public collections. This was the first privately held copy they'd tracked down.

'So is this extra?' asked Thijs from his desk. 'Besides the library copies?'

'Yes! It was imported by a Dr Gerard Bromley, of St Ives.'

'*Godskolere!* Do we have a squad on the way?'

Jo calmed down a bit. 'No, he's not our killer. He's ninety-two and in a nursing home. Angelo and Cooper just rang from there. Still sharp as a tack, but he doesn't get around much anymore.'

'Still, it could be a worker out there.'

'Or family.'

'Maybe. Apparently he keeps it under lock and key. Nobody even knows he has it. Angelo's running a background check, though, just in case. Staff and family.'

'It doesn't sound like you think it's a lead,' said Amy.

'No, I don't.'

'So why so excited?'

'I'm just stoked we've found one. We still have about forty addresses on the NSW list and about a hundred interstate. Any one of them could be it.'

'Fair enough.'

'Do you need more help?' asked Thijs.

'Could we call up some uniforms to get through the list? The boys have just been checking for me as they get the chance.'

'No worries, there's still some spare provision,' said Thijs. 'I'll let Spud know.'

'No that's okay, I'll ring him,' said Jo. 'I want to ask him a favour anyway.' She knew her brother would rain on her parade – it was his default reaction – but she'd learned many years ago that he was less of a pain in the arse if he was involved in some way. She only had to give him a job to do and he'd be fine.

Tuesday 8 January – morning

Murphy hadn't thought much of Jo's fancy customs play, chasing this one edition of a 500-year-old book, because it seemed unlikely to him that anyone planning a killing spree would fill out his importation forms correctly. But he had to admit, his sister had hit the bullseye. Not that she had any idea.

Their telephone conversation had been pretty typical – her naive academic enthusiasm colliding with his streetwise scepticism – until she'd asked him to check an address on her list. It was a long shot, she'd said: a billing address for a credit card that had paid the rental on a post office box in Hornsby, where one of the expensive book shipments on her list had been sent.

'You're out west somewhere, aren't you?' she'd asked, only vaguely aware of what he was up to and where he was up to it. 'Could you check on it while you're out there?' Then she'd read him a street address in Seven Hills.

It was the address of the Denison Bank warehouse, the very building he was sitting in at that moment.

He'd had that sensation of clarity, then, when an idea crystalises in your mind and you realise you already knew it in your gut. It came from months of getting inside the killer's head, of seeing the world the way he did, of hunting connections. From a thousand half-seen impressions, half-felt hunches and half-grasped strands. From learning what it meant to surveil and be surveilled inside the Denison Bank computer network.

Murphy didn't believe in coincidences. Not on this scale, anyway. He was dead certain.

His killer worked for Denison Bank.

***

The first thing Murphy did was to lock the door and push a set of drawers against it. He felt like an arachnophobe waking up covered in spider webs – he was surrounded by potential serial killers. No way was he going to be next cab off the rank.

He drank straight from the whisky bottle to calm himself, then grabbed the keyboard to the bank mainframe terminal and lit up the sign-in screen. He picked up his mobile and dialled.

'Adams here.'

'Tom, it's Spud.'

'Mate, how's it going? Have you got him?'

'Not yet, getting there.'

'You still at Sevo?'

'Yeah I am. Listen, I need your login, Tom. The spook-level one.'

'Nah, mate, can't do that.'

'If you let me in now I'll be gone by the end of today. As in, never coming back.'

'Spud, you got no idea what that login can do. There's no way.'

'I don't want to do anything, just look around, like you did the other day.'

'For what?'

'I'm playing a hunch.'

'Tell me what you want and I'll look into it for you.'

'Come on, Tom, you know that's not how it works. I have to get in there myself and follow my nose. I won't make any changes. I wouldn't know how, anyway.'

'That's what worries me. You wouldn't know if you did.'

'I'm not a complete dope. I just need to have a look.'

But Adams was resolute. 'No, Spud, I can't. It's a sacking offence, A-grade.'

Murphy sighed. Enough fucking around: time to go nuclear. 'Yeah, mate, and shooting a fucken suspect in the face for a bag of cash is a fucken sacking offence too. Even in the Armed Robbery Squad.'

Murphy pictured the blood draining from the former cop's face. 'Spud, come on.'

'You murdered a thief for money, Adams. You involved me by doing it in front of me. Then you tried to bribe me with half the cash.'

'Please, mate, don't—'

'And then you threatened my family, to keep me quiet.'

'I never threatened you! You told me you'd let it go if I went quietly!'

'That'll be your word against mine, mate. Your weapon, your slug, your prints. Your record of violence and graft.'

'Fuck you, Murphy. I retired, as we agreed. We even handed the money in.'

'At my insistence, because I'm not a fucken thief.'

'Pascoe was a killer anyway. He had it coming, you said so yourself.'

'Pascoe was a fucking scumbag, but that won't impress the court, will it?'

'Fuck you, Murphy,' Adams repeated.

'That's two strikes, Adams. I know you're upset, but you want to think very carefully before saying that to me again. There's a lot at stake for you. We will not be having this conversation again.'

There was a long pause, then an anguished groan. 'Half a mil, Spud. Each! They never would've known.'

'Like I said, mate, it's not my way.' Murphy softened his tone. 'Here's the deal: you give me the login. I use it strictly to look around, press no buttons. Just this arvo, then I'm gone. Never coming back.' He paused for dramatic effect. 'And you're off the hook for Craig Pascoe.'

'For real?'

'For real, Tom. For good. Far as I'm concerned, you do this? You'll've repaid your debt to society better than any prison term. We square this thing today, for all time.'

'Jesus.' Adams was sobbing. Murphy cringed but kept silent. 'I ... okay, Spud.'

'The people thank you, Tom.'

'Just today and you're gone, right?'

'That's right.'

'No matter what you find?'

'Yes, mate. You've done enough.'

'Okay, okay. Just don't fuck this up for me, Spud, I'm not kidding. They'll fire me if they find out. I'll never get another job.'

'They won't know a thing. It'll be like I was never here.'

'I'm going to have to wipe your search soon as you're done. I can't have any trace left behind.'

'No worries.'

'There'll be nothing for you to use in court.'

'I understand. I'll do my work and leave, and you'll wake up from a bad dream.'

Adams sobbed again – Murphy had held a lien on his future for so long he must've forgotten what freedom felt like. When he could speak again he rattled off the login string and the password. Murphy typed, and he was in. He promised to text Adams when he was done, and hung up.

Murphy found the user monitoring system, but then he stalled. Adams had revealed Murphy's activity by tracking the fake user ID, but Murphy needed to come at it from the opposite angle, finding the user ID based on activity. He tooled around until he found a way to trace search activity by query target. He entered a few names – Anthony Williams, Laura Newman, Brendan Evans – and looked at the search histories. He soon established that each one had been the subject of detailed queries in their final days. He ran Patrick Hall, Damien Henley and Amber Darcy through as well, and came up with the same thing. Finally, fucken finally, something concrete that linked the victims to one another.

None of this had shown up in the routine searches. Homicide always checked victims' financial records for anomalies, including account maintenance. They'd all come up clean: no address changes, no account closures, no large transfers, no cigar.

Yet someone had run numerous search queries on these six customers in the days before each one had died. Someone logged in as SP07M378.

Murphy returned to the main menu, found the staff files and entered the user ID.

Stephen Samuel Porter.

Systems Monitor and Help Desk Operator, Systems First Response. Sydney Computer Centre, Alexandria.

Tuesday 8 January – afternoon

The police commissioner was hunched over a speakerphone along with his senior subordinates, with an irate premier and a tense police minister on the other end.

'The opposition's hammering me and you're getting nowhere,' fumed the premier. 'The only thing that's working is this anatomist angle, and that was my idea.' That raised some eyebrows, but nobody contradicted him. 'Maybe this Murphy character isn't up to it, is that the problem?'

'No, sir, he has the best clearance rate in the country, and he leads a very effective team,' said Commissioner Carr.

'Is he off his game for some reason?' the police minister chimed in. 'Something at home?'

'I don't think so, sir,' said the superintendent, Murphy's line manager. 'He's stressed about the failure to apprehend, but that's all.'

'Well what's the fucking problem, then?' barked the premier.

Deputy Commissioner Hughes leaned in. 'The perpetrator's extremely well prepared, sir. He's reduced his exposure to the minimum. But sooner or later he will be seen or disturbed, it's just simple probability.'

'So he's a sneaky prick. Murphy's a sneakier prick, I bet,' said the premier. 'You're the cops, just work something out. I can't tell the voters our best idea is to let him keep killing them until he fucks up.'

'We understand, sir,' said the commissioner.

'I go to the polls in eleven weeks and this needs to be ancient fucking history before I stroll over to see the governor. You need to wrap it up now, you hear? Not Easter, not Christmas – now.'

The line dropped out and the three brass sat in silence for a moment. 'All right,' said the commissioner. 'If what distinguishes our perpetrator is his preparation, then we disrupt his preparation.'

'Murphy's already working that angle, sir,' said Superintendent Manning.

'Then he needs to work it harder,' said the deputy commissioner. 'We can give him more uniformed help. Clearly we have the green light.'

'No, I'm afraid that's not enough.' The commissioner sighed. 'I hesitate to say this, with a character like Murphy, but it's time to set him loose.' He raised his eyebrows at his deputy.

Hughes held his gaze for long enough to convey her misgivings about letting a rogue like Murphy off his leash, but her boss didn't waver. 'All right,' she said eventually. 'I'll speak with him.'

Tuesday 8 January – afternoon

'Stephen Fucking Porter,' said Murphy to the staff profile. 'You're fucked now, sunshine.' He poured a celebratory mug of whisky and nearly rang Janssen, but caught himself in time. This knowledge was entirely illicit: he had to bring Porter in by legitimate means that would stand up in court. Nobody could know.

First he checked Porter's recent activity to see if he was researching his next victim. Murphy was disappointed to find everything quiet – had Porter already selected his target, it would have been a simple matter of setting an ambush and waiting. Murphy was going to have to do this the hard way instead, by working out the killer's method.

Porter had collected a prodigious amount of information on each of his victims, but Murphy still didn't know how he'd selected them in the first place. While patiently exploring Porter's surveillance history in pursuit of that question, Murphy had discovered another twenty-odd customers the killer had studied over the past year, but who'd somehow avoided dissection.

Nothing seemed to differentiate Porter's searches on the two kinds of subjects, so Murphy turned to the customer records themselves. He compared the file of a survivor named Richard Elliott with the late Brendan Evans. Flicking back and forth between them, Murphy found that Porter had cancelled Elliott's credit card at the point he'd stopped his research, while Evans's card had not been cancelled. It was the same for all the others: the credit cards of the living had been cancelled by Porter, while those of the dead had not been cancelled, by Porter or anyone else.

Murphy eventually noticed a field called *Open MCR* that was starred for the victims, but empty for the survivors. The system's online user manual told him it stood for 'open missing card report': an electronic report had been opened but never filed, so it was flagged as incomplete.

Murphy stepped through the process mentally. The customers would report their credit cards lost or stolen, and Porter would filter them as potential candidates, on some mysterious criteria. Then he did his homework, excluding three out of every four, for whatever reason. For those he rejected, he cancelled their cards and they were none the wiser: they received their new cards and life went on. For those selected to die, he left the missing card report unactioned.

Adams had mentioned that most staff had to open an action report in order to gain access to a customer's detailed record. Some kind of privacy measure, presumably. Porter may not even have realised that abandoned reports left this tiny permanent trace.

Then Porter would show up at the victim's home, probably claiming to have their new credit card for them. With Amber Darcy he would have produced the Hordern's card he'd lifted, but the mechanism was the same: the MacGuffin was a credit card. Once they opened the door to collect the card, it was goodnight, Irene.

Murphy had a disturbing thought, and navigated to his own Denison Bank file. Sure enough, there was the *Open MCR* flag: Porter had looked into Murphy's own customer records months ago. Well, it figured – his name had been attached to the case since the beginning – but it unnerved him all the same. The serial killer wasn't the worst bad guy who knew where Murphy lived, but most of the others were guests of Her Majesty.

Murphy took another swig and shook it off. There was no time for paranoia. He returned to the staff system and wrote down Porter's data: home address; date of birth; home and mobile phone numbers; car rego, make, model, colour. He recorded everything he could find – bank account numbers and balances, historical mortgage details, emergency contact and next of kin (blank), tax file number – using the unlimited access while he had it. He found the systems monitor roster and checked where Porter was at that very moment: not at work, it turned out. The killer had finished a night shift early that morning and was now not due in until the weekend. Murphy noted down Porter's shifts for the current fortnight and the next.

Now Murphy had to fabricate an alternative story for the benefit of his squad and the court about how they'd found their killer. He'd have to be very careful: everything from now on would be raked over minutely in the trial. He couldn't workshop this with his unit. He had to lead Homicide to Porter along a plausible chain of deduction, without anyone realising he already knew the way.

He could say they were playing a hunch about the way Denison Bank kept cropping up, and how the killer seemed to know everything going in. They'd had plenty of those discussions, like Harris and Jo going on about the odds. Their suspicions were not nearly enough to obtain a warrant, but that was immaterial with the cooperation of the Fort's security chief. A raid and lockdown was out, but an exploratory visit timed for Porter's shift could work.

He wargamed the encounter. If they went to Alexandria, they had to leave with Porter in custody, no question. But that would mean bringing serious firepower, while claiming to be there only for information. The defence lawyers would smell a rat, and the crown prosecutor would be antsy, too.

Moreover, Murphy would need a reason to make the arrest. If they were lucky, Porter would panic and give him a pretext, but their killer seemed a pretty cool customer. So Murphy would have to re-enact his breakthrough about Porter's method during the visit – in real time, with his detectives watching over his shoulder, without anyone realising that he already knew what he was looking for. Not likely, with only a day's practice in the bank's staff surveillance system.

So, scratch option one.

Murphy reached again for his whisky. Perhaps he could lead Porter to the unit, instead of leading his police to the killer? Murphy could wait for Porter to select his next victim, then nab him in an ambush. But that would involve watching his search activity, and after today his high-level spook access was finished. Murphy had pushed Adams as far as he would go: any more stress and he could freak out and blow the whole thing apart. No, an ambush wasn't going to work. Anyway, involving civilians was always untidy – they were too unreliable. People often got hurt, or worse.

A snare-trap, then? Dangle a victim so juicy that Porter would rise to the bait. It avoided civilians, and Murphy could steer the trap towards a time and place of his choosing. Being unable to see Porter's activity on the bank's system was less of an issue with a known target. All he'd be missing was whether or not Porter had taken the bait. The lure would just have to be irresistible.

But a snare-trap would be an official operation, requiring brass approval and a lot of personnel. Murphy would need to explain the reasons for his confidence. The question wasn't whether anyone in the squad would suspect he knew something he wasn't sharing – someone would suspect, for sure – the question was how far he could go before they couldn't keep those suspicions to themselves. It would be delicate, especially during the trial.

Ah: but what if it never came to trial? Because snare-traps had other advantages, in Murphy's view. Set up right, a deadfall snare allowed you to close the case right there, old-school. Justices Smith and Wesson presiding, with half a dozen jurors of the .357 Magnum variety. Saved the taxpayer a whole lot of time and money.

'Yeah, yeah, yeah,' Murphy muttered to himself, topping up his mug. This was a promising line of attack. Bring him in, let him make his move, and shoot the fucker dead. Problem solved.

A resolution at the point of capture would give Murphy the latitude he needed on prior intel, and otherwise it would be mostly just logistics. He knew Porter's method, he only had to bait the trap right. Going off the Hordern's tape and what the families, neighbours and colleagues had told them, the victims were all pretty much arseholes: that told him how to get on Porter's shortlist. Since a fake customer profile was out of the question – it would need the bank's assistance – Murphy would have to be the bait himself. He just had to get under Porter's skin, spur him into action and lure him onto a killing ground that Murphy could control.

His main problem was that he was running out of time – he had to work out all the details right then, before he left the warehouse, because there was no way Adams was going to let him back into the system.

He checked his watch – coming up to half past two. That ought to do: he could plot this out in three or four hours. But he had a niggling feeling, like he had something to do – a meeting he'd forgotten about. The commissioner? No. Then he remembered – he was thinking of Sylvia's gynaecology appointment, at 2.45 this afternoon. He'd seen it on the notepad that morning.

He tried to get his mind back onto planning, but he was distracted now. Something wasn't right. Then it hit him: Sylvia had seen her gyno only recently. Usually she saw this Christel at the hospital – they worked together at Prince of Wales – but for some reason last time Sylvia had needed to go to her private rooms in Paddington, and Murphy had dropped her off. Why would

Sylvia need to go back to the cunt doctor so soon? She hadn't said anything about tests or a follow-up, and she hadn't mentioned any trouble down there. It didn't make sense.

Unless.

And then Murphy remembered how Sylvia had eaten like a horse at Christmas. They'd even joked about it. Admittedly, Cath was a fucken outstanding cook, but Sylvia had eaten more than Murphy had. And she'd had a healthy appetite since then, too. It was definitely out of character.

Unless.

What about her period? He tried to remember when Sylvia had last been on her rag, but he drew a blank. That didn't mean anything, though: he never paid attention to that business.

What about the booze? She'd been pretty pissed at Christmas, to the point they'd had to leave the car behind. Murphy had walked back to Rocky's the next morning with a Cabernet hangover to pick it up. Surely that clinched it in the negative?

But that was the last big session of hers he could remember, and it had been a long while since the one before that. They used to knock off a bottle at a sitting, easy – two on a good night. She'd been tapering, he realised, and he'd been picking up her slack without noticing. On reflection, he hadn't seen Sylvia drink at all for at least a week, maybe two. Unusual in summer. She loved a G&T on a hot afternoon.

Unless.

Okay, he told himself, *don't jump to conclusions.* Be rational, consult the evidence. He pulled out his mobile phone, opened Sylvia's calendar and searched for 'Christel': every twelve months like clockwork, almost to the day, then this one only seven weeks later. He pulled the indented notepad pages out of his pocket and unfolded them, looking again at the rubbings. The two entries appeared to have been written on the same sheet, with a similar degree of pressure coming through. The notes were both scrawled, rather than neatly formed in Sylvia's usual style. He could see no reason why she'd be agitated while writing down a doctor's appointment.

Unless.

There was no obvious connection between appointments with a gynaecologist and a divorce lawyer.

Unless.

Then he remembered the vomit on the underside of the toilet seat the other day. It had obviously splashed up from the bowl and he'd assumed it was his, from New Year's Day. He'd idly thought it was unusual the cleaner had missed it, but now he realised he hadn't noticed it before then. And he would have – he lifted that seat every time he pissed. But Sylvia had no need to lift the toilet seat, so she wouldn't realise the spew was there. Hard to figure why she wouldn't mention throwing up.

Unless.

And then he'd complimented her on the buoyancy of her tits in the pool on the weekend, but she hadn't let him near them. Said she was tired and had a headache. His working theory had been that she was just frosting him out.

Unless.

Unless unless unless.

The bitch was fucken pregnant.

Murphy picked up a dusty old rotary telephone from the adjacent desk and threw it at the wall. It went straight through the plasterboard and wedged into the cavity. He reached for a tubular stacking chair, but then thought better of the racket and quelled his rage. He sat and seethed instead.

It all fitted together. Sylvia had been so distant lately because she'd been fucking around behind his back. And now that she'd gotten herself knocked up, she was going to take Murphy to the cleaners and piss off with half his fucken assets.

'Not on my fucken watch, sweetheart.' He was not about to be robbed, or deceived, or abandoned. He was not about to be humiliated.

At least she hadn't been at it in his own home. He'd been keeping tabs on her through the spy camera recordings for months now, and there was never anyone else there, apart from his sister every now and then. Even when Sylvia was getting around half-naked it was all very innocent. Clearly she was careful. Cunning. Fucken devious.

Murphy picked up the whisky and poured, the mug surrounded by his scrawled notes on the trap he was going to set for Porter. He had a nagging sensation, like a sneeze that wouldn't come: a notion, ancient and new, swimming around beneath the surface. He looked down into the mug and found the design in the peaty depths: the intricate machinery laid out in blueprint, the gears and vectors, the causes and effects.

Oh, brilliance. Yes. This was the better plan. A modified snare-trap: no permissions required, no explanations necessary. Draw his quarry in, send the prick straight into the hands of the squad. And deal with his other little matter in the process. Murphy drank off the rest of the whisky and stepped it through from start to finish, but he already knew. It was beautiful.

But did he dare? There was no coming back from something like this. He'd killed people before, but they were bad guys, in everyone's eyes, and he'd been given medals for those shootings. This could not be more different. It was a launch out into clear space, a sovereign act in defiance of everything around him, a stroke of finality that would cut him off from the realm he was sworn to protect.

He looked back at Sylvia's notes. That bitch. Fuck it. He was entitled to protect his property, protect his freedom, protect his rightful place as the man of the house.

His plan was dicey, to be sure, but he would remain in the shadows, out of sight. And it would solve both his problems at one inspired stroke. There were a good many moving parts to it, and it would require careful curation, but he held all the levers now. He knew he could make it work.

'Oh, Murphy, you absolute cunt,' he growled, downing the last of the Islay malt. 'You're a fucken genius.' He logged out of the system and sent Adams a text:

—*Elvis has left the building.*
Thank you very much.

Tuesday 8 January – afternoon

Sylvia bounced out of her doctor's office feeling the best she had in days, months, years. She understood she had a long, hard road ahead, but fuck it, from now on she was going to smell the roses whenever they were at hand. And they were at hand today, great bundles of riotously coloured, richly fragrant hybrid tea roses.

Her baby was growing, her body was in the form of its life for the task ahead, and her gynaecologist could not have been happier, medically speaking.

But it was specifying a due date that had brought it all home to her. She was due in early September: her child's birthday would fall in Sylvia's favourite time of the year, when Sydney was particularly gorgeous. It all made perfect sense.

She couldn't wait to tell Jo, as soon as she'd sorted out the Murphy stuff. She knew her sister-in-law would support her through it all. They'd held one another's hair for much less than this.

For the first time in weeks, as she walked across a courtyard back to her shift in Emergency, she caught herself humming. She laughed out loud, closed her eyes and held her face up to the sun. It was going to be good. So good.

Tuesday 8 January – afternoon

Murphy took the back way to Parramatta to avoid the breathos, tracing the railway line towards a sneaky rat-run he knew that shadowed Victoria Road. He dialled Deputy Commissioner Hughes.

'Good afternoon, detective,' she said. 'I was just about to call you. Do you have a breakthrough for me?'

'Sorry, ma'am, no – but I do have an idea. I'd like to consult the Operation Scintilla team.'

Scintilla was the Victorian Police operation that had nailed the country's last serial killer four years earlier. Variously described as 'inspired', 'unorthodox', 'problematic', 'unethical' and 'borderline illegal', it had nevertheless apprehended the culprit, tried him cleanly and put him away for life. Hughes had been Scintilla's supervising brass: she'd been recruited north of the Murray River on the strength of its achievement.

'Shouldn't you be asking Superintendent Manning?'

'I wanted to seek your advice before formalising a request, ma'am. Since you know the case and the people.' She had to know he was blowing smoke up her arse, but he was confident she'd see the angle. Murphy didn't much like the deputy commissioner, and the feeling was clearly mutual – she thought he was a cowboy, he thought she was a bull dyke – but he respected her pragmatism. She wanted results, and they both knew he could deliver them.

'Is this another piece of premier-friendly innovative design thinking?' she asked.

'It is if you want it to be. But I also think it will help for real.'

'All right, do it. I'll tell the commissioner. Do you know Josh Kelly?' Kelly had led the Scintilla investigation, and was now head of Victorian Homicide.

'I do, we've been on courses together.'

'Okay. Tell Manning I've approved it. Make your arrangements.'

'Thank you. And there's something else, ma'am.'

'Yes?'

'It might be time to escalate our use of the media.'

'Through the media unit?'

'I was thinking more informally.'

'Ah. You want to activate that scheme of the attorney-general's.'

'Kind of. Only, strictly in-house.'

'So you're not wanting to involve those press secretaries?'

'Fuck, no! Ma'am.'

'Glad to hear it. But it's still a risky play, detective.'

'True, but so's waiting for him to strike again. "Doing nothing," as they call it on the news.'

He gave her time to silently weigh the public relations consequences of each option. They were damned either way, of course. 'All right. But nobody speaks to the press apart from you. I want no repeats of the fingerprint debacle.'

'Yes, ma'am.'

'We need to close this one out, Murphy.'

'Yes, ma'am. Thank you.' He hung up before his voice betrayed him. As if he needed schooling on that point.

He phoned his superintendent to give him the substance. Manning understood why Murphy had gone over his head, but it was better to tell it direct.

He still had a few calls to make, so he turned off the main road and drove through Balmain to the London Hotel. It was a good place to think, and nobody would ever look for him here.

Murphy took a schooner of Old onto the pub balcony and regarded the Harbour Bridge while blowing the froth off. His mind turned back to the last time he'd sat there, with Sylvia at his side – he had a photo of that afternoon somewhere on his phone, actually, Sylvia laughing with the bridge in the background. He pulled up the picture and a twinge of anticipatory regret ran through him. What he was planning was pretty fucken full-on – maybe he was going too far. Could he protect his interests another way: shut her down but let her live on?

But then he imagined her at other pubs, with other men, laughing and flirting with all and sundry, going home with whichever prick had inseminated her, and his bile rose and he cursed, then hardened his heart and focused his attention on the job at hand.

He extracted Porter's shift roster, then opened the calendar app on his phone to compare. He pondered for a moment, then opened his Fort banking app and cross-referenced with a few recent credit-card transactions. Ten minutes later he had a preferred date and a rough time of day and no more beer. He texted Kelly, the Victorian Homicide chief, asking for a quick chat, and was just back from the bar with another schooner and a packet of salt-and-vinegar chips when Kelly rang. Murphy pitched his request for a technical briefing on Scintilla, in Melbourne. Kelly was enthusiastic: there'd be some reflected glory when Murphy made his collar, and a nice reportable in the meantime. Early the following week would work. Murphy locked it in.

He drained his glass and jumped in his car, taking the back streets to Victoria Road. He phoned police ops admin to arrange the flights and a hotel: down to Melbourne early Sunday afternoon, back to Sydney late Wednesday afternoon, staying at the Windsor. He promised to submit the paperwork in the morning.

Crossing the Anzac Bridge, he hesitated before making the next call. This was the point of no return, and the enormity of his plan pressed down on him. But then he looked to his right towards Glebe, as was his habit, and saw some ranga bitch in the car next to him giving the long-suffering bloke in the driver's seat a proper serve, and he hit dial.

Hollier from the *Sydney Envoy* answered on the second ring. They'd done a lot of favours for one another over the years, too many to keep track of. Murphy offered the journalist an exclusive on the case, with all the juice. The story was an open-cut gold mine, done right, with a book in it and a shot at a Walkley Award. Hollier made the statutory complaint about short notice

– always a bit fucken rich coming from a journalist – but his heart wasn't in it, not with Saturday's front page in the frame. They arranged to meet late that night at the Hero of Waterloo.

Murphy decided to avoid the office. He needed to think through his strategy for handling the unit before seeing them, and he had a lot of slander to invent about their killer before meeting the reporter. Plus he was definitely well pissed by now, with a couple of quick schooeys chasing probably half a pint of malt. Not the best look.

He headed for home. He had some work to do there, anyway, including a major clean-up of the greatest-hits reel on his computer from the backyard spy camera.

Besides, he could do with some fucken peace and quiet after a big day. According to the calendar on his phone, Sylvia would be at work for hours yet.

Saturday 12 January – afternoon

Porter lifted the Saturday newspaper by its edge, as though it were smeared with excrement. Which it was, metaphorically. He moved from the system monitor's desk to a nearby bench, as much to prevent contamination of his workspace as to utilise the broad flat surface.

He opened the newspaper to the double spread, a lurid indulgence of distortion, fabrication and titillation. The centrepiece was a précis of each Volume, the bare facts obscured by an embroidery of supposition, misinformation and patent deceit. All manner of insult was heaped upon him, all born of ignorance and steeped in malice. While the byline was Hollier's, behind each slur stood Detective Senior Sergeant David Murphy.

Porter sighed at how far this venerable newspaper had fallen. The *Envoy* of old would never have countenanced this. Hollier had quoted

Murphy extensively and relied on him entirely, displaying not a shred of professional scepticism. Porter wondered momentarily where the journalist did his banking.

Predictably, the dominant theory was of profound sexual deviancy, starting with the usual insinuation of sadistic homoeroticism. Porter was not offended by the suggestion that he was homosexual – he was not, as it happened, but he didn't care who thought he was. However, he loathed the sly, bigoted conflation of homosexuality and sadism.

And then there were the lies about the women. Murphy ostentatiously refrained from providing any explicit detail, but he was willing to imply that Porter had wrought the most vile degradations upon Laura Newman. Between these lies and a stunningly hypocritical sermon on misogyny, the picture editor had seen fit to print a pair of gratuitous photographs of Ms Newman playing beach volleyball in an especially economical bikini.

Amber Darcy's maturity, by contrast, was established by an unflattering picture taken towards the end of a long, hot day at the races. Any gynaecological interest in a woman of her age and aspect, went Murphy's insinuation, proved conclusively that Porter was an absolute monster. He found this as insulting to the late Mrs Darcy as to himself.

Porter understood that his examination of the reproductive and gastrointestinal paraphernalia unavoidably exposed him to salacious innuendo at the hands of the police, the media and the public. The extension of this focus to the other specimens, however, lacked even this glimmer of excuse.

He particularly resented the accusation of cruelty. He derived no pleasure at all from the small suffering his candidates experienced, notwithstanding how unendurably obnoxious they had each been to him before he had propelled them into immortality. He took great care to minimise their pain – a scruple of which Murphy must have been aware, from the forensics, yet one that he had chosen to ignore or suppress.

Porter knew that today's 'exclusive' was only the opening salvo – there would be more when the Sunday paper took its turn. Not to mention all the reaction pieces, on television and radio, and in all the other newspapers. It would run for weeks.

He was beyond furious.

He glanced at the clock and remembered several routine tasks he had yet to complete before his twelve-hour dayshift ended. He ran through the task list quickly, confirming that the bank was still operating normally. Everyone's money was nice and safe. A little less so their longevity, after today's provocation.

Sunday 13 January – morning

Murphy lay doggo until Sylvia left for brunch, then bounded out of bed. Avoiding the back of the house, he showered and dressed in ten minutes. He drove down the hill and parked at Woolies, then found a table up the back of a dodgy milk bar across the road from Industry Beans. Not trusting the coffee, he ordered a pot of strong tea and settled in to watch the table of four women inside the cafe over the road.

***

Freya stood as soon as they'd finished the quiz in the *Envoy*. 'All right, girls, I'm off to buy Dani's wedding present.'

'What are you going to get?' asked Sylvia.

'I have no idea; they already have everything.'

'Hmm, two lawyers in their early thirties...' said Jo.

'What about those round wine glasses?' suggested Katie. 'You know, with no stems.'

'No, if they don't already have them it's because they don't want them.'

'What about a wine decanter?'

'Does anyone really decant wine?'

'True. Who can wait?'

'A whisky decanter, then?'

'Oh, I don't know.' Freya sighed. 'Hence Peter's of Kensington.'

'Actually, can I come too?' asked Katie. 'I need a birthday present for Dad.'

'Don't buy anything else,' warned Jo. 'That place is dangerous. You both have too much crap as it is.'

'It'll be a ruthless military operation,' said Freya.

'Speak for yourself,' laughed Katie. The two women settled their portions of the bill at the counter, waved their goodbyes and left.

'So, how's life in the Ice House?' Jo asked Sylvia after a moment of silence.

Sylvia still wasn't ready to tell Jo all about it, not until she'd seen the lawyer. 'Things are still frosty, but at least it's calm. He's been wrapped up in paperwork every night. I'm just keeping out of his way.'

'Yes, he's been offsite a lot lately, out in the suburbs. Trawling data, we think. All very mysterious.'

'Oh, fuck.' Sylvia frowned out through the window. 'Speaking of.'

Jo turned to see her brother standing in the middle of the street, waiting for a break in the traffic. 'What's he doing here?'

He trotted across the road, smiling widely as he strode in and straight to their table, taking Freya's chair. The room shrank a little.

'Morning, Sylv.' He kissed her on the mouth, then gave his sister one on the cheek. 'How you goin', Jo?'

'Pretty good, Dave, how about you?'

'Yeah, great. Double ristretto, thanks, darlin',' he said to the barista who'd drifted over, before she could even ask him what he wanted.

'And can we have the rest of bill, please, Sorcha?'

'No worries, Sylvia.'

'You're all over the papers this weekend.' Jo nodded at the lurid

Sunday tabloid front page. 'Sure that's a good idea?'

'Perps make mistakes when they're angry, you said it yourself.' He shrugged. 'It's crude, but it works.'

'What if he goes ballistic, though?' asked Sylvia.

'He won't. He's fucken insane, but he's not a psychotic berserker on ice. He's a planner.'

Jo agreed with that assessment, on balance, but she wouldn't bet the house on it. 'When was this cooked up? I didn't know.'

'Nobody knew,' Murphy told her. 'Strictly between me and the brass.'

'Still seems dangerous to me.'

Murphy shrugged: he didn't care what the women thought. 'How'd you go in the quiz?'

'Eighteen and a half.'

'How many halves?'

'Three.'

'Any bonus points?'

'One.'

'So sixteen, really.' Murphy shook his head as his coffee arrived with the bill. He did not approve of their system of bonuses and half points.

'Hey, what did Woody Harrelson's father do for a living?' Jo asked him.

'No idea. Carpenter.'

'He was a hitman!'

'How 'bout that,' said Murphy, clearly not giving a shit. 'You all set?' he asked Sylvia.

'Soon as you're done.' She turned to Jo. 'We'll have to shoot off in a minute. I'm taking Dave to the airport.'

'Where're you going?' Jo asked Murphy as he stirred in the crema.

'Melbourne. Talking to the Operation Scintilla people.' He noticed her blank look. 'The Homicide task force on those nightclub killings.'

'They did an *Underbelly* of it,' said Sylvia, riffling through her purse.

'*Australian Psycho,*' added Murphy. 'They took an unusual approach, got results. Could be useful.'

'You kept this quiet, too.'

'People get antsy about official travel.'

Jo nodded, but she was distracted by Sylvia's increasing agitation. 'All right, sis?' Sylvia just muttered in reply. Jo turned back to Murphy. 'When are you back?'

'Late Wednesday,' said Murphy, downing his espresso.

'Shit!' said Sylvia, at last.

'What's up?' asked Jo.

'I can't find my credit card.'

'When'd you use it last?' asked Murphy. Jo rolled her eyes. Never off duty.

'Yesterday, to buy petrol, but now it's gone.'

'Did you leave your purse lying around? In the car?'

'No, I came straight home and haven't been back out until this morning.'

'Maybe it's at the service station?' suggested Jo.

'No, I remember putting it back. I almost jammed the receipt in there with it, see?' She flourished a crumpled receipt.

'It's probably at home,' said Murphy. 'Like last time.'

'No, I put it away and didn't touch my purse again until now.' She was getting testy. 'You didn't use it, did you?' she asked him.

'Why would I use it?'

'You could phone the service station,' suggested Jo.

'It's not at the bloody service station!'

'All right, keep your shirt on,' Jo said. 'So call up the bank and report it, then.'

'Yeah, I s'pose. Bugger.' Sylvia pulled out her phone. 'Dave, can you cover me for this? It's about twenty-five.'

'Nah, I'll get it,' offered Jo.

'All good, sis,' said Murphy, pulling out his wallet. 'But check at home before you ring them, Sylv. It's a bloody hassle, getting a new card.'

'It's just gone, David, okay? Don't worry, I'll get you to your bloody plane.' She put her hand out. 'Give me your card.'

'Why?'

'I need the phone number off the back. Just go pay Sorcha, will you?'

'Who's Sorcha?' he asked, handing her his credit card.

'She's one of the baristas who's been making you perfect fucking ristrettos for the past three years.

Jesus, Murphy.' She turned the card over and started dialling.

Murphy made his *women!* face and went up to pay.

'If it's gone it's gone, best to cancel it and get another one,' said Jo. She picked up the arts section and turned to the book reviews.

'Yeah, I know.' Sylvia sighed. She pressed a few buttons and reached the telephone queue. Murphy came back, stuffing a couple of banknotes into his wallet. Sylvia returned his credit card.

'Still waiting?'

She nodded, then raised a finger and turned aside. 'Yes, hello, Stephen, I need to report a lost credit card. That's right. My name is Sylvia Elizabeth Murphy, and I live at 37 Morgan Street, Randwick.'

Sunday 13 January – morning

Porter ended the call, pressed the *Away* key and removed his headset. He walked calmly to the kitchen, put the kettle on, scooped two measures of tea into his teapot, and rinsed out his mug. Then he sought the privacy of the men's room.

He emitted a gasp of joy, his fists clenched in excitement, his eyes aglow in the mirror. He could not believe his good fortune. Immediately after Murphy had insulted Porter's integrity, impugned his character and misrepresented his practices, his wife Sylvia had volunteered for service.

He splashed his face with water, finished making his tea, and returned to his desk. He swept yesterday's newspaper into the bin, declaring the innings on his attempt at dispassionate analysis. The time had come for a more trenchant response.

He knew from his prior research on the Murphys that the job was plausible:

good layout, no security firm monitoring, lots of privacy, no children. He'd established rapport with the candidate just now, which would surely advantage him relative to the previous Volumes. All he needed was the opportunity.

Timing was the major hurdle, so he started with Sylvia Murphy's work roster. Porter soon discovered that the hospital's facilities management was contracted to a company in Botany, and the back office further subcontracted to a remote service in Phoenix, Arizona. Within minutes he was inside the hospital's main server and looking at Murphy's wife's shift roster. Reading it against his own roster, he saw that Tuesday morning looked promising. She would very likely be at home resting between late shifts, her husband would be at work and Porter would be on a three-day break.

He then ran his usual due diligence process. A check of the candidate's diary revealed no commitments on the Tuesday. The housing documents confirmed there was no security system. There were no current building approvals for the neighbouring premises.

Their cleaner wasn't due until late Wednesday morning. While inside Murphy's airline account, he discovered a flight booking to Melbourne for that very afternoon, returning on Wednesday evening.

This was perfect – it afforded Porter a day and a night. While the Volume would still be performed in haste, this windfall nocturne would enable a more fitting depth of study.

Sunday 13 January – afternoon

Murphy looked out the window as the plane powered along the runway. This was the closest he would come to death today, all going well, and he enjoyed the frisson. The rumbling gave way as the aircraft left the ground then leapt ahead of itself, pulling into the sky on a wide bank to the right. They cleared the old oil refinery at Kurnell, rusting tanks in gravel clearings among the marsh and scrub, then the dunes of Wanda Beach – scene of the Force's oldest cold homicide – then the shining surface of Port Hacking, carved by the curving wakes of a hundred motorboats. Then it was all orange sandstone cliffs with murky black streaks, and a carpet of green stretching back to the freeway, the Royal National Park laced with tracks to beaches, waterholes, the Wattamolla lagoon. They passed Bald Hill – some mad bastard hurling himself into space on a hang-glider, no more than a tent fly stretched across a Hills hoist – then the contours of the Seacliff Bridge, then they crossed the coast above Bulli and finally levelled off.

After they landed, Murphy withdrew some cash from his Fort account at an airport ATM, then found the unmarked outside the terminal. Kelly briefed him on the way. Much of the schedule involved cops behaving badly, but some of it sounded useful. At the Windsor Kelly headed for the Cricketer's Bar to join the others while Murphy checked in, using his Denison Bank credit card for incidentals. He went upstairs, unpacked and rang Sylvia, but neither had much to say. He asked if she'd found her credit card and she hung up on him. *Fine. My flight was smooth, thanks for not asking. Bitch.* He went downstairs to join the reception committee in the bar.

Sunday 13 January – afternoon

Sylvia was taking full advantage of the opportunity for a long, uninterrupted session on her guitar. She was still a little rusty from her long hiatus but she was just getting back to the point where she could drift away in a piece at the level of expression instead of concentrating on the physical movement of her fingers. When the phone rang she almost didn't answer it, but she had to get ready for work soon anyway.

It was Murphy. He was tense, distant and distracted. She asked what the Windsor was like, but he didn't seem to register the question.

'Did you check the sofa for your credit card?' he asked, instead of answering. 'Wasn't that where it showed up last time?'

'Yes I did, it's not there.'

'It could be fucken anywhere, for all the care you take of things.'

'I've cancelled it, David, it's not a big deal.'

'Yeah but it keeps happening. You're bloody hopeless.'

She hung up on him then, something she'd never done in her life, not even to her father. But the grim cloud of spiteful negativity Murphy carried around was just too much to bear.

Maybe she should just get out now, she mused, take advantage of a couple of days' head start. Not having her credit card in hand made it tricky – Murphy handled all the money, otherwise – but surely she could get access to the savings account? She could confide in Jo, perhaps stay with her?

But that all sounded complicated and uncertain, and a false start might alert Murphy to her plans. Besides, it was no small thing to come between family members, no matter what Jo said. Sylvia decided to stay the course, seek professional advice, set it up right and make the move when everything was ready.

Not long now.

Monday 14 January – morning

Murphy slept poorly and woke at dawn. It was already hot and dry, the start of a classic Melbourne scorcher. He walked north into Fitzroy and found a cafe serving breakfast beside an Airstream caravan, surrounded by home-grown vegetables and sheltered by camouflage netting. He had baked eggs and a couple of coffees, then continued up Brunswick Street until he came across a bookstore. It was early, but there was someone unpacking stock and she let him in. He found the authors his sister had recommended but they didn't appeal, so the bookseller asked him what sort of books he liked and suggested Peter Temple. When he paid for the book she told him how to get to Docklands by tram.

***

Murphy found the briefings helpful, and he welcomed the absorption. He kept his mind mostly on the job and took copious notes. He checked in with Janssen in the afternoon who told him there'd been a surge in hotline calls after the media attention, but it had yielded nothing yet. Janssen asked whether Murphy had anything for them from his end.

'No, why should I?' he snapped.

'No reason, sorry. Just wondered.'

Murphy took a deep breath. He was too agitated; he needed to regain control. 'I'm just digesting it all, mate. These Mexicans run a slick operation. We should compare notes more often.'

The day rolled on. Sylvia phoned Murphy just before her late shift, but she sounded as distracted as he was. Probably preparing for her feminazi lawyers, he figured.

That night, the whole Melbourne City Homicide team went out for steaks. The women came along – it was more or less compulsory – but they made their excuses after dinner, along with the softer cocks, so it was just proper blokes afterwards. Murphy ate on the corporate card but used his own plastic for beer.

Soon they were eight or so rounds in at a loud beer hall in Southbank with a row of giant arty flues out front regularly emitting balls of flame. They were all parched by the time the next shout finally arrived, a cop called Douglas returning from the bar with half a dozen jars or tubs or whatever they called the children's size in Victoria.

'Took you long enough, Dougie,' said one of his mates.

'Got talking.'

'Yeah I was gunna ask who's your fat chick.'

A few heads turned and someone said, 'The dirty blonde in the red stripy thing.' She looked over while they were all checking her out, and she blushed scarlet.

'Oh, fuck, mate. You can't be thinking of taking that home?'

'If you try to leave with her, Dougie, I'm staging an intervention, I swear.'

'Nah, fat chicks over forty are great,' said Douglas, 'I fucken love 'em.' There were groans of disgust. 'Even better if they've got kids.'

'You pervert!'

'Not like that, you fucken ... what is *wrong* with you, Jonesy?'

'Well, fucken explain yourself, then.'

Douglas spelled it out deliberately. 'Because they shave their pussies, and they'll let you fuck 'em in the arse.'

That shut them up as they weighed the percentage.

'Yeah, okay. They're desperate.'

'Zackly,' said Douglas.

'Like Taylor's "Go ugly, early" policy.'

'Tried and true, mate,' Taylor responded, tilting his beer in salute.

'Makes sense, I s'pose, but Jesus.'

'Yeah well, your missus doesn't shave her snatch for you, does she Robbo?'

'How the fuck would you know, Dougie?'

'We all saw her at Torquay that day. Fucken jungle down there.'

'Taking back the plantation.'

'You shouldn't let her wear a bikini in that condition, mate.'

'Maybe I like the seventies vibe,' Robertson replied.

This elicited further howls. 'Enjoy camping in Melinda National Park, do ya?'

'Every chance I get, mate.'

'What do you reckon, Spud?' asked Kelly, tilting his head at Douglas's blonde hopeful, who was still throwing glances their way. 'Piss-poor standards or cunning strategy?'

Murphy shook his head. 'My missus is smoken hot and thirty-three, so I'm not much help on tactics.'

'True, she's a fucken knockout,' Kelly confirmed for the others. 'I met her at the PFA show last year.' The national cop awards night was a very glamorous affair: tuxedos, ball gowns, red carpet, the lot.

'She wasn't the one in the blue dress, was she, Spud?'

'Yeah, she was,' he replied. 'Why, did you fellas see the photos?'

This was disingenuous: Murphy knew very well that every male cop in the country had seen the photos, and had probably downloaded them onto their computers. Her red carpet shots were popular, but there was a ripper of her leaning across the table. Her tits very nearly had the better of the neckline.

'So you get the idea, then. And she goes the full Brazilian for me, I'll give her that.' He drained his glass and set it on the table. 'I'll leave you gentlemen with that image. See youse tomorrow.' He headed for the door, relishing their groans.

But thinking about her body had put his head wrong. He had to stop thinking about her. Fuck. Fuck it. It was in motion. Let it run.

He crossed the Yarra and walked along the riverbank, passing under the road near Flinders Street station instead of going up to street level. It was a mistake. He came out in a gloomy, deserted stretch of pathway, disoriented and suddenly aware of how drunk he was.

He was pissing like a racehorse against a bluestone wall when a couple of punks approached, talking overloud. He turned around just as they closed on him, fast and aggressive. Murphy pissed all over the first punk, then shoved him hard onto his arse on the bitumen footpath. The other one threw a wide uncontrolled roundhouse that Murphy easily ducked, buying enough time to tuck himself in and zip up. Then he really let loose, kicking and punching both punks with unmediated savagery, aiming for the soft parts, roaring in fury, until they gave up and took off. 'Fucken mad cunt,' one yelled as they ran away, and Murphy howled with manic laughter.

He left the riverbank, found Flinders Street again and walked along the tramway in the middle of the road. A storm swept in from the bay as he climbed the Spring Street hill, his adrenaline draining away as he approached Collins Street. He was dead on his feet by the time he made the Windsor. The doorman bade Murphy a formal good night, pretending not to notice that his guest was all wild and dishevelled and soaked through.

Tuesday 15 January – morning

Sylvia had just pressed play on a Ukrainian *bel canto* piece she was learning with the hospital choir when there was a knock at the door. She grabbed her swimming keys and padded up the hall. She unlocked the deadbolt and opened the door to a dorky middle-aged man bearing an insipid smile and a masonite clipboard.

Her hand went automatically to the screen-door latch: locked. 'Can I help you?'

'Good morning, I'm looking for Mrs Sylvia Murphy.'

'What's this about?'

'I'm Stephen, from Denison Bank – we spoke on Sunday. When you reported your card missing?'

'Oh, right. Yes.'

'You're on my way to work, so I thought I'd save you some trouble by dropping in your replacement card.'

'Oh. Well, thank you, Stephen, that's kind of you.'

'It's no trouble, Mrs Murphy.'

She gestured towards his clipboard. 'Do I need to sign for it?'

'Yes you do, and I need to record some ID. You know, for the files.'

'Will a driver's licence do?'

'Yes, please. And a recent bank statement, if you have one to hand.'

'No problem. Back in a sec.'

'Oh. Okay, Mrs Murphy.'

He clearly wanted to come inside, but he could wait right there. She closed the door on the man from the bank and went to the back of the house, where she rounded up her driver's licence and the mortgage documentation she'd collected for her meeting with the lawyer on Thursday.

She came back up the hall and opened the front door, unlatching the screen door and handing him the mortgage papers through a narrow gap. 'Is this okay from the bank? It's all I have in hard copy.'

'That'll be fine,' he said. She stood behind the screen door while he juggled his clipboard and copied down a number from the paperwork. He handed back the documents through the gap, and she crumpled them into one hand with her keys while handing him her driver's licence with the other. He stepped back a little to compare her face with the photograph, then recorded the licence number. He held the card out to return it but he was still a step away, so she pushed the screen door wider and reached for it.

His outstretched hand retracted slightly, and she tipped forward a touch to follow it. Then in a blur of motion the hand released the licence, clenched into a fist and flew straight at the middle of her face. Then there was a second punch before she could react, much harder, and an explosion of pain and light as her nose shattered and her orientation deserted her, and she was only falling, falling.

Her head hit the hardwood floor and a jet of thick rich blood swamped her face, gushing into her mouth. She rolled onto her side and spat, heaving in a deep breath and pulling herself upright. She rotated fast and lunged towards the door, blinded by blood and a wash of tears but aiming for the rectangle of light, filled now with a looming shape that she attacked with a ferocity she hadn't known she possessed. She tore at flesh and fabric but the rectangle was narrowing, so she shoulder-charged and ricocheted off him towards the light. But he was inside now and the screen door was latched and she collided with the mesh, face abloom again in white bursts of pain. He was dragging her back into the room as she groped for the doorhandle but missed, slipping on bloodied paper and keys, falling backwards again onto the floor, then he was shoving her across the timber further into the room, the heavy wooden front door closing behind her.

She hauled herself upright on the hall table, opening the drawer and reaching for the heavy marble pestle lying inside, but he grabbed her by the waistband and heaved her around, the weapon flying from her slippery grasp as he threw her down again, a hand clasping a cloth against her face, wet with some acrid chemical. She twisted away and pulled in a lungful of air, desperate to yell out, but he kneed her hard in her ribs and knocked the wind out of her. She bucked and kicked, but he had all the leverage and a renewed grip over her shattered face, so she opened her mouth and bit down hard through the wet pad until she tasted blood – new blood, his blood – and he roared in pain and wrenched his hand away.

She twisted out from under him once more and pushed him over and away, blinking the blood and tears from her eyes until she found the pestle, grasping it by its haft and lifting it high above her head and bringing it down onto his temple, as hard as she could with no hesitation: she knew what this was she knew who he was she knew what she was fighting for. But he turned aside before the blow connected and he caught it instead on the jaw and neck, there was no crack but it laid him out on the floor and it was enough. She was on her feet and working the handles and she was through both doors, outside and making for the gate. But then her T-shirt went drum-taut around her shoulders and wrenched her backwards, clean off her feet, her back crunching onto the concrete path. He was pulling her by her arms back towards the door, her legs scrambling for purchase, her hands flailing. She heard Clare's voice in strident command: 'Leave her alone! I'm calling the police!' and he dropped her weight to the ground and she looked straight up and read his face as he assessed his options, saw him give up his assault as a lost cause, saw the afterthought dawn, saw what was coming.

She closed her eyes tight as he dropped her torso and cradled the sides of her face, lifting her head up, up, pausing at the top of the arc to stroke her left cheek with his thumb, once, gently, then smashing her head down to earth with a terrifying velocity. And there was nothing in the world but an explosion of searing pain, an awful crack, a blinding white light, an annihilating mortal fear; then everything dissolved to a merciful, consuming blackness.

Tuesday 15 January – morning

Porter let go of Murphy's wife's head and scrambled to his feet, turning towards the side fence, but as soon as he stepped away from the inert form he was struck hard on the elbow by half a paving stone. The old woman was reciting her address into a cordless telephone while crouching down below her camellias, before coming up with another chunk of stone from the border of her garden bed. He evaded the second missile and retrieved his clipboard from the front step, shoving it into his Gladstone bag. He gathered up everything the candidate had dropped when he'd punched her and shoved it all into the bag. As he closed it, he collected another paving stone on the side of his neck, and he turned and crashed through the flimsy picket gate, the neighbour screaming blue murder behind him.

Porter ran diagonally across the road towards a side street, a final paving stone bouncing on the road behind him, and he risked a look back as he rounded the corner. The neighbour was crouching over the motionless candidate, still talking into her phone. He cut left as soon as he could and threaded through the maze of streets, slowing his pace to a brisk walk as he worked his way back to where he had parked.

Porter's outward calm was a complete fiction, his disappointment only eclipsed by his self-loathing, and he choked back a sob as he approached his car. With anyone else he would have aborted the attempt once entry had become problematic. He would have simply found another candidate upon whom to perform the Volume. But this one was special. The Tribute had become personal. So when she had failed to let him in, he had escalated to violence, assuming she'd turn and run inside like Laura Newman, retreating further into the trap of her home. But she'd stood her ground and fought to gain the greater safety of the outside world.

And now he had been seen, had fled instead of walking away. It was a serious setback, but he would not fail Vesalius. Or let Murphy off the hook. He made a silent, solemn vow that he would complete the Tribute, no matter what. And he would make Detective Senior Sergeant David Murphy pay.

Tuesday 15 January – morning

Murphy woke up fairly dusty on Tuesday morning, but three doppios and a proper hot breakfast at Cumulus sorted him out.

The cool change had come in overnight and he walked down Flinders Lane towards the police headquarters in a very light shower. Typical Melbourne. It had only a little more weight to it than mist: less rain itself than a metaphor for rain. He'd never admit it to a Mexican, but it was actually quite pleasant.

The morning at Vic Homicide lacked the energy of the previous day, as the novelty of an interstate visitor started to wear off. Late morning found him in a forensic lab, his mind wandering, in desperate need of another coffee.

Then a door behind him crashed open, and everybody turned around, and Murphy knew immediately that something had gone terribly wrong with his plan back in Sydney.

'Detective Senior Sergeant Murphy?' It was one of the juniors from last night. He'd told this young copper to go home when he'd started looking green around the gills. He looked a lot worse now.

'What is it, son?'

'Your ... it's ... you need to talk your office, sir.'

'Are they on the phone now?'

The boy nodded, gulped. He looked as clammy as warm cheddar.

'Which line, constable?'

He held up two fingers.

Murphy crossed to the flashing handset. They would have called his mobile, vibrating uselessly in a basket outside the lab door.

This couldn't be good. It was a day too early; she wasn't supposed to be discovered until Wednesday. What had happened? Was it done? Was Porter in custody? Was Murphy under any suspicion himself?

Only one way to find out.

'Murphy here.'

VOLUME VII

THE BRAIN

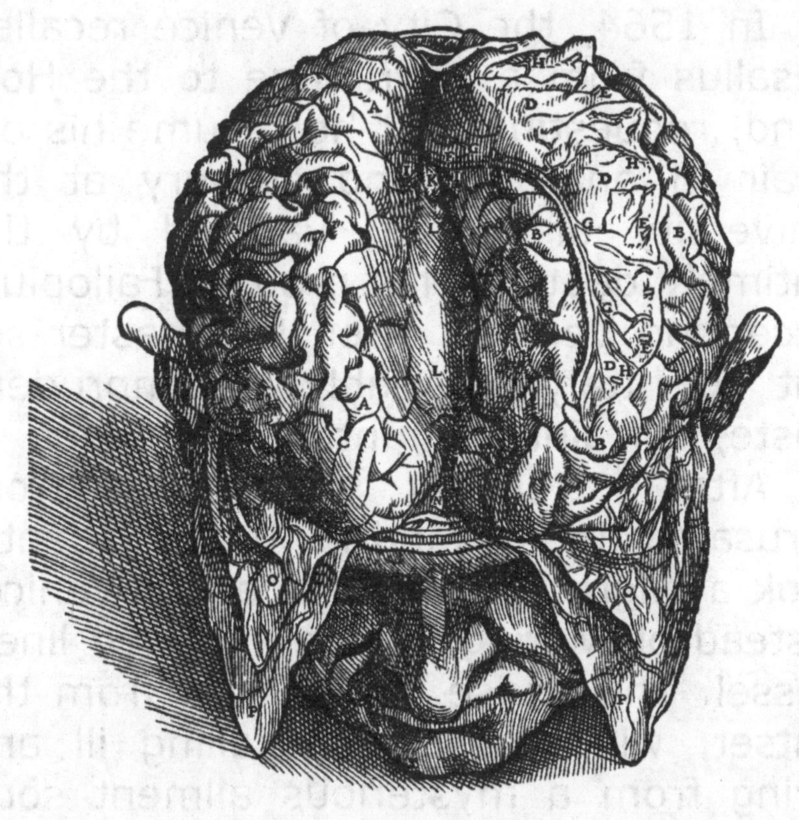

In 1564, the City of Venice recalled Vesalius from a pilgrimage to the Holy Land, requesting that he resume his old chair in anatomy and surgery at the University of Padua, vacated by the untimely death of his protégé Fallopius. Accepting Venice's offer, the Master set out for Italy, arguably in imprudent haste, certainly by unreliable means.

After trekking overland from Jerusalem to Alexandria, he impatiently took a pilgrims' charter boat for Venice, instead of waiting for the Venetian line's vessel. The cruise was cursed from the outset, with passengers falling ill and dying from a mysterious ailment soon after they'd embarked. Then the ship was delayed for weeks in the Ionian Sea, safe within Venetian waters but frustrated by recalcitrant winds.

By strange coincidence, a thunderstorm had been brewing when Vesalius was himself struck by illness. Then – we owe a debt here to C.D.

O'Malley, who translated the deposition on Vesalius's death – then the storm broke, with a violent flash of lightning and an appalling crash of thunder. As the disease ravaged the Master's body, the ship struck rock off the island of Zante, and Vesalius leapt out and swam for the deserted shore. When he nerved himself to turn, the storm had done its work: the ship was lost. Despite his weakened condition, the Master stumbled to the city gate, only to succumb at the threshold of salvation. He was forty-nine.

The historical account suggests that the mysterious ailment was scurvy. Records show that the malaise on the unfortunate ship was concentrated on the poorer travellers, pointing away from infection and towards a factor that was a function of wealth. Absent violence, diet was the most likely culprit. It was common for all but the very wealthy to forego fresh food on Mediterranean voyages, which were typically of only a few days' duration. The early deaths may be attributable to an equally impoverished desert caravan diet prior to boarding. As the voyage dragged on, both morbidity and mortality increased rapidly.

Scurvy may be considered guilty civilly if not criminally, as it were: the case is not beyond doubt, but on the balance of probability, that hypothesis best explains the distribution and timing of the ship's calamity.

As everyone knows now, but nobody knew then, scurvy is a long-term selective malnutrition caused by a deficiency of vitamin C. It befell those forced to rely for long periods on preserved rations: sailors, soldiers, overland traders. It took centuries for medical science to resolve. While long observed, this expensive disease was not properly described until 1753, two centuries after the death of Vesalius, by Royal Navy surgeon James Lind in his *Treatise on the Scurvy.* The culprit had evaded deductive reasoning due to the coexistence of two independent factors: the quite random assortment of foods containing vitamin C, obscuring any trend; and the propensity of vitamin C to degrade under preservation, such that the same food might or might not have been a source, depending on its treatment. As Lind observed: 'I do not mean to say that lemon juice and wine are the only remedy for the scurvy. This disease, like many others, may be cured by medicines of very different, and opposite qualities to each other.'

Most animals are not susceptible to scurvy, because they can manufacture L-gulonolactone oxidase, the enzyme required to synthesise vitamin C. Simians – including humans – and certain birds, fish and other mammals have lost this ability along the way. In humans, the necessary DNA code is missing from the *p* arm of chromosome 8, which is strongly connected to brain development and function, and also happens to be highly mutagenic.

This high rate of mutation on a chromosomal fragment fundamental to brain development is one of the critical factors that enabled the rapid evolution of the human brain. There is some evidence that mutations at location 21, where the nonfunctional gulonolactone oxidase pseudogene is found, are implicated in schizophrenia.

Scurvy and schizophrenia, then, may be the genetic price that humans pay for our intelligence.

Once Lind had identified the cause of scurvy, eradication was straightforward. The disease has all but disappeared today. It can be easily prevented by the consumption of foods rich in vitamin C, including citrus, guava, strawberries, whale skin, cabbage, oysters, spinach, horse meat, capsicum, adrenal glands and potatoes.

Another fine source of vitamin C is the central nervous systems of animals, including humans.

Tuesday 15 January – noon

Murphy had to admit, the Mexicans handled the situation bloody well.

They let him vent his shock and fury, then waved away his apologies. Victorian Police ops admin liaised with their New South Wales Police counterparts to change his flight. They put him in a pursuit vehicle with their best wheelman and sent a couple of blue-and-whites ahead up the freeway to clear the express lane.

He phoned Janssen back from the car.

'Sorry about that.' All his deputy had managed to tell Murphy earlier was that their perp had savagely attacked his wife in his own home, putting her in hospital, and had fled the scene. Murphy had cut him off by slamming down the lab's telephone in fury.

'You don't need to apologise, David.'

That conveyed the gravity more than anything. Janssen had never called

Murphy by his given name, not even once, in all their dozen years.

'How is she?'

'She has serious injuries to her head and upper body, but the ambos reckon she'll pull through. Your neighbour was on scene; she did all the right things until they arrived.'

'Is she conscious?'

'Not last I heard, no.'

'Probably better off. She at Prince of Wales?'

'Yes, they've pulled out all stops.' Sylvia would get the royal treatment, at her own hospital. 'And I've posted guard – a couple of our spare uniforms.'

'Good. Does my sister know what happened?'

'Not yet. Chartier's on her way to tell her.'

'No, I want to tell her myself. Get Chartier to just bring her in.'

'Okay.'

'Something I don't follow,' Murphy said. 'What makes you so sure her attacker is our guy?'

'He dropped a cloth soaked in midazolam in your front room.'

'Oh, thank Christ. Finally Mr Perfect fucks up.'

'Yes, he left in a hurry. And your neighbour said he ran off with a Gladstone bag – looked heavy.'

'His bag of tricks.'

'I'd say so.'

'Circumstantial, but I like it,' Murphy said, nodding.

'We've got a lot of blood here, too. We're hoping some of it's his.'

'How much is a lot?'

'It's pretty messy, Spud. She put up a hell of a fight.'

Murphy cursed. This was not the plan. It was all supposed to be rapid, clinical, virtually painless: a shock, a few seconds of fear, then nothing. Like a light going out. But instead it had been violent, ugly, traumatic.

Not to mention that she was still alive. He had no idea what that was going to involve. He hadn't wanted her to suffer, particularly, but he hadn't wanted her to fucken survive, either. What if she was a vegetable? What if she wasn't? Neither prospect was enticing.

Janssen interrupted Murphy's gloomy reverie. 'And the neighbour said she hit him with a couple of paving stones.'

'Who did, Sylvia?'

'No, Clare Vaizey, your next-door neighbour. She chased him off while she was on the phone to 000. Not bad for ninety-odd.'

Murphy grunted, reluctant to give credit. 'So he'll have lost some skin.'

'Mack's confident we'll get some DNA at last, one way or another.'

'Good.' Murphy paused for a moment, then dropped his trump card. 'But we also have video.'

'What? How?' Janssen's excitement was palpable.

'Security cameras, front and back. Motion-activated. They record onto the PC through the wifi. The picture's very good.'

'Where do I go?'

Murphy directed Janssen to his study and talked him through downloading the week's footage that was automatically saved by the system.

'Okay. So, how did he get to her?' Murphy asked while Janssen worked the camera program. 'Did she let him in?'

'No, it all happened right at the front door. It looks like she's opened the door and he's forced his way through.'

'The famous twelve red roses.'

'There's no sign of flowers, but something like that, yes. Did she order anything to be delivered?'

'Not that I know of, but that doesn't mean much.'

'We'll check the financials.'

'And ask Jo when she comes in.'

Janssen blew out a long breath. '*Nondedju*. That's not going to be good.'

'It is not. Okay, I've gotta go, we're almost there.' Twelve minutes from the police headquarters to the airport: he doubted that could be done from Surry Hills to Mascot, and this was three times the distance. This driver was good.

'I'll be there when you land,' said Janssen.

'No, you stay there; get Harris to pick me up. We'll come to you.'

'I'll send Harris, but you can't come here, boss.'

Murphy arced up at that. 'Don't fucken patronise me, mate. If you're so worried about my mental health let me catch the cunt.'

'It's not about that, Spud. Your home is a crime scene. You know the protocol. You're off the case, officially.'

'Fuck protocol.'

'Really, Spud? You want the prosecution thrown out of court?'

Murphy had no plans for Porter to see trial, but he couldn't very well say that to Janssen. And not in the back seat of a police car, in another jurisdiction. He chose another tack. 'You can't lock me out of the case, mate.'

'Of course not, it's just a formality. But you can't go to the house. You know the brass will be watching. It's both our necks.'

'Fuck. *Fuck.*' Murphy punched the seat beside him. He fumed, but he knew his deputy was right. 'All right. Meet me at the office when you're done.'

He hung up and glared out the side window until he recovered his composure, then faced forward again. The driver and his offsider were scrutinising the landscape as carefully as if they were scanning the Fallujah roadside for IEDs. They'd exchanged silent glances during Murphy's conversation, but hadn't reacted overtly. Smart fellas.

The head of airport security was waiting out the front. Murphy was able to cut the queue at the scanners, and a courtesy cart took him to his gate. Someone must have primed the airline: they gave him an upgrade and he was first on the plane. An attractive young blonde offered him a drink before he even sat down.

Tuesday 15 January – noon

Porter stood in the front foyer of his house for the last time.

He had tended to his injuries and destroyed the incriminating driver's licence and papers from the Randwick debacle. He had retrieved his go-bag, a tactical backpack stuffed with equipment, supplies and rations – including $10,000 in used banknotes – to keep him going through a range of fugitive scenarios. He had a canvas weekender with several changes of clothes, his running gear and another $50,000 in cash beneath a false bottom. The bulk of his money was spread innocuously across a dozen bank accounts in a variety of false names.

The rest he would abandon: his home, his art, even his precious *New Fabrica.* He had his high-quality photocopies of Volumes VI and VII, and the beautiful new edition was a liability now. He had to harden his heart to all sentiment, other than his thirst for revenge. That he would nurture, cultivate, slake.

He would honour the Master by continuing his Tribute, striking quickly in the quarter least anticipated. The police would expect him either to flee the city, or to make another attempt on Murphy's wife, who was stable in intensive care, according to the radio. They would never predict the move he was about to make.

He collected his bags and went through the front door without a backward glance, pausing only to lock it behind him. No point making it easy for them.

Tuesday 15 January – afternoon

By unspoken agreement, Murphy and the suit in 1A ignored one another until they landed, when it was safe to exchange comradely banter about the relative merits of Sydney and Melbourne with respect to weather. Then he was first off the aircraft and straight into another cart. Within minutes of docking he was striding across the footpath through the humidity to the waiting unmarked.

'Any progress?' he asked Harris by way of greeting.

'Shit, yeah.' Harris was grimly pleased as he drove away. 'Niko's got a dozen really clean stills from your security video. He's running scans with Roads now, on the driver's licence photo bank. The Feds are searching the passports database.'

'Same bloke from the Hordern's footage?'

'Niko says so, yeah.'

Murphy's phone rang: it was Janssen. He hooked into the car's stereo and answered. 'Where are you?'

'Surry Hills. But, boss: we've identified him.'

'You fucken beauty! Who is he?'

'Stephen Samuel Porter. Lives in Marrickville, works in Alexandria.'

'Have you despatched?'

'Nguyễn's doing it now. Which one do you want?'

'You're closer to Alexandria. We'll take Marrickville.' Harris changed lanes accordingly.

'17 Helena Street, off Sydenham Road,' said Janssen. 'And get this: he works for Denison Bank.'

'Wait. Oh, fuck,' said Murphy, clicking his fingers. 'Sylvia lost her credit card on Sunday. She rang the bank to report it. Jo and I were with her.'

'The Fort?' asked Janssen.

'Yes, the fucken Fort.'

'I knew it,' said Harris.

'I owe you a beer, son,' said Murphy.

But Harris was in no mood for laurels. 'Let's find the bastard, first.'

'Listen, Janssen: phone Tom Adams before you go in. Tell him about this lost card angle.'

'Might be better coming from you, Spud. I don't really know him.'

'I couldn't take it, mate, he'd be all tea and sympathy. Besides, it's your case. *Protocol,* remember?'

'Fair enough. I'll call him on the way.'

'Any news about Sylvia?'

'Yes, Mack spoke with them a short while ago. Critical but stable. They're keeping her unconscious for now, to minimise brain swelling. She has a number of injuries but the main concern is the blow to the back of her head. It was quite severe.'

Murphy took a deep breath. 'Do they think there's permanent damage?'

'The scans were inconclusive. Mack says there's no way to know for sure until she wakes up and starts talking. She's in a private room within ICU. I don't think you can see her yet.'

'Okay. I should wait for Jo, anyway. Have you heard from Chartier?'

'No, her phone's going straight to voicemail. I've left some messages but haven't heard back.'

'Keep trying.' They hung up.

Murphy's phone rang again immediately. It was Hollier, the *Envoy* journalist. Murphy took as much of the journo's contrition as he could handle, declined a request for an exclusive follow-up and hung up.

Then the commissioner phoned. 'We're all thinking of your wife, Detective Murphy. She'll be guarded around the clock, as long as she's in hospital, and of course we're deploying every resource to catching him. You need to know this is personal now, for all of us. You have the entire Force at your side.'

'Thank you, commissioner; that means a lot. We have a positive ID. My team's on the way to both residence and workplace.'

'Yes, about that. You understand you're off the case now, don't you, detective?'

Murphy seethed, but kept his tone level. 'Yes, sir, I understand.' Harris shot him a questioning look, but Murphy waved impatiently at the road beyond the windscreen – *just keep going.*

'You can stay in your office and do some desk work on the case, but Janssen's in charge and you're confined to barracks, do you understand?'

'Sir.'

'No interference, detective, or I'll bring you out to headquarters. I mean it.'

'Of course, sir,' said Murphy. 'Thank you, sir.' He hung up before his relief made the commissioner think again.

Harris checked his mirror to change lanes. 'So, back to the office, is it?'

'Nah, fuck that,' said Murphy. 'You're off to see where this prick lives, Detective Harris. I'm just sitting in the passenger seat. Anyway, what the brass don't know.' He was not about to be locked up with the bosses in the executive offices out at Parramatta, but keeping away from the investigation wasn't an option either.

Harris returned to his original lane and put his foot down.

From then on the phone rang non-stop, with the entire police command expressing their concern. They meant well, but sweet Jesus. After the police minister's office rang, Murphy diverted all calls except those from Homicide. *Fuck's sake. It's not as if she's died.*

Porter's place was fifty metres down from Sydenham Road on a T-intersection supervised by a quiet neighbourhood pub. It was a modest brown-brick house from the thirties with geometric stained-glass casement windows, a deep front verandah and a roof of lichened terracotta tiles.

The block was cordoned off by half a dozen patrol cars and a swarm of uniforms. A tactical unit executed an orthodox frontal assault. Murphy was third man in, even though he wasn't officially there.

They found the house unoccupied and cleared out. Murphy phoned Mack.

'I hear Niko identified him?' said Mack.

'Yeah, I'm at his house now. Dunno what you're gunna find; it's freakishly tidy. Looks like he's shot through.'

'If he lived in it, we'll find plenty.'

Murphy had his doubts, but just grunted.

'Spud, I'm so sorry about Sylvia,' said Mack.

'Thanks, Mack. I appreciate you keeping up with her condition.'

'No bother at all. Head of Emergency's an old mate. We interned together in Tamworth.'

'I'd be grateful if you could keep tabs on her, Mack. I'm going to have my hands full trying to catch this bastard.'

'Of course, Spud.'

'Can you give me a bit more detail? What's with this head injury?'

'Well, it isn't good, but they're saying it isn't terrible.' Mack clearly hoped to leave it there.

'Come on, Mack. Do you want me to read about it in the *Tele?*'

The medico drew a deep breath. 'She's in an induced coma, Spud. She had a lot of head trauma, so the main worries are swelling and the risk of a bleed. So far the scans are clear but anything can still happen. Staying under in ICU gives her the best chance of stabilising.'

'And then what? Will there be any brain damage?'

'It's hard to tell yet but I'm told the prospects are good, as long as there's no bleeding.'

'What else did he do to her?'

'She had multiple facial fractures including a badly broken nose. A few broken ribs, a couple of broken fingers. Dislocated right shoulder and right thumb. And that nasty occipital fracture.' Mack cut himself short.

Murphy wasn't having it. 'Come on, Mack, what else? Did he put her under?'

'No, she avoided the midazolam.'

'Then what?'

'Just...' Mack hesitated. 'He pounded her head into the concrete, Spud. Your neighbour saw. After he knew it was all over. He took the time to break her skull before he ran off.'

'Fucking ... *cunt.*' Murphy smashed a fist into the kitchen bench beneath him, then went quiet for a long time. Porter had broken the rules, turning his clinical little parlour game into a violent common assault. On his fucken wife. It was personal now.

Murphy eventually tuned back in, sensing Mack's distress at the other end. 'Thanks, Mack. Let me know of any changes, will you?'

'Of course.'

Murphy hung up and calmed himself down, then rang Janssen. 'Nothing here at his house,' Murphy said.

'Same at his work,' his deputy replied. 'He's not rostered on until Friday. They'll detain him if he comes in.'

'Is their security detail up for that? A fugitive serial killer?'

'They've got a guard who's ex-British SAS. Adams says he was in Belfast during the Troubles.'

'Okay. But surely we've blown it now anyway. Porter won't show up.'

'I think you're right. There were cars and uniforms all over the place, everyone at the windows.'

'Might as well go public, then. Throw out the net.'

'I'll get the media unit on it.'

'What did Adams say about the lost card theory?'

'He's concerned about the bank's liability. He's going to phone you about it.'

'Any idea of Jo's whereabouts?'

'No, I still can't reach her – or Chartier.'

'Keep trying. See you back at the ranch.'

Twenty minutes later, Murphy and Harris were standing in the unit's briefing area with the rest of the detectives, minus Amy Chartier. Nikolaidis projected three crisp colour photographs of the same man: a corporate head shot, a still from Murphy's security camera and a passport photo. Nikolaidis added the best still from the Hordern's CCTV footage for comparison.

'Our perp's a middle-aged Caucasian male, you'll be shocked to hear. Name of Stephen Samuel Porter, forty-four years of age, as of two weeks ago. Works in Alexandria, lives in Marrickville, alone as far as anyone knows.' Nikolaidis raised his eyebrows at Murphy and Harris, who both shrugged and nodded.

'No whereabouts as yet. We'll watch his house and his workplace, but the media unit is hitting the TV and radio bulletins, so we're not expecting him to turn up.'

'What about his use of the bank's computer system?' asked Janssen.

'We're preparing a seizure brief now for his access records,' said Nikolaidis.

'No need for seizure,' said Murphy. 'We'll sort it out with Tom Adams. The bank'll want to position Porter as a rogue player.'

'Fucken oath they will,' said Harris. 'An employee bumping off customers...'

'It's a PR nightmare,' finished Nguyễn.

Nikolaidis continued. 'There's nothing on him in CrimTrac. He has a sister in Wagga but we haven't been able to reach her. We've got locals there on it.'

A phone rang and Nguyễn picked up. 'Homicide ... Oh, Christ ... Thanks, Gately.' She hung up and turned to Murphy. 'Chartier found Jo. They're on their way up.'

'Does she know about Sylvia?' asked Nikolaidis.

Murphy shook his head. 'Just that there's another crime scene. Get on with it, everyone, but don't stray too far. Janssen, come with me.'

Tuesday 15 January – afternoon

Porter observed the raid on his home from the front bar of the Ern Malley Hotel, an odious public house whose sole virtue was its affordance of an unobstructed view along the length of his street. He'd spent several hours here after each Volume, watching his house. Now, he witnessed the end of his settled life with resignation and disappointment: he'd known this day was coming, but he'd hoped to complete the Tribute first.

Above all, he was annoyed with himself for so thoroughly mishandling Volume VI, despite all his planning. Having been identified, despite all his precautions, would make things exceedingly difficult.

He watched from the gloom of the noisome bar as Murphy and his thugs demolished his front door. It had taken him days to sand that door back and repaint it. They were brutes and fools who clearly watched too much television.

At least he'd had the foresight to withdraw his equity prior to embarking on the Tribute, by selling the house and renting it back. He'd enjoyed the convenience of staying in his own home without risking the forfeiture of his capital.

He sighed deeply and turned his attention to Sylvia Murphy's keys. He'd grabbed them more or less by instinct, from where they'd landed on the bloodied bank papers. But it had been an inspired instinct, for they held the twin prospects of redemption and revenge. He toyed with the Sydney University medallion, which suggested that the three coloured keys would give him access to Joanna King's apartment.

Which, in turn, would give him access to the contents of Joanna King's cranium, in a somewhat more literal way than the meeting of minds he had proposed in April.

He left nearly untouched a glass of attempted pinot grigio and departed through the beer garden. It was no longer safe for him here, and he had a theory to test.

Tuesday 15 January – afternoon

Jo strode rapidly from the lift to Murphy's office. 'Could you give us a minute please, Thijs?'

'Of course.' He stepped outside to join Chartier, who'd followed in Jo's wake.

Jo closed the door then leaned across her brother's desk. 'Why would you try to keep this from me, David?' Her voice quivered with anger.

'Oh for ... It's not all about you, Joanna.'

'That's my point, exactly.'

'What's that supposed to mean?'

'You wanted to tell me about Sylvia yourself, just to indulge your taste for melodrama. And you say *I* watch too many movies.'

'Come on, Jo, don't get hysterical.'

'You do not call me hysterical, mate.'

'Look, sis, let's not—'

'You push people around to suit your own agenda. Try to control everyone.'

'I don't—'

'And how could you expect Amy to keep this from me? She's my *friend*.'

'She's a police—'

'Shut up, will you, I'm talking. I know this is awful for you, but it's awful for me, too. Just ... release your grip a little. Let us each handle things our own way? Please?'

He walked around the desk and put his arm around her. 'I'm sorry if I upset you, sis. I just wanted to be with you. We're family.'

The wind was out of her sails now. She punched him half-heartedly on the chest, then collapsed into it and sobbed. 'She spoke to that bastard while we were right there, Dave,' she sobbed. 'Remember? I told her to ring the Bank.'

'Come on, it's not your fault.'

'Is she going to be okay?'

'I don't know. They're keeping her under for now. It's going to take a while before they can tell.'

She wept into Murphy's shirt while he looked over her head at Janssen and Chartier outside his office, conducting a muted but intense discussion. *What fresh hell?*

***

Janssen ended the phone call with Mack. Chartier looked at him, dumbfounded. 'How are we going to tell him that?'

Janssen shook his head. 'I have no idea; it's too much. I'll deal with it later.'

She looked down. 'I'm sorry about today.'

'I tried ringing you all day, Amy. He became very agitated.'

'Thanks for taking the heat.'

'What happened?'

She shrugged. 'Phone battery must've died.'

Janssen glanced at the mobile in her hand. 'Seems okay now.'

Chartier looked him in the eye. 'I couldn't keep her in the dark and just haul her in here, Matthijs. I mean, could you?'

'Probably not.'

'So what would you do? Under the circumstances.'

'Turn my phone off and take care of her,' he admitted.

'Right.' Chartier relaxed visibly then. 'She wanted to go to the hospital, but I rang and they told me Sylvia was in isolation. So I took her home. She was a fucking mess. Finally, she settled down and I said I had to come in. She insisted on coming with me. I tried to make her stay but she didn't want to be alone. Tell you what, she's pissed off with Spud.'

'It's probably shock as much as anything,' he said. 'I'm glad you were with her, Amy. You did the right thing.'

Something in his voice made Chartier look up then, and they held one another's eyes for a long moment of recognition. Janssen nodded, in his serious way, and Chartier flushed slightly.

They looked up as Murphy's door opened. 'Come in, both of you,' he said.

Chartier went straight to Jo and pulled her into a hug. Jo buried her head in her friend's shoulder, then detached from Chartier and drew Janssen to her. Murphy cleared his throat.

'So I think we're all straight now,' he said to Chartier, absolving her for going dark on him. 'Jo tells me she wants to stay on the case.'

'Oh, honey,' said Chartier. 'It's too much.'

'What else am I going to do? I can't go back to work.'

'Take some time off,' suggested Janssen.

'And just sit there picturing it? I'd rather help catch the fucker.' Janssen and Chartier both nodded doubtfully. 'We're fine, if that's what you're worried about,' said Jo, nodding at her brother. The detectives were visibly unconvinced of that, too.

Murphy wore a look of strained tolerance, waiting for all the feelings to dissipate. 'Let's just get on with it, can we?'

'He's right,' said Jo. 'Can we?'

'Of course,' said Chartier, squeezing her arm. 'Whatever helps.'

'But you should see our counsellor,' added Janssen.

'It's a good idea,' said Murphy.

'You too, boss,' said Chartier.

'Yeah, nah, I think I'll pass. I understand that humans find it helpful, but that shit doesn't work on me.'

Jo snorted a reluctant laugh and wiped her nose. 'God, you're annoying,' she told her brother. 'I wish I could just hate you.'

'So listen,' Murphy asked her, 'how are you set for company overnight?'

Jo felt the others' radars step up to high sensitivity. She very deliberately kept her gaze on her brother. 'What do you mean?'

'The SOCOs are still at my place.'

'Oh, right. Yeah.' In a normal family, Jo supposed, a sister would offer her brother her spare room as long as he needed it. Instead, she waited for him to continue.

'So I was thinking about staying at the pub over the road here. Close to the action. But if you need the company I could stay with you instead.'

'No, that sounds best,' she replied a little too quickly. 'Thanks anyway.'

'No worries,' said Murphy, oblivious. He'd done his fraternal duty and had been excused. Perfect outcome.

'So, what can I get started on?' Jo asked the detectives.

'Denison Bank's sending over all the relevant data, but it's in proprietary formats,' said Janssen. 'Maybe you could figure out how it all works, so we can put it into spreadsheets.'

'Okay, I'll get started.' She left the office and headed downstairs.

Murphy closed the door. 'All right, is there anything you two want to tell me now she's not around?'

'Yes,' said Janssen, 'but I'd prefer to tell you when you're not around, either.'

'No time for that. Let's hear it.'

Janssen looked at Chartier, who frowned grimly, then back at Murphy. 'Spud, Mack says Sylvia was pregnant. Five weeks.'

'The baby didn't make it,' said Chartier. 'I'm so sorry, boss.'

Murphy buried his head in his hands so they couldn't see his face. He found it cold comfort to have been proved right. He looked up to find his subordinates exchanging an alarmed glance. Perhaps he was overdoing it.

'Does Jo know about this?' he asked.

'I doubt it,' said Chartier.

'Well, someone better tell her.' Chartier moved to leave – in Murphy's world this would definitely be women's work – but he stopped her. 'No, you stay. You do it,' he told Janssen, who nodded and left.

Murphy lowered his voice. 'I'm told you reviewed the security footage over the past week. Before the attack.'

Chartier breathed out slowly and shifted her focus. 'That's right.'

'So what did you find?'

'Nothing, really. She was just going about her days. You know, cooking, housework. Reading, swimming, guitar. Nothing relevant.'

Murphy weighed the wisdom of the next question, but he had to know. 'Did she have any company?'

'No,' replied Chartier, puzzled. 'Were you expecting any?'

Murphy straightened and waved a hand. 'Just the old woman next door. Never mind.'

'Oh. Well, no. It was just Sylvia. And you, of course.'

'All right. Off you go.'

Chartier nodded and left the room.

Murphy locked the door behind her and closed the blinds on the internal window. He drew a fresh bottle of Lagavulin from his bottom drawer, cracked the customs seal and pulled the cork. He put the bottle to his lips and took a decent swig, rolling the burn around his mouth.

The big question was what to do now. What if she came out of hospital fucken brain-dead? He'd be expected to care for her. Feed her baby food, shower her, wipe her fucken arse. Not likely.

Even if she pulled through with no permanent damage, there'd be a long convalescence. Months of living with her, looking after her, knowing the whole time that she'd planned to take off with some cunt who'd knocked her up; knowing she was probably still planning to take off once she was back on her feet. Fuck that, too.

But he couldn't exactly walk in there and rip out all her wires, either. And Porter wasn't going to finish the job, not with a police guard on the ward. No, he'd have to bide his time, see what shape she came out in, and figure it out from there.

He poured a decent measure of whisky into a mug and recorked the bottle. Better pace this one. He felt exhausted, strung out, overwhelmed.

But fucken vindicated.

Tuesday 15 January – evening

Porter checked in to a modest flat in Clovelly, all organised online to avoid face-to-face contact. After attending to his injuries, he spent several hours changing his appearance, applying tonal makeup and discreet facial prosthetics, and giving himself a completely new hairstyle. He turned on the television and found himself all over the evening news, but it was a face that the casual observer would not recognise in the new one in the mirror. The TAFE course on theatre production he had taken in preparation for this day had been well worth the time invested.

He was not surprised to learn that Sylvia Murphy had a heavy police guard on her hospital room, but neither was he discomfited. He had every intention of fulfilling his Tribute by dissecting the heart of Murphy's beloved, but she would keep for another day: for now, he would turn his attention to the brain of Murphy's intellectual sister. The poetic symmetry was irresistible, after all, and it compensated somewhat for the unfortunate necessity of proceeding out of order.

Once night fell he painted his fingertips with clear nail polish, then went out to the car and swapped his old number plates for a clean pair he'd found in a questionable auto wrecking yard. He drove to Coogee, checking the route and scoping the streetscape. He parked near King's apartment block, then walked to the top end of the beach and back, admiring the luminescent foam on the island in the middle of the bay beneath the nearly full moon. He slowed as he approached the park opposite King's place from the north, exploiting a lull in the passing foot traffic to dash into a thick stand of heath banksia beneath a low-growing clutch of honey myrtle. The vantage point was well hidden but had a clear view of her building's front door.

He didn't have long to wait. King and a tall plainclothes policeman arrived in a late-model sedan and entered her building. One of the Homicide detectives, no doubt. The lights went out soon after, but the policeman did not emerge. Porter hadn't anticipated an overnight security detail, but he wasn't overly concerned: they wouldn't keep that up for long.

He crept out of his hiding place, crossed to the building and tried the keys from Murphy's house on the frosted-glass lobby door. The yellow one turned the barrel, confirming his hunch. He suppressed a shiver of excitement and slipped inside to look around, but there was nothing to see beyond the letterboxes and a few forgotten items stored beneath the stairwell.

This was enough risk for one night. It was time to rest so he would perform optimally when the time came. He left the building and walked away down the hill, exhilarated at the audacity of his plan, before circling back around the block to his vehicle and driving to his anonymous apartment.

Wednesday 16 January – morning

'We compared DNA from the skin and blood at the scene with cell tissue from his home,' Mack told the morning briefing. 'It's conclusive: Stephen Porter is our man.' There was a rumble of approval. 'We also found a spotless copy of the *New Fabrica,* locked away. You nailed it, Jo.'

'It was Sylvia's idea, really.' Jo dragged her eyes away from the blown-up photos of the killer and turned back towards the group.

'So who is this prick?' Murphy asked. 'What's his backstory?'

Nguyễn read from her notebook. 'It's fairly unexceptional, actually. He grew up in Dulwich Hill, just him, his mum and his big sister. No dad on the scene. He went to the local primary school then Fort Street High. After matriculation he studied medicine at Sydney—'

'I knew it!' Murphy turned to Mack. The SOCO raised his eyebrows in reply.

'Yeah,' said Nguyễn, 'but we were too narrow, looking for graduates: he dropped out in third year. Then he did odd jobs – watch repairs, bar work on Taverner's Hill, selling insurance. Enrolled at the Sydney College of the Arts. It's part of Sydney Uni, too.'

'But not on the main campus,' said Jo. 'They're in the old psych hospital in Rozelle.'

'How appropriate,' Nikolaidis said.

'He specialised in anatomical drawing,' continued Nguyễn. 'We found the catalogue for the graduating exhibition in his honours year. All stuff like the *Fabrica*.'

'Let me guess: his thesis was on Vesalius?' asked Jo.

'We don't know yet, Dr King,' chimed in Harris. 'The college is asking for a court direction to access his academic records.'

'That's bullshit, Harris,' said Murphy. 'It's a murder investigation and those are relevant files. The case law is clear.'

'That's true, boss,' said Chartier, defending the rookie. 'But these places don't hire lawyers to answer the phones.'

     'The commissioner seems to know the vice-chancellor quite well,' said Jo dryly. 'Why don't you get him to ask her?'

     'I don't need the commissioner to hold my prick while I piss,' said Murphy. 'This is bread-and-butter stuff.'

     'All right, then. I know the provost, I can try her,' said Jo.

     'Do that. See about his med-school files while you're at it, will you?'

     Jo nodded. 'Do we know anything else about his art career?' she asked Nguyễn.

     'Yeah, looks like it never really took off. Not enough to live on, anyway. He'd been part-time with the insurance firm through art school but went full-time after graduation. They were eventually swallowed up by Denison Bank, and he moved to the back-office side. Ended up in tech support. He's worked there ever since.'

     'So how would we find out if he ever sold any art?' asked Jo.

     'Fraud Squad have an active fine-arts brief,' said Nikolaidis. 'Cox will know how to find out. Why?'

'I just can't shake the feeling he looks familiar,' she said, looking again at the trio of photographs fastened to the board.

'You might know people he knows,' suggested Janssen. 'Someone could know his haunts.'

Jo nodded. 'It might help to see what he was painting. Did he have a studio at home, Dave?'

'No. There was an easel in a sunroom but there was nothing on it.'

'Did he have any of his own artwork up?'

'Didn't really notice what was on the walls, to be honest.' Murphy looked at Harris, who shook his head.

'We photographed everything,' said Mack. 'I'll show you later. He has a few original pieces I didn't recognise, a couple of reproductions tending to the anatomical. A fairly gruesome pietà.'

'Mantegna's *Lamentation,* I'd bet. The foreshortened one.'

'That's it.' Mack nodded. 'And your *Dead Christ.* The frame looks new.'

'He sticks to his 'hood, doesn't he?' Harris broke in, studying the city map. 'Raised in Dulwich Hill, high school in

Petersham, bar job on Taverners Hill, med school in Darlington, art school in Rozelle, lives in Marrickville, works in Alexandria. D'you reckon he has issues?'

'Living in the inner west is not a psychiatric condition, Harris,' said Nikolaidis, who lived in Erskineville.

'Still, it's interesting that he's ranged all over town on the job, while living in such a tight pocket,' said Nguyễn.

'He broke all the rules by killing someone in Glebe, then,' observed Janssen. Conventional wisdom held that serial killers tended to keep a prudent distance between home and their crime scenes. There was a theory that with enough victims, an unwitting serial killer would eventually draw a ring around their own district.

'Maybe he's read the same books we have,' suggested Chartier.

'Was there anything from the doorknock?' asked Murphy.

'Just the usual stuff,' said Nguyễn. 'He's quiet, keeps his yard tidy, brings your bin in, keeps to himself...'

'"Can't believe a nice fellow like him is mixed up in something like this"?' suggested Nikolaidis.

'Exactly.'

'Same at his workplace,' added Janssen. 'Model employee, reliable colleague, happy to help with a swap – maybe a little boring.'

'What about the sister?' asked Murphy.

'Dead end,' said Chartier. 'She's in a care facility: late-stage lung cancer. Hasn't seen her brother for six or seven years. Not close to begin with, apparently, then they fell out over some family dispute. She's got two daughters, one still at home. I'm told the girl literally spat on the ground when asked about her Uncle Stephen.'

'Crikey,' said Nguyễn. 'Where's the other daughter?'

'Los Angeles.'

'Actress?' asked Murphy.

'Entertainment lawyer. Apparently he sends presents to her kid, but that's it.'

'Okay, scratch that,' said Murphy. 'What else?'

'One unusual move,' said Nikolaidis. 'He sold his house September before last, then rented it back.'

'Smart,' said Murphy. 'Got his equity out to avoid seizure.'

'And cash to run with,' added Harris.

'How about the car?' Jo asked.

Nikolaidis smiled sadistically. 'White ten-year-old Corolla sedan.' Everyone groaned. It was the most common vehicle on the road in every category: age, model, body and colour. 'His plates are flagged with Metro Traffic, and we're canvassing all commercial carparks equipped with plate readers.'

'I bet he's swapped plates,' said Janssen. 'He's a planner.'

'Yeah, it's what I'd do,' said Murphy. 'What about travel records?'

'We've got his credit card statements going back eighteen years,' said Nikolaidis. 'Bankies are very steady in their financial habits, apparently.'

'Discount interest rates,' said Jo.

'He's done all his banking with the Fort his entire working life. We're combing through it now. If he goes to ground, chances are it'll be somewhere he's been before.'

'Could be someplace he hadn't been for a while,' said Chartier.

'Yeah, but we figure he'll have gone back for a fresh recce once he started planning all this,' said Nguyễn.

'Makes sense,' said Murphy. 'Let's check for flights and get camera data for country New South Wales roads as well.'

'How far back?'

'We know he was planning in earnest when he put his house on the market,' said Janssen. 'Start a few months before then.'

'That's a lot of computation,' said Nikolaidis.

'You think our system's not up for it?' asked Murphy.

'It can handle it, but it'll take a while.'

Murphy turned to Jo. 'While you're talking to this prefect of yours, maybe ask if the uni's got a big fuck-off supercomputer we could get some time on.'

'Provost,' said Jo. 'Okay.'

'What if he bought another house in a different name?' asked Nguyễn.

'No, he might have dropped some on a bolt-hole, but what he really needs now is a lot of cash,' Murphy said. 'His money's in a bank somewhere, sure as there's shit in a cat.'

'Not Denison Bank, but,' said Harris.

'Probably not, although we should check Fort accounts opened by his user ID,' said Janssen.

'Both good points,' said Murphy. 'Let's feed his basic backstory to the media; follow up last night's bulletin. Get to it.'

Murphy caught Mack's eye as the team dispersed and cocked his head towards his office. They went in and Murphy shut the door. 'I have a technical question for you, Mack. Strictly confidential.'

'Sure.'

'Janssen told me about the pregnancy.'

'I'm sorry, Spud,' Mack said gently.

'Thanks, Mack. Look, I know this is a strange question.'

'That's okay. Anything you want to know.'

'Don't pass this on. That I'm asking.'

'Of course not.'

'Can we find out who the father was?'

'Whose father?'

'Whose do you think, Mack? Christ.'

'What are you talking about? She was yours, Spud.'

Murphy shook his head. 'That can't be right.'

'The lab matched the DNA against your exclusion sample. It's standard procedure.'

'How reliable is that result?' asked Murphy.

'As near a hundred per cent as doesn't matter.' Mack gave Murphy a quizzical look. 'What's this about, Spud?'

'Just ... how's that even possible? I had the snip years ago.'

'Ah, I see,' said Mack, with manifest relief. 'Recanalisation. It's where the tubes regrow over time. Not common, but not vanishingly rare, either.'

'They told me about that, but I thought it only happened in the first year or so? I did some follow-up tests.'

'Usually that's right. But it can also happen after trauma, like surgery or an injury. Didn't you take a knock down there last year?'

Murphy thought about it. 'Yeah, I got me balls stomped on in a collapsed scrum. Some fucken Manly prick. Laid me up for the weekend.'

'You probably ruptured something, and the vas deferens re-established during the healing process.'

'Fuck me, I really had no idea. So I've been shooting live rounds ever since?'

'Sounds like it,' Mack said.

'Damn, I'll have to get it done again.' Mack was taken aback, so Murphy added, 'It's like a kick in the balls, mate. I'm not that keen for another one.'

Mack raised his forehead and blew out both cheeks. 'It's not the most comfortable procedure,' he eventually agreed.

Murphy recognised his error, so he bent his head and turned from the SOCO. 'Sorry, Mack, I'm all over the fucken place. There's just too much going on.'

Mack placed a hand on Murphy's shoulder. 'It's all right, Spud. Everyone understands.'

Murphy wasn't entirely convinced he'd recovered his ground but he turned back around and nodded his thanks. 'So—' he croaked. He cleared his throat and tried again. 'When can I have my house back?'

'This afternoon will be fine,' said Mack, clearly happy to change topics. 'My crew's about done there, and the clean-up detail will only take a couple of hours.'

'And what about Sylvia? When should Jo and I go up there?'

'You could go now if you want to, but she's still in a coma. I'm told she looks pretty rough. She's definitely recovering, though, so there's no urgency.'

'So what are you saying, keep away?'

'I'd wait until she's conscious. There's no benefit to Sylvia in you going now, and it will just be traumatic. Better to go when she knows you're there.'

'Okay, good advice,' Murphy said, trying not to sound relieved. 'Would you mind telling Jo that yourself? She'd take it better from you.'

'Okay, I'll talk to her.'

'All right, that'll do for now. Thanks, Mack.'

Mack regarded Murphy with an appraising gaze then turned and left the office. Murphy closed the door then sat down heavily behind his desk, holding his head in his hands for a moment, in case anyone was watching through the window. But when he looked up, it was all just detectives going about their detecting, so he opened his drawer, poured a decent measure of whisky into his coffee cup and drained it in one go.

Just when you thought you had the measure of the game; just when you thought you could see all the pieces in play. Something always snuck up behind you to fuck you up. This homicide business was full of fucken surprises.

It dawned on him that Sylvia would've known about the recanal thing last winter. She was a fucken nurse – of course she knew. All that time she was pretending to care for his tender balls, she was just trapping him into giving her a baby.

Then the penny dropped. It had *never* been about happy families: she'd probably been planning this all along. Trick him into knocking her up then shoot through; take him to the cleaners with the paternity to hold over him. That fucken scheming bitch.

Wednesday 16 January – morning

Jo looked at the piece of folded notepaper in her hand, her stomach plummeting and her mind reeling at its significance. Inscribed by a finicky hand were the words **VESALIUS** and *Stephen Porter* over a Sydney phone number. She remembered him now, that odd but oddly forgettable Vesalius buff who'd approached her after her public lecture last year. A trainspotter, Sylia had called him.

And she'd had his number all along.

Medium everything and unremarkable in every way, but he'd looked familiar when she'd first seen his face blown up on the Homicide Squad incident board yesterday afternoon. Now she knew why: she'd met him, spoken with him, taken his phone number. Then folded the piece of paper and promptly lost it among her scrappy pile of lecture notes. She hadn't given the man a moment's thought since, until now when she was finally sorting through all her case notes.

She stood frozen with indecision. She felt an urge to tell someone, even an obligation, but she was afraid of her brother's reaction. Thijs would feel compelled to tell him; Amy too, very likely. Her face flushed as she realised her oversight could find its way into the newspapers. But there was no doubt it was a pertinent fact. She needed to talk to her brother anyway: she'd wing it on whether or not to tell him, depending on his mood. She walked over to Murphy's office and knocked on the door, pulling him out of some grim reverie.

'What is it, sis?'

'I've just spoken with Mack,' she said. 'What do you think?'

'About what?'

'About visiting Sylvia. Or not visiting her.'

'I think we should follow his advice.'

Jo was unconvinced. 'She needs us, Dave. She'd want us there.'

'She'd want us here, trying to catch the fucker. Mack says she's oblivious. What if it throws us off our game?'

Jo exhaled. 'All right. But let's talk about it again tomorrow.'

'Okay,' he said, but she could tell he would be of the same mind then.

She lifted a sheaf of papers. 'I've figured out the bank's file formats.'

'Have we got the data converted into spreadsheets yet?'

'Angelo's writing a script for it.'

'Who?'

'Niko.'

'Oh, right. Great.'

'And the provost is sending all Porter's central records over by courier now. They're rousting the medical faculty and the art school, too, to see what they've got locally. I have a contact in her office for anything else we need.'

'Thanks, Jo.'

'And I helped Amy go through the week's video from your backyard camera. There's nothing relevant.' Murphy raised an eyebrow, but Jo didn't expand.

She'd been heart-warmed and saddened in equal measure, watching her friend at home, unselfconscious and free. Sylvia had read, cooked, played guitar, talked on the phone, dipped in the pool, danced around a little to a soundtrack Jo couldn't hear. Sometimes she just sat there, happily stroking her belly. Other times she'd been pensive and tearful, but each time she'd pulled herself together. Murphy had brought a stultifying weight to the mood whenever he'd appeared, the tension tangible even through that tiny, silent aperture. But mostly it was a documentary film of a week in Sylvia's most private life, spent in peace and calm, in sadness and occasional joy. Jo had made herself a copy.

'I'll look through the university files when they arrive,' she continued flatly, 'but I'm not sure what I'm meant to do after that.'

'What do you want to do?'

'I want to wake up and for all this to not be happening.' She teared up again and he motioned to come around to her, but she waved him down. 'I still want to help,' she continued once she could speak. 'But I'm not sure how to be useful.'

'Stay here, sis, we need you. There's always work on an investigation for a sharp pair of eyes and a good brain.'

'That's the nicest thing you've ever said to me.'

'Don't let it go to your head.'

Jo laughed and almost told him then about Porter's note, but she remembered something else and went the other way. 'Dave, did you know Sylvia was pregnant?'

'No. Did she tell you?'

'No, she didn't.'

'I'm surprised,' he said.

Jo shrugged, but she was hurt to have been kept in the dark.

Her brother ventured a line. 'I suppose she hadn't decided yet.'

'Decided what?'

'Whether to keep it.'

'She'd have wanted to keep her, Dave. She would've been worried about you.'

'That's not fair, Jo. I never even knew.'

'Yeah, no shit.'

'What does that mean?'

'She wouldn't have been able to bring it up. You were always so unyielding.'

'About what?'

'About not having children.'

'There's nothing wrong with knowing your limitations, Jo.'

'But you wouldn't even discuss it with her.'

'We did discuss it,' he objected. 'Several times.'

'No, you just shut her down and ruled it out. That's not discussion, Dave.'

'So she complained to you about it?' he asked, exasperated.

'She's my best friend.'

Murphy sighed. 'I can't believe we're fighting about this.'

'We're not fighting, it just makes me sad.' Jo wiped her eyes on her sleeve. 'That poor little girl.' She turned away without looking at him. She couldn't confide in Murphy like this. She'd keep the phone number story to herself, for now.

Jo was nearly out the door when Murphy said, 'Actually, there is something you could do.'

She turned back.

'Reckon you could contact Sylvia's family, let them know?'

'Why would we do that?' she asked. Sylvia seldom mentioned her childhood in Western Australia. Jo knew there was some sort of unpleasant backstory that Sylvia never talked about, and she'd had bugger-all to do with her family since coming to Sydney. Jo really couldn't see why that should change now.

'They'll only see it on the news otherwise. I don't need the static.'

'I've never even met them, Dave. Shouldn't you do it?'

'Nah, they don't like me. And they're creepy.' Murphy had only met them the once, as far as Jo knew, over an intensely awkward lunch in Margaret River. 'At least you're neutral. Anyway, you're good at that sort of thing.'

'What, because I'm a woman?'

'Exactly.'

Jo snorted.

'What?'

'You really don't have a clue, do you?'

'What'd I do now?' he asked, his arms opened wide at his sides, palms facing forward. His stance reminded her fleetingly of one of the standing figures in the *Fabrica*. She turned and walked out without another word.

Wednesday 16 January – afternoon

Porter spent the morning in neuroanatomical study then returned to Coogee, lunching at a homely cafe at the northern end of the bay while he caught up on the news. He was unsettled to find his face on all the front pages but he was satisfied that his disguise was holding up. Sylvia Murphy was still in an induced coma, due to her brain injuries, but the doctors were cautiously optimistic. Apparently she had been pregnant, but was no more. Porter felt no regret at that detail – if anything it simplified things for later, when he would return to claim her heart.

He paid his bill and strolled along the boardwalk. The beach was crowded – had none of these people a job? – but he enjoyed its demotic feel in comparison to the tedious beautiful-people tone of certain other beaches nearby. He climbed the hill at the southern end into the park opposite

King's apartment, hoping to reconnoitre the terrain at his leisure. It proved more difficult than he'd hoped.

He found it necessary to keep moving, due to factors he'd failed to anticipate. There was a playground directly opposite her building, for one – always a difficult setting for a middle-aged man to linger in without attracting suspicion. Then a leisurely pause at the top of the rise earned him a disgusted admonition from a passing jogger, and he realised that the nearby cliff-face overlooked the women-only sea baths. No loitering was possible here, either, especially on a hot summer's day when the baths below would be well patronised. To make it all worse, the long-sleeved shirt he wore to cover his wounded elbow was as conspicuous in its way as the livid bruise and nasty graze on his neck.

He wandered around the southern headland and into the back streets until dusk, then ate dinner at a small Thai establishment. After dark, he collected his Gladstone bag from his car and returned to the park, seizing a quiet moment to settle into his vantage point within the brush.

It was a tiresome wait of some duration. The moon was full and creeping into the canopy of the Norfolk pines by the time King finally returned home at 11.30, once again escorted by a plainclothes security detail; a woman this time. Porter sighed with frustration while they passed inside, then settled down to wait for his chance.

Wednesday 16 January – night

Murphy couldn't fucken believe it. Finally on his way home for the first time in days, nine o'clock at night, and he runs into the fucken crone next door at the local supermarket. The shopkeeper had helpfully pointed her out, so he'd been obliged to make a great public fuss over her heroic rescue of his poor unfortunate wife, and then he'd had to give her a lift home. A pain in the fucken arse it was, being a pillar of the community.

He settled her into the passenger seat and latched a seatbelt he'd have sooner wrapped around her scrawny throat. As he pulled out of the carpark, she murmured, 'Dear Sylvia; she deserves better.'

'Yes it's horrible, what happened,' Murphy mumbled. 'Lucky you were there.'

'That's not what I mean, Mr Murphy. I mean, she deserves better than you.'

Murphy twisted to look at her. She gazed levelly back. 'I beg your pardon?' he asked.

'Watch the road,' she said, and he turned back to the front. 'I know how you treat her. You're a big man out there in the world, Mr Murphy, but it's who you are at home that counts. And I know what kind of man you are.'

'Oh yeah?' Murphy sneered, glaring over again. 'And what kind is that?'

The old hag smiled tightly and shook her head. 'I don't use that sort of language.' She looked out her side window at the full moon breaching the ocean horizon. 'Your wife is lovely,' she said softly. 'She deserves much better.'

They didn't exchange another word. He parked in front of his house and she struggled out of his car with her pissant bag of groceries. Not so much as a thanks for the lift. Murphy let her fuck off inside her place before he got out. Fucken witch.

Then, finally, he was inside his house, front door shut, every fucken arsehole and criminal and spiv and politician and pathetic fucken civilian on the other side. He stood against the door, head tilted back, eyes closed. Home.

Alone.

After a long moment he pushed off and made for the back room. 'Time for a fucken drink,' he said aloud.

He shrugged off his jacket and removed his shoulder holster, sliding the weapon into its drawer. He could hear Sylvia nag him – *Why do you want to keep it in the kitchen, Dave?* – completely missing the point of having a portable fucken Howitzer on the premises.

He dropped his keys into the big marble mortar, watching them land beside Sylvia's sprawling main bunch of a dozen keys and tags and fobs. *Must weigh half a fucken kilo,* he mused. No wonder she kept the streamlined set to take swimming. He took the bottle of Lagavulin and a glass over to the couch. He sprawled across it diagonally, his head supported by the low armrest, his neck supported by a small cushion, and his soul supported by Islay whisky, the early tendrils of soothing oblivion reaching into those provinces of his brain that really needed to shut the fuck up and give him a night off for once.

He tried to empty his mind. Like Sylvia and her bloody meditation. Better than sex, she said. Fucken, as if. Reckoned she could empty her mind for hours at a time, away on retreat. Away from *him.* His response was always that she had an unfair head start on an empty mind.

Sylvia.

What the fuck was he going to do about her? He had no idea where things went from here. Sooner or later Sylvia would wake up and come home, looked like, and either she'd need nursing for the rest of her life – in which case sorry, but fuck that shit – or she'd let him help her recover fully then waltz back out the door. And then where would he be?

Fucked, that's where.

No. He'd started it. He had to finish it, somehow. He just had to find a way.

He let the idea settle on him, then he told himself to leave it alone for now. It was too soon; he needed to know the scenario before he could build a plan. He just had to trust himself.

He drank more whisky then slid down on the couch, looking up through the window at the high, silvered clouds. He closed his eyes and tried visualising the Gatting Ball, the young Elle Macpherson in that Tab commercial, the car chase from *Bullitt*. Anything. His mind tuned out at last and he dozed, dreaming in blue.

But then he came back to periscope depth, and a single concrete realisation that had been needling for attention for days finally broke through. He lifted his hips to pull out his wallet and removed Sylvia's Denison Bank credit card. It'd been risky to carry it around this long, but he'd been reluctant to destroy it in case the narrative needed it to show up, and he couldn't leave it anywhere in case it was found. It was the little things that always fucked people up. What to do with it now? Lost in the home, he decided. He polished the card with his shirt and went to the laundry. He flicked on the light and leaned over to peer down behind the washing machine. It was all lint and dust back there. He dropped the card into the gap. Some repairman could find it one day. It'd fit the story perfectly.

He went back to the sofa but he was wide awake again now, so he topped up his glass and turned his mind to Porter. He'd be unpredictable now he was on the run, but Murphy knew they'd have him soon. They'd harvested a ton of data in the past couple of days, and since they'd released his identity the hotline had been busy with all sorts of people who'd known him. Somewhere in there were the details that would lead them to him. It's always in the details.

In theory, Porter could go to ground and live out his life as Mr Nobody in Buttfuck, Nowhere. But in Murphy's experience, crims never had the patience to sit tight and lie low. Sooner or later, every bad guy raised his ugly mug above the parapet. And Murphy would be there when he did, waiting to blow it away.

At that happy thought, his exhaustion pulled him back under. He slept deeply on the sofa for a couple of hours before the dark dreaming started again, thrashing him about until he gave up. The moon was way up now, shining brightly on the courtyard and the pool.

He drained his glass and looked up through the canopy of the Sydney red gum in the yard behind. Something was still not right. His gut knew what it was, but his brain wasn't listening. He sat up and grabbed the Lagavulin, tipping the last two fingers into his glass. He nearly dropped the bottle when the realisation hit him.

Sylvia's swimming keys were missing from the big marble bowl. The set with Jo's front-door keys on it. He went over to check, pulling out his own set, with Jo's back-door key on it, and Sylvia's big bunch. The pared-down set of keys was definitely gone.

And he knew with a sickening certainty where they were.

Sylvia must have used that set to open the front door to Porter. The crime scene team hadn't found them, so Porter must've taken them when he ran. Maybe he'd spotted the university crest and guessed whose keys they were.

A chill ran through Murphy then. Porter could let himself into Jo's place at any time. He could be there right now.

No, that wasn't right: Porter *was* there right now. Murphy knew it in his bones.

He scrambled into action: pulling on his shoes, grabbing his keys, retrieving his revolver from the kitchen drawer and bolting for the front door.

Fuck, he hoped he'd make it in time.

Wednesday 16 January – very late

The lights went out in King's apartment just before midnight. The policewoman left the building, walked up the hill to an unmarked car and drove away. Porter waited another full hour before creeping across the road and letting himself into the lobby. He glided up the stairs to the top floor. The red key didn't fit, but the green key slid into the lock and rolled the tumbler on its axis. He opened the door and was halfway inside when he saw Joanna King lying on her couch, not three metres away.

***

Murphy drove recklessly fast down Dudley Street, straight over the top of two low-profile roundabouts, police lights flashing. At Beach Street he switched into stealth mode: headlights off, coasting down the hill to park next door to Jo's block. He looked up at her place three storeys above. Her lights were off, but he thought he saw a brief flash on the balcony ceiling. Probably his imagination. The main thing was there was no mad fucker looking down, watching him arrive. He grabbed a can of graphite spray from the boot, ran down the side of Jo's block then quickly scaled the external staircase at the back of the building.

***

Porter stood unmoving until he was sure King was asleep. He was reassured by a near-empty bottle of red wine alongside two glasses, one half-full and one drained.

He came completely inside and closed the door silently behind him. He opened his Gladstone bag and eased the keys down inside, all the while watching his quarry. She was utterly still. He donned a pair of gloves, then removed the gauze pad from the sandwich bag, crossed to the sleeping scholar and clasped the gauze firmly to her face. She woke immediately, of course, all struggle and grunting and bulging eyes, but her panic was brief. Once the midazolam took effect and she was out cold, he worked quickly under torchlight to prepare the other pharmaceuticals.

***

Murphy waited a moment to gather his breath outside Jo's door, then squirted the lubricant into the hinges and keyhole. He drew his revolver, thumbed the safety off and pulled the hammer back. He slid his key silently into the lock, turning it steadily, then pushed lightly. The door opened with only the faintest squeak. He looked around the small rear storage room, his eyes adjusting to the darkness inside after the bright moonlight. Empty. He withdrew the key, slid the bunch into his pocket, slipped inside then closed the door silently.

Murphy held still, trying to tune into the space above the sound of his own pounding heart. He thought he could feel the presence of someone there, sharing the air of the apartment, listening for him. Jo? Porter? His imagination?

Only one way to find out.

***

Porter was preparing Joanna King's cubital fossa for the sodium thiopental when he registered a tiny sound at the back of the apartment. It might have been nothing – these old buildings shifted constantly – but then he had an uncanny feeling, a heuristic response to a shift in air pressure and in the sounds coming from the street. He switched off his torch and listened. A moment later, the street sound diminished slightly, and a kind of flatness returned to the air around him. There was no doubt about it: a door or a window had opened then closed, somewhere out the back.

Porter cursed himself silently. He had failed to consider the possibility that the apartment had a back entrance: it was unusual, certainly, but not rare in blocks of this vintage. In his haste he had come underprepared. Losing access to the bank network had robbed him of many resources, but he could have at least found a floorplan online.

But it was too late for recriminations. Now it was all about survival. He looked around, assessing sight lines and shadows, but his major problem was weapons. He had enough pancuronium bromide to kill a man twice over, and it was even effective injected directly into muscle instead of a vein, but a syringe was a meagre weapon in hand-to-hand combat, no matter its contents. His Gladstone bag held a loaded pistol, but it sat squarely in the line of sight of the hallway, bathed in moonlight: if the intruder had made any progress at all, he'd be looking at it right now.

My kingdom for a ballpein hammer.

A floorboard squeaked slightly down the hall. It had to be Murphy. Who else would have a key to the apartment and an inclination to stealth? A boyfriend would not be so sneaky; any other cop would storm the front door.

It was time to commit to a course of action, right now. The kitchen was his best bet, with the refrigerator providing some cover from the hallway, and an armoury of weapons.

Holding the syringe of pancuronium bromide, he crawled to the kitchen counter, then slid up onto it. He swivelled across it, quickly but quietly, casting a brief shadow on the rear wall of the kitchen, out of sight from the hallway. He let his body down softly. He set the syringe on the bench, and levered an impressive meat cleaver from the magnetic strip on the splashback. This would be the weapon to finish with, but the first blow demanded something hard and heavy. He found a mortar, identical to the one at Murphy's house, but with its pestle in place. How poetic. He could still feel the effects of its twin on his jaw. He switched the knife to his left hand and hefted the pestle with his right.

***

Murphy crept steadily along the hallway. Jo's floor was squeaky as fuck – he knew from experience – so he stepped with a wide gait, his footfall hugging the skirting boards to minimise the travel of the ancient floorboards.

At Jo's studio he dropped his body, braced his shoulder against the door jamb and his right foot on the far wall, and slid his head around cautiously down at hip height. The theory was you got a quick peek without having your head blown off. In practice, poking your head inside a room occupied by a fugitive serial killer bore a fair degree of inherent risk, and there was only so much you could do to mitigate it.

But there was no serial killer in sight. There were plenty of places to hide, but the ambush risk was too great for him to go in and clear the room. He played the percentages and pressed on.

He was creeping forward again when he noticed a vintage leather doctor's bag just inside the front door. He'd never seen it before. Certainly wasn't Jo's. Presumably it was the famous bag of tricks. Then the moonlight on the wall ahead undulated briefly. It wasn't a shadow, exactly, more like a ripple passing across the surface of water. The trees were on the far side of the street-lighting and Jo's balcony plants were small. That meant someone was moving around in the living room. He moved quickly up the hall.

***

The gun came first, the muzzle poking out of the hallway past the refrigerator. It was tentative, as though sniffing out danger, then came forward again. The barrel just kept on coming, lengthening to an almost comical extent, and in his heightened state of anxiety Porter nearly giggled aloud. Murphy and his pathetic masculinity issues. Eventually there came the cylinder, then a finger curled around the trigger, then the butt and the hand. Then the fragile wrist, the point of least stability.

Porter was tempted to strike now, but the aspect of the gun's approach indicated that Murphy thought his quarry was in the living room rather than the kitchen. So Porter held out for the decisive head-strike, pestle raised high. Murphy kept coming: too late, he glanced into the kitchen, just as Porter brought the pestle down onto his skull.

***

Looking to his left to clear the kitchen, Murphy caught a glint of light on steel just before he sensed the body next to him. He reeled back, but an explosion of pain over his left ear sent him flying. He held his feet somehow and staggered into the living room, taking a blow on his left shoulder then the back of his head. Porter had thrown his club: it would be a knife next, or worse. Murphy caught a glimpse of Jo on her sofa – dead or alive, he couldn't tell, but definitely out of commission. Too bad: he could do with the help.

He turned to take a shot but Porter was right on top of him, a meat cleaver in one hand and a syringe in the other. They collided at full pace and crashed onto the coffee table, Murphy catching the edge on the middle of his back with Porter's full weight on him. His gun flew out into the darkness, and he heard the knife fall as they tumbled together onto the floor. Murphy sat up and punched down at Porter, hard on the side of the face. Porter rolled away, slashing at him with the syringe, tearing Murphy's shirt and tracing an arc across his chest. Porter pushed Murphy back against the coffee table, then got to his feet and ran for the door. Murphy attempted a diving tackle from his knees, but missed. Porter snatched up the leather bag and disappeared through the door.

Murphy tried to stand, but his vision swam, so he stayed down for the moment. His head hurt like fuck and his upper body was battered, but at least he could see and move. He held his hand to his clamouring left ear and felt the blood pulsing out of his scalp. There was another nasty gash at the back, but he'd survive.

He crawled over to Jo on the couch. He put his ear to her mouth and sensed nothing, but with his head still roaring that wasn't surprising. He hovered an open eye over her mouth until he could feel her breath on his cornea, shallow but regular. Thank fuck. He shook her with one hand while checking her arms for needles and feeling around her head and torso for injuries. She seemed intact. Eventually she groaned and opened her eyes.

'You all right, Jo?'

'Think so,' she said, her speech syrupy. 'Gave me mizlam. Tastes awful.'

'He was getting ready to inject you.'

'Fuck.' She laid her head back. 'Thanks, Dave.'

'No worries, sis.' He felt around for his revolver.

'Where is he?'

'Took off. I'm going after him.' He re-emerged from under the coffee table, gun in one hand, the other moving to a sticky mess of blood congealing on the side of his head.

'Shit, Dave, doesn't that hurt?'

'Only when I laugh.' He came cautiously to his feet. He was unsteady, but upright; it was going to have to do. 'You stay here,' he said, and stumbled out the door.

Thursday 17 January – early hours

Jo was still a bit groggy, but the soporific was wearing off quickly, so she slipped on some shoes, grabbed her keys and followed her brother, closing the door behind her. She raced down the stairs then peered cautiously outside and saw Murphy half-sitting in the passenger seat of his car, his legs poking through the open door.

'Get down, he has a gun,' he stage-whispered at her. *Well yeah,* she thought, *he's a serial killer: of course he has a bloody gun.* But she crouched behind the bonnet like she was in the 'Sabotage' video and scuttled across to him.

'I thought I told you to stay put.'

She ignored that. 'Where'd he go?'

But Murphy was already slithering further inside, his arm up under the driver's seat, then he pulled out and handed her something compact and dark as he got out of the car. 'If you're out here, you're going to need this to wave around.' She recognised the police-issue Glock 22, the model she'd fired at the range. Only it was way too light. 'Don't fucken use it, and don't fucken lose it.'

'But, Dave, it's not—' she started, but he cut her off.

'Call it in on the radio, then go back inside,' he said. 'Tell them he's gone into the Ladies' Baths.' Then he was off, running around the front of the car and across the road, through the playground and into the shadows above the cliff.

She got into the car and inspected the police radio. One green LED glowed, but it was otherwise dark and silent. Was it even on? There was no obvious power button. She lifted the mic and pressed the button on the side. 'Hello?' Not even static. She tried again, more declaratively: 'Hello.' Silence. She felt ridiculous.

She looked across the road at the shadows obscuring the gate to the Ladies' Baths. *Nah, fuck this.* She checked the Glock's chamber was clear then ejected the magazine. She opened the glovebox and swapped the empty for Murphy's spare magazine, pushing it into the butt until the catch clicked. She pulled the slide back and let it spring forward to chamber the first round. She weighed the loaded gun in her hand. *Might not be able to work the stupid radio, but I can load a bloody pistol.*

She got out of the car and closed the door quietly, then took off across the road, keeping to the shadows beneath the tall, straight Norfolk pines. She held to the line of their trunks, curving around to join the footpath, until she reached the gate to the Ladies' Baths. It was swinging open.

Okay. They were on her turf now. She went in.

Jo held the gun in both hands out in front, moving steadily and smoothly down the path alongside a brick wall. She peered around the corner at the end, scanning for movement. She was looking along the front of the change rooms, brilliantly lit by the full moon almost directly overhead. Beyond was the maze of lawn and bushes and paths and rocky shelves of the steep, terraced hillside above the ocean pool.

She ducked between the rails of a wooden fence, slid down the grassy knoll and leaned cautiously over the proper fence at the bottom. The pool glistened beneath her, an expanse of flatrock and sand with the odd clump of seaweed, its surface riffled by a light breeze. There was nobody in the pool or on the steps below her, although the far steps were mostly out of sight.

She made her way along the fence, past the top of the pool steps and towards a retaining wall beneath a small grassed terrace. She stopped and looked around: from where she stood, a short flight of steps led down from just beyond the wall to a wide concrete platform that served as the baths' central intersection. She paused to inventory the various alcoves, platforms, shrub screens and pathways around it that had sprung up over the years. It was a complicated space for such a confined area – Porter and Murphy could be anywhere in there, stalking one another, coming within metres of each other without realising it. She took a deep breath and reminded herself that this was her terrain: she knew these grounds well, while the men had never so much as set foot in here.

If Murphy and Porter were moving around at all, sooner or later they'd have to come through the concrete plain before her. She moved quickly over to the cover of the retaining wall, leaning her head against the brick for a moment. Her heart was pounding hard and fast. She told herself to calm the fuck down. Listened, for once.

She looked around the edge of the wall and nearly lost it as she saw Porter standing with his back to her not ten metres away, on the wide expanse of concrete where seconds ago there had been only moonlight. She pulled back to her cover, her heart lurching then restarting in a trip-hammer beat. She peered around once more.

Porter hadn't moved a muscle: he was standing in a tense parody of a television gunfighter's stance, like Elvis in that Warhol silkscreen, aiming an automatic pistol across the expanse of concrete into the shadows beyond. He was utterly transfixed. Jo couldn't see whatever he was looking at, but it could only be Murphy.

She took a slow breath to steady herself then stepped out silently from behind the wall, creeping across the path to a small lawn that sat above the concrete platform but was screened from it by a row of banksia. Murphy came into her view through the shrubbery, facing Porter in a more relaxed but equally lethal posture. The two men were as rigid as statuary below her, utterly absorbed by their stand-off. It was clear neither one had seen her through the brushes.

She moved further to her right, stepping carefully, to gain a better bead on Porter, then secured her stance on the ground. She now had a clear, open shot at his chest. She slid her left index finger inside the trigger guard and pulled cautiously until she felt the trigger safety lever give. One more breath.

THE EPITOME OF ANDREAS VESALIUS

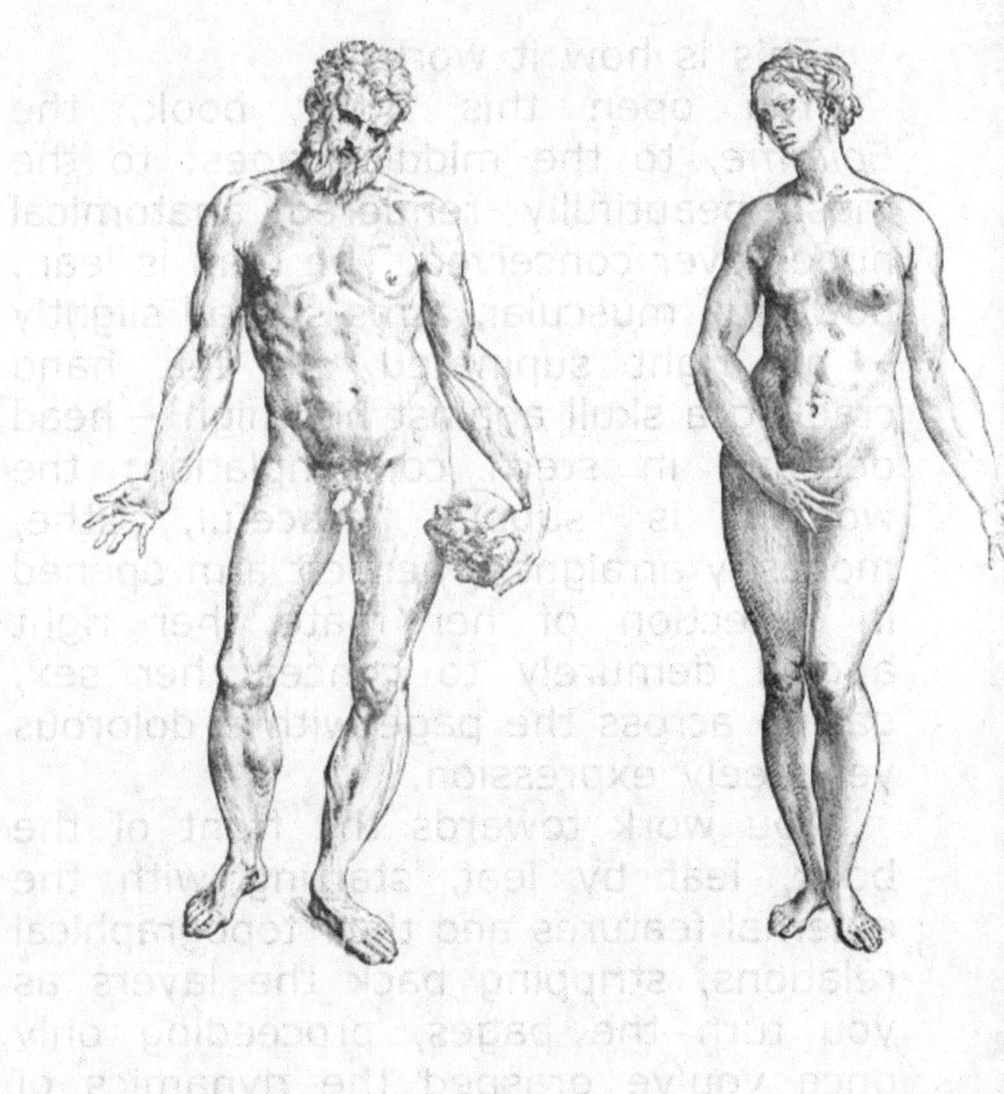

This is how it works.

You open this other book, the *Epitome,* to the middle pages: to the most beautifully rendered anatomical nudes ever conceived. The man is lean, powerful, muscular, arms spread slightly – his right supinated, his left hand cradling a skull against his thigh – head declined in stern contemplation; the woman is supple, graceful, lithe, modestly arraigned, her left arm opened in reflection of her mate, her right angled demurely to conceal her sex, gazing across the page with a dolorous yet steely expression.

You work towards the front of the book, leaf by leaf, starting with the external features and their topographical relations, stripping back the layers as you turn the pages, proceeding only once you've grasped the dynamics of each tier and their attitudes relative to the layers already comprehended. Stratum gives way to stratum as the muscles are stripped back, deeper and deeper, until you reach ligaments, cartilages, bones. By now the student knows where every tendon attaches; which muscles overlay every process and protuberance; which fibres generate every motion; which line and curve and prominence of the naked human body owes to every combination of sinew and bone.

Then you return to the central pages and begin again, now working towards the back, this time with veins and arteries and nerves, the viscera and organs of life and thought and promulgation, again moving from superficial to deep.

Thus are acquired the two crucial aspects of anatomical knowledge: the principles of organ functionality, and the precise location of every tissue relative to the surface, the bones and the other organs.

De Humani Corporis Fabrica Epitome was published by Johannes Oporinus in 1543, immediately after the *Fabrica*'s first print run, and sold to students at a much cheaper price than the fabulously expensive *magnum opus*. It is the workbook to the *Fabrica*'s magisterial text, and includes cut-outs that can be assembled into three-dimensional models. It features many of the original's plates, its production values every bit as impressive as those of the *Fabrica*.

The *Epitome* echoes, distils and completes the *Fabrica*. It takes the Master's empirical knowledge out of the library and into the field. While the *Fabrica* is for study by candlelight, the *Epitome* is for use at the dissecting table, scalpel in hand, among the blood and meat and fluids of the body.

The *Epitome* brought the new Anatomy to a far broader audience than the *Fabrica* could have done alone, and this dissemination ensured that Vesalius's radical movement was not only momentous in intellectual essence, but also revolutionary in effect. Vesalius foresaw the democratisation of knowledge – he facilitated a German translation of the *Epitome* in Basel by Alban Thorer, published immediately after the Latin version – and anticipated the evolution of mechanical reproduction. He understood that while a work's integrity is absolutely crucial, so too is its reach.

The publication of the *Fabrica* secured Vesalius's reputation among his illustrious peers and the mighty elite of his day, but it was the mass publication of the *Epitome* that saw Vesalius immortalised in the annals of intellectual history.

Thursday 17 January – early hours

'Lower your weapon,' growled Murphy, his pistol aimed straight at the fugitive, but Porter stood frozen in place. 'Fucking *now,*' Murphy shouted, and that did the trick. Porter pointed his pistol at the ground between them. Murphy dropped his own revolver down by his hip, in a show of good faith, then tilted it back up imperceptibly as he stepped forward. Jo kept her Glock trained on the serial killer, her trigger finger a hair's breadth from the break.

As the detective advanced, Porter retreated slowly until his back bumped against the fence high above the ocean pool. The detective following him, stopping about five metres from his quarry, watching him through narrowed eyes.

Murphy was in command, comfortable and at ease. Porter was edgy, desperate and dangerous. Jo was the novice, hiding unseen in the bushes, just barely holding her nerve. She had no field experience, but she'd seen the movie. She was about to find out what that was worth.

Porter recovered some composure, visibly calculating his options. They can't have looked good. He relaxed into a fatalistic stance, all reckless and unpredictable, and broke into a deranged, malevolent smile. He looked down at the ground then back up through an exaggerated pan-and-tilt towards Murphy, like some fugitive lunatic gone feral in a Stephen King fun house, Dennis Hopper's Frank Booth with a dash of Heath Ledger's Joker. It scared the shit out of Jo in her hiding place, but her brother practically yawned.

Murphy raised his revolver a touch. Porter responded in kind. Porter's lips began moving, sub-audibly.

'What's that, retard?' called Murphy. 'Speak up.'

'You imagine you have me at a disadvantage, detective.'

'Yeah, I reckon I do, dickhead.'

'You're wrong, so wrong.' Porter chuckled. 'You can never take from me what I have taken from you.'

'I'm gunna take *every*thing from you, Porter. I'm gunna make you fucken burn.'

'You have thwarted my Tribute, Murphy, but I invaded your very *home*. Your sister's home. They are lost to you now. I win.'

'I don't think so, fuckwit.'

Porter sighed. 'Are you really so stupid that you don't understand? The worse you treat me, Murphy, the sweeter it becomes.'

'I'm happy to test that theory.'

'I stole your *manhood,* detective,' Porter said with a snarl, suddenly animated and vicious. 'I stole your progeny. I stole your wife's baby and any respect she could have for you. Where was her protector, while I was pounding her head onto your front path? I put her in a coma, Murphy, while you were waking up with a hangover in Melbourne beside some spangled whore.'

'Enough,' barked Murphy. 'Put the gun on the ground.'

But Porter raised his weapon instead. 'You're not going to arrest me, you pitiful little policeman.'

'Suits me, arsehole.' Murphy raised his own gun further.

Porter laughed aloud at the tension. 'It was your elderly neighbour who did your man's work for you, detective. She has spirit. But you? You're a lightweight.' Porter spat on the ground. 'A wretched, pathetic excuse for a man.'

'Shut it!'

'Actually, you're no man at all, Murphy. You're just a grub, an insignificant, disgusting, foetid little grub.'

Then Murphy went utterly calm, his edgy tension yielding to an ominous supple poise, his anger morphing from a hot, animal temper into an icy, ethereal rage. Jo stifled a gasp: she had seen this once or twice before, but not for years. It had never ended well.

Murphy smiled then, warm as a shark. 'You could not be more wrong, Porter.'

'Wrong about what?'

'About who fucked who.' Murphy's eyes gleamed even as they narrowed.

'How so?'

'There are two kinds of people in this world, my friend,' said Murphy with lethal composure. 'The players, and the pawns.'

Porter cocked his head quizzically.

'SP07M378,' recited Murphy.

This meant nothing to Jo, but Porter reeled. 'My staff number?'

Murphy smirked while Porter's arrogance dissolved, his mind apparently turning until some dark knowledge emerged, the killer stumbling back in appalled comprehension.

'You knew!' Porter accused. 'You knew all along!'

'Yes I did.' The detective nodded, encouraging the killer to put the final piece in place. 'But more than that.'

Porter's eyes widened further and he cried, 'You set her up!'

Murphy's face broke with a vicious sneer. 'You think you're so fucken smart, Porter; all your meticulous planning. But you never had a fucken clue. I hunted you down and smoked you out and pointed you in the direction I chose.'

'You sent me to kill her!'

'That's right, cunt. You were never in charge. It was always me.'

Jo staggered, taking the blow in the centre of her chest as she understood what her brother had done to Sylvia: what he had tried to do. She cried out in anguish and rage, her wail shocking both men from their death stare, turning them towards the screen of banksia that hid her from their view.

Murphy started to speak, but Jo shrieked over his words, refusing to permit him any single word. And in his alarm he nearly missed the glint of moonlight on gunmetal in his peripheral vision, as Porter's weapon came up and around.

Nearly.

Thursday 17 January – early hours

Then it was on, finally, and it was the old state of flow, adrenaline surging and focus snapping in, sharp and sure, like a warrior, like a predator. Murphy had been here a hundred times, his motion like mercury: all fluid grace and cruel intent. He was clarity, precision; he was perfect Vengeance, with all the time in the world.

Murphy lifted his Smith & Wesson through a smooth vertical arc to sight between the dead man's eyes, his trigger finger moving through the takeup to the very edge of the break. He exhaled and held steady while Porter levelled his Browning and opened his mouth to curse.

Then Murphy squeezed a fraction more and it was all thunder and lightning, the barrel kicking up in his fist through his sightline. He lowered his revolver and saw the corona of scarlet mist hang for a moment in the bright moonlight, before the light breeze snatched it away.

The body careened into the wooden fence behind, firing the pistol once into space in some final convulsion before fracturing the top rail and tumbling out into air; a suspended moment of silence, then a crash into the water below.

Murphy swivelled towards Jo, who had come around the screen of bushes above the platform, her Glock – *his* Glock – aimed at the centre of his chest. He motioned her down the steps with his Magnum, and she descended warily to the concrete, her aim never wavering.

'For fuck's sake, Jo, why didn't you stay at home, like I told you?' He shook his head and sighed. 'You weren't supposed to hear all that. See it.'

His sister just stood there, silently pointing her empty weapon at his sternum, waiting for him to act. He thought his next move had to be pretty obvious, in the circumstances, but she'd always avoided the harsher facts of reality.

'What a fucken mess.' Murphy shook his head ruefully. 'I don't suppose we can sort this out at all?'

Jo said nothing and did not waver, holding his gaze with coldsteel fury.

'No, I didn't think so,' muttered Murphy. 'Why are you so fucking unreasonable, Jo?' He lifted his pistol and took his aim at her. 'Do you see what you made me do? I never wanted—'

She squeezed her trigger then, and a ten-gram bullet fled the chamber at well over a thousand kilometres per hour.

Murphy recoiled in surprise at the impossible flash from the unloaded Glock, then a tremendous blow to his chest propelled him backwards and he was overwhelmed by searing pain. He stumbled, then crumpled, his legs collapsing beneath him. He fell heavily to a seated position, then listed to his right, the side of his head striking the concrete. A huge crimson tropical flower bloomed in time-lapse across his white shirt-front.

Jo moved across to him and stood firmly on his revolver, still grasped in his right hand. He couldn't let it go, couldn't move, couldn't speak. He looked up at her, his lips quivering. The dark glistening pool grew beneath him, bubbling out of a gaping crater where the back of his ribcage used to be.

'When it's time to shoot, just shoot,' she said. 'Don't talk.'

Jo looked out into the bay at Wedding Cake Island shining brightly in the vivid moonlight. With a sudden bellowing crash, a great plume of white shot up out of the sea and inundated the island. There was another boom two beats later as the same wave hurled itself onto the rocks beneath them, then the sizzling hiss of the water running off and home.

Thursday 17 January – early hours

Jo didn't look down until the gurgling stopped. It was worse than she'd thought. Vacant eyes staring into the night sky. Trickles of blood leaking from his ears, nose, mouth; his face a twisted sneer of pain. Features so familiar to her, now entirely alien. No living face could look like this. Murphy was gone.

The shirt was entirely soaked, a deep velvet burgundy. Only the left sleeve was still white. He lay in a wide pool of clotting blood and spongy flesh, with flecks of white here and there that must have been fragments of bone. She retched.

Yeah, it really was time to go.

Jo heard a siren in the distance and felt her adrenaline kick up a notch. Fuck, she had just shot a cop. She needed to focus and keep moving. There would be time later for grief, guilt and nausea. Right now she had to think and act.

She crossed to the shattered fence and peered down at the ocean pool, where Porter floated serenely face-down, arms and legs spread wide. His head was a shiny blackness at one end of a slick running across to the landward steps. She spotted his handgun in clear water, midway between his body and the seawall.

She ran down to the steps leading into the southern end of the pool, then waded over to Porter's pistol. Jo ejected the magazine from her Glock, scrubbing it all over with her T-shirt before reinserting it. She scrubbed the rest of the pistol as well, taking particular care around the trigger, mindful of the round in the chamber. She placed the Glock on the floor of the pool and picked up Porter's weapon. She inspected it in the moonlight, found the safety lever and flicked it on. She untied the knot of her trackpants, threaded the cord through the trigger guard and retied it, then slid the Browning inside her trackies while pulling the right pocket inside out, pushing the gun into the makeshift pouch.

She climbed over the seawall and onto the rocks. The water was a little rough, but she had no real choice. Shots had been fired, people had been killed, and this was the only other way out of the baths. She eased herself into the waves, scrambling ahead when she could and holding her ground when they broke around her. Eventually she pushed off from the rocks between sets and moved quickly into open water.

She swam towards the leeward side of Wedding Cake Island until she found a suitable satellite rock she could stabilise against as she untied the knot and let the pistol fall away into the water. She took off her ballet flats and crammed them into her pocket, pushed off from the rock and swam north. She couldn't help thinking about that movie, all alone in the open sea at night, but she ignored it as best she could and set a strong, steady rhythm across the back of the bay.

Twenty minutes later, Jo climbed the steps near Our Lady of Coogee fence and slipped on her ruined shoes. She legged it to Sylvia's house, pausing only to let a cruising taxi disappear down

Coogee Bay Road. She had the shakes something fierce and was still dripping wet, but she didn't think she'd been noticed.

It took her three attempts to pull her keys from their zip pocket, and she immediately dropped them, then she couldn't hold still enough to get the key in the lock. She eventually managed to let herself in and moved quickly to the back of the house, closing the hallway door before turning on the lights. The clock on the oven said 3.28. She poured a decent measure of vodka into an old-fashioned glass and downed it in two good throws, the warmth spreading across her chest and up her neck. Her eye found Sylvia's guitar across the room, but she clamped down hard on her emotions. Any momentum lost now would not easily be recovered.

Clean up first. Jo stripped and shoved her T-shirt, trackies and undies into the washing machine, setting it on the fast sport cycle, then put her damp shoes into the tumble dryer and started it on warm. She showered in the main bathroom, running it hard and hot for a long time, until she felt almost human again. The washing machine still had six minutes left to run, so she made buttery toast with a thick smear of Vegemite. She groaned aloud at the indecent pleasure of it: it was that fucking good.

Once the washer was done, she added her wet clothes to her still-damp shoes and set the dryer to run for another hour. She poured another glass of vodka, switched off the lights and went to bed in the spare room.

Thursday 17 January – dawn

Jo was wrenched from the deep by an insistent pounding on a door. She sat up, clutching the damp sheet while the remnants of an unpleasant dream receded. She oriented herself: Sylvia's spare room.

Sylvia. Murphy. Fuck.

The urgent knocking resumed.

'Hold your horses,' she called out as she pulled herself upright and wrapped the bath towel around herself. She unlocked the front door to find two uniformed police she didn't recognise wearing serious expressions that she had no trouble emulating.

'Hi,' she croaked, before trying again. 'Hi.' The cops looked at one another.

'Good morning, Dr King,' said the senior one. 'Sorry to disturb you at this hour.'

'It's okay. What time is it?'

'Quarter past six.'

Just over two hours' sleep: no wonder she felt like shit. 'I'm sorry, it doesn't look like Dave's home.'

'Yes, we know. We need to speak with you, ma'am. It's urgent.'

'What's the matter?'

'It would be better if we could come in, please.'

'Of course. Give me a sec?'

'Certainly, Dr King. We'll wait here.'

She closed the door and ran to the laundry, where she retrieved her clothes from the dryer and raided Sylvia's laundry basket for a bra. Close enough. She dressed quickly, dropping her ravaged shoes in the spare room on the way back to the door.

'I'm Senior Constable Carroll,' said the policewoman as they entered. 'This is Constable Moody. We're from Eastern Beaches Local Area Command.'

Once inside they looked around, trying not to be obvious about it, though they clearly knew what had happened here. Jo gestured down the hall and followed them into the living room. Carroll was about Jo's build, although she was encumbered by a lot of gear, but the young policeman filled the entire available volume. Where did they get these boys? *Beef country.*

'Please, sit down,' said Jo, realising she was delirious with exhaustion. She needed to be very careful with what she said. 'Would you like some tea?' She headed around the kitchen bench, while the cops sat on the couch.

'Yes please, if you're making some.'

Jo filled the kettle. 'How can I help you?'

Carroll spoke without preamble. 'Dr King, I'm very sorry to inform you that your brother has been shot and killed in the early hours of this morning, in the course of apprehending Stephen Porter.'

'Oh, fuck.' Jo groaned, slumping against the kitchen bench, glad of the support as her face drained of colour. She tried to speak, failed. Tried again. 'Where?'

'At the Ladies' Baths in Coogee. Across the road from your flat.'

'What on earth was he doing there?'

'We were hoping you could tell us,' said Moody.

Jo shook her head. 'What happened?'

'We're not exactly sure yet.' As far as they could tell, Carroll explained, both Murphy and Porter had been in Jo's apartment last night. It was not clear why they were there. There had been a fight: there was broken furniture and a lot of blood. Evidently there had been a pursuit. They'd ended up inside the Ladies' Baths, where it appeared they had killed one another in some kind of shoot-out. Their bodies were found when the baths opened at sunrise.

Jo made the tea while the policewoman spoke. Sylvia's Dutch teapot had been a thirtieth birthday present from Jo's mother, not long before she died. A lifetime ago. Two lifetimes ago, if you counted Murphy.

'So Dave shot Stephen Porter?'

'Yes, ma'am,' said Moody.

'Dead?'

'Yes, ma'am.'

'And you said Porter shot my brother.'

'Yes, ma'am.'

'What, at the same time?'

'That's how it looks.'

'I thought that only happened in the movies.'

Carroll shrugged. 'It appears Detective Murphy has been shot with his own service weapon.'

'But ... so how did he shoot Porter, then?'

'He had another registered firearm. A revolver.'

'That wasn't his service weapon?'

'No, that was his own. He had a police-issue sidearm as well. We think Porter stole it from here when he attacked your sister-in-law.'

'Bloody hell.' Was this as simple as it sounded, or was it a trap?

'We understand it's a massive shock, Dr King, especially just after the attack on Mrs Murphy.' Moody cleared his throat and opened his notebook. 'But we need to ask you a few questions.'

'Of course. I'm not sure how I can help, but whatever you want.'

'Dr King, when did you last see your brother?' asked Carroll.

'Well, Amy brought me home last night. Detective Chartier.' They nodded. 'I went to sleep but when I woke up she was gone. I couldn't face being alone, so I came around here.'

'When was this?'

'I'm not sure. Round midnight.'

'How'd you get here?'

'I walked. It's twenty minutes.'

'What happened then?'

'We had a drink, talked about Sylvia. I wasn't hungry but Dave made me eat. Then I went to bed in the spare room. He was still up.' She pointed at the whisky bottle on the coffee table.

'And that was the last time you saw him?'

'Yes.'

'And what time was that? When you went to sleep.'

'I don't know. Oneish?'

'And did you hear him leave at all?'

'No.'

'Did you sleep through?'

'I went to the bathroom at one point.'

'When was that?'

'About 3.30.'

'Was Detective Murphy here then?'

'He wasn't up, but I assume so.'

'And when did you get up this morning, Dr King?'

'Just now.'

'You told us he didn't seem to be home.'

'He didn't come to the door for you. And their bedroom's empty, as you saw.' The bedroom door was wide open, the bed neatly made.

'Did Detective Murphy have a key to your place, Dr King?' asked Moody.

'Yes they have a full set, front and back.'

'Does anyone else have keys to your apartment?'

'No.'

'Do you know why Detective Murphy has gone to your place in the middle of the night, Dr King?' asked Carroll. 'Something you discussed last night, maybe?'

'I have no idea. We just talked about Sylvia's condition, when we should visit her in hospital.'

'Anything to do with her that would send him there? Photos, maybe?'

'Not that I can think of.'

'Any papers relating to that anatomy book?'

'No, everything's with the Homicide Squad. He knew that.'

'Nothing else about your academic work?'

'No, I'm sorry. I agree it's strange he was there, but I really have no idea why.'

'Will you keep thinking about it, please, Dr King? It's the main blank patch in our understanding.'

'Of course. But can I ask: how did you even know they'd been in my flat?'

'When the Baths called in the incident, a flag came up in the system, since it's on your street. We were concerned for your welfare, so we gained entry.'

Gained entry. Jo wondered if she'd have to repair that later.

'Dr King, do you know where Detective Murphy's gun safe is?' asked Moody.

'Sorry, no. I didn't even know he had one.'

'Did you ever notice what he did with his sidearm when he came home?'

'Yeah, he keeps it in here,' said Jo, waving at the kitchen drawers. 'Drives Sylvia nuts.' The police exchanged a disapproving frown, and Carroll came over to the kitchen. 'Third drawer down.' The policewoman opened the drawer with a pen and sniffed inside. She nodded at Moody.

'You're welcome to look around for the safe if you like.'

'That's okay, a site team will be over later,' said Carroll. 'They're at your place now, I'm afraid. The detectives will let you know when you can go home.'

'And they'll have to formally interview you, Dr King,' added Moody. 'There are a lot of gaps still.'

'I understand. I'll ring Detective Janssen.'

Moody stood and approached the framed St George rugby league jersey on the wall. 'That's quite a piece. Is it original?'

'Yes. From the 1977 premiership. My father bought it for Dave at a charity auction when he was a boy. He's had it on the wall ever since.'

'Your dad a St George supporter?'

'No, but Dave's father was. He died in 1978. That was his last grand final.'

'The replay against Parramatta.'

'That's right. Craig Young wore that jersey in the tied match. Are you a Dragon?'

'Used to be. More a Waratah these days.'

'Detective Murphy would've been young when he lost his father,' said Carroll.

'Yes, he was five years old.'

'What happened, if you don't mind me asking?'

'He was a police officer, shot in the line of duty. Still unsolved, I believe.' That brought all conversation to a halt.

After they left, Jo closed the door, leaned against it and slid to the ground. She took shallow, measured breaths until she heard the patrol car drive off, then she let herself go, sobbing and heaving.

Swatches of mid-grey, little more than the sensation of light, soft and diffuse within the enveloping dark. A dreamlike floating, mostly pleasant but with a darkness there, ominous, ever crouching just behind, waiting. Background sounds, a brisk clattering, the odd raised voice, utterances that are no words. What is this place?

***

Red first, then yellow, and painful slashes of white. Words without meaning, questions without answers. The dark lurking presence now shows itself at night: it is her pain. Her suitor, her betrothed. They keep it back for her but it is patient. Time is on its side. Oblivion protects her, for now, but not for much longer.

***

A simple cartoon face, a child's watercolour ruined by rain, framed within the aperture; kindly, smiling. The mouth opens and she recognises its voice, from before. She cannot remember, yet she knows he has watched over her, here in this place.

She opens her mouth without realising it, croaks noiselessly: 'Mack.'

***

Then one afternoon she returns to the world intact: to this empty room that she still can't see properly. Shapes and colours, yes – and movement – but only right in front. She can make out objects but only up close, and not at all clearly.

But she can hear the sounds on the ward. She understands them. She knows who she is. She remembers. She knows where she is, and why. Her right hand by instinct moves to stroke her belly, but before she even touches it she knows, she knows. She weeps for her lost child, slides back into the black.

***

She is all cried out. She thinks she might be ready. She knows it will be a hard road back – that people will want a lot from her. The doctors, the police. Her husband. She has to hold him at bay somehow, until she can think. The work will be her cover. The work of recovery, of witnessing. Her pain will help; her pain will steer her.

She is tired already, but she knows she has to make a start. She reaches for a cable, finds it and follows it to a small box, presses the button at its centre. The door is flung open. There's a figure in blue, in deep soft focus. 'Sylvia!' It's her friend Lucia, crying, hugging her tightly. 'You're back.'

She asks for Jo.

***

The world she came back to was not the one she had left. Her baby was gone: the central fact of her life before the attack was now a yawning void. She knew she should have been pleased when the doctors told her she'd make a full recovery, but she could not yet feel good about that without her little girl.

Then on the third day, when she cautiously asked where Murphy was, Jo told her that he was dead: apparently shot by the man who had attacked her. It upset Sylvia deeply that Dave had been killed, and she cried for him, not for herself. She had never wanted him hurt, she had just wanted to live in peace.

Nor did she take any consolation from the death of Porter. She was glad that his series of killings had been stopped, but she was appalled at the idea that Murphy had executed him.

Before long, Sylvia in her turn told Jo about her own decision to leave Murphy, before the attack. She told her all her reasons, and why she hadn't confided in her at the time of the attack. Jo was supportive of Sylvia, but had little to say about Murphy directly. Sylvia was at first surprised at Jo's muted response – she had always been forthright about her brother's shortcomings – but then, Jo was grieving too. She had lost her last family member.

Sylvia gave bedside evidence to the police, but it had little relevance to the coronial inquest or the internal inquiry into the dual shooting. Sylvia wasn't called to either hearing; Jo was called to both, but the questioning was perfunctory, a recapitulation of her witness statement. The forensics supported the standard theory of grossly unprofessional conduct on Murphy's part, resulting in mutual homicide. Despite the cloud hanging over him, the New South Wales Police Force buried Murphy with full honours while Sylvia was still in hospital.

***

Sylvia was discharged at last and she went home to Randwick. Jo came to look after her. Neither of them loved being there, with the shadow of Murphy hanging over the house, but Sylvia was not yet up to climbing the four flights of stairs to Jo's place. Once Sylvia was up and about, though, they started getting the house in order to put it on the market.

Autumn had called a cease-fire for the Anzac Day holiday: it was a mild, still, clear blue Sydney day, the air washed clean over weeks of squally weather. The morning sun streamed into the back of the house as Sylvia cleaned out the laundry alcove. Jo was working in another room, as had become their habit. By silent consensus they were avoiding mention of him, but the result was that Murphy loomed over every conversation: he had finally placed the distance between the sisters-in-law that he had never managed to in life. Jo had spent the occasional night with either Amy or Thijs, to give Sylvia a little space, but it only accentuated their caution with one another when they were together. Neither of them seemed to know what to do about it.

Sylvia put all that aside for the moment to concentrate on her work. Every nook and corner was encrusted with dried laundry powder, beneath strings and balls and pellets of dense, hardened lint. She pulled the washing machine right out from the wall to get in behind and something clattered to the floor. As she bent to pick it up, she saw it was a plastic card.

Her Denison Bank credit card.

Sylvia froze in place, staring at the object in her hand. She tracked back over that time, and knew without doubt that she hadn't lost it in the laundry. Her memory was fully restored, and she had given it a lot of thought at the time. There was simply no way her card had found its way there by accident.

Which meant someone had put it there on purpose.

It could only have been Murphy.

It might have been just another gaslighting exercise. But as she considered those final days and saw how it all fitted together, she knew that it wasn't.

Sylvia didn't remember crossing to the sofa, but that was where Jo found her: head down, her hands dangling between her legs, holding the card.

'What's up, sis?' asked Jo.

Sylvia looked up, her face streaked in tears. 'He set me up,' she croaked.

There was a long pause while Jo absorbed this. 'What do you mean?' she asked, haltingly.

Sylvia lifted her hands, holding out the credit card for Jo to see. Sylvia tried to find the words to explain what it meant, but when she refocused from the card to her sister-in-law's face, she could see it already written there. Jo's skin was drained of all colour, her mouth open in a silent gasp of horror.

'You knew what he did,' whispered Sylvia.

Jo nodded slightly, unable to speak.

Sylvia held Jo's eyes for a long while. 'When?' she asked.

Jo opened her mouth, paused, spoke. 'At the end.'

'You were there?' A question.

Jo nodded again. Her fear was all over her now.

Sylvia thought about that. 'Oh.' She looked up. 'It was you.' A statement.

Jo was rigid, stricken. Then she nodded again, just once.

Sylvia looked down, took a deep breath and let out one harsh, anguished sob. Then inhaled again and stood. Moved to Jo. Opened her arms and held her tight.

Jo fell into her sister-in-law's embrace and let it flow, for the first time in months, for the first time since that night. She cried for days and days, and Sylvia held her close until she was done.

FINIS

Author's Note

Caution: here be spoilers.

It probably goes without saying that there is a bit of me in each of the characters in this yarn – in a couple of cases, I feel the need to emphasise, just a *tiny* bit. I'm left-handed, like Jo, and schooled in the humanities, although I can't draw to save my life. I take my coffee as a double ristretto, like Murphy, and while I seldom drink, the only whisky you'll find at my place is from Islay. Even their homes are known to me: Sylvia and Murphy live in a version of my former PhD supervisor's place, and Jo lives in my brother's former building – specifically the flat upstairs, then occupied by a celebrated actor and her young family.

I also spent three years studying medicine at Sydney Uni before dropping out and working odd jobs. Then I paid my way through my arts degree as a systems monitor on a bank help desk. Sound familiar? I've never killed anybody, and my interest in Vesalius is intellectual rather than pathological –

but, yes, there's something of me in Stephen Porter.

I'm coming to my point, but we need to turn left here for a sec. In med school we had this much-loved biochemistry lecturer named Vivian Whittaker. Both a scientist and an experienced medico, he was also a musician, a humanist and a terrific raconteur who gave dazzling lectures, full of dry wit and erudition. His annual lecture on porphyria was a legendary virtuoso performance attended by hundreds of people from all over the university. He used to set these diabolical exams – impossible to complete in the allotted time – on the indisputable premise that in an emergency situation, when we needed to know the diagnostic and therapeutic implications of some biochemical process we couldn't go look it up in the library. We would need to know it *then.*

One day in third year, not longer after exams, I was crossing the campus when I ran into Dr Whittaker. I asked him, with not a little trepidation, whether he recalled how I'd done.

'Ah, yes, I remember your paper. You write rather well, you know.'

'Oh, really?' This sounded promising.

'But you must remember the first rule of writing, Mr Byron: to write about what you *know*.' At which he tipped his hat, wheeled about and kept walking.

This, of course, was both devastatingly brilliant, in a Wildean way – I was honoured to have been the object of such a great line, delivered *ex tempore* and *con brio* – and moderately deflating. I say moderately because I had already been floundering for a while and this news only reinforced my growing conviction that I was not on the right path. For the record I scored 58 per cent for Biochem III, which neatly enumerated my ambivalence about that career trajectory. Would you want to be treated by a doctor who'd been so unconvinced of their vocation that they barely passed everything? Me neither. I left.

A decade later I had absolutely inhaled a BA Hons at Adelaide Uni. (The big lesson here is, only ever study what you're actually interested in learning.)

I was back at Sydney Uni, starting my PhD in English, so I looked up Viv Whittaker and took him to lunch. I reminded him of our exchange ten years earlier and he roared laughing, appalled at himself. He apologised profusely 'for being such a bastard'.

On the contrary, I replied, it had been one of several illuminating moments around the time that had helped me find a much better path. I regretted none of it.

'Well, that's good to hear and kind of you to say, but it's still unforgivable,' he replied. 'And anyway, it's *lousy* advice. Especially in the humanities. You should write beyond yourself, surely. Isn't that the point? You write to find out what you don't already know.'

And so it is with this story. I was very fortunate to grow up in a house where violence was never used as a means of doing family business. It was really only during my teenage years, as I heard and saw things in the homes of some of my peers, that I began to realise just how fortunate we were, and perhaps how unusual.

In more recent years, stories like these have come out from behind closed doors and into widespread community awareness, which is certainly a positive development.

But their incidence does not seem to be diminishing, so the people who are perpetrating the various forms of domestic asymmetrical warfare haven't yet got the message – which is, to be clear: it isn't fucking on, and you need to fucking stop. The coercive control, the gaslighting, the financial abuse, the social isolation, the negging, the disrespect, the intimidation, the marital rape, the non-marital rape, the beatings, the murders: it has to end now, and end for good.

While there are certainly adult male victims of intimate partner violence, we all know that the overwhelming majority of perpetrators are men. Although nearly all the anti-DV advocates are women, this is men's business, fundamentally, because we are the ones responsible. With vanishingly few exceptions, we are the abusers, we are the attackers, we are the rapists, we are the murderers. This epidemic won't stop until men stop it. That's up to us, not our victims.

And yes I mean we, us, our. I've never raised a hand in my life, but I'm in this too. All men have to be part of sorting this out, because this is about the licence we extend to one another, the expectations we set, the standards we accept. It comes through in the chat, the banter, the jokes and the anecdotes. The silences that may well stem from discomfort or disapproval, but that are read as permission, even encouragement.

A significant contributor to the problem is the stories that men tell ourselves and each other *about* ourselves and each other: stories that excuse bad behavior; that deny its possibility even when it is going on right under our noses; that shrug and turn away; that weigh abuse and predation against professional success and popularity; that enable a culture of impunity that in turn permits and facilitates the abuse, the control, the violence.

So I wrote this novel to explore the mythology about the top blokes, about the tough-but-fair, hardworking salt-of-the-earth types, about the family men next door and the pillars of the community who everyone swears would never abuse their partners, not in a million years. Like fuck they wouldn't. I spent eight years in a boys' school and several more working in our federal parliament; I know perfectly well what those men are capable of, especially the ones who slide right into the skin of confident, entitled adult masculinity. I wanted to contribute a counter-narrative from a male writer that exposed from the inside the utter bullshit from which this behavior takes its nourishment. Fuck those men and fuck their *omertà*. It's beyond time to blow the lid off this.

Because the moment our country is in right now is an opportunity for men to recast their relationship with power and control, and to commit to carrying themselves with dignity and genuine self-respect. Not the risible swagger of the macho poseur, but the calm, centred poise of the man in possession of himself. Anyone can dominate someone physically weaker than themselves, anyone can be mean, and anyone can succumb to their anger: that's easy. The tougher work is to control your own behavioural response. That's where self-respect comes from, and the respect of others.

If you need help learning to take control of yourself, make that phone call. You're not alone, and asking for help is an expression of strength. The only shame comes from the weakness of submission and self-indulgence.

Master that, and you'll know how good it feels to treat her right. Yeah, even on her bad days. Even on *your* bad days. *Especially* on your bad days.

Be safe out there, people, and be kind to one another and to yourselves. Life can be hard enough and short enough as it is.

1800 RESPECT National helpline 1800 737 732

Lifeline 13 11 14

Men's Referral Service 1300 766 491

Mensline 1300 78 99 78

Acknowledgements

This has been a long time coming. Thank you for support, encouragement, advice and inspiration, over many years and in ways you don't even know: Alister Air, John Aldhouse, Deborah Anton, Georgina Arnott, Kathy Bail, Amanda Barbosa, Angela Barney-Leitch, Christine Barnicoat, Emma Barron, Fiona Bastian, Becky Batagol, Rosie Batty, Amanda Bell, Dave Bloustien, John Birmingham, Jan Borny, James Bradley, Rosi Braidotti, David Bromley, David Brooks, Dani Brown, Joe Burke, Andrew Burns, Charlie Burton, Erin Byron, Gary Byron, Josh Byron, Lachlan Byron, Mark Byron, Michael Byron, Paul Byron, Kim Carr, Cath Carroll, Ian Chubb, Ruth Clare, Tom Clark, Sharon Clews, Peter Coaldrake, Taasha Coates, Clare Corbould, Kay Cox, Nicole Cox, Ravi de Costa, Sabina Curatolo, Glyn Davis, Tori Dixon-Whittle, Susan Dodds, Rebecca DuField, Robyn Dunne, Sean Dunne, Orianne Dutka, Monique Earsman, Kate Eltham, Hilary Emmett, Alison Faulknor, Emily Forrest, Kate Fullagar, Pat

Gallagher, Peter Garrett, Andrew Gately, Malcolm Gillies, Nicole Gilroy, Kári Gíslason, Dawn Godbee, Meg Gulbin, Harry Gupta, Julie Hare, Margaret Harris, Michael Heyward, Amanda Hinkley, Freya Hohnen, Peter Høj, Nathan Hollier, Stephanie Holmquest, Claire Hooker, Sue Hosking, Ellie Hughes, Sheena Ireland, Jessica Jones Irons, Bill Junor, Karen Junor, Kate Junor, David Kelly, Mary Anne Kenny, Simon Kent, Cath Kevin, Michael Kirby, Natalie Kon-Yu, Emma Koster, Alan Lawson, Dave Leys, Iain McCalman, William McInnes, Kate Mackinnon, Clare McLaughlin, Karen Mann, Tim Mann, John Manning, Marlene Manning, Libby Martin, Brett Mason, Adrian Melillo, Liz Mercer, Gerard Moody, Judy Mundine, Jennifer Murphy, Mark Murphy, David Myton, Katy Nebhan, Andrew Nette, Jade O'Donohue, Tina Parolin, Kate Pasterfield, Hilary Pearse, Deborah Pike, Angela Pratt, Kerrilie Rice, Leisa Ridges, Christel Romano, The Rookies, Jorge Salavert, Lizzie Schebesta, Julianne Schultz, Fiona Scott, Lucia Scurrah, Tom Sear, Margaret Sheil, Kimberley Shrives, Jag Sidhu, Zora Simic, Greg Smith, Nic

Smith, David Spencer, Natasha Stott Despoja, Jen Talamini, Rebecca Taylor, Mandy Thomas, Giovanni Tiso, Millie Tizzard, Graeme Turner, Michael Upton, Julienne van Loon, Michael Vanderlaan, Ella Vines, Katie Webbe, Andrew Wells, Mike Whelan, David Whish-Wilson, Terri-ann White, Andrew Wilkie, Tarrin Wills, Ed Wright, Farley Wright and Andrea Yapp-Byron; and the late Srinivas Aravamudan, Jo Chartier, Ian Donaldson, Scott Ewing, Dennis Godbee, Heather Kerr, Jack Mundey, Susan Ryan and Vivian Whittaker.

To my beta readers, whose generous and insightful commentary over several iterations vastly improved the manuscript–Kim Carr, Kate Fullagar, Emily Forrest, Nathan Hollier, Iain McCalman, Hilary Pearse, Tom Sear and Julienne van Loon (x4) – my deepest thanks, and a complete indemnity on the result. Double, even.

For ristretti, kindness, enthusiasm and gracious accommodation of long writing sessions, my thanks to the excellent people of: Industry Beans, Fitzroy; Assembly, Carlton; Heartattack and Vine, Carlton; Fireworks, Austinmer;

Merlo, QUT; Rudy's, Surfers Paradise; and especially Mark, Tim and their awesome staff at Grub Food Van, Fitzroy (vale). To my lovely friends of the Brunswick Street Bookstore in Fitzroy – Nina, Marie, Sam, Leni, Bella and Anna – I cannot tell you what your faith and goodwill have meant over the years. I hope I've delivered.

Huge thanks to the judges of the 2019 Victoria Premier's Literary Award for an Unpublished Manuscript, Jaclyn Crupi, Elizabeth Flux and JP Pomare, who shortlisted an early (and much longer – sorry about that) version of this book, alongside the works of my Affirm stable-mate, Wayne Marshall, and the winner, Victoria Hannan, in a benediction that opened doors for all of us. Thanks to the Wheeler Centre who ably administer the awards, and thanks in particular to successive Victorian governments of both stripes who have supported Aussie writing through these awards since they were established by John Cain in 1985. The affirmation of creative work, especially the encouragement of new writing through the unpublished manuscript award, is of inestimable value. A special mention to Andrew Nette (shortlisted 2010) for the timely and canny advice to have a crack at it.

Enormous thanks to my literary agent, Catherine Drayton of InkWell Management, who already believed in this story back before the whole VPLA thing, and whose astute editorial advice over several drafts tightened the manuscript considerably before we even took it to market.

My publisher, Martin Hughes of Affirm Press, absolutely grasped the point of the novel from the outset, and made some critical suggestions that improved it no end. My partner in editorial crime, Ruby Ashby-Orr, worked with nous, sensitivity and an unbelievably sharp eye to help me make this the best book it could be. Then the rest of the Affirm Press team made it beautiful, brought it into being and took it into the world with verve and enthusiasm – thanks to Sasha Beekman, Sandy Cull, Elena Gomez, Susie Kennewell, Laura McNicol Smith, Kevin O'Brien, Lauren Ravida and Keiran Rogers. You took this rookie in hand with generosity, professionalism and über-loveliness. I can't thank you all enough.

Special thanks to Erika Brunner, rights and permissions manager of S. Karger AG of Basel, Switzerland, for generous permission to use the gorgeous digital renderings of Vesalius's illustrations that were created for the *New Fabrica,* and for the supply of high-quality files. Those images are integral to the novel's coherence and we are very grateful for their inclusion. Karger has made a profound contribution to the history of medicine by commissioning that supremely accessible new English translation. Lavishly illustrated, beautifully designed and scrupulously annotated, the *New Fabrica* is the true and fitting tribute to Vesalius's landmark contribution. Seek one out in a library and you'll see what I mean.

Finally and above all, thanks to Julienne van Loon, to whom this book is dedicated, who has given so much of her exceptional professional expertise to its development, but whose principal contribution is the love, companionship, wisdom, joy and courage that she shares with me every day. I'm so grateful we found one another, my love. Long may we prosper.

This book was written on Aboriginal land. Always was, always will be. Most of the action takes place in the stunning home of the Gadigal people of the Eora Nation – lands and waters that were never ceded. Respect to those all over this ancient continent who've been looking after Country since time immemorial, well before Spud Murphy's bread-thieving ancestors showed up.